BURN

BURN

CARLIE GUERRERO

kindle direct publishing

For Mum and Dad

Burn

Text copyright © Carlie Guerrero 2024

All rights reserved. No part of this publication may be reproduced, distributed, or transmitted in any form or by any means, including photocopying, recording, or other electronic or mechanical methods, without the prior written permission of the publisher, except in the case of brief quotations embodied in critical reviews and certain other non-commercial uses permitted by copyright law.

For permissions requests, write to the publisher at carlie.guerrero98@gmail.com.

This book is a work of fiction. Names, characters, places, and incidents either are products of the author's imagination, or are used fictitiously. Any resemblance to actual events or locales or persons, living or dead, is entirely coincidental.

ISBN: 9798321404515

Carlie Guerrero García
Printed in Spain.

Part I: Burn

The heat sticks to her back as the colour of the tree bark shifts from a living, deep brown colour to a blackened state. The sound of fire cracking draws closer. Footsteps are heard. She turns around to meet the gaze of a shadow...

1

A flashlight dangles from a tree branch, somehow unaffected by the gentle breeze. Soft footsteps echo behind me, causing my heart to skip a beat. I turn around slowly, only to be swallowed by darkness as a pair of eyes pierce through me.

I wake up with a loud gasp, my heart racing with adrenaline.
For some unknown reason, those eyes feel familiar, but can't wrap my head around it. *Have I seen them before?*

A flickering sound startles me, and I turn to see the curtains flapping next to my bed. I've left the window open again. Shit. I tiptoe towards the window, planning to shut it, but something outside catches my eye.

It's a faint light just across the street—in Mulkiwa Park. What's weird is it's moving in a circular motion, as if it's hanging from something. Puzzled, I grab my hoodie from the foot of the bed, yanking the hood over my head before returning to the window.

Maybe some fresh air will help me get back to sleep.

I swing my legs out of the window, using the oak tree by my side for balance before taking a leap to the ground.

A quiet grumble escapes me as my feet meet the damp grass, and I curse under my breath. Note to self: jumping from the second floor wasn't the brightest idea.

The late September breeze follows me as I cross the road, reaching the gates of Mulkiwa Park. I'm not sure what our mayor, Mayor Glenn, was thinking when he installed the fence, because it hardly keeps people out.

I hesitate, wondering if I should take a walk instead of breaking into the park. But the light radiating from the park pulls me in, and I realise it comes from the information cabin near the lake. Impulsively intrigued, I examine the gate before giving it a push, the rusty hinges creating an ear-piercing screech.

People say curiosity killed the cat, so maybe following a mysterious light on a whim isn't the smartest move. Despite that, I find myself walking deeper into the park. The light from the information cabin becomes clearer in the darkness, and I can't help but stay fixated on it.

Within a few steps, I'm at the front of the wooden cabin, and I notice a flashlight hanging from the door handle. I grab it, giving the trunk a tap with my finger. The batteries are almost flat.

The snap of twigs startles me, causing me to jump. Spinning around, I point the flashlight at the source with my heart racing.

"Shit," a guy says, shielding his eyes. "You shouldn't be pointing those things at the naked eye." My heart races from the shock, and the flashlight trembles as I lower it.

"You shouldn't be sneaking up on people in the middle of the night," I shoot back, defensively. The guy smirks, amused by the edge in my tone. He's around my age, with a chiselled jawline and light-brown hair styled into a quiff.

"Maybe you should lose the hood. It gives off a shady vibe," he suggests, his hands tucked into his leather jacket. Damn it, he's got a point.

I push my hood back, letting my blonde hair tumble, bringing my necklace with it. The guy raises an eyebrow, a soft smile forming on his lips.

"Do I know you?" I ask, crossing my arms. He chuckles, looking down at his muddy Converse. Strangely, I have never seen him around, and I know almost everyone in this town.

"I'm Theo," he says. There's a pause, like he's waiting for me to introduce myself. I remain silent, lowering my gaze. That's when I notice the flashlight in my hands—it's the one from my dream. The *recurring* dream.

Theo chuckles awkwardly.

"No name, huh? Why are you staring at your flashlight?" he asks. I meet his gaze, dropping my arm to my side.

"I, um... found it," I stammer, realising how odd it sounds. Theo raises an eyebrow.

"Sounds like you stole it," Theo teases, his tone playful. I smile, hoping it eases the awkwardness, but I suddenly realise something.

"What are you doing out here?" I ask, raising a brow. Theo shrugs, gazing up at the sky.

"I can't sleep. And it's a full moon tonight," he replies, causing me to look up, too. The moon's brilliance reflects on the lake, a shimmering beacon. Theo's gaze makes my cheeks flush with a crimson hue.

"I should head back. I have school tomorrow," I mention, breaking another silence. Tomorrow is my first day of senior year and I need to wake up early. Theo raises his eyebrows in surprise.

"Oh you're in school, too?" he asks.

"Yeah. I'm a senior."

"Huh, me too. I just moved here from LA," he says, studying me with curious eyes.

"Oh, nice. I'll see you tomorrow, then," I reply, offering a soft smile.

"Yeah," he grins. I glance at the park gate, shooting Theo a quick smile before making my way towards it.

"Hey! What was your name?" he calls out. I turn to face him.

"Cora."

•••••

Questions swirl in my head as I reach the gates of Barren High. *Was last night another nightmare? Did I really meet that guy?*

I push the thoughts aside and join the flow of students entering the building. The first day back is always a bit chaotic, but this year the hallway seems different. Maybe I'm viewing school through what my dad calls 'senior year glasses'—an optimistic perspective as graduation draws near. His theory makes sense now, I suppose.

Squeezing through a group of younger students, I make it to my locker a few minutes before the bell. I enter my code into the lock, but as usual, it refuses to budge.

"Shit," I mutter, smacking my hand against the locker. I roll my eyes, trying the combination once more. It's been like this for two years, but my dad said he can't buy me another one.

Just when frustration sets in, a shadow falls over my hands on the lock. I lift my chin, a grin spreading as I see my boyfriend Chris. He's waiting for me, Economics textbook under his arm.

"Not opening again?" Chris asks, flashing his signature dimpled smile. I sigh, stepping aside to let him give it a try. Chris enters the code, and the locker opens without a hitch.

"Okay. It's official. It hates me," I moan, making Chris laugh.

"Oh, yeah. For sure," he beams, poking my ribs. The first bell chimes, its noisy echo filling the building. The moment feels surreal; everyone still seems stuck in 'summer mode'. Chris gives me a quick peck on the cheek before we head off to our respective classes.

The first half of the day drags on, but nothing I'm learning seems to stick. The only thing on my mind is last night: my worsening insomnia, the information cabin, the flashlight, and Theo.

I find it odd that Theo would choose to move to a small town like Barren. It's tiny, with a large forest dividing the territory into different areas, featuring lakes and a modest population of around 7,000 people. Although it's just a county away from New Jersey City, it's still pretty quiet—especially for someone who moved from a big city like LA.

During lunch, Chris and I make our way to the cafeteria as usual, joining his friends. I'm not a fan of Chris' friends, but the problem is, I don't have any other. They chat about their weekends, as if they hadn't spent it with each other, and I feel my mind drifting away.

"Babe, can you pass me the ketchup?" Chris' voice pulls me from my thoughts.

What if I didn't have to pretend everything was fine? What if it could all just disappear?

Suddenly, everything goes black.

I jolt upright with a gasp, as if I'd been holding my breath. The clock on my laptop reads 3:52 P.M. I'm back home, sitting at my desk. It's as if someone pressed the 'skip' button on a remote. I have no memory of the past four hours. Damn, how the hell did this happen? Is it happening again?

No, this can't be happening. If I lose control, I'll go back to last year. I really *don't* want to go back there.

Swallowing hard, the front door creaks open. My dad usually comes home from work at 6 P.M., but it's only 4 P.M... Could it be him?

Tiptoeing downstairs, I catch the sound of rustling paper coming from the kitchen. Just as I am about to call out for my dad, I spot him unpacking groceries. His face lights up with a smile as soon as he sees me.

"Cora! Can you give me a hand?" he asks. I furrow my brows, staring at him in confusion. He never smiles at me. His face is usually etched with permanent frown lines, ones that indicate he hasn't been happy in a long time. But today, there's a soft smile on his lips, and his hair is neatly pushed to the side.

"Is... Something wrong?" I ask, lending him a hand.

"Why would there be?" he replies, unloading the last bag.

There has to be something wrong. He just came back from the grocery store, meaning it would have taken him at least half an hour to get there. Judging by the amount of food he bought, I'd say it took him an hour. Then there's another half-hour drive back home.

"Why did you leave work so early?" I ask, opening the fridge as he places some groceries inside.

"Did I not tell you? I wrapped things up early today," he responds, but something about it doesn't sit right with me. Not trusting my only parent drives me insane, but this lack of trust hasn't always been there.

My mom died when I was only 10, and I don't remember much about her. My dad told me her car drove off a cliff near the gas station. No one could explain how or why she lost control of the car that day. Since her passing, my dad has been my only guardian. If I had any more memories of my mom, therapy must have repressed them all. The only memory I have is the necklace she gave me, which I always wear.

"How's your day been?" Dad asks, sensing the silence in the room. Should I tell him I don't remember four hours of my day? No, he'll freak out. I don't want him to know they're back. The blackouts. It would mean we're back to square one, and I don't want to believe that.

"Good."

Another awkward pause. Suddenly, I want to run to my bedroom and forget this entire conversation. Our conversations are always like this, mainly because I hardly tell him anything.

"Did you know we have a guest coming over tonight?" he asks, and I furrow my brows.

"Guest?"

"Yeah, one of my colleagues from work is coming over. You'll be thrilled to meet her," he says, his deep brown eyes glimmering with excitement.

"Her?" I gulp, feeling a wave of nausea. It's not the first time I've had to meet one of my dad's 'colleagues'. I must be a huge failure to him since, so far, I haven't approved of any of the women he's seen.

"Yeah, she's really sweet. You'll like her," my father coaxes, sensing he's on thin ice. That's why he went grocery shopping and put on a Polo shirt, as if he actually likes that type of clothing.

"I actually have to study for a test," I interject, tucking a strand of hair behind my ear. "I should get back to that."

I'm on the verge of escaping upstairs to avoid more questions when my father's voice stops me.

"But you'll be done by dinner, right?" He sounds like I just scolded him. I turn to look at him for a moment, meeting his anxious gaze. He really wants me there tonight. However, the paranoia about not remembering four hours of my day kicks in again. I have to remember.

"I'll try," I reply before rushing upstairs. Closing my door, I take out my phone and realise Chris has texted me.

> **chris ♥** 2h ago
> *cora, are you alright?*
>
> **chris ♥** 2h ago
> *why didn't you tell me you went home??*

> **chris ♥** 1h ago
> *text me pls*
>
> **chris ♥** 40m ago
> *Hope you're home alright. I hate seeing you like this.*

I went home? Is that why I don't remember the rest of the day? Wasn't I having lunch with Chris and his friends?

> **me**
> *What happ*

I delete the message. I take a deep, frustrated breath. Just do it, Cora.

> **me**
> *What happened?*
>
> **chris ♥**
> *You went to the nurse because you were dizzy*

Reading Chris's message, the wildest thing is that I can't remember going to the nurse's office. My fingers tap out a reply, my palms sweaty with a mix of fear and anxiety.

> **me**
> *Yeah. Don't worry, I'm fine now*
>
> **chris ♥**
> *Good. I love you*
>
> **me**
> *love you too.*

Tossing my phone across the bed, I lie down and exhale. The sun is setting outside my window, signalling the end of the first day of senior year. I can't shake the fact that I don't remember anything from this afternoon, the gut-wrenching fear settling in my stomach.

But what's about to come is almost as bad—the last thing I want right now is to meet my dad's new girlfriend downstairs. A wave of drowsiness suddenly washes over me, my eyes closing softly as I drift into a deep sleep.

•••••

My footsteps come to a halt as I reach my front picket fence. The moon hangs overhead, a gentle breeze ruffling my hair. The sound of approaching footsteps catches my attention, and I glance over to see Theo walking towards me. His steps stop when he reaches the fence, a soft smile playing on his lips. I stare at him blankly for a moment, unsure if I'm imagining this. What is he doing in front of my house at this hour?

"I don't understand why, but I trust you," he says, his voice smooth. His intense sapphire eyes focus on me, causing my breath to catch in my throat.

"Really?" I ask, surprised. He takes a few steps towards me until our bodies are almost touching, his face hovering just above mine.

"Yeah. I guess I have a hunch about you," he says, a soft smile lingering on his lips.

"You must use that line on every girl who talks to you," I mutter. He laughs under his breath.

"I thought we were just friends," he murmurs, causing my cheeks to blush.

"We are. I know guys like you," I fire back, his lips lingering just inches from mine. His gaze drifts from my eyes to my lips, a smirk playing on his face.

"No booty call, then?" he whispers, a certain irony in his tone. I can't help but scoff at his comment.

"In your dreams," I mutter, feeling my face heat up. I try to usher him across the street with a playful push to his chest, but he remains still—his strength overpowering mine. Theo bites his lip, holding back a smile as he takes hold of my wrist. Our lips are mere inches apart, and I can feel his breath gently brushing against my skin.

"Don't push me," he purrs with a mischievous grin. My pulse quickens, and I respond with another playful shove. Theo laughs, biting his lip.

"I can push you as much as I want," I assert, determination in my eyes. His eyes meet mine, the intensity behind them causing my surroundings spin.

"I'm warning you, it's a game you can't win," he teases, giving me a flirtatious smile. With my heart thumping in my throat, I roll my eyes before letting him go.

He bites his lip, a smile playing on his face, before his shadow fades into the night.

All of a sudden, my eyes snap open. My body jerks up from the bed, a strange feeling coursing through my veins. While I'm relieved I didn't sneak out to talk to Theo, the dream felt incredibly real. Uncertainty settles under my skin, and I furrow my brows, my gaze flickering to the window next to my bed.

Why did I dream about the guy I met last night?

2

My dad is furious with me. I expected him to be disappointed for missing dinner with his new girlfriend, but it's escalated into a series of arguments about me not wanting 'his life to fall back into place'. Frankly, that's not my biggest worry—what does concern me is the fact that I lost four hours of my day yesterday. The infamous blackouts seem to have returned.

Before junior year, I experienced them every now and then—infrequently—and a few months after meeting Chris, they stopped completely. So, why would they come back now? One thing's for sure, I'm terrified of losing control again, just like one year ago. I can't go back to that.

The school halls are bustling with people rushing from one class to the next, chatting with friends or at their lockers. Making my way to my English class is a struggle, having to push past people. Searching for my seat from yesterday, I realise somebody's already taken it.

It's Theo. Theo is sitting in my seat.

A crowd of girls gathers around Theo, forming what seems like his fan club—they fiddle with their hair and giggle at him like schoolgirls. He doesn't notice me glaring at him as I walk past, too distracted by his admirers. The rest of my classmates pour into the classroom, chatting among themselves as they take their seats. I feel isolated—I'm the only one in the room with no one to talk to.

Hesitating, I grab the last available seat at the front of the class. Everyone hates sitting at the front, including me. Thankfully, the chatter of girls behind me is silenced the moment Mr. Woods enters the class.

"Good morning. Are you all ready to delve into 'The Merchant of Venice' today?" Mr Woods scrawls the title of the play in chalk. The class remains silent, reluctant to start the lesson. English class is one of my favourites because of Mr Woods. He manages to make the subject interesting.

"Contain your excitement, ladies and gents. Let's start by examining Antonio's character. What do Antonio and Bassanio want from Shylock the Jew?"

I raise my hand, knowing the answer immediately.

"Miss Danvers," Mr Woods calls out.

"They want a loan from him so Bassanio can court Portia. But Antonio had a conflict with Shylock in the past, which is why he's hesitant," I respond. I hear a gentle scoff behind me and turn around to see Theo smirking at me, playing with his pen.

"Well done, Miss Danvers. I'd like to see more of you focused. I know it's Friday, but it's no excuse to zone out in my class."

"Sir, but the football match is tonight," I hear Damon call out. Damon is the school jock, the guy that every straight girl is in love with. He's always talking about football. In fact, I think his entire brain is taken up by football.

"You said it yourself, Mr Martin. *Tonight* is the key word. Until then, you pay attention," Mr Woods replies smartly. Damon sighs, sinking lower into his chair.

The bell rings, prompting me to dart out of class without hesitation. Seeing Theo after that lesson is the last thing I want. Every time I answered a question, he'd either stare at me or chuckle under his breath.

I run into Chris at my locker, his usual lopsided grin on his face when he sees me, and I blush when he kisses my cheek.

"How's my beautiful girlfriend doing?" Chris asks. I smile, sliding a few my books into my locker.

"English was boring," I say, surprising myself.

"What? *You*? Finding English *boring*?" Chris laughs, shaking his head in disbelief.

"Well, the new kid in my class he kept stopping my teacher." I sigh. Theo was constantly interrupting Mr Woods to explain each part of the plot, which was irritating.

"Damn. What's his name?" Chris asks, wrapping an arm around my waist.

"I have no idea," I reply, suddenly spotting Theo at the end of the hallway. His eyes lock with mine, a smirk appearing on his lips. If that's the game he wants to play—where we act like we've never met—I'm more than happy to go along with it.

"The game is tonight, so I need to go to practice today," Chris says, but he's not referring to football. He's talking about his band, The Rebellions. They have a gig tonight at the local bar, the go-to spot for everyone from school. They're very casual about selling alcohol to minors, which is a big incentive for most people. Chris really wants me to go see him play, but I guess I'm too scared to tell him I don't like rock music.

Any other girl in my school would fall head over heels for a bass player, but those labels never caught my attention.

"Cora?" Chris calls out, snapping me out of my trance. I meet his gaze, realising I was staring at my locker.

"Sorry. What were you saying?"

"If you could make it by six, that would be great. The bar gets pretty crowded on Fridays," he says, pushing his dark brown hair away from his face.

"Sure," I respond, shutting my locker.

"Is something up? You've been zoning out a lot these past days."

"Have I?" I genuinely ask. I had noticed, but didn't realise he noticed it, too.

"Yeah. Hey, do you think we'll be able to hang out on Sunday at your place?"

"On Sunday? Why not Saturday?" I ask, puzzled.

"I have work to do on Saturday. Plus, tonight's gig will end pretty late." What he means is, he'll likely be hungover on Saturday. I hate Chris' drinking habit. I really do. It makes it hard for me to trust him sometimes.

"Okay. Sunday's fine," I reply with a forced smile.

"Great! You'll finally see me play the new set."

I've been delaying this plan for three weeks because I don't want to see him play. I know it's not a nice thing to say, but I just don't enjoy it. Being around his friends and the bar crowd isn't my thing. I've been sneered at several times by creepy old men.

"Yeah," I sigh, feeling defeated. Chris gazes at me, lifting my chin with his index finger.

"What's wrong?" Chris asks. In my peripheral vision, I spot Theo watching from a distance with his hands in his pockets. But as soon as he notices me looking, he swiftly averts his gaze back to his locker.

"Nothing." I force a smile. "Just really tired today. Let's go for lunch?" I ask, changing the subject. Chris beams, grabbing my hand as we walk past Theo and towards the lunch hall.

While Chris chats with his friends at the lunch table, my thoughts drift to the recurring dream. It happened again last night—the forest, the flashlight hanging motionless from a tree branch, the chirping of crickets, and the mysterious eyes among the trees.

The dream has been replaying in my mind for the past six months. It's almost surreal that the exact same dream would resurface so many times. Or maybe I'm losing my mind. The blackouts are becoming too frequent. It happened again today during breakfast. I glanced at the clock: it read 6:45. A minute later—or what felt like it—the clock showed 7:30.

Shit. I'm going crazy.

Laughter surrounds me, bringing me back to reality. That's when I realise all of Chris' friends, including him, are staring at me. Some of them are laughing.

"She zoned out, bro. She high?" It's Jason, one of the guys I dislike the most. Luke laughs at Jason's comment, and Chris chuckles, saying something to his other friend. I scowl at Jason, rising from my seat in frustration. I leave the lunch hall as quickly as possible, pushing past people until I reach the bathroom. My hands shake as I lock the cubicle door, and I feel a tear rolling down my cheek. What is happening to me?

The overwhelming stress of being out of control returns. I have no one to talk to about this. I haven't had friends of my own since sophomore year; I've always stuck with Chris since we started dating, sacrificing my own friendships.

I take a deep breath, allowing the embarrassment to fade. I exit the cubicle, only to collide with someone's back.

"Shoot, sorry…" A tall brunette with curly hair glances my way, offering me a sheepish smile, as if it were her fault I crashed into her.

"I'm sorry," I mumble, my face burning with embarrassment, before quickly leaving the bathroom.

In the loud hallway, I look around, trying to figure out where to go until my next class. It suddenly hits me—I have no one to turn to. Embarrassment drops in my stomach like a pang, recalling Chris and his friends laughing at me. I can't go back there.

Maybe some fresh air will help me calm down. As I step outside, a warm breeze tousles my hair. People are scattered everywhere—some engaged in a game of football on the grass, others lounging in the shade. I pull out my phone before settling on the steps, aiming to pass the last 20 minutes of lunchtime.

> **chris ♥**   3m ago
> *Cora? Where are you? I swear we were only kidding!*

Anxiety kicks in and the embarrassment returns.

> **me**
> *Fuck you*

I delete the message. I type it again.

> **me**
> *Didn't seem like a joke to me.*
>
> **chris ♥**
> *Oh come on, don't be mad at me* 🙂
>
> **me**
> *well I'm mad at you*
>
> **chris ♥**
> *I didn't mean to upset you, I'm sorry.*

I scoff at his response, locking my phone. I gaze ahead, and a group of seniors captures my attention. They stand front of the Barren High sign, talking and laughing amongst themselves. I remember seeing them together last year—they're one of the three popular groups—but one of them stands out. It's the girl from the bathroom, Helena Corey. She's chatting with them—no, she's friends with them.

As if she could read my thoughts, Helena notices me. She doesn't just look in my direction; she waves at me. Shit. Now she'll probably think I'm a real loser for sitting here alone. A few guys in the group turn around, fixing their gaze on me. I recognise the other girl as Beth Wilds, Helena's best friend. Her flawless mocha skin is complemented by straight black hair, and she glances in my direction before whispering something to Helena.

"Hey!" Helena calls out, still smiling at me. I respond with an uncomfortable smile, but she gestures for me to come over. Shit.

I rise from the steps, attempting to appear confident as I walk over to the group. I'm not a fan of new people, especially in large groups. I can feel all their eyes on me as I stand next to them, feeling awkward.

"What's your name?" Helena asks in a chirpy tone.

"Cora. Yours?" I ask, even though I already know.

"Helena. But everyone calls me Hel," she replies, her eyes crinkling as she speaks, as if she's used to smiling all the time.

"You see, it has two meanings," Matt, one of the guys, interjects. His chocolate curls are slicked back into his baseball cap, and he sports a nose stud and a lip ring. Matt is one of the few people who can make theatre look cool.

Helena laughs.

"That's my boyfriend Matt. Don't worry, he's not as bad as he seems," Helena teases him, and Matt rolls his eyes.

Another guy, whose name I don't know, muscular with bleached hair and walnut-toned skin, shakes my hand.

"I'm Mason," he says.

Hel points at a dirty-blond surfer guy and the other girl in the group.

"This is Daniel and that's Beth," she explains, and they both smile politely. Helena and Beth are two of the most beautiful girls at school, and they somewhat resemble the main characters from Clueless. They often wear matching preppy outfits that make them stand out from the hoodie-wearing students. Chris mentioned in the past that they were shallow, but I somehow find it hard to believe.

"Nice to meet you all," I say with a smile.

"So, how long have you been at Barren High?" Hel asks. I'm surprised by how little she knows about me compared to how much I know about her group. I've heard they rented a cabin last Easter and got so wasted that they ended up prank calling every teacher in school.

"Since freshman year," I reply.

"Seriously? That long? I'm genuinely surprised I didn't know you from before," she says, furrowing her brows. Maybe the clichés are accurate; popular people don't care about non-popular people. Especially when you have been home-schooled most of high school.

"We took different classes, I guess."

"Maybe. What subjects do you take?" Hel asks.

"AP English and Econ, Math, Sociology and American History."

"Dude, that's a lot of subjects," Mason comments, sounding impressed.

"My dad told me to take extras," I explain, feeling somewhat embarrassed. The last thing I want is for them to think I'm a nerd.

"Why? Are you going to college?" Daniel asks, leaning coolly against the Barren High sign.

"I don't know yet. Probably," I answer. The truth is, my parents would talk about me going to college every day when I was a child. They never had the chance themselves, which is why they were so insistent. However, since my mother passed away, my dad hasn't brought it up again.

"You must be pretty smart, then." Beth beams, revealing her perfectly straight teeth.

"I guess?" I chuckle.

The sudden, jarring ring of the bell startles us, leading a few guys to curse under their breaths. Hel turns to me with a friendly smile.

"What lesson do you have now?" she asks.

"American History. You?"

"Huh! Looks like we're in the same class," she chirps. Hel links arms with me, chatting excitedly about the upcoming weekend as we make our way to class. I didn't expect Helena and her group to be so welcoming after what Chris told me about them. Even though the vibe is nice, I can't shake the thought of blacking out, casting a shadow on our cheerful conversation.

The last time I blacked out, they almost didn't find me.

3

As we wait for class to start, Helena complains about how difficult American History is and how she's contemplated dropping the class multiple times. Despite that, I find her company relaxing. I guess I'm not used to having someone to talk to, besides Chris.

Hel and I grabs seats at the back of the class before the others arrive. Yet, the only thought in my mind is Chris. How should I fix our situation without hurting his feelings?

"So, are you going to watch the match tonight?" Helena asks, pulling my attention back to the present.

The deafening noise of people talking fills the classroom as a group of popular girls enters. Even Helena doesn't like them; she scrunches her nose in disgust. I roll my eyes when I spot Theo amid the commotion, wearing a smug smile as he finds a seat towards the middle. He must be relishing the new-boy attention.

"What's wrong?" Helena asks, glancing over at the group of girls, which now surround Theo's desk. "That guy?" she asks, arching an eyebrow.

For some reason, I can't keep my eyes off him as he flirts with the girls. It's as if his entourage of admirers has sucked away the anger I felt towards Chris. This is what would happen if Chris and I broke up—and I'm not prepared to confront that reality.

"Hey," Helena says, tapping my arm. I turn to her, feigning indifference about Theo's obnoxious fan club.

"What?"

"Something's up with you and the new guy," she whispers, wiggling her brows at me.

"I don't know him," I lie, but for some reason, Helena isn't fully convinced. She clicks her tongue in amusement.

"If I weren't in love with Matt, I'd say he's hot. Apparently, he moved from California."

"Huh," I mutter, pretending not to know about his recent move from LA.

"He seems really popular already," Hel says.

"I've noticed," I mutter, my thoughts drifting to the night at the park. He seemed charming enough, but after seeing him around the cheerleaders, I'm starting to change my mind about him.

"Knowing the cheer team, he'll be part of Damon's pack within minutes," Hel says, rolling her eyes in annoyance. For some reason, Helena's popular group doesn't like the jocks. Maybe they know better than that. The final bell chimes two seconds before Mrs Sanchez shuffles into the room, a broad stack of books clutched to her chest.

"Good afternoon, class. We have a new student with us today! Stand up, come up here!" Mrs Sanchez exclaims. Theo walks towards the front of the class, a few whispers circulating in the room. He stands next to Mrs Sanchez, and I find their significant height difference amusing.

"Hi, I'm Theo Rhodes. I just moved here from California, and football has been my life for the past few years. I look forward to meeting you all and being a part of the team," he announces.

Damon and his friends cheer loudly, celebrating as if Theo had just won a championship. The rest of the class joins in with applause, but I remain expressionless. Theo's gaze locks with mine for a couple of seconds, a smirk playing at the corners of his lips. His eyes wander away from me before he returns to his seat.

"Thank you, Mr Rhodes." Mrs Sanchez beams at Theo before clearing her throat. "Today we'll be looking at the Montgomery Bus Boycott."

"You're such a bad liar," Helena whispers. I give her a puzzled glance. "He was totally checking you out."

Oh, I know he was. It's not the first time he's done it—and I'm definitely not the only girl he does it to. I shake my head, opening my textbook. Theo's eyes seem to drift to me during the lesson, and I try my best to avoid it. He probably feels frustrated because I'm not giving him the same attention as his female admirers.

The bell rings, signalling the end of the lesson, and I follow Helena out of the room, feeling relieved that the day has come to an end.

"So, are you going to the football match?" Hel asks again.

"No, I can't. I'm going to watch my boyfriend play," I reply. I kind of wish I could attend the game instead, but I promised Chris I'd be there.

"Play? He's in a band?" Hel exclaims with bright eyes. I nod, strolling towards my locker with her.

"They're called The Rebellions."

"You're kidding! They're *so* famous right now."

"Really?" I ask, raising a brow. Chris had mentioned our local bar being supportive of their band, but I didn't know they were *famous*.

"Yeah! I've heard they might be touring the entire East Coast next month."

"Weird, Chris has never talked to me about that..." I mutter, raising an eyebrow. Hel's eyes widen in surprise.

"Chris Matthews is your *boyfriend*?" she exclaims. It's surprising how, after four years at this school, nobody had noticed that I was Chris' girlfriend.

"Yep," I reply, tossing my books into my locker. I'm taken aback when I see Chris' face as I close my locker, and I let out a surprised gasp.

"Shit, sorry for scaring you," Chris mutters with an apologetic smile. He gives Helena a nervous glance, as if her presence makes him uncomfortable.

"Can I talk to you in private?" he asks me, his voice above a whisper. When I turn to face Helena, I realise she's already walked away.

"About?" I ask, avoiding his gaze by zipping my backpack.

"I'm sorry about what happened, okay?"

"I don't care, Chris."

"But I do, okay? I love you, and I'm really sorry," he pleads, making me feel somewhat appreciated. If Chris and I broke up, my sanity would drain faster than water. I'd never be prepared for that. I exhale, trying to calm down.

"Okay," I say, giving in. Chris grins at me, releasing a relieved exhale. "But I don't like it when you laugh at me," I add.

"I wasn't laughing at you; I was laughing at Jason's comment. But you were really out of it, babe."

"The fact I looked 'out of it' and you haven't bothered to talk to me makes me angry," I snap, feeling my anger return. Chris' eyes widen. I've never been angry at him. I usually go along with what he wants, being submissive and tolerant. Could it be that, since I started blacking out, I've started losing control of my words, too?

"Okay. Something's going on," Chris says, crossing his arms. "You've never been mad at me."

"Maybe because I never speak up about it," I fire back. Chris is perplexed by my reaction—his lips are slightly parted, and his eyes have widened.

"Are you saying this because you don't wanna see me play tonight?" he asks, his tone hurt.

"No. I do want to see you play," I lie.

"Then, what is it?"

"I can't let you keep treating me like shit. That's what it is," I retort. Shit, I'm running my mouth, but I can't help it. I've reached my breaking point. Chris scoffs, rubbing his freshly shaven chin. He takes a deep breath, but the anger resides in his tone.

"How am I treating you like shit? You're the one that doesn't talk to anyone except me. If anything, you treat yourself like shit, Cora."

"Don't talk to me like that," I snap. I'm about to storm off when Chris grabs my arm, pulling me to him. We lock eyes, but his anger physically fades when he sighs.

"Look, I'm sorry. I'll hang out with you more. I've just been busy with the band." Chris cups my cheeks, pressing his lips against mine. I force myself to not recoil, hiding my anger.

"Okay, but promise me you won't get drunk tonight," I say, aware I could be at the verge of making him angrier. But much to my surprise, he nods.

"I won't get drunk," he insists. He cups my cheeks, his hazel eyes lingering on mine.

"Good," I say, smiling. I go on my tiptoes to kiss him, his hands dropping to my waist. Something at the corner of my eye catches my attention, but it's not just 'something'—it's Theo. He's staring at me from the other side of the hallway, his backpack slung on his shoulder. His focus remains on me momentarily before walking away.

"What's up?" Chris asks, glancing behind him, but Theo has disappeared.

"Nothing," I respond, pursing my lips. Why did Theo look angry at me?

"Okay, I feel like we should really talk about what's been going on. You've been zoning out way too often. Are they back?"

I release a deep sigh. He's the only person who knows about my flashbacks. The psychiatrist who diagnosed me at the age of ten labelled it as Post-Traumatic Stress Disorder.

"Yeah," I lie. The truth is that I have no clue why the dream of the forest has persisted in my mind for six months or what it symbolises. However, what terrifies me more than the dream is the blackout from yesterday.

Chris nervously runs a hand through his hair. Neither of us likes the return of my instability.

"What do we do?" Chris murmurs under his breath. He knows what could happen to me if the flashbacks return. He knows how severe things have gotten in the past. But this isn't just flashbacks—it's worse.

"I don't know," I say, sighing. "Shit." I smack my palm against my forehead. "I have gym tonight." Chris' expression darkens.

"At what time?" he asks. The final school bell reverberates through the building, and students spill out of the classrooms with haste.

"Now,"

"Go. If you're a few minutes late to the gig that's okay," Chris says, giving me a peck on the cheek. I hug Chris before watching him disappear into the crowd of students.

•••••

Entering the female changing room, I toss my gym bag onto the bench before getting dressed. I tie my hair up into a high ponytail, slip on some shorts and a sports bra, and lock up my belongings.

Walking into the gym, my eyes widen in surprise as I see Theo on the benches lifting weights. He only realises my presence when I step onto the treadmill, his gaze making my cheeks flush. Quickly plugging in my earphones to avoid conversation, I start my run.

I don't realise I've lost track of time until I realise the sun has already set. I blacked out again. Fuck. Theo raises a brow, sitting up from the benches, his forehead damp from the exercise.

"Holy shit," he mouths, but my music drowns out his voice. Popping out my earphones, I step off the machine and try to regain my breath. I ignore his eyes on me and wipe the sweat off my torso with my towel. Our eyes meet instantly when I look at him, making my heart race.

"What?" I scowl, feeling somewhat intimidated.

"You've been running for an hour straight," he breathes. He sounds impressed, but from his built physique, I know he's capable of running for longer.

"So?" I reply coolly, shrugging.

"You're quite the athlete," Theo teases, making me roll my eyes.

"You're a jerk," I fire back, sitting down on the ground to regain my breath.

"And you're annoying," he replies in a light-hearted tone before grabbing the weights again. He lifts them a few times, and I find my gaze fixated on the rhythmic movement of his muscles, the sweat rolling down his arms.

"You're staring," he purrs, smug that he's caught me looking at him. My cheeks turn crimson, but I brush off his comment with a scoff. Without saying a word, I rise from the floor, and head towards the changing room.

As the warm water cascades over me, I try to wash away the thoughts of Theo and his rhythmic weightlifting. Dressed in fresh clothes, my mind remains tangled in a web of confusion. Why does he make me nervous? No, this is wrong. What would Chris think?

I shake off the thoughts before leaving the changing room, but I'm taken aback when I see Theo standing outside, his bag strapped to his shoulder and a smirk on his face.

"Are you done?" he asks in a playful tone.

"Are you stalking me?" I ask back with a smirk. "First the park, now this." Theo laughs, shaking his head.

"You wish," he replies. His gaze lingers on me as I check my phone and realise it's 5:13 P.M.—just enough time to make it to Chris' gig.

"Do you want to get some food? Gym people need to stick together," he suggests. A realisation hits me—I might have crossed a line.

"I'm sorry, but I have a boyfriend," I clarify, feeling guilty. Did Theo think—

"What makes you think I was asking you on a date?" he chuckles.

"Why would you want to hang out with me? You can't stand me," I joke. Theo laughs softly, a smirk forming on his lips. Closing the distance, he steps towards me until our bodies are mere inches apart. My heart races, and my cheeks flush from his proximity.

"Because you and I have more in common than you think," he whispers, his gaze intense.

"You and I have nothing in common," I retort. I feel his ocean eyes follow me as I walk away, not saying another word.

4

I take a deep, anxious breath as I step into the old-fashioned bar. The crowded atmosphere makes my heart race, and I instantly regret coming here. I head toward the stage, feeling the weight of people's scrutinising glares on me. Their eyes seem to pierce through, giving me the uncomfortable sense that they're silently critiquing my every move. Laughter, chatter, and occasional singing fill the air as everyone eagerly awaits the band to take the stage.

For someone who doesn't black out and lose track of time, this atmosphere might seem normal. However, in my eyes, the dim glow from the oil lamps distorts people's silhouettes, casting a villainous threatening air over the setting. It's my paranoia, creeping up the back of my neck and colouring my perception. The sensation of being in a constant 'fight or flight mode'—a surreal experience to an ordinary person. I shoot a text to Chris, informing him that I'm early.

> **chris ♥**   now
> *Great. I'm excited to see you.*
> *I love you* ♥♥

The crowd's enthusiastic cheers interrupt my thoughts as The Rebellions take the stage. My paranoia turns into excitement as Chris waves to the lively crowd, and he notices me with a wide grin.

Jason, the main singer, thanks the crowd for coming, and the band starts their first song with a crescendo of strumming strings. I can't help but feel a sense of awe for Chris's passion for playing bass, wondering how he manages to be with someone who isn't a fan of rock music.

When the song ends, the crowd roars, including me. Maybe I should have more faith in Chris. Maybe he can help me overcome my recurring dream of the forest fire, just like he helped me overcome the flashbacks.

As the crowd begins to pour out of the bar, I head towards the back of the stage, where I spot Chris downing an entire bottle of water. I run up to him, wrapping my arms around him from behind. He turns around, his face lighting up with a wide grin as he kisses the top of my head.

"Hey babe," Chris exclaims, his skin glowing from the performance.

"That was amazing! You were so amazing!" I congratulate him. He seals the moment with a kiss, his arms wrapped around my waist. In that moment, everything feels perfect, as if it has always been this way.

But as Chris walks me home from the bar, the anxious thoughts start to creep back in. I can't shake off the fact that I blacked out at the gym, and even Theo noticed. It's possible that there is a connection between the blackouts and my insomnia, something I hadn't considered until now. My mind wanders as Chris discusses his band, but Helena's words about their upcoming tour suddenly come rushing back to me.

"Chris, I wanted to talk to you about something," I say, my anxiety already creeping in.

"What is it?" he asks, his brows furrowed with concern. The clouds part in the sky, unveiling the ivory-coloured moon behind the forest trees, casting a subtle glimmer of tranquillity. My heart pounding, I take a deep breath, bracing myself for what's to come.

"Is it true your band is going on a tour?" I ask. There's a pause before Chris cusses under his breath. I suddenly feel nauseous. "It's true?" I shriek. Chris lowers his gaze, guilt written all over his face. He sighs.

"I wanted to tell you, but it's not finalised yet," he mumbles.

"Finalised? Someone told *me* about this. Someone who apparently knows more about you than I do," I snap, my temper bubbling.

I can't believe he hid this from me. That's not who we are. We don't keep secrets from each other.

"Who told you?" he asks, stopping his footsteps. As I look up at the moon, a sudden yet terrifying realisation sinks in. I can't keep lying to myself. I'm not sure if I feel the same way about Chris anymore.

"It doesn't matter who told me. You've been hiding things from me."

"Hiding things? Cora, it's just some stupid tour," he argues, crossing his arms. I shake my head with an ironic laugh.

"Yeah, well, the stupid tour is your *life*, Chris. Do you know what you're gonna do after high school? I mean, we're seniors, and you have no idea what to do," I shout at him. Chris' face scrunches up in anger, the emotion visibly building up within him.

"You know what? Fine! I'm not like you, Cora. I'm not smart and I hate studying. The only thing I have is music," he yells back. The anger within me simmers, reaching a boiling point as I feel close to my breaking point.

"I'm not criticising your passion. I'm saying this tour is so important to you. Why didn't you have the guts to tell me? Why did you hide this from me?" I exclaim, my eyes filling with tears. I make a conscious effort to pause and take a deep breath. Shouting in the middle of the street at midnight isn't the solution.

Chris recognises the need for both of us to calm down, and he nervously chews his lip.

"Because..." he mumbles in a deep voice, lowering his chin. "I knew it would make you really upset. So, I was going to tell you in the least painful way possible."

"So, hiding it was the least painful way? God, Chris. I'm not some grenade about to explode. I can handle shit like that."

"I never said you couldn't, Cora," he says, pressing his lips together.

"Yes, you are! That's why you didn't tell me."

"No, Cora. I've seen how you've been acting this whole week. You're blacking out, not remembering things. It looks like you haven't slept well in days. I didn't want you to get worse. We've been in this situation before," he explains.

He's referring to the night I ran away to New Jersey City. It was a year ago, when the flashbacks of my mom's death resurfaced. It was the day I lost control—but things are different now.

"It's nowhere near the same. I'm different," I murmur. My voice quivers, similar to a frightened ten-year-old girl who just lost her mother. Chris shoots me a scowl.

"Yeah, that's where you're right. You keep starting arguments with me."

Something inside of me snaps. I can't do this anymore.

"Okay. Fine!" I shout. I storm off into the night, not daring to look back at him.

The only glimmer of light as I cross the road comes from the soft glow of the streetlights. Inside my house, the lights are off, meaning that my dad is already asleep. The eerie emergence of fog sends shivers down my spine as I climb the porch steps.

I wonder if my dad realised I was out all afternoon, but then again, it wouldn't surprise me if he didn't. Silently unlocking the front door, I tiptoe to my bedroom with tears in my eyes, still upset from the fight with Chris. I lie down on the bed, hoping I'll be able to forget what just happened.

•••••

I'm awake. I don't know why. I'm suddenly overcome by an inexplicable urge to get out of bed. Putting on my hoodie, I head to the window and jump, landing on the ground with a soft thud. It's as if my body is moving on its own, my mind strangely blank. Glancing back at my house one last time, my feet guide me to the park, adrenaline coursing through me. Stepping over the low fence, memories of the last time I was here flood my mind.

The flashlight. The cabin. Theo.

I feel an inexplicable pull towards the lake in the horizon, quickening my pace towards it. The moon, which was concealed by clouds only a few hours ago, now gleams serenely on the lake, and the distant hum of crickets fills the air. I settle down at the edge of the lake, dipping a finger into the lukewarm water. Soft ripples form on the surface, similar to creases on gentle skin, while a breeze dances through the trees.

In that moment, a glistening object in the sediment captures my attention. On impulse, my feet plunge into the water and sink into the upper sediment as I stride through the lake toward the shiny object. Scooping the object out of the water, my eyes widen when I realise it's an antique gold watch.

Why would this be underwater?

Examining the watch, I notice grime covering the wristband and the face of it. Suddenly, my foot sinks deeper into the sediment. I curse under my breath, looking down at my foot. I almost let out an ear-piercing scream when I see a milky-white hand underneath the sediment.

•••••

I called the cops. The moment I stepped out of the water, I knew I had to tell someone. However, I hadn't thought of a plausible explanation as to why I found a dead body at 5 A.M.— and now my alibi is flimsier than water.

I'm in an interrogation room with the Sheriff and his Deputy, my hands trembling from anxiety. I've been here for almost an hour. Bureaucracy, the Sheriff called it.

"Let's go over your statement again. You mentioned being outside at 5 A.M. on Saturday, because you couldn't sleep. You saw a glistening object in the water, went to retrieve it, and that's when you discovered the body," the Sheriff reads my handwritten statement.

"That's correct," I reply. I feel a knot form in my stomach as I glance at the clock behind the Sheriff. Shit. It's almost 6 A.M., and my dad must be awake by now. The Sheriff and the Deputy exchange a look, and the Deputy clears his throat.

"So, you're saying you woke up in the middle of the night and found the body?" the Deputy asks as if he were trying to convince himself.

"Yes, sir," I reply politely, realising how suspicious my statement sounds. Do they think I killed the woman in the lake? The Sheriff nods, sliding a few pictures of a man across the desk.

"Do you recognise this man?" he asks, eyeing me. I study the picture, trying to see if I recognise the man, but his face is unfamiliar. Thick black hair and a moustache—a stranger to me.

"No," I say, feeling a chill that reaches my toes.

"We have her husband in custody. He's had a criminal record since he was a teen," he states. After a pause, the Sheriff exhales, gathering the pictures.

"Thank you for your help. I will escort you to the front office. If your parents ask why you're late, say you had to speak to me."

As the Deputy guides me out of the interrogation room, my throat dries up like sandpaper. We pass by the jail cell, and behind the glass, a man in his late forties with dirty hair, a thick moustache, and menacing eyes glares at me. A name echoes in my head, one I can't remember ever hearing.

Robert Harris. He murdered the woman I found at the bottom of the lake. Wait. How could I possibly know that?

The jailed man's sinister gaze has been etched into my mind, sending an unavoidable shiver down my spine. I head out of the police department, following the narrow road that leads me home. My phone buzzes, making me jump.

> **chris ♥**   now
> *I'm so sorry about last night. I feel like I was such an asshole to you.*

I sigh, locking my phone. If Chris found out about this, he might think I'm a psychopath.

Maybe I am.

•••••

The questions circle endlessly in my mind as I approach my house, the sunrise blending in with the night sky. How could I have known that a body would be sitting at the bottom of the lake? How did I know the man's name?

A tense atmosphere fills the air as I quietly unlock the front door. My heart nearly halts when I find my father standing in the hallway, arms crossed and a disappointed scowl on his face.

"Where on Earth have you been?" my father demands, frustration evident in his tone. I muster the strength to reply without revealing the panic bubbling within me.

"I went for a walk," I mutter. I meet his shattered gaze, instantly regretting the lie that slipped through my lips.

"Okay, what about last night? You didn't even come home for dinner."

"I went to the bar to watch Chris play. Don't worry, I didn't drink," I say, rushing up the stairs. My excuses are paper thin, and I can tell that he doesn't believe me. But I'm not emotionally stable enough to talk to anyone after finding a dead body.

"Come back here, we're not done talking." My dad's words stop me from going to my room, the guilt catching up to me again. I sigh, walking down a few steps and making eye-contact with him.

"Okay," I say, crossing my arms. The worst part is, I can't tell him about last night. He'd send me to a therapist again if he suspected anything—and that is the last thing I need.

"I was quite upset that you didn't meet Isabelle," he starts, making me roll my eyes. I can't believe he is still holding onto that.

"I told you, I fell asleep. I had a very tiring day."

"I've noticed you haven't gotten as much sleep as you used to. You should talk to me about this, Cora. Is something wrong?"

"I'm fine!" I assert, trying to convince myself. The reality is, I'm not sure if I'm fine. I'm losing my mind, and that is the only thing I'm certain of.

"Are you sure?" he asks, his brows furrowing.

"Yes, Dad. I'm sure. It's been a hectic first week, that's all." I insist.

"Alright." He sighs, worsening the guilt within me. "I believe you, kiddo."

"Good. So... How was the dinner?" I ask, even if I don't want to know the answer.

"It was great. I can't believe I didn't mess up the lasagne," he chuckles. I give him a tight, awkward smile.

I'll never understand how my dad moved on so quickly since my mom's death. Sure, it's almost been a decade, but just as I don't want another mom, I can't fathom why he wants a new wife. Maybe I'm just a broody teenager.

An uncomfortable silence fills the room before I break it with a subtle clearing of my throat.

"Well, I'm gonna go upstairs. I have some work to finish," I say.

"Okay, kiddo," he mutters, and I head upstairs. Collapsing onto my bed, I release a heavy sigh. The exhaustion settles in, and I let my body disconnect. Fatigue seeps through my bones from having slept only a few hours, and I can sense my body disconnecting. Resting my head on the pillow, I instantly fall into a deep sleep.

I wake up around noon, letting out a yawn as I sit up in bed. Checking my phone, I find messages from Chris.

> **chris ♥** 10m ago
> *cora, we need to talk. it's important*
>
> **chris ♥** 10m ago
> *don't ignore me, okay?*
>
> **chris ♥** 10m ago
> *i love you*

me
sorry, i've been busy, whats up?

chris ♥
can i come over right now?

Me
my dad is home

chris ♥
it's okay, i can sneak in. it's not like it's the first time i've done it 😊😊

me
is 5pm okay?

5

My phone buzzes as I type the final words of my history paper, and I see an Instagram notification. It's Helena—she probably found me by searching my name and surname.

> **helenacorey**
> *hi girl! have you done the history homework?* 😊

> **coradanvers**
> I'm on it. It seems to take forever 😒😒

> **helenacorey**
> hahahaha ikr. Im almost done with it tho.

> **coradanvers**
> awesome

> **helenacorey**
> hey um did you see what happened on the news?

> **coradanvers**
> what news?

> **helenacorey**
> *OMG!! you must check it out N O W.*

I stare at the reply, puzzled about what Hel could be freaking out about. Just as I contemplate checking the local news, a knock on my window startles me. Leaning against the window, I gasp softly when I see Chris outside, holding a pebble. I open the window, letting in a cool breeze that ruffles my curtains.

"You're gonna smash my windows," I groan, making Chris laugh.

"Can I come up?" he asks, holding onto the tree next to my window.

"Be careful," I warn, observing him clumsily climbing up the tree. He nearly slips a few times but manages to reach my window frame. He lands on my bed, backside first, wrapping his arms around me immediately. He starts to nibble on my collarbone, making an involuntary moan escape my lips.

"Chris! What are you doing!" I giggle, giving him a playful shove. His emerald eyes meet mine, and he pouts.

"Kissing you. Is that okay?" he asks, his eyes filled with desire. I playfully dodge a few kisses, pushing him away.

"We haven't exactly made up," I tease, not letting him off the hook that easily.

"Let's do that now," Chris suggests, running a cold hand up my shirt. I laugh, swatting his hand.

"That's too easy," I say, a grin spreading across my face. I grab his arms, pinning him to the bed. We share a chuckle as we playfully wrestle, laughter echoing in the room. But Chris is far stronger than me, and he ends up on top of me.

"Isn't your dad home?" Chris whispers, his face inches from mine.

"He is, which is why we have to keep it down," I whisper back, playfully poking his nose. Chris beams, gently stroking my cheek with the pad of his thumb.

"Well... What we just did wasn't exactly being quiet," he whispers.

We share a quiet moment, his eyes locked onto mine with a comforting warmth. It feels like the chaotic events of the past few days have temporarily faded away—arguing with Chris, my dad, my blackouts, and the dead woman I found at the bottom of the lake. I can't break up with Chris, not when he is the only person that stabilises me.

A sudden, overwhelming desire to have him close to me washes over me. I press my lips against his, my tongue brushing against his bottom lip. Chris lets out a moan, gripping my hips in response. With a swift movement, I straddle him, planting hungry kisses on his neck. His hands snake up my shirt until he reaches my bra strap, causing goose bumps on my skin.

"I love you, Cora," he whispers, his eyes filled with longing.

"I love you, too," I whisper back. But as he starts to fiddle with my bra strap, my body instinctively jerks away from him. It feels like his touch triggered a powerful wave of repulsion within me. My body moves instinctively, rolling off the bed, confusion flooding my thoughts. Why did I do that?

"Did I do something wrong?" he asks, a hint of sadness in his voice.

"I don't know," I mumble, avoiding his gaze. "I really don't know," I repeat, but Chris sits up, a concerned expression on his face. He can tell I'm not being honest.

"Cora, I'm being serious. What's going on?" he insists.

A sudden throbbing pain strikes my temples before I can answer. Closing my eyes, I wince in pain, and my heart skips a beat as I realise I'm standing in Evergreen Forest. A flashlight hangs on a tree branch, and the tree bark is covered in dense black soot. A twig snaps behind me, causing me to spin on my heels. There's a shadow among the trees, but I can't make out its identity. The faint scent of burnt wood lingers in the air.

My eyes snap open, the echo crackling fire fading away. I'm back in my bedroom, and Chris is staring at me as if he had seen a ghost.

"Cora?" he says, his tone filled with worry. The air is sucked out of my lungs as I replay what I have just seen. It feels like I was there, in that very moment, witnessing the fire unfold. The hesitation is evident in my eyes as I avoid meeting his gaze; there's no way I can tell him what just happened.

"Yeah?" I ask, pretending nothing is wrong, but my voice trembles when I speak. Chris bites his lip in worry, concern etched on his face.

"Are you okay? What happened?" he asks. He's afraid. So am I. I've started losing control in front of him—but a thought lingers in the back of my mind. Some details were added to my dream. Was it even a dream?

"Yeah. I was just lost in thought," I lie. I wish I weren't lying to his face. Chris's lips part, as if he's about to say something, but he closes them again, scratching his head in puzzlement.

"With… With your eyes closed?" he stammers. He doesn't believe me, and I don't blame him. This is happening too frequently now, but I can't confess that to him.

"Yep, just lost in thought with my eyes closed," I fib again. "You seem a bit alarmed," I note, trying to downplay the strangeness.

"You were out of it for more than a minute," Chris replies.

"I was just deep in thought, Chris," I snap, frustration bubbling up. He sighs at my sudden outburst, massaging his temples.

"Maybe you could use some rest," he suggests, his tone earnest.

"But I'm fine."

"You practically fell asleep standing up," Chris chuckles. I roll my eyes at him.

"Fine, I'll go to bed after dinner," I reply. Chris grins, pulling me into a tight hug.

"I should head home. My mom is probably wondering where I am." I nod, partly grateful he's leaving. I wish I could tell him what's going on, but the last thing I want is him worrying about me.

"Let me help you out," I offer. I push the window open, observing as Chris clings to the tree trunk. His eyes meet mine, a gentle smile gracing his lips.

"I'll see you on Monday," he says, releasing his grip. He lands on the grass with a thud, offering a wave before fading into the shadows.

•••••

Dinner with my dad is typically awkward, especially now that he's aware of my disapproval toward his girlfriend. I haven't explicitly voiced my dislike, but I'm pretty sure he picked up on it from my body language.

I shove the last bite of steak into my mouth, my eyes glued to the TV screen across the room. My dad, who has already finished his meal, places his plate in the sink. The TV show I was absorbed in is cut off by flashing headlines, making me drop my fork onto the plate.

The news hits me like a cold wave, sending shivers down my spine as the anchor announces, "Jorna Harris's body discovered at Mulkiwa Park following a neighbour's tip-off. Robert Harris, the murderer, formerly served as an information officer at Mulkiwa Park. Found guilty in court, he's sentenced to life imprisonment, facing accusations of sexual abuse and drug possession."

The photo of the man I glimpsed in jail appears to the right of the reporter, and my stomach churns with shock. Panic sets in. How did I know Robert Harris killed his wife? More importantly, how did I know his name?

A chilling realisation settles in the pit of my stomach.

Without uttering a word, I dash upstairs to my bedroom. Rifling through a few drawers, my heart races in my chest when I find Robert Harris' flashlight—the one I found at Mulkiwa Park.

I grab my phone and message the last person I'd ever consider reaching out to—the only person who was at the park when I found Robert Harris' flashlight.

•••••

It's official—I can't sleep. The news headline has had me tossing and turning for the past few hours, my head swirling with horrifying questions. How did I recognise Robert Harris when I saw him in jail, and how was I so certain he murdered his wife? How do I justify having his flashlight to the police? How am I going to explain to anyone what is happening to me?

The vibration of my phone on the nightstand startles me, causing me to bolt upright on the bed. Glancing at the message, I hastily throw on a hoodie and quietly walk downstairs. Stepping into the night, the loud chirping of crickets surrounds me as I make my way to the front gate. I shiver in my thin pyjamas, the darkness of the night heightening my unease.

A shadow catches my attention as it approaches from across the street, and I start fidgeting with my sleeve. The silhouette gradually turns into Theo's outline, and my teeth chatter by the time he reaches me. He's wearing the school's football hoodie, his hair half-wet as if he had just showered.

"What do you wanna talk about at this hour?" Theo asks, a smirk tugging on his lips. Shit, I just realised he might interpret this as a booty call—but I need to ensure my hands are clean if the investigation continues. Theo is the only one who witnessed me taking Robert Harris' flashlight.

"I didn't expect you to text me back at this hour. I was thinking more of an 8:30 meetup," I whisper, feeling my cheeks flush with embarrassment.

"Sorry, I've only just finished practice," he says, gesturing to the gym bag slung over his shoulder. He crosses his arms over his chest, waiting for me to speak.

"I'm not sure if you've seen the news…" I murmur.

"About the dead woman? Yeah, it's pretty messed up," he nods.

"Listen…" I say, taking a deep breath. "Turns out I accidentally took his flashlight. Please don't tell anyone," I plead, desperation creeping into my tone. His eyes widen in surprise.

"It was his flashlight?" he whispers. "Why don't you want to tell them you found it?"

I nervously bite my lip, scrambling to come up with a reasonable excuse.

"Because…" I trail off. *It's not too late to back out, Cora. You don't have to tell him-* "I was the one that found the body. They might think I was involved." Surprise flickers across Theo's eyes.

"Wait… How did you find the body?"

The question lingers in the air like a dense fog. I'm at a loss for how to respond. There's no clear explanation for how I found Jorna Harris' body at Mulkiwa Lake. But I need to say something, or he might suspect my involvement.

"I…" I stammer, unsure what to say. "I couldn't sleep, so I went for a walk. And that's when I found it," I confess, soon realising how suspicious I sound.

Theo tilts his head, as if questioning whether to believe me. Then, his face drains of colour. He shoots me a panicked look before burying his face in his hands.

"Oh, my God…" he mutters.

"What?" I ask, my voice squeaky with fear. Theo exhales deeply, rubbing his temples.

"We were there the night of the murder."

"What?" I gasp, my face draining of colour. "You mean…"

Theo nods, biting his lip.

"You found his flashlight the night it happened," he says, locking eyes with me. "You can't tell anyone about that flashlight, Cora."

"I-I won't," I stammer, realising the gravity of the situation. If the police suspected our involvement, everything would untangle. A criminal record, the town finding out—we'd lose it all.

Theo nods, the seriousness in his expression heightening my anxiety. Just a week ago, he was a stranger, and now we find ourselves temporarily entangled in this mess. There's a brief pause between us before Theo decides to break the silence.

"I don't understand why, but I trust you," he says, his voice softening. My heart skips a beat as our eyes connect, noticing the intensity of his gaze.

"Really?" I ask, surprised. Closing the distance, he steps towards me, and now we're only half a foot apart. His height makes him tower over me. He nods.

"Yeah. I guess I have a hunch about you," he says, a soft smile tugging the corners of his lips. Wait, I swear we've had this conversation before. All of a sudden, it feels like we're standing a bit too close.

"You must use that line on every girl who talks to you," I tease, hoping to remove the seriousness of the conversation. Theo lets out a chuckle.

"I thought we were just friends," he says, in a playful tone. A blush creeps onto my cheeks.

"We are. I know guys like you," I retort. Why am I repeating words I'm sure I've said to him before?

"Oh yeah?" Theo challenges me. "What do you think we're like?"

My legs start to tremble from his proximity, his blue eyes locking onto mine. I find the strength to stand my ground.

"Arrogant, cocky. You think every girl wants to be with you just because you're a jock," I retort, anger burning in my eyes. Theo laughs, biting his lip to hold back a chuckle.

"Arrogant and cocky mean the same thing," he corrects me. I roll my eyes.

"You just proved my point."

His gaze drifts from my eyes to my lips, a smirk playing on his face.

"No booty call, then?" he teases. I respond with a scoff.

"In your dreams," I retort, my face heating up from his comment. I try to guide him across the street by playfully pushing his chest, but he stands firm—he's much stronger than me. Theo bites his lip, suppressing a smile as he grabs my wrist. Without thinking, I tilt my chin up, bringing his lips inches away from mine.

"Don't push me," he purrs with a mischievous grin, his sapphire eyes glimmering under the moonlight. "I'll tell the cops about the flashlight."

My heart races, and I give him another playful shove—but it only elicits a stifled laugh from him.

"I can push you as much as I want," I retort, determination in my eyes. Our eyes meet for a moment, and the intensity of his gaze leaves me feeling lightheaded.

"I'm warning you, it's a game you can't win," he teases, a smirk playing on his lips. Rolling my eyes, I let go of him, my heart still pounding in my throat. Crickets chirp in the distance as he crosses the street, and I find myself unable to look away. Once he reaches the other side of the curb, his footsteps come to a halt. He turns to face me, a smile playing on his lips while he shakes his head. I'm relieved that he can't see my blushing face as his silhouette vanishes into the night.

I'm a hundred percent sure this has happened before. But that's impossible. I must be losing my mind—that's for sure.

6

Laughter reverberates through the linoleum-floored hallway, mingling with the sounds of excited shouts and conversations. The shrill sound of the first bell pierces through the chaotic hallway, dulling the surrounding noise. My temples throb from the sudden noise as I make my way to class. I spent the entire Sunday wondering how on Earth I dreamt of Theo coming over to my house—and a week later, the dream actually happened.

It's impossible. Biologically impossible. There's no way it could have happened. What's more, strange dreams have been unsettling my sleep. I found myself in Dr Fleming's office, being scolded for some unknown reason. The dream was so vivid; felt as though I were physically present. Perhaps it's my subconscious telling me to bring my grades up again.

"Cora!" a voice calls out from behind. I turn to see Hel, smiling broadly at me before she pulls me into a hug. I stand awkwardly until she releases me, my thoughts too distracting to engage in small talk.

"Hey," I murmur, my voice croaky. Going out in the middle of the night in my thin PJs might not have been the best idea. Usually, I'd take a few even breaths and push back any thoughts of Theo—but today, I find myself unable to. What worries me the most is that I dreamt about it a week before it happened.

Hel follows me into the classroom, the students' chatter intensifying the throbbing ache in my head.

"You seem tired. Is something wrong?" Hel whispers, following me towards the back. I shake my head.

"I think I have a cold," I mutter, settling into my desk. "So, what was the news you mentioned last night?" I ask, steering the conversation in a different direction. She looks at me, raising a surprised brow.

"Didn't you see the news?" she whispers loud enough for me to hear. "Robert Harris murdered his wife. The cops said it was an open-and-shut case."

"Huh, I don't know him," I reply, which is partially true. I happen to know his name without ever meeting him, but that doesn't mean I *know* him. It's a paradox.

Hel nods, observing as students pour into the classroom and take their seats.

"He was an outsider. He was my dad's neighbour when he was a child," she whispers. Her eyes glimmer with excitement, prompting me to raise a brow.

"You seem enthusiastic about this," I say with a nervous laugh. If Hel knew I found Jorna Harris' body, she'd think I'm a psychopath—or worse—that I was involved.

"This is the most exciting news we've had in Barren since microwavable pizza. You're kidding!" she gushes.

In that moment, the room falls silent. Theo makes his entrance into the classroom, accompanied by Damon Martin by his side, instantly seizing everyone's attention. Damon's egocentric aura prompts an eye roll from both Hel and me. She was right—it was only a matter of time before Theo joined the jocks. Theo smirks at a few popular girls before casually slumping into his seat beside Damon.

Can I truly trust him with a secret as serious as withholding evidence?

Theo turns his head to look at me, a sly smirk on his lips—but the moment is fleeting. Hel notices, shooting me a wide-eyed look.

"I swear he likes you," she whispers.

"I'm sure he doesn't," I mutter. "Plus, I have a boyfriend."

"Shit, that's true." Hel sucks her teeth, her gaze drifting to her notebook. "Did you do the homework?" she asks. As if on cue, Mrs Sanchez rushes into class. As usual, her glasses are perched on the tip of her nose, carrying dense textbooks in her arms.

"No," I mouth to Helena, whose eyes widen. She subtly slips her answer sheet to my desk seconds before the teacher speaks.

"Good morning everyone. Who's done the homework?" she asks, a charming smile on her face. Mrs Sanchez is the type of teacher who supports student participation as a way of learning. Out of the corner of my eye, Theo's hand shoots up. Mrs. Sanchez beams at him, delighted that, for once, a student is eager. "Mr Rhodes. How about you answer the first question?"

"Why was Rosa Parks one of the most important icons in Black history? I said she helped many African Americans establish confidence in fighting for civil rights."

Theo's detailed answer silences the whole class, which doesn't surprise me. Maybe he's not the typical jock who doesn't care about grades.

"Very good, Mr. Rhodes. How about question two?" Mrs. Sanchez asks, a hush falling over the classroom.

I decide to stay low-key for the rest of the lesson until the last few minutes, when Mrs. Sanchez interrupts our work.

"For the next lesson, you'll prepare essay questions in pairs. I've already chosen your partners so there won't be any... drama," she announces with a proud smile. She reaches for a sheet on her desk, calling out some names. Every time a boy is paired with a girl, a few murmured words echo through the classroom.

"Damon and Cora," Mrs. Sanchez reads out. A few chuckles spread, and I clench my fists, feeling the tension as Damon Martin turns to look at me. Surprised that he knows who I am, his devil-like smirk forces me to look away quickly, grabbing my books before the bell rings. My heart pounds in my chest as I rush out of class. The memory of the woman's pale corpse flashes in front of my eyes, making me instinctively clutch Helena's arm as we leave the room.

"Damon Martin, huh?" she comments, her eyes flickering to my hand. "You look like you're about to faint."

Feeling the awkwardness, I swiftly drop my hand to my side, cheeks flushed.

"Is he really that bad?" I ask with scepticism. Honestly, being paired with Damon Martin is the least of my worries. The question lingering in my mind is: What drove Robert Harris to murder his wife? I feel like I might have a clue, but how could I? Coming across the body was purely accidental. Or was it? Hel's laughter interrupts my thoughts.

"He's gonna make you do everything. Mark my words," she says with a knowing glance.

Amidst the chaotic swarm of students exiting the school building, Hel leads the way towards the picnic tables where the seniors gather. I notice Matt and the others at the nearest table, but instead of joining them like Hel, I find myself drawn to Chris's table. A moment of hesitation lingers—I'm aware his friends don't like me, but after flipping out on Chris last night, I feel compelled to make more of an effort.

I freeze when a familiar, yet unexpected voice calls my name from behind. Turning, I find Damon Martin, clad in his football gear, sprinting towards me. Droplets of water cascade down his forehead, as if he just stepped out of a shower or ran a marathon. His hazel eyes meet mine, and the oddity of the situation draws the attention of onlookers.

"I've been looking for you," he purrs in a honeyed tone. I instinctively take a few steps back, feeling slightly intimidated by his closeness and flirtatious tone. I can't help but sense Chris' eyes on me as well.

"Is this about History?" I ask, trying to appear indifferent.

"Yeah, we got a lot of that," he chuckles, stealing a glance at the jocks behind him. They're all staring at us, including Theo, whose expression is unreadable. My stomach churns with unease, praying Chris can't overhear this conversation.

"Last time I checked—no," I retort, making sure my answer is loud enough for people to hear. Damon theatrically places a hand on his chest, as though I had shot him with my words. Laughter ripples through the jocks, drawing the attention of Chris' group. But Damon isn't one to give up easily. His eyes linger on me as if I'm a slab of meat.

"That was harsh. Should we hang out after school to work on the, uh, research?" he asks.

"It's okay, I will do my half at home," I reply dryly. Jak Oban, Damon's trusty sidekick and the ultimate meathead, bursts into laughter. Damon confidently steps closer, a smirk playing on his face.

"Is this about Emma? Because I swear that's a stupid reason to be rude," he says.

The name makes my heart sink to my stomach, causing me to chew my lip in discomfort. Emma was my childhood best friend and the only person I trusted when my mom died. In sophomore year, she developed a huge crush on Damon Martin, who exclusively dates cheerleaders. The word got around to the jocks, and soon, to Damon. The jocks laughed at her about it, spreading a rumour that she stalked him.

"I think that's a pretty good reason," I fire back. "You made her change schools."

Theo's eyes lock with mine, and a wave of disappointment washes over me. I cannot believe he's part of Damon's group after everything they've done. I can only hope he doesn't tell the police about Mulkiwa Lake.

Chris, who has been observing from afar, storms towards us with his fists curled.

"What's this about, Martin?" he spits. Damon nonchalantly shrugs, pretending innocence as he rubs his chin.

"We're discussing homework," Damon replies. Chris scoffs, a smug smirk on his lips.

"Jeez, Damon, you shouldn't be using your entire vocabulary in a sentence," he shoots back. Chris' best friend, Jason, approaches us from the side-lines. He rests his hand on Chris' shoulder.

"Leave it, Chris. No need for drama," Jason says, giving Damon a stern look. Chris elbows him away, clenching his jaw at Damon. I don't like the look of this.

"You were hitting on my girlfriend. You think you own everything, don't you?" he growls.

Just as I'm about to intervene and suggest it's not worth arguing, Theo swiftly pulls me away. Chris swiftly aims his wrist at Damon, landing a lightning-fast punch on Damon's jaw. Damon stumbles backwards, unleashing a string of muttered curses. I stare, wide-eyed at the scene, a sense of fear intensifying within me.

"Stop, Chris! You're-" Jason begins to interject, but his words are abruptly stopped by a blow to Chris' face. A chill courses through my veins as I witness Chris' nose starting to bleed. Damon's friends cheer him on, chanting his name over and over. Several phones hover around, capturing every movement of the brawl.

"You think this is funny, huh?" Damon taunts through gritted teeth. My immediate instinct is to move toward Chris, but my heart freezes as his hand comes flying toward my face. Theo intervenes just in time, pushing him away before he can land a hit on me.

"You almost hit her!" Theo shouts, clutching Chris by the shirt. Blood trickles down Chris' face, his eyes sunken from Damon's punch. The cacophony of the crowd's chants makes my head spin, but I need to intervene and separate them.

"Theo, please stop!" I plead, tugging his arm. Theo's angry gaze briefly meets mine, and the desperation in my expression prompts him to release his grip on Chris. A wave of terror washes over my face as I observe Dr. Fleming pushing past students. In that very moment, Chris' clenched fist connects with Theo's jaw, causing a gasp from the crowd. My face turns pale as I realise that Dr. Fleming has witnessed the altercation.

"Mr Matthews!" Dr Fleming's voice echoes, parting the crowd as he enters. The crowd's excitement vanishes abruptly in the principal's presence, leaving behind an eerie silence. "Come to my office right now!" he booms.

Chris, with his bloody nose and clenched fists, exudes an aggression I've never seen in him before. Theo's jaw is swollen, and Damon's eye now resembles the colour of an eggplant.

"Damon Martin started it," Chris protests, his tone wavering as he tries to catch his breath.

"I don't care who started it! Fights are not the Barren High way and you *all* know that," Dr Fleming asserts, pointing his finger at the crowd with a furious scowl. "Instead of breaking up the fight, you're recording it?! Mr Martin and Mr Rhodes to my office. And all of you—homecoming is cancelled."

The students express their annoyance with groans, and the crowd quickly disperses. It's as if the crowd were flies and Dr. Fleming's words were insect repellent. Damon Martin shoots me a furious glare, as if blaming me for it all, before trailing behind Theo and Chris toward the principal's office. But before I can dash towards Helena, whose eyes are wide with shock, my vision goes black.

7

The first thing I notice is the grey sky adorned with fluffy clouds. The second is the dulling pain at the back of my head. The third is Hel, Matt, and Beth peering down at me from above.

"Cora?" Hel asks, her tone laced with worry. A helping hand assists me in getting up, my palms pressing into the asphalt as I sit upright.

"Are you okay?" Matt asks. The sharp pain in my skull makes me wince, and I gently touch the area where a bruise is sure to form soon.

"What happened?" I murmur, my voice cracking on the last syllable.

"You kind of passed out," Beth replies, helping me rise from the floor. Despite my aching bones, I muster the strength to stand upright.

"Fuck…" I curse, relying on Hel's arm for balance. The courtyard still seems to be swirling around me.

"Let me take you to the nurse," Matt offers, gripping my arm to provide support.

"I'm fine," I insist, shaking my head. I take a series of steady breaths, regaining my balance. Hel observes me with concern in her eyes, motioning for Beth and Matt to step away.

"I'll take her to get a drink. You guys can go," Hel says. Beth and Matt nod, heading off to class. Hel releases a sigh, motioning for me to sit on the picnic bench. "I'll fetch you some water."

Hel rushes to the nearest water fountain, filling her plastic bottle to the brim. She hurries back to the table, handing me the bottle. I take a few satisfyingly large sips, my eyelids closing in bliss.

"Thank you," I hum, flashing her a smile. She settles beside me, her coffee-coloured irises locking onto mine.

"I can't believe that just happened. We haven't had a fight in Barren in like 10 years... Did Chris hit you?"

I shake my head.

"No, Theo pushed him out of the way."

Hel shakes her head in disgust, anger evident in her eyes. I don't think I've ever seen her angry before.

"Man, that's messed up," she mutters.

She's right. There's something unsettling about Chris' sudden aggression, and I don't feel like talking to him about it just yet.

"I think it was just a reflex. He didn't even see it was me," I say, attempting to convince myself, but she shakes her head.

"Still, he owes you a major apology. None of that was okay. I'm just glad Theo intervened and moved you out of the way; those fights can turn really ugly," she adds. I raise a brow at that, considering that just a few days ago, she was fangirling over Chris and his band.

"I thought you liked Chris."

"Girl, what he did was wrong. He started a brawl," she argues. She's got a point. It's made me see him in a different light, but at the same time, I'm terrified of approaching him about it.

"You're right," I mutter with a sigh. "He's going to be suspended for a very long time."

Hel nods in agreement, her lips forming a thin line. She stands up from the bench, extending her hand to me.

"Let me take you to class," she says. I nod, taking her hand before getting up. Our pace towards the school building is slow, hesitant. Neither of us is eager to return to class after the brawl. Before we say goodbye outside my Math class, Hel tugs my arm.

"Are you sure you're feeling better?" she asks. It takes me a few seconds to reply because I'm unsure of the answer myself.

"Physically, yes. Emotionally? Not quite."

•••••

By the time lunchtime rolls around, my anger towards Chris has simmered—somewhat. Hel is right. He needs to understand that what he did was unacceptable, and I'm still uncertain if I want him back.

Hel's group and I sit at the cafeteria, and although nobody mentions the morning's fight, I sense that they want to discuss it.

The conversations revolve around mundane things—weekend plans, homework, Hel's Math grade... but I know what they must be thinking—Cora's boyfriend got into a fight.

With each passing second, my embarrassment intensifies. I finally muster the courage to confront Chris about it. The last thing I want is for my new friends to start avoiding me because of his mistake.

me

> *We need to talk about what*
> *happened. You really messed*
> *up, Chris.*

chris ♥
I didn't fight myself.
There were 2 other people involved

chris ♥
What's really pissed me off is that
Damon and his stupid puppy didn't
get half the amount of shit I got.

"So… Tell us about yourself, Cora. We don't know that much about you." Hel's voice prompts me to leave Chris on read, and given what's just happened, it might be a reasonable solution. I feel all their eyes on me, waiting for my answer. However, the tension eases when Hel swats Matt's arm for chewing on his fries too loudly.

"What do you wanna know?" I ask, taking a swig from my juice. Maybe they're trying to make me feel less awkward after Chris' fight and my sudden fainting. Matt wraps an arm around Hel's waist, planting a kiss on the top of her head. He then locks eyes with me.

"Have you always lived in Barren?" he asks.

"Yeah. Born and raised."

Beth gives me a curious look, arching her flawless, microbladed brows.

"That's strange, I didn't see you until freshman year," she says, making me realise something. They did notice me in the past, they just didn't approach me.

"I was home-schooled until high school," I reply. The reason my dad decided on home-schooling was because of my mom's death. The trauma made it difficult for me to socialise as a child.

"I used to live in Evergreen Forest, actually," I add. Mason raises his brows in surprise.

"I heard that house has been abandoned for years," he mutters, shoving a forkful of pasta into his mouth. I nod, finishing the last of my sandwich.

"It was," I murmur. After my mom died, we couldn't maintain our house because my dad's job couldn't cover the expenses. We tried to sell it, but the banking crisis didn't help. Eventually, my childhood home was left deserted.

"Someone bought it recently, though," Matt says.

"Really? My dad didn't-" I stop myself from finishing the sentence. "Who told you that?" I ask.

"My mom told me. She's a real estate agent," he says, resting his chin on Hel's shoulder.

"Huh…" I mumble, still in disbelief. Memories of the house rush back, bringing a pain to my chest. After we were forced to give up our house, my dad crumbled into money problems and had to sell his family business. He started working at Bern's Surveillance five years ago, and things have been *somewhat* better since then.

I suddenly remember I haven't replied to Chris' message. I hesitate. I want to avoid arguing with him, but I have this inner urge to assert myself.

me
i didn't know about that. but you shouldn't have hit either of them.

chris ♥
you looked uncomfortable and he was harassing you.

chris ♥
it wasn't harmless banter.

·····

Instead of heading for the exit after class, I navigate through the crowd of students eager to go home, making my way towards the lunch hall. I had noticed him heading in that direction after class, which is convenient since I wanted to talk about the fight with him in private. The moment I spot Theo's figure behind the glass door, my heart starts to race.

He's on his knees, scraping gum from under one of the lunch tables. His face is scrunched up in disgust, and he sighs repeatedly in frustration. It takes him a minute to notice me, and for a few seconds, he seems embarrassed. I glance at the bucket filled with chewing gum, a wave of nausea making me look away.

"I see you've figured out your spot," I joke, biting my lip when I realise how rude I sounded. Theo chuckles as if my meanness were just a part of my sense of humour.

"I guess you're right," Theo says with a sigh. He casually tosses the knife used for scraping off gum onto the floor and removes the latex gloves with a swift motion. "How did you know I was here?" he asks, grabbing the mop to clean the sticky tiles. I'd rather be suspended than clean this mess.

"I saw you come here after class," I answer, hoping I don't come off as a stalker. I clear my throat, mustering some courage. "I wanted to tell you something."

"Sure," Theo replies. His usual flirtatious tone is absent, and his focus is entirely on the rhythmic motion of the mop.

"Thank you for..." I trail off, creating a brief silence. Theo pauses his actions to look at me.

"Stopping Chris from hitting you?" he asks, his choice of words making me wince. When he puts it like that... I had never pictured Chris as the kind of guy who deals with his problems through violence.

"Yeah," I mutter, feeling embarrassed.

"How could I not? You're my friend," he says, avoiding my gaze. *Friend.* The word sinks into my gut, but I'm unsure why. He stops his mopping, meeting my gaze with a smirk. "Even if you think I'm an asshole."

I can't help but laugh, shaking my head.

"I don't think you're an asshole," I say shyly, a tinge of remorse for being too harsh. A smile tugs at the corners of his lips as he continues mopping the tiles around me.

"Anyway, if you don't mind, I want to finish this and go home," he says, making my cheeks flush red.

"Right, sorry. I'll leave," I mutter. Exchanging a brief smile, I make my way out of the lunch hall.

Walking through the empty school halls, the day's events swirl in my mind—the heated fight, the confrontation with Chris, and now the unexpected conversation with Theo. The day has been a rollercoaster, and I can't shake the feeling that it's far from over.

As I reach the main entrance, to my surprise, I spot Hel, Matt, and Beth waiting for me. Their expressions are a blend of curiosity and concern.

"Cora, what happened?" Hel asks, her eyes searching mine. "We thought we'd check if you're okay after you fainted today."

I take a moment to gather my thoughts, sighing.

"It's been a crazy day," I say, offering a weak smile. "Let's talk about it outside."

We exit the school building, finding a quiet spot on the steps. I recap the day's events—the escalating conflict between Chris and Damon, Theo's intervention, and the aftermath in the lunch hall. Hel's eyes widen as she listens, Matt's jaw tightens, and Beth shakes her head in disbelief. The heaviness of the day lingers in the air, and I sense the tension among us.

"So, what now?" Matt finally asks, breaking the silence.

I glance at each of them, uncertainty clouding my thoughts. I need to assert myself in front of Chris, but it's my first time doing so, and I'm unsure about how he'll react.

"I need to talk to Chris about all of this," I say, my voice determined. "But I have no idea what to say."

The three of them exchange glances, a silent understanding passing between them. I'm a bit hesitant to know what they might be thinking. Hel places a reassuring hand on my shoulder.

"Trust your gut," she says, offering a supportive smile.

•••••

Gently knocking on Chris' front door, I hope he'll be the one to answer and not his mom. Chris has been living with his mom since childhood, ever since his father abandoned their family for another woman. Perhaps that's why Chris and I have such a dysfunctional dynamic.

To my relief, Chris opens the door. An uneasy silence hangs in the air, leaving us both uncertain about who should break it. I take a deep breath, summoning the courage to speak.

"We need to talk about what happened today," I say, my voice steady. "The fight, your reaction—I can't pretend it didn't happen."

He gazes blankly at me before gesturing for me to come inside. I follow him to the kitchen, where he pours a glass of water for me. Seated on the couch, I awkwardly stare at the drink in my hands. Chris takes a seat across from me, his hands resting in his lap, and his green eyes locked onto mine. He sighs, running a hand through his messy hair.

"My mom is furious," Chris mutters. In all honesty, I can empathise with her. Chris has been a handful to raise—his mom used to complain about it even a few years ago. But not once did she say that Chris was violent.

I bite my inner cheek, mustering the courage to continue the conversation.

"Look, Chris. I deserve an apology," I say. He takes a deep breath, burying his face in his hands.

"You're right," he mumbles. "I'm sorry for almost hitting you. I thought it was Damon."

"You can't just use that as an excuse, Chris," I say firmly. "Even if you thought it was Damon, violence is never the answer."

Chris looks down, his expression a mix of guilt and frustration.

"I don't know, Cora. It just happened. I lost control."

"That's not good enough, Chris," I assert. "I can't be with someone who resorts to violence when things get tough."

I can feel the desperation in his eyes as he shakes his head.

"I know, Cora. I messed up. I just... Please forgive me."

Seeing him in this vulnerable state is unusual for me, but it might be because I had never challenged him until now. Remorse shines in his green eyes, and a pang of guilt hits me—but Helena's words echo in my mind. Taking a deep breath, I brace myself for what I'm about to say next.

"I didn't just come here to discuss the fight. I think we need to take a break," I state. Chris looks up, his eyes widening in surprise.

"A break?" he repeats, disbelief evident in his tone. I nod, the weight of the words heavy on my shoulders.

"Yeah, a break. This fight, everything that happened today—it's just too much. I need some time to think, to figure things out."

The atmosphere in the room becomes heavy with tension. He leans back on the couch, sighing in frustration.

"Cora, we've been through a lot. Can't we just work through this?" he pleads. His persistent attitude suddenly overwhelms me. I let out a sigh, irritation etched on my face.

"Chris, it's not just about today. It's about us. Our relationship has become toxic, and we both need space to breathe."

Silence hangs in the air as Chris processes my words. I can see the hurt in his eyes, and it makes my heart ache. But deep down, I know it's the right decision—for both of us.

"Have you seen your therapist lately? Because I've noticed you've gone back to old patterns," he remarks.

"Not since last year," I reply. Chris furrows his brows.

"You should. They can give you pills for your situation, Cora. They help repress memories, too."

"I don't want to forget that my mom died," I interject, crossing my arms. Chris shoots me a sympathetic glance, realising he's touching a sensitive subject.

"I know... You know, when my dad left us, all I wanted was for things to go back to normal. I wished he would come back, but... The truth is, we can't change people's minds," Chris utters, sighing. He continues, his gaze lingering on a distant memory. "I tried so hard to hold on to the idea of my parents being together, but sometimes holding on hurts more than letting go. It took me a while to accept that some things are beyond our control."

I nod in understanding, appreciating the vulnerability in his words. It's a shared moment of silent acknowledgment between us, each carrying the weight of our own pasts.
Chris looks at me earnestly, his concern etched on his face.

"I want to help you, Cora. But I don't know how to. I don't know if I should even go on this tour."

A mix of emotions swirl within me. It's comforting to know he wants to be there for me, but I can't stop him from going on tour.

"You have to. I don't want you to put your dreams on hold for me. Besides, some distance might help us figure things out," I explain.

Chris sighs, his emerald eyes locking onto mine. He moves closer on the couch, enveloping me in his arms.

"I'm so sorry for almost hitting you. I swear to God I didn't see you," he murmurs into my hair. A lone tear traces down my cheek, landing on Chris' shoulder.

"I forgive you… but we need this break." I sniffle, pulling away from the hug. He avoids eye contact as he rises from the couch, the pain in his expression making my heart clench.

He walks me to the door, both aware that his mom could walk in at any moment. Standing awkwardly in the hallway, I find myself at a loss for words. I suppose there isn't much to discuss with someone you've just ended a relationship with. Chris breaks the silence with a hesitant smile.

"Take care, Cora. I'll… I'll see you around."

I manage a small nod, my throat feeling tight.

"Yeah, you too."

With that, Chris retreats into his house, leaving me alone on the porch. The weight of the moment settles on my shoulders, and I take a deep breath, trying to gather the strength to move forward.

The night air is cool, and I wrap my arms around myself, both for warmth and a sense of comfort. The break-up was necessary, I tell myself. It's a step toward healing, toward figuring out what is happening to me. Yet, the ache in my chest tells a different story.

As I turn to leave, I can't help but glance back at the closed door, knowing that behind it, a chapter of my life has just closed. With each step away, I try to shake off the past, embracing the uncertain but necessary journey that lies ahead.

Mid-step, my heart jolts as my phone vibrates in my back pocket. Fumbling to retrieve it, I can't help but wonder who could be reaching out at this hour.

8

Theo's name illuminates my screen, and I realise he's just followed my Instagram. A mix of surprise and curiosity floods over me. It's as if the universe is weaving an intricate web of connections between Theo and me, and I find myself entangled in its threads. My thumb hovers over the phone, accepting the follow request.

> **theorhodes**
> *Can't believe how filthy students are.*

> **coradanvers**
> *It looked pretty gross.*

> **theorhodes**
> *I'm sorry your bf got in trouble didn't know what Damon was up to. I didn't know Chris was going to escalate things too.*

> **coradanvers**
> *It's fine.*

I tuck my phone away, releasing a heavy sigh. The uncertainty surrounding my decision to end things with Chris makes my heart ache, as if I'm missing one of my limbs.

I walk home, the cold night air biting at my skin. The streetlights cast long shadows on the curb, creating an eerie atmosphere. As I approach, my two-story house comes into view. I notice the lights are on downstairs, signalling that my dad must be home.

Unlocking the door, I'm drawn to the soft murmurs coming from the kitchen. Moving quietly, I tiptoe towards the source of the conversation. My heart quickens as I spot a blonde woman sitting with my dad at the dinner table. He looks up as he hears my footsteps, and the woman, probably in her mid-forties, delicately wipes her mouth with a napkin.

"Cora, you're home," my dad smiles, a wine glass in his hand. My dad rarely drinks wine; he's more of a beer person. He's clearly trying to make an impression on the blonde woman, whose gaze is fixed on me. She extends her hand, offering me a perfect smile.

"Hi, sweetie. I'm Isabelle," she introduces herself warmly. She seems familiar like a face I've glimpsed at the supermarket or during her dog walks. Her beauty is undeniable, and it's clear why my dad is drawn to her. Yet, an unexpected surge of anger rises within me, remembering my mom and the life we had before.

I force myself to shake her hand, my expression stoic—but the moment our skin grazes, my vision plunges into darkness.

I see it again. The flames, my flashlight on the tree branch. I find myself surrounded by towering trees, the air heavy with the bitter scent of smoke. The crackling sound of burning branches echoes in my ears, and the flames paint the landscape in an orange glow. The taste of ashes lingers on my tongue, intensified by the overwhelming scent of burning wood. The pine trees in the distance succumb to the fiery embrace, the heat clinging to my clothes.

Amid the swirling smoke, the moon emerges from behind dark grey clouds, casting an eerie glow. A soft crunch of twigs startles me from behind. Turning slowly, I face a shadow—a pure black silhouette that I cannot distinguish.

"Cora?" a distorted voice calls out. The forest fire scene begins to blur around me, and I find myself back in the kitchen. My dad and his girlfriend stare wide-eyed at me, their faces pale with shock. A sudden, bone-chilling coldness takes hold, making my teeth chatter.

As if driven by an animalistic instinct, I sprint up the stairs and lock myself in my bedroom. I hadn't even noticed that my breathing had become ragged, only the throbbing pain striking my temples. Am I having a mental breakdown? The dream has never been this intense before. I'm losing my mind.

I can still feel the tremors in my hands from the adrenaline, the scent of burning bark lingering at the tip of my nose.

I rummage through my drawers, desperately searching for a notebook to record what I witnessed. A sigh of relief escapes me when I find my diary from last year. I run my fingers over the muddy purple cover, tracing the intricate mandala pattern etched into it. This journal was my refuge when I started dating Chris—whenever I felt overwhelmed, I would pour my thoughts onto its pages. I flip through the filled pages until I find a blank one.

I should draw it. That way, I won't forget.

I scramble for a pen, my lower lip caught between my teeth. The instant the tip meets the blank paper, my wrist seems to have a mind of its own. I draw the trees, the flames devouring them, and the shadow lurking behind me. The flashlight dangles from a branch, frozen in my sketch.

Understanding every detail seems crucial; knowing anything could be useful in unravelling the mystery behind this recurring dream. I'm determined to uncover why this vivid vision continues to haunt me.

The familiar buzz of my phone interrupts my thoughts, drawing my attention back to reality.

> **theorhodes**
> *I just heard on the radio*
> *Robert Harris was found guilty.*
> *Open and shut case.*

A momentary relief washes over me, but the closure of Jorna Harris' murder case doesn't provide answers to the darkness unfolding within me.

•••••

It's been three days of silence with Chris, and the loneliness is starting to take its toll. It's the longest period I've gone without talking to him, and I'm not used to it. I've been experiencing panic attacks at school, and I find myself compulsively checking my phone every five minutes, hoping for a message from him. But there's nothing.

Breaking up with him seemed like a clear decision at first, but with each passing minute, the pain in my chest intensifies. The anxiety over the daydream about the forest fire only adds to the turmoil within me. I can't shake off the unsettling feeling that there's something more to these vivid dreams.

It's also been three days of avoiding my dad, having takeaway food at the park instead of facing dinner with him. I'm not ready to confront him just yet. I completely zoned out in front of him and his girlfriend, making myself look like a total mess. She probably thinks I'm a basket case.

The bus comes to a stop outside the school building, and the familiar sounds of chatter and laughter spill out. I head to my first class, my backpack weighed down by textbooks and the diary I now plan to take everywhere in case I have another dream.

Hel's face brightens at the sight of me, and I hurry to secure a seat before the rest of the class joins.

"Did you hear the police closed the Jorna Harris murder case?" Hel whispers, her eyes widening with a mix of surprise and relief. "They found some new evidence or something. The whole thing seemed to wrap up quite suddenly."

I feel a mix of emotions—relief that the case is resolved, but also a lingering unease I can't wrap my finger around.

"That's unexpected," I mumble, feeling a knot tighten in my stomach. "But Robert did it, right?" I ask, hoping I am wrong. Hel nods.

"Yeah. It's strange, isn't it? Like, what happened in those woods that night?"

A chill runs down my spine at the thought of Robert Harris murdering his wife. There's something eerie about the situation, especially considering how little usually happens in Barren.

In that instant, Damon Martin's entrance into the classroom disrupts my thoughts, drawing the attention of the entire class.

Rumour has it he was suspended for three days for instigating the fight, but because he didn't physically harm anyone, he 'won' against Chris.

Damon exchanges handshakes with Theo and his other jock friends before sinking into his chair. I catch a glimpse of the words 'The Damnation' on the back of Damon's hoodie. Jak enters the classroom, followed by Mrs Sanchez. I notice Jak wearing the exact hoodie Damon has on, sparking my interest.

"What's *The Damnation*?" I whisper to Hel, who gives me a surprised glance.

"You don't know? It's an exclusive Instagram account where the jocks post pictures of their parties and stuff," she explains, rolling her eyes. "It's like their gang name or something."

Helena shows me the account, filled with pictures of alcohol, half-naked girls, and drugs. It's disgusting. I give the back of Damon's head a death glare, entirely blaming him for Chris' suspension.

Mrs. Sanchez jots down the date on the board before turning around, her tiny glasses perched on the tip of her nose.

"You are going work on the group projects together today. Get in your pairs, and I'll give you the title for the research," she announces. Sighs echo around the class, mine included, as the realisation sinks in—I'm stuck with Damon Martin.

The class searches for their assigned partners, but I'm adamant—I refuse to work with Damon. As I head towards Mrs. Sanchez to protest, Theo intercepts me, blocking my way.

"Hey. I spoke to her yesterday and..." he pauses, seeming somewhat embarrassed. "I hope you're cool partnering up with me instead of Damon.

"You told Mrs Sanchez?" I ask, raising an eyebrow. I'm unsure why he would do me a favour, especially after my kind-of-ex-boyfriend thew a punch at him. Theo affirms with a nod.

"She said Dr Fleming had already told her," he replies, speaking above a whisper. His kind gesture makes my cheeks flush.

"I don't know what to say... Thank you, Theo."

He responds with a casual shrug, a smile playing on his lips as we take our seats at the back of the classroom. I catch Helena's gaze from across the classroom, but I choose to ignore it. I'm well aware she'll bring it up and ask me about it later.

The intensity of Theo's gaze feels like it's burning through my skin as I rummage through my backpack for a pen. In the process, my diary slips out, landing spine-first on the floor. It opens to a page with writing, and I quickly bend over to retrieve it. The last thing I need is for someone to get hold of my diary—I'd be in deep trouble.

"Do you need help?" Theo asks, his eyes following me as I hurriedly stuff the diary back into my bag.

"No, thank you," I mutter. Tucking a strand of hair behind my ear, I try to focus on the essay titles rather than Theo. Fortunately, they're all from my summer reading, and I silently appreciate the time I spent going over them.

"Seems like the case has been solved," he comments in a serious tone. I nod, thankful that the situation didn't spiral out of control. I gather the courage to meet his blue eyes.

"Thank you. For everything."

"It's my pleasure," he smiles, his gaze focused on me. "So… What's this about?" he asks.

"It's about the conferences in 1945, Yalta and Potsdam."

"You actually did the summer reading, huh?" he mumbles, smirking at me. I feel a flush of embarrassment creep up my face as I give him a sheepish smile.

"Come on. Can we please do the first question?" I groan, and Theo responds with a lopsided grin.

"It's only been two minutes. Relax," he laughs. His smile is contagious, and I find myself smiling back at him. Even though a part of me feels a twinge of guilt for being so comfortable around Theo lately, the reality is, we're just friends.

We dive into the first question, exchanging thoughts and brainstorming ideas for the essay. I'm impressed by how well Theo understands the material, and the assignment turns out to be more interesting than I thought. Maybe he's not the typical jock who's indifferent about school.

Time slips away, and before we know it, we've completed the entire assignment. Surprisingly, we're the first group to finish, and Mrs. Sanchez praises our work in front of the class.

"See, that wasn't so bad," he remarks, a satisfied grin on his face. I chuckle, feeling grateful for his help.

"Thanks for making it bearable," I say, gathering my things as the bell signals the end of the class. As we walk out together, I can't shake the feeling that there's something unspoken between us. Our friendship has become more comfortable, and I find myself thinking about the blurred lines. But when I look at Theo, I feel better knowing I have someone I can trust. I didn't even think about Chris during class, which is a significant upside.

We share a brief smile before he disappears into the crowd. I see Helena waiting for me at my locker, wearing a puzzled smile.

"He's way better," she says, giving me a knowing look.

"Anyone's a better student than Damon Martin," I respond with a laugh. Helena shakes her head.

"I meant he's better than Chris."

A flicker of doubt creeps in—Is Chris the right person for me? While it's true I've had panic attacks since we stopped talking, does that automatically mean I love him, or do I just need him?

I remind myself that Theo and I are just friends. Nothing more.

"Are you heading to the gym?" Hel asks, interrupting my thoughts.

"Yep. You?"

"Same, let's go!" she smiles, locking arms with me.

•••••

I finish up at the gym with Helena, the workout providing a temporary escape. However, as soon as I'm alone, the familiar grip of a panic attack tightens its hold. Being without Chris for such an extended period is new for me, and I'm unsure how much longer I handle it.

Taking deep breaths, I quicken my pace, trying to push through the rising anxiety. Carrying my gym bag over my shoulder, the chilly wind tousles my hair, and I feel my teeth chattering. In Barren, temperatures can plummet to 44 degrees Fahrenheit at night during this time of year, even though it's the end of September. My breath fogs in the cold air, and I find myself wrapping my arms around for warmth. Although a few neighbours are out walking their dogs, it's not exactly the kind of weather to be strolling around.

Walking by Mulkiwa Park, I still sense a peculiar connection to the place. There are lingering mysteries surrounding the night I discovered Robert Harris' flashlight. What compelled me to go there? Is it somehow tied to the recurring dream that haunts my nights?

As I cut across the street, my heart stops when my phone buzzes with a text message. I take it out, and a wave of relief washes over me as I see the sender's ID.

9

The TV hums in the background as I make my way towards the kitchen. My dad slouched on the sofa, his phone in hand, unfazed by the football match on TV. As soon as he hears me come in, he straightens up in his seat. It's been three days since our last conversation, and I've come to the realisation that I can't keep avoiding him much longer.

"Hey," I greet him, leaving the keys on the counter. A mix of frustration and sadness crosses my dad's face.

"I haven't heard from you in three days," he says in a serious tone. I wish I could tell him that I'm far from okay, that these past weeks have been a war with myself—but I can't. I can't let him know about the blackouts and strange dreams

"I've been studying for a test," I lie, but my dad doesn't buy it. He turns off the TV, his anxious eyes studying me.

"I'm worried about you, Cora. When Isabelle came over the other day, you were unfocused. I don't want a repeat of what happened last year," he says. I shift uncomfortably under his gaze, his concern weighing on my conscience. I know he only wants to help, but if he knew what was truly happening, he would probably insist on sending me to a mental institution.

"I'm fine, Dad. It's just stress from school and stuff," I insist.

He exhales heavily, a mixture of frustration and fear evident in his eyes.

"Cora, I need you to be honest with me. What's really going on? I can't see you go through that again."

I feel the tension in the air, the unspoken understanding of the events that unfolded last year, events that neither of us wants to revisit. The danger I face is that if I don't tell in my dad, I might end up in that situation again. But telling him that I've been dreaming of a forest fire for the past six months would cause concern for anyone.

Taking a deep breath, I meet his gaze.

"Dad, there's just a lot on my plate right now. I promise I'll talk to you about it, but I need some time to figure things out."

His expression softens, and he nods, though the worry lingers.

"Okay, sweetie. Just remember, I'm here for you, no matter what."

"I know."

"And if you don't want to tell me, you should see your psychiatrist," he says.

"I swear, I'm fine."

When my mom passed away, the trauma weighed so heavily on me that my dad took me to a psychiatrist. I remained silent for the first six months after her death; I guess I just closed up. Losing a parent, especially at the age of 10, is not an easy thing to go through.

Suddenly, I remember what the group was discussing today: the sale of our old house. I'm surprised my dad never mentioned it. That house was his most significant achievement, and we both know how much it means to us.

He leans forward in his seat, his expression a mix of curiosity and concern.

"Are you really sure? You seem distracted."

I take a deep breath, contemplating whether to bring it up.

"I overheard the group talking about our old house being sold. Why did you never tell me?" I ask, a touch of accusation in my tone. He looks away, guilt clouding his face.

"I didn't want to burden you with it. The decision to sell was tough, but it seemed like the right thing to do."

"When did this happen?" I ask, frustration in my tone. I can't believe he didn't tell me about this. My dad sighs, scratching his bearded chin.

"I've been trying to sell it for the past two years, and a few months ago, somebody bought it."

"I just can't believe you didn't tell me," I say, feeling a knot tighten in my stomach. He looks at me with a mixture of regret and understanding, placing a hand on my shoulder.

"I should have talked to you about it. I'm sorry if it upset you, kiddo."

"Who bought it?" I ask, my voice quivering. The idea of someone else living in the home my mom and dad spent years building is too much to bear. It makes me feel sick just thinking about it. He shrugs.

"I don't know. Either way, it's none of our business. We've moved on," he says, observing my reaction. "I still think you should see your psychiatrist from last year," he adds.

The reason I stopped seeing her was that, after I started dating Chris, the flashbacks of my mom's death came to an end. I exhale, realising I have to do this for him, not just for myself. Our relationship was never the same after my mom died, and I must admit I haven't always been the best daughter to him. But if this makes him happy, I'll do it, even if I never tell my psychiatrist about the dream.

"Fine. Just a couple of sessions and that's it," I reply. My dad's expression softens with gratitude.

"Thank you, kiddo. I just want to make sure you're taking care of yourself," he says, a blend of concern and love in his eyes. I offer a small nod, understanding the depth of his worry.

"I'll schedule an appointment soon, Dad.

His smile widens, and he envelops me in a hug, catching me by surprise. It's been years since he's done that.

"That's all I ask, sweetheart."

My phone's buzz interrupts the moment, reminding me that I need to hurry. I sling my backpack over my shoulder, taking a few steps toward the stairs.

"I'm going to take a quick shower. I'm meeting some friends after," I say.

"Okay," my dad replies with a smile, and I quickly ascend the stairs.

•••••

The doorbell's chime echoes through the house, prompting me to hurry downstairs. For a few seconds, I forget about my paranoia and my recent blackouts. Unlocking the door, my heart flutters as I'm greeted by Chris standing outside, a grin on his face. We cross the street toward Mulkiwa Park in silence, both uncertain of who should speak first.

"Thanks for texting me back. I know it's late," Chris says, casting a glance my way.

I didn't expect him to text me when I got home, but a wave of relief washed over me when he did. Although I still feel upset about the fight, my panic attacks had become unbearable. Besides, now that we have both had a chance to cool down, I'm open to hearing him out.

"You said you wanted to make it up to me before you go on tour," I say with a soft smile.

"I promise you, I will. I've really missed you, Cora," he beams, wrapping an arm around me.

"I've missed you, too," I reply with flushed cheeks. He releases his hold on me, effortlessly hopping over the park fence. With a friendly smile, he extends a helping hand, inviting me to join him on the other side.

As we stroll through Mulkiwa Park, Chris's presence brings a comforting sense of familiarity. The scent of recently watered grass lingers in the air, and the moon's glow casts shadows from the surrounding pine trees onto the turf.

"You must be excited about leaving Barren for a while," I mention as he guides me toward the lake. However, with each step, the lump in my throat grows as memories of Jorna Harris's body resurface.

I suddenly realise that Theo is the only person who knows I found the body, apart from the Sheriff. Perhaps I shouldn't have told him, but for some reason, I felt like I had to.

"Yeah, I really am. I can't believe we're touring the East Coast in a week," Chris replies. He leads me to the lake's edge, where a picnic blanket is laid out on the grass. I can't help but gasp in excitement.

"Did you set this up?" I chirp, glancing at the wicker basket and paper cups. Chris grins, settling on the blanket before handing me a cup.

"I told you I was going to make up for it," Chris says. His eyes glimmer in the dim light, and I can't help but gush at him. Grand gestures like these aren't typical for him, making it an enjoyable surprise. I scoot closer to him on the blanket, flashing him a smile.

"This is really sweet, Chris."

Our smiles reflect the warmth of the moment, and my anger from a few minutes ago dissolves. Chris hands me a fruit salad, pouring hot tea into my cup. We sit in silence for a few moments, gazing at the water ahead as gentle ripples form on its surface. Memories of the moment I found the body in the lake intrusively enter my mind. I push them away, focusing on eating to distract myself.

"What's on your mind? You seem distracted," Chris asks, stealing a glance in my direction.

My cheeks redden as I think of an excuse. He's not the first person to say I seem distracted. The first thought that pops into my mind is, "What's going on between you and Damon?

His initial reaction is furrowing his brows, but he quickly masks any annoyance with a casual shrug.

"We used to be good friends until he started bad-mouthing my band. It happened around the time you and I started dating," he explains.

"Why didn't you tell me?" I ask, giving him a puzzled glance. He shrugs again, taking a swig from his cup.

"Because it's not important. Anyway, enough about Damon Martin. I brought you a surprise," he says, his face lighting up. He retrieves his dark blue bass from behind him, and my eyes light up in surprise.

"Your bass!" I chirp.

"Yep. I'm gonna play one of our new songs. I wrote it last week, actually," he says, tuning the bass. His focused expression fascinates me, and I can't help but watch in admiration.

"Let's hear it," I say with a smile. He continues to tune the bass, his eyes locking with mine. He locks eyes with me, a sheepish smile on his lips.

"You know, a lot of my songs are about how I feel when I'm with you," he confesses. I am taken aback by this revelation; I had no idea Chris had ever written a song about me.

"I hope it's not *Kick to the Curb,*" I tease, playfully swatting his arm. I remember the somewhat aggressive lyrics to that song. Chris laughs, shaking his head shyly.

"No, Jason wrote that one. I was thinking more about *Southern Constellations* and *Blank*," he explains.

"Really? Those are pretty great," I reply with genuine admiration. He nods, warmth in his green eyes.

"Yeah, they're about you," he says, a smile tugging the corners of his lips. He strums the first few notes, meeting my gaze. "This song is called *Open Heart*."

As he begins playing, I'm captivated by the song. The peaceful surroundings of Mulkiwa Park create an ideal setting for Chris's heartfelt performance. I become entranced by the melody, savouring the emotions embedded in every note. The tension between us fades away, replaced by the shared connection of this intimate moment. I find myself lost in the moon's pale reflection on the lake's water as I sway to the beat, a peaceful smile gracing my lips.

But in that instant, my vision blurs, and the haunting memory returns. The pale hand of the deceased woman, trapped in the sediment, with her jewellery glinting under the moonlight, flashes before my eyes. Even submerged, the stench of the corpse lingered on the surface. Her colourless, beady eyes beg for mercy, while her blue lips are frozen in sheer terror. The image only lingers for a moment, but my heart races in my chest as I snap out of the trance.

The memory of the rotting corpse lingers, causing an uncomfortable shift in my attitude. Adrenaline seeps into my veins, and I find it challenging to push away the haunting image. Glancing over at Chris, who is still engrossed in the song, I realise he's oblivious to my internal struggle.

The worst part is that I will never be able to tell him about what's happening to me, not after what happened last year. I don't know how much longer I can keep playing this game, trying to convince myself that staying with Chris is the right choice.

Ever since Jorna Harris's murder, something within me has been awakened.

·····

The cafeteria's scent, a mix of fries, hot dogs, and fresh milk, always fails to awaken anyone's appetite. I stand in line with Hel, my mind wandering to the events of last night. Chris was enthusiastic about us staying together, even with his upcoming tour, and he vowed to be a better boyfriend multiple times. It seemed like a good idea last night, but this morning, the euphoria had dissolved.

Hel and I find the group at our usual table, absorbed in their own conversations. I slide in between Mason and Dan, both offering me welcoming smiles.

"Hey, girls. We were just discussing Damon Martin's supposed rivalry with Chris Matthews. Honestly, it ain't even that deep," Dan rants, shrugging.

"The rivalry from middle school? It *was* deep, Dan," Hel emphasises, delicately placing her food tray on the table and taking a seat next to Matt.

I raise a brow.

"What rivalry from middle school?" I ask, surprised that Chris had never mentioned it. Helena theatrically waves her fork in the air, clearing her throat as if she was about to deliver a lecture.

"Damon and Chris were best friends. They did everything together. But one day, Damon found out his mom was getting remarried. Guess who she was getting married to," Helena insinuates.

She gazes at me, anticipating a response. Then it hits me. Chris' dad left his family when Chris was in middle school.

"So, Chris and Damon are stepbrothers," I blurt out, my jaw dropping. Hel nods, a mischievous glint in her eyes. Is that why Damon started the fight with Chris? For revenge?

Beth shrugs, momentarily tearing her eyes away from her phone.

"Honestly, I don't think it's a big deal. People become stepsiblings all the time," she pipes in.

"True, but they were best friends," Matt interjects. He twirls a strand of Hel's hair with his fingers, making her blush.

As I watch, I can't help but reflect on my relationship with Chris. There was a time where I felt that same joy, but this year has been with nothing but arguments between us. There are some things that are still unclear about Chris, too. If he lied about Damon being his stepbrother, what else could he have lied to me about?

My focus shifts when I spot Theo at the jocks' table, engaged in a lively conversation with a blonde cheerleader, a wide grin on his face. A pang of unease hits me, but I'm unsure of the reason behind it. The jocks rise simultaneously, and the cheerleaders follow suit, playing with their hair to capture the guys' attention. Theo has a cheerleader clinging to his arm, and I watch them with a cold gaze as they head to football practice.

Beth's touch on my arm snaps me back into the conversation.

"Sorry if we were boring you with Matt's play," she says, offering a sheepish smile. Matt responds with an eye roll.

"I wasn't bored at all. I just had something on my mind," I respond, giving Matt a reassuring smile.

"Hold on, Beth, don't you have cheer practice?" Hel asks, gathering her food scraps on the tray. Beth's eyes widen in surprise, and she quickly rises from her seat.

"Shit! I totally forgot."

She looks around nervously for her cheer team, but they've already left. Beth gives us a quick wave before dashing out of the lunch hall, drawing a few glances as her short skirt flaps.

Matt groans, unwrapping his arm from Helena.

"I have to host the auditions today," he says, pouting sweetly at her.

"Have fun, babe," Hel replies with a smile.

They share a quick peck on the lips before Matt leaves the lunch hall, holding a stack of scripts.

"Should we head out to the bleachers, guys?" Mason suggests as we toss out our food trays.

10

"Man, the weather is so nice this year," Dan says, squinting at the sun.

Instead of tuning into the group's conversation, I can't help but think of my dad. Perhaps, if we had been closer over the past two years, my dad might have told me about our house. As much as I hate to admit it, my relationships are deteriorating because I can't understand the dreams I keep having. But I know I have to figure it out on my own.

The bleachers are filled with enthusiastic sports fans, eagerly anticipating Damon and his group's practice. We grab seats near the front where there are only a few spots left, and the conversation shifts to Mayor Glenn's new political speech.

Everyone in Barren loves Mayor Glenn. His focus has always been on improving our quality of life and ensuring our safety. In fact, his latest policy is about putting up CCTV cameras all over Barren in the next few months.

"I just think that, after Jorna Harris' murder, it's about time they installed cameras," Hel says. She's right; in a negative way, it implies that people in Barren are feeling unsafe after the murder. And installing cameras isn't just beneficial for our safety; it's also good for my dad's job since he works at Bern's.

"I agree," I reply.

"Looks like someone's finally joining in on political discussions, huh?" Hel nudges me, wearing a proud smile.

The crowd roars as the jocks step onto the field in their jerseys, greeting us as if they were celebrities. Damon Martin steals the spotlight, as usual, waving at his female admirers while the others disperse across the field. The jocks begin practicing for the mid-term finals, set for tomorrow night. Our school team, the Hawks, is known for being the best in the county, and their games typically end in victory.

But in that moment, the football field blurs, and the cheers of the crowd distort, leaving me breathless. Suddenly, the setting changes to underneath the bleachers—I glimpse the back of Theo's head, his arms around a girl with jet-black hair. I blink in disbelief, and just as quickly, the scene returns to normal. Coach De La Vega blows the whistle, and the crowd buzzes with excitement.

A coldness seeps into my bones as I process what just happened. Was what I witnessed a creation of my imagination, or am I on the brink of losing my sanity? My stomach churns with anxiety, and fear envelops me.

Hel's gentle voice interrupts my panic attack, bringing me back to the present.

"If Theo Rhodes wasn't friends with Damon, I'd say you guys would be cute together."

I suddenly remember that people think Chris and I broke up. In that moment, I feel too embarrassed to tell Helena the truth.

"Don't start," I mutter with a dry laugh.

Theo glances my way briefly before rushing back to his position. A strange feeling overwhelms me. Is it possible that I have feelings for Theo?

It can't be. I just got back together with Chris, and he promised to change for me. We've been together for a year, and he's been my rock since we started dating. I can't be feeling this way about a guy I met just a couple of weeks ago.

Practice is nearly over, and the cheerleading squad lines the sidelines with their pompons ready. Beth takes the lead, approaching the football team while fluffing her pompons. The remaining girls follow suit, rehearsing their choreography on the side while the jocks conclude their practice.

I'm about to head to the bathroom when I notice Theo jogging away from the match, disappearing behind the bleachers. Nobody seems to notice him, as Damon Martin is under the spotlight, but I do. I crane my neck to glance behind me, my lips parting in shock when I see Theo kissing Madison Cortese.

All colour drains from my face, and an inevitable, sinking fear seeps into my bones.

Did I just witness something minutes before it happened?

•••••

I remained speechless for the rest of the day, even when Mr. Woods asked me a question in front of the class. The horrifying feeling has taken residence inside me. How did I witness Theo kissing Madison minutes before it happened?

It's impossible. I must have experienced a moment of déjà vu. Déjà vu is normal, right? It can happen to anyone. Maybe I'm overanalysing things. I must be. But there's a part of me that doesn't buy it. I saw it right before my eyes, as if I were a part of the picture.

As the last bell rings, I walk out of class in a daze, my heart pounding in my chest. Nausea washes over me, and just as I'm about to hurry to the bathroom, someone grabs my arm.

It's Helena.

"Hey, are you okay?" she asks, her grip on my arm gentle. "You look really pale."

I shake my head, unable to find the right words.

"I want to go home," I manage to say, but I feel completely detached from my body.

"I'll walk with you," she says, her expression filled with concern.

As we walk, Helena tries to engage me in conversation, but my responses are distant and distracted. The world outside appears blurry, and I can still feel the unsettling weight in my chest, as if something is seriously wrong. Night has already fallen, and a dense fog begins to envelop the quiet residential streets. As we approach my street, my breaths grow heavy, as if an imminent danger lingers in the air.

"Cora?" Helena asks, her eyes widening with worry. I hadn't realised I had stopped walking, and I'm panting heavily.

"Yeah?" I manage to whisper between breaths. Helena's worried expression intensifies, and she grabs both of my arms in a comforting gesture.

"I think you're having a panic attack," she says, but all I can focus on is the image of Theo kissing Madison. I saw it happen before it happened. How is that possible?

"I'm okay," I mutter breathlessly, trying to regain control of my breathing. Helena glances around nervously before returning her gaze to me.

"Look at the sky. Describe in your head what you see," she instructs. My heart is pounding at a thousand beats per minute, and my vision is becoming blurry.

I force myself to take a deep breath and look up at the night sky. It's filled with countless stars that sparkle like diamonds. The moon, shining brightly, adds a gentle glow to the darkness. As I breathe in, I feel the air returning to my lungs, and my head gradually stops spinning.

"Good. See? The moon is in the Waxing Crescent phase right now," Helena says, her voice soft. My breath slows down, and my anxious thoughts also begin to ease. As I start to feel better, I shift my gaze to her. The worry that was there before has vanished, replaced by a soft smile.

"H-how did you do that?" I stammer, sensing the colour returning to my cheeks.

"My brother used to experience panic attacks growing up. I would always tell him to focus on something," she explains.

"Well, it really helps," I say, offering her a soft smile, which she returns.

"Are you okay to walk? We're almost at your house," she asks, and I nod.

As we approach my doorstep, I turn to her with a grateful smile, feeling significantly better.

"Thank you, Helena. I don't know what I would have done without you," I say sincerely. She responds with a warm smile, enveloping me in a hug. The warmth of Helena's hug lingers as she eventually pulls away.

"Anytime, Cora. Take care of yourself, okay?"

I nod, grateful for her support.

"I will. Thanks again."

Helena waves, giving me a smile before heading off into the night. As I step inside my house, the unsettling events of the day flood back into my thoughts. On my way to my room, I notice my dad asleep on the couch, the light still on. With a heavy heart, I cover him with a blanket and switch off the light as he snores. I hurry to my bedroom, feeling my anxiety rise with every passing second. Collapsing onto the bed, I release a deep exhale, staring at the ceiling. Guilt blends with fear as I realise that it's only a matter of time before this situation will come crashing down on me. My mind keeps echoing the same words: *I saw Theo and Madison kissing before it happened.*

I need to see a therapist before I am too far gone.

•••••

Coughing violently from the airborne ashes, I navigate through the dense smoke with blurry vision. I take a few steps towards the cacophonous sound of burning wood, my heart in my throat. The tangerine flames radiate intense heat, causing beads of sweat to trickle down my forehead. The crackling fire draws nearer, prompting me to turn around.

I jolt awake as if someone drenched me with a bucket of ice-cold water—suddenly, gasping for air and fully alert.

A sudden realisation washes over me, one that could potentially be more dangerous than being psychotic. What if my dream of the forest fire is similar to what happened today at the bleachers? What if I'm witnessing something that hasn't happened yet?

I stagger toward my desk, reaching for my diary tucked beneath a pile of books. Flipping through the pages, I find the drawing from a few weeks ago, meticulously observing every detail. In that moment, Helena's words from earlier echo in my head.

The moon is in the Waxing Crescent phase right now.

The moon I sketched resembles a thin, curved fingernail, revealing only a small portion of its surface. I look out my window to see how it matches its current phase.

Breathing anxiously, I hurry to grab my laptop, searching for a diagram of the moon's phases. I instantly make the connection. In the dream, the moon is at Waning Gibbous, whereas currently, it is at Waxing Crescent. My heart races in my chest as I open my calendar, counting the days until the moon reaches Waning Gibbous.

Twelve days. That's less than two weeks. A surge of terror courses through me as the realisation sinks in.

If my dream is a premonition, what does that mean for me?

●●●●●

Eleven days.

The Damnation has gathered in the school hallway, all wearing dark green hoodies with their names displayed on the back. I swiftly walk past them, keeping my gaze lowered to avoid Theo. If he's dating Madison now, there is no way Damon would approve. After all, Damon and she were together for two years; some teacher seven believed they would end up married. I thought Theo was better than that, but maybe I was wrong.

While opening my locker, a letter falls to the floor, and I quickly scramble to retrieve it. The envelope's front is blank, but I don't hesitate to tear it open. Leaning into my locker for privacy, I examine the contents. An inaudible gasp escapes my lips as I pull out a wad of green banknotes, counting them frantically. 200 dollars.

I take a sharp breath when I find a small piece of paper between the money and the envelope, reading: *D.M. A deal is a deal.*

Is Damon Martin dealing drugs in school? I glance at the approaching jocks, including Damon and his sidekick Jak. They are too absorbed in their conversations to notice me. Damon opens his locker, shoving his expensive backpack inside before slamming it closed. Shit. Someone must have mistakenly slipped this into my locker instead of his. I'm on the verge of saying something when they both disappear into the crowd.

·····

Halfway through first period, I excuse myself from the classroom, pretending to 'go to the bathroom'. I realise that if I want to talk to Damon in private, I'll have to skip class. I make my way toward the football field, cutting through the empty lunch hall. As I step outside, I'm greeted by the soft sounds of their practice on the field. Coach De La Vega blows the whistle, signalling the end of practice. Taking cover behind the bleachers, I observe Damon stretching, his jersey emphasising his well-defined muscles. I can't resist rolling my eyes at him.

I decide to wait near the changing rooms for Damon, aiming for privacy without arousing suspicion from coach and his friends. The football team streams into the hallway, their camaraderie echoing through the walls. I pretend to sip from the water fountain until Damon makes an appearance, accompanied by Jak and Theo. Ignoring Theo's burning gaze on me, I tug Damon's arm to grab his attention. He turns towards me, a smug smile playing on his lips as our eyes lock.

"Hey, can we talk?" I ask, a moment of stillness hanging between us. Damon hesitates briefly before nodding to Jak and Theo, signalling them to walk away. They disappear into the changing rooms, leaving Damon and me in the quietness of the hallway.

"Let me guess," Damon purrs, a smirk playing on his lips as he leans against the lockers. "you're gonna ask me if I have a girlfriend."

My eyes widen in surprise, and my face flushes into a deep shade of red.

"Actually, no. I came because somebody left this in my locker," I mutter, handing him the blank envelope. Surprise flashes in his eyes as he swiftly tucks it into his shorts' pocket. He glances around nervously before leaning in.

"You need to forget about this, Cora. It's none of your business," he whispers. I furrow my eyebrows, not satisfied with his vague response.

"Why do you have this much money in an envelope?" I ask, uncertain if I want to know the answer.

Damon smirks, a hint of arrogance in his eyes.

"Curiosity killed the cat, Cora. Just leave it alone if you know what's good for you." Before I can press further, he straightens up and gives me a dismissive look. "I've got a game to prepare for. Don't dig where you don't belong."

With that, Damon walks away, leaving me standing in the hallway with more questions than answers.

Just as I'm about to head to my next class, my vision fades to black.

11

A shiver of dread courses through me when I open my eyes. I'm walking towards the school building, like everyone else, but something feels off, and I can't figure it out. Fear grips me as I check my phone, gasping in panic when I see the date on my screen—it's Friday morning.

I've almost skipped 24 hours of my life.

My throat tightens with panic, a cold sweat forming at the nape of my neck. I try to recall what I did last night, but my stomach drops as the realisation sinks in.

Nothing. I remember nothing.

I have no recollection of finishing the school day, of having dinner with my dad or waking up in the morning. The only memory I have is talking to Damon outside the locker room.

As I make my way through the crowd and enter the building, horror tightens its grip on my racing heart. Why can't I remember? Should I tell someone? The realisation hits me the moment I step into the hallway—something terrible has happened. Chaos reigns with students talking loudly, crying, and shouting. The atmosphere is dark, as if a door to another dimension has been opened.

I spot Helena and the others gathered outside a classroom; their attention focused on their phones. As I approach, their heads turn, and the fear reflected in their expressions sends my heartbeat into overdrive.

Mason's question, "Where were you last night?" intertwines with Helena's inquiry, "Did you hear what happened?", which only intensifies my panic.

"What's going on?" I manage to croak, my throat feeling dry. Not only did I black out for several hours last night, but the sombre expressions on their faces tell me something dreadful has happened.

Silence hangs in the air as they exchange glances, and only Helena has the courage to respond.

"Cora... Damon was shot last night," she mutters, her eyes glistening with tears. "He's in critical condition. They don't know if he'll make it."

My heart pounds in my chest, and the world around me blurs. The weight of the news presses down on me, and a mixture of shock, fear, and guilt floods my senses. I feel a lump forming in my throat, making it difficult to breathe. I stagger back, gripping a nearby locker for support.

This can't be real. It must be one of my surreal dreams.

"I-I don't understand. What happened?" My voice comes out shaky, and Helena takes a step closer, placing a comforting hand on my shoulder. Matt swallows hard, his Adam's apple moving in a visible bob.

"They found him unconscious in the school parking lot after the mid-term game. No one knows who did it, or why," he mutters.

This can't be real. These things don't happen in Barren. The room spins as I try to process the information. Damon, shot near the school, and I have no memory of what happened. A sudden wave of guilt envelopes me, but I don't know why. A chilling question seeps into my bones, filling me with dread.

Did I do something?

The hum of students' voices abruptly interrupts my thoughts, seizing all of our attention. The Damnation gathers around Damon's locker, their heads bowed in mourning. Among them, Theo stares blankly at the ground, disbelief etched on his face. Jak Oban opens Damon's locker, pulling out one of Damon's football jerseys. The navy-blue jersey with the number 19 and 'Martin' written on the back sends an overwhelming terror through my core.

My vision blurs with tears, and the air is knocked of my lungs as the setting around me begins to change.

I find myself in the dark of night, muffled speaking slicing through the fresh air. The sharp crack of a gunshot reverberates through the parking lot, and seconds later, a body lands on the asphalt with a thump. Yet, from the darkness, I'm unable to see the victim's face. The perspective shifts, and my heart somersaults as I witness Theo cradling Damon's bleeding body.

As I blink again, the school hallway replaces the haunting scene. Thoughts race in my head, my breaths quickening with desperation. It feels like the air I breathe isn't enough, and the instinct to flee courses through my bloodstream.

Theo's sapphire eyes lock with mine from across the hall, his expression unreadable. He found Damon's body, but wait, how do I know that? The school bell's shrill ring sends shivers down my spine, hushing the entire hallway.

Dr Fleming's announcement cuts through the palpable tension in the air.

"All students to the gym hall now. I repeat, all students to the gym hall *now*."

Helena and I share an uneasy look before we join the flow of students heading towards the gym hall, where an unsettling silence has settled. As we enter, we spot Dr. Fleming standing at the podium with a microphone in his hands. His face is etched with grief, intensifying the sense that something terrible has happened.

I try to shake off the overwhelming thoughts crowding my mind, but it's impossible. How could I know what happened last night when I can't remember anything? A haunting question circles in my mind, and my face turns pale at the mere thought of it.

Was I somehow involved?

Dr. Fleming's voice interrupts the turmoil in my head as he clears his throat before speaking.

"Students of Barren High, I know many of you are confused and scared, and I wish I could provide answers. Last night, we experienced a tragic incident. Damon Martin was found injured on school grounds after the football game. He was taken to the hospital, and despite efforts to save him, he succumbed after his comatose state was terminated. The authorities are investigating the circumstances surrounding this event."

A collective gasp echoes through the gym. My heart pounds in my chest, and the guilt within me intensifies. I glance at Helena, her eyes mirroring the shock and fear I feel.

"As we await more information, I ask you all to support each other. Counsellors will be available for those who need someone to talk to. We will get through this together as a community," Dr Fleming explains.

The weight of Dr Fleming's words hangs in the air, and the gym's atmosphere shifts to one of discomfort and anxiety. This can't be real—Damon can't really be gone. Dr. Fleming finishes his speech, his voice trembling slightly as he announces, "Miss Cortese has a few things to say."

Madison Cortese, Damon's girlfriend for two years, steps up to the podium, her jet-black hair glistening under the fluorescent lighting. Despite her outfit that could grace a magazine cover, her black eyeliner is noticeably smudged beneath her lower lashes. Madison, who is known for her tough exterior, never shed a tear— even after breaking up with Damon after he cheated on her. Witnessing her vulnerability, especially in front of the entire school, feels surreal. She takes the microphone from Dr. Fleming before he settles into a seat in the front row.

"Damon Martin was the star of the football team. He was the man of my dreams..." Madison begins, a few tears streaming down her cheeks. She wipes away some mascara-streaked tears away before continuing. "Whoever did this... I hope you rot in hell," she hisses, her voice brittle.

Madison leaves the microphone on the stand, soft sobs escaping her lips. She dashes for the gym hall door, weaving through the crowd of staring students. A melancholic silence hangs in the room, and Dr. Fleming seizes the opportunity to take hold of the microphone.

"There will be a memorial this evening in honour of Mr Martin. The funeral will take place in the upcoming days. That's all. Thank you," he concludes.

I shift my gaze to Theo, seated in the row ahead, his expression perplexed as he stares vacantly at the ground. The final bell rings, signalling the end of the assembly, but the panic persists. I blacked out again, and this time, something has happened.

A killer is amongst us.

•••••

The rest of the day unfolded with teachers expressing condolences, students placing flowers in Damon's locker, and football practice getting cancelled. Even Coach De La Vega took a day off to grieve. It's all a blur, and panic grips my stomach. The same questions whirl in my mind.

Where was I last night? Who could have killed Damon, and why?

Damon Martin was a just another jock, with high expectations, money, and influence. But after the envelope incident, it's possible he might have been dealing drugs, which could be a solid reason for someone to want him dead—especially if he had enemies and things got out of hand.

I hurried home right after class, unable to bear another person talking about Damon. Yesterday's blackout was terrifying, and it's been haunting me almost as much as Damon's murder. It's hard to believe that someone in Barren could be twisted enough to kill a seventeen-year-old. The mere thought of it makes me sick.

I sink onto the leather couch and tie my hair into a messy bun. A few minutes later, my dad arrives and starts bombarding me with questions like a detective.

"You're not going out after sunset," he declares, giving me a stern look. I sigh, rolling my eyes at him.

"Where would I even go?" I ask. He narrows his eyes, unamused by my response.

"I don't know, but until the police arrest the killer, you stay home after school. It's not safe out there," he insists. I slump back into the couch, a mixture of frustration and fear settling within me.

"Fine," I mutter reluctantly. The truth is, I can't bring myself to tell him that I don't remember 20 hours of my life.

My phone buzzes in my pocket, catching me off guard as I retrieve it. Hel's name lights up on the screen, making my pulse quicken. My dad glances over his shoulder, suspicion evident in his expression.

"Hey, Hel," I answer. My dad pretends to be engrossed in the snack cabinet, attempting to eavesdrop on my conversation.

"Hey. I was wondering if you're coming tonight," she says. I raise an eyebrow, not quite sure what she's talking about.

"To what?"

"Damon's memorial, remember? Everyone's going," Hel answers. I nervously chew my lip, realising this might not be the best move. Damon's secret life as a drug dealer life is now in my hands, and not showing up might make people think I was involved. And that's the last thing I want, especially when I am unsure myself.

"What should I wear?" I ask, anxiously biting my lip.

"Well, it's a party. Smart-casual, I guess."

My eyes widen in shock.

"A party? He *died*!" I exclaim. How can Damon's friends be fine with drinking and having fun after he was murdered? Maybe none of them cared enough about him.

"I know, but it's a school fundraiser for his funeral. There won't be alcohol," she explains.

I release a breath, contemplating whether I should go. Maybe I'll recover fragments of my memory, like when I saw Damon's football jersey. The mere thought of being involved and not remembering makes me nauseous.

Shit. I must remember what I did last night.

"I'll come. What time?" I reply, glancing over my shoulder. Fortunately, my dad isn't there anymore. I promised him I wouldn't go out after sundown, but I need to do whatever it takes to remember.

"Want me to pick you up in an hour?" she offers. I glance at the clock, relieved that my dad is usually asleep by 10. I can slip out without him noticing.

"That'd be great. Thanks Hel," I say in a hushed tone.

"No problem, I'll see you then."

·····

Hel and I walk toward the school building, an uneasy silence hanging in the air. It's strange to think that just 16 hours ago, one of our classmates passed away, and now we're going to campus at night for a memorial 'party.' As we enter, our footsteps echo in the empty, dimly lit hallways, creating a sense of unease. The vibrant posters on the bulletin boards contrast with the sombre mood, and the usually bustling lockers remain closed and untouched. As we approach the gym hall, we notice a queue of people standing outside.

"What's this?" I ask Helena, furrowing my brows.

"It's for Damon's funeral. They're asking for donations," she replies.

The crowd shifts until we find ourselves next in line to pay. To my surprise, Theo and Jak Oban stand at the entrance, each clutching a glass jar to collect donations. The stark contrast between them grabs my attention. Theo stares expressionlessly at the floor, while Jak greets me with a smile. Who would've guessed Jak and Damon had been best friends since middle school?

Helena opens her wallet, inspecting the bills tucked inside.

"How much is the entry?" she asks.

"20 dollars," Jak replies.

"Wow, that's a lot," I mutter, glancing at my half-empty wallet. The memory of Damon's drug money surfaces, sending a shiver down my spine. I push the thought aside and hand the money to Theo instead of Jak.

"Enjoy," Jak coos, giving me an amused look. I sense Theo's eyes on me, but I choose to ignore it. He's with Damon's ex-girlfriend now, meaning I have nothing to talk to him about.

Exchanging a glance with Helena, I push the door open. The gym has been transformed into a memorial with pictures and memorabilia of Damon. The entire school is present, teachers included, all dressed in black. The atmosphere is eerier than I anticipated. People gather in the centre of the room, enjoying light snacks and engaging in quiet conversation. My eyes scan the room, searching for the seniors. Helena spots the group toward the back and grabs my hand, pulling me along as she manoeuvres through the crowd.

The discomfort is evident on their faces as they sip from cups of what I assume is alcohol-free punch. Matt gives me a quick hug, and Beth manages a slightly uneasy smile—clearly not in the mood for a party. Helena's gaze wanders around the room, her voice barely above a whisper.

"It's surreal, isn't it? Seeing the gym like this."

Matt nods in agreement.

"Yeah, never thought we'd be here for something like this…"

"Hey, did anyone figure out what really happened? The rumours are all over the place," Mason mutters, taking a swig from his cup. Helena lets out a sigh, fear evident in her eyes.

"I don't know, but it's unsettling. Feels like we're in the middle of some mystery. First Jorna Harris, and now this."

"And the fact that it happened in our town, in our school... it's just crazy," Beth adds. Silence lingers between us, acknowledging that she's right. Nothing's ever happened in Barren before, and now we've had two murders in two weeks. The worst part is that I am somehow connected to both.

"I can't wrap my head around having a memorial 'party.' It just feels wrong,'" I murmur, trying to steer the conversation. They nod in unison, recognising the strangeness of the situation.

"They're doing it for the donations," Matt explains with a shrug.

"True, but it's still hard to wrap my head around the whole thing," I reply.

I look around the room, searching for Theo. The image of Theo holding Damon in his arms remains etched in my brain. The only logical explanation is that I remembered a part of what I saw last night, but what was I doing in the parking lot with Theo?

I spot Dr. Fleming speaking with a few parents across the hall. My heart suddenly drops when I remember something.

Chris. Chris is Damon's stepbrother. I completely forgot to check up on him.

I'm about to call him when Mayor Glenn steps onto the podium, hushing the entire room.

"Students, parents, and staff of Barren High. Today, we gather to remember Damon Martin, a young life lost too soon. Damon was not just a student; he was a son, a friend, and an important part of our town. In these tough times, let's support one another and cherish every moment. Damon's passing reminds us of how fragile life is. As a community, we've shown resilience and unity. Let's continue supporting each other. Together, we can navigate through these challenges and keep Damon's memory alive. May we find comfort in each other as we say goodbye to a bright soul gone too soon. Thank you."

A moment of silence hangs in the air before the crowd erupts into applause.

"He's so great," Hel whispers into my ear, wearing a proud smile. Mayor Glenn steps away from the podium, making way for Jak to take the stage. A few of his friends cheer him on by chanting his name. He's wearing his The Damnation hoodie over his black clothes, and his eyes are bloodshot. I can't tell if he's been crying or if he's just high. He clears his throat, capturing the attention of the hushed crowd.

"Thank you, Mayor Glenn, and thank you all for being here to remember Damon. I know it's not easy to come to school on a Friday night," he says, earning a few laughs. His expression turns sombre as he continues. "Damon was like a brother to me. When I had a bad day, he was always there for me. But Damon wouldn't want us to be sad. He'd want us to remember him with a smile and keep living our lives." He raises his glass, drawing a few whispers from teachers. "So tonight, let's raise a non-alcoholic toast for Damon."

The crowd shares a chuckle before raising their glasses in unison, including teachers.

"To Damon. You'll be missed, brother," Jak concludes with a bittersweet smile. The crowd cheers as Jak steps down from the stage, and I exchange an uneasy glance with Helena and Matt.

Madison steps forward, a mixture of grief and determination in her eyes. The atmosphere of the room changes as she approaches the podium, seizing everyone's attention. She's dressed in a little black dress paired with a fur jacket, and her makeup is immaculate.

"Thank you, Jak, for those words. Damon was truly special to all of us," Madison begins, her voice steady but tinged with emotion. She continues, "Damon was not only my boyfriend, but the love of my life." I can't help but raise my eyebrows at that, remembering I saw her kissing Theo behind the bleachers the day Damon was shot.

As Madison continues her speech, Mason passes me a glass of fruit punch, shooting me an ironic look.

"This can only be endured with alcohol," he whispers, and I arch an eyebrow.

"Wait, I thought the drinks were alcohol-free," I whisper back.

"We added vodka to ours to make it through the night," he confesses. I accept the drink, downing it within seconds. If I have to endure Madison's twenty-minute speech, I need to be at least tipsy.

"Damon's motto was always: Make the days count. Unfortunately, his days were numbered," she chokes out, pausing her speech. Madison wipes away a tear from her cheek, her eyes heavy with emotion. She composes herself with a few deep breaths, but traces of tears still glisten in her eyes. "Damon was right. We need to make the most of our lives because we never know when they might end. Tonight, Damon wants us to celebrate, not mourn, because that's who Damon was."

The crowd erupts into cheers, and Madison steps down from the podium. As she passes by, I catch a glimpse of her exchanging glances with Theo in the crowd. Dr. Fleming takes the stage, his eyes scanning the room.

"Thank you all for being here tonight. We gather not just as a school but as a community, united in grief and remembrance." The sombre tone of his voice resonates through the gym hall, casting a momentary hush over the crowd. "As we remember Damon Martin, let us reflect on the impact he had on each of us. A student, an athlete, a friend—Damon wore many hats, and he wore them with pride."

He continues, "In the face of tragedy, we often find strength in unity. Tonight, as we come together to honour Damon, let us also reflect on the strength of our community. We've prepared some food and refreshments for the night, so feel free to enjoy them."

He gestures to Jak and Madison, who are standing on the sidelines.

"Additionally, as per the requests of Mr. Oban and Miss Cortese, we'll be playing some of Damon's favourite songs."

The crowd applauds gently as Dr. Fleming steps down from the stage. Gradually, the crowd disperses, and the hum of people's conversations fills the hall.

"I can't believe Madison went up there to talk about her ex while she's hooking up with Theo," Beth whispers with an uncomfortable glance. I gulp at her comment, feeling a churn in my stomach. Why does it bother me that Madison and Theo are together? We're just friends.

Suddenly, the speakers start blaring some old-school hip-hop. It's an unexpected choice for a memorial, but it's probably Damon's playlist they're playing. Matt's head starts to move to the beat of the music, almost in an ironic way, and Helena can't help but chuckle.

"It's turning into a rave, y'all," Matt announces, pouring himself another glass. "We even have the booze.

"Shh, we gotta keep that quiet," Mason warns, shooting him a glance.

I distance myself from the group, grabbing my phone to send Chris a text. I can't believe I forgot to text him earlier. It's been a few days since we last spoke, and the news of his stepbrother's death might not be the best way for him to start his East Coast tour.

me
*chris, i'm so sorry
about damon. are you okay?*

Just as I hit send, I feel an intense stare from across the room. My heart skips a beat when I realise it's Theo, standing at a distance from the crowd with a glass of punch in his hand. He opens his mouth as if about to say something before he starts walking towards me, but Madison interrupts him by wrapping her arms around him. His eyes lock with mine as she whispers something in his ear, and my heart sinks as she kisses him. Standing awkwardly with my phone in hand, a sudden urge to leave overwhelms me. I turn around, searching anxiously for my group—but just as I spot Matt and Helena, the ambiance takes a horrifying turn.

Armed police officers storm into the gym, their forceful presence plunging the room into silence. My heart races as I blink rapidly, hoping to wake up from this nightmare. The horror sets in when I realise I'm not dreaming.

"We're here to make an arrest for the murder of Damon Martin," one of the policemen shouts. The sudden announcement sends shockwaves through the gym. My eyes dart towards the staff, catching the bewildered expression on Dr. Fleming's face. Panic spreads through the crowd like wildfire as the police move purposefully through the students and teachers, and my heart drops to my stomach as they approach Madison and Theo. Madison steps back with wide eyes as the police officer flashes his badge at Theo, whose face has gone pale in terror.

"Theodore Rhodes, you are under arrest for the murder of Damon Martin," the officer declares. Dread seeps into my bones, and fearful murmurs ripple through the room. Theo glances around frantically, his eyes meeting mine for a moment before the metallic handcuffs encircle his wrists. As Theo is taken away, the crowd buzzes with questions, and the predominant one on everyone's mind is:

Did Theo kill Damon Martin?

12

Nine days.

The events from last night are hazy in my memory—not due to the alcohol, but because none of it made sense. I haven't slept a wink since I got back from the memorial. My mind races with a thousand thoughts as I read another article about Damon, my eyelids heavy with exhaustion.

According to the Barren News website, the police seem to have gathered enough evidence to convict Theo of murder. They found a gun near the scene, and Theo's prints were on Damon's uniform. Another article mentions that the police searched Theo's house and discovered his football jersey with faded bloodstains. According to the police, Theo shot Damon and made a run for it.

I've refreshed the website ten times this hour, hoping for a new statement, but the latest update still focuses on Theo's stained clothing. I slump back into my study chair, the question from a few hours ago still swirling in my head.

Why would Theo kill his friend? There's something off about the news, as if the truth goes beyond what the police have seen. Could it be that I trust Theo's word after he promised not to talk to the police about Robert Harris' torch? Or could it be because I might have feelings for him?

I nervously chew my lip, releasing an annoyed sigh. I should really get some sleep, but my mind is a whirlwind of thoughts. The built-up distress has created a dull ache in my temples. A warm shower might be just the thing to help me fall asleep.

I make my way to the bathroom, realising that the more I think about Damon's murder, the less sense it makes. Yet, there's a small voice inside my head that argues, 'how could it *not* make sense?'. Maybe there's a part of me that remembers what happened that night when I blacked out. There's a nagging thought in the back of my mind telling me I could have been involved, but I'm too terrified to face it.

The warm shower water caresses my face, its comforting warmth easing the tension in my muscles. Exhaustion starts to weigh on me, and my eyelids begin to flutter. Yet, the moment I close my eyes, an intrusive, bone-chilling image materialises in my mind.

It's the Barren High mid-term finals. The school's parking lot is dimly lit by a nearby streetlamp, casting an orange glow that accentuates the hazy air. The light falls on Damon's football jersey as he stands with his back turned. The gravel crunches, cutting through the crisp air as a series of footsteps approach. Three men in suits stand behind Damon, their faces hidden in shadows. The moment is fleeting, shattered by the imminent crack of a gunshot. The sound pierces my eardrums, transporting me as if I were present in that very moment. Theo emerges from the shadows, panic evident on his face as he rushes toward Damon. The three men have vanished—but the terror has only just begun.

My eyes snap open, and I release a loud gasp. I cling to the shower walls for stability, an intense cold sweeping through my body. Reaching for a towel, I realise that what I have just witnessed is no figment of my imagination—it's *the truth*.

Theo didn't kill Damon.

I slip into my clothes, my teeth still chattering from the chilling sensation that has enveloped my body. A frightening realisation sets in. If it wasn't Theo, who are those tall, suited figures? I couldn't make out their faces, but malevolence exuded from them like an ominous aura.

All I know is Theo is innocent. I can't let him take the blame for Damon's murder.

I glance at the time before hastily pulling a sweater over my head. I don't have much time. My legs move quicker than the rest of me, nearly stumbling as I rush downstairs. With a racing heartbeat and anxious thoughts, I run towards the Barren Police Department.

•••••

The Police Department's receptionist eyes me with curiosity as I quickly fill in a form at her desk, probably wondering why anyone would be here on a Saturday at 6 A.M. My breaths are uneven, and my face is sweaty and flushed from the sprint, but I'm aware that the clock is ticking against me. I slide the form across the desk and settle into a seat in the waiting room. Anxiously fiddling with my phone case, my gaze darts to the clock on the wall. The seconds seem to crawl by, perhaps too slowly. I'll be waiting for a considerable time before the Sheriff reviews my statement, which declares I have evidence about Damon's case.

Fifteen minutes pass.

When Sheriff Holm swings open the door, I've already jumped to my feet and circled the room a dozen times. There's a certain 1970s vibe to Sheriff Holm, thanks to his sideburns and moustache—indescribable yet unmistakable. He walks toward me at a leisurely pace, like he's not in a hurry at all.

"I read your affidavit. Follow me," he instructs.

Sheriff Holm guides me through a narrow hallway adorned with antique paintings, each one older than the previous. In just a few steps, we arrive at the interrogation rooms, and the atmosphere turns eerie. My blood runs cold as I spot Theo in one of the rooms, handcuffed to the desk like a criminal. His shoulders slump, and dark circles frame his tired eyes.

The Sheriff leads me into the interrogation room adjacent to Theo's, shutting the door behind us. I settle into the chair, swallowing the lump in my throat. Holm sinks into the seat across from me, placing his hands on the table.

"I've understood that you're here to corroborate with Mr Rhodes' story," Sheriff Holm asserts. From his tone, I gather that not many people think Theo is innocent. I nervously clear my throat.

"Theo Rhodes is innocent."

Sheriff Holm raises a surprised brow, scratching his stubbled chin. Even if my statement might sound unbelievable, I'm already ten steps ahead of him. Sheriff Holm leans back in his chair, studying me with a discerning gaze.

"I'm all ears," he challenges. My heart races in my chest, and I take a deep breath before speaking.

"My father, Archie Danvers, has access to the surveillance footage in Barren," I answer, my words sounding hurried. Holm's brows knit in confusion as he leans forward in his seat.

"How so?" Sheriff Holm asks, his tone a mix of scepticism and curiosity. I gulp, maintaining eye contact.

"He works at Bern's Surveillance, and he can pull up the footage for the specific time Theo is being accused," I answer.

Sheriff Holm sits back, processing this information.

"We found his fingerprints on the gun and Damon's blood on his jersey," he challenges.

The reality is, I can't reveal how I know Theo is innocent. All I can do is show him the evidence—how those men in suits made their entrance and fired the fatal shot at Damon. I choose my next words carefully.

"Sheriff, the truth is in the surveillance footage. I'm genuinely surprised you're accusing a seventeen-year-old without watching it," I challenge, crossing my arms. I remember Helena saying Mayor Glenn installed security cameras in Barren as part of his election strategy. It's surprising the Sheriff hadn't considered this until now.

Sheriff Holm takes a moment, anger visible in his expression.

"Alright, let's see this footage of yours. But it better not be a waste of my time. Is your father at work?" he asks, and I nod. "We're going to need a warrant. Stay here," he adds, rising from his seat.

As Sheriff Holm leaves the room, I'm left in a whirlwind of anticipation and nerves. A part of me wishes the Sheriff could prove me wrong, that I imagined those three men in suits shooting Damon. Yet, another part hopes I'm not losing my sanity, that my flashbacks might hold some significance. The seconds feel like minutes until he returns, holding a piece of paper—a search warrant. That's when I notice two guards trailing behind him, escorting Theo.

My heart leaps out of my chest when our eyes meet, a surge of relief flooding over me. But worry sets in as I notice his state—broken, with tired eyes framed by dark circles. He seems like he hasn't slept, incredibly pale and worn out. It's surreal to see Theo, tied to a table, with handcuffs around his wrists.

Sheriff Holm takes his seat in front of us, wearing a stern expression. He probably isn't thrilled about two teenagers questioning his work, but if I'm being honest, they haven't done a great job. The tension between Theo and the Sheriff is palpable. Beads of sweat form on the sheriff's pink forehead, indicating his anxiety.

"Mr Rhodes, Archie Danvers from Bern's Surveillance has granted us access to their CCTV footage. I'd like to show it to both of you before you answer some questions," the Sheriff declares. Panic wells up my chest. If the footage disproves Theo's innocence, it means I've officially reached insanity.

"Okay," Theo replies, his voice steady. I exchange an uncomfortable glance with Theo as one of the guards hands Sheriff Holm a laptop. The Sheriff turns the laptop around, presenting the screen to us. The image is black, and the anticipation makes my palms sweat.

The video starts rolling. The image quality is low and grainy, but I can make out the setting—it's the parking lot of Barren High. At the bottom of the screen, the date 28/11/17 frames the image—the night Damon Martin was shot. The image remains static for a few seconds, and my eyes widen as a shadow enters the frame. Clutching onto the armrest of the chair, I feel the hair on my arms stand up. The shadow gradually transforms into a clearer image within seconds. My grip tightens around the armrest as I notice the distinct features of the school's dark green football jersey.

Number 19. Martin.

Damon's back is turned to the camera, his footsteps confident as he approaches his white Porsche. He fumbles for the car keys, but his actions abruptly stop. I furrow my brows in confusion, but in an instant, Damon staggers back. My jaw drops, and a gasp catches in my throat as Damon collapses beside his car.

My blood turns to ice when three shadows enter the frame. They're tall—dark. Even Sheriff Holm's complexion drains of colour. In the darkness of the parking lot, the three figures blend with the shadows of the cars until they vanish. The shadows feel like an optical illusion—like a trick my brain is playing on me.

Twenty minutes later, another shadow enters the scene. The indistinct figure hurries toward Damon's body, and my eyes widen when I realise it's Theo. He crouches on the floor, but the camera's graininess obscures the details. Theo rises, pulling out his phone. He hesitates, as if contemplating making a call, before his shadow rushes out of the frame.

A heavy silence settles in the room, confirming the tape's importance in the investigation. The Sheriff is speechless, as if someone had taken the words from his mouth, and embarrassment is etched on his face. With trembling hands, he extracts a document from a folder. Theo and I exchange an anxious look. It seems the footage has frightened Holm as deeply as it has frightened us. He hastily writes a few words on the document, adds a scrawled signature, and briskly exits the interrogation room.

As silence fills the room, a shared question hangs in the air: Who are the men in suits? They could be anyone, and they could be anywhere.

As one of the guards leads me out of the interrogation room, I catch a snippet of their conversation: "Mr. Rhodes, you are being released."

The guard escorts me to the sliding doors and sets me free with a formal nod. Stepping out of the police station, I notice it's the crack of dawn, and the light fog is beginning to dissipate as the first rays of sun creep into the sky. My breath forms mist in the cold air, and my teeth chatter as I try to make sense of what just happened.

I'm not only relieved that Theo is innocent; knowing I'm not going crazy offers some comfort. But the unsettling thought of the men in suits lingers in the back of my mind. There was something eerie about the way they walked or how composed they were when they shot Damon.

A sudden realisation hits me. Maybe Damon's murder is connected to that envelope of money in my locker. It's possible he owed some gangsters money, and they came for him. Either way, digging deeper into this case will only lead to more problems.

The automatic doors slide open, interrupting my train of thought. My breath catches in my throat as Theo steps outside, his eyes meeting mine instantly. Relief washes over his expression, and the tension from moments ago dissipates. On impulse, my arms wrap around him, catching him off guard. A soft chuckle escapes him, blending with the strands of my hair. In that moment, all I feel is relief. We pull away from the embrace, our faces mere inches apart. His ocean eyes express gratitude and relief, their intensity quickening my heartbeat.

"I-I'm sorry, I..." I stammer, feeling a tinge of embarrassment for throwing myself on him. A soft smile tugs at the corners of his lips.

"Don't be. I can't thank you enough. You just saved me from a lifetime of prison," he says.

"You were innocent," I reply softly. Our eyes meet for a few seconds, the intensity of the moment colouring my cheeks. For a moment, I feel a flutter in my chest. I take a step back, clearing my throat. "I just wanted to do the right thing," I add casually.

Theo's sapphire eyes gleam in the streetlight, and silence surrounds us. I can't shake the memory of Theo helping Damon in the parking lot. I wish I could ask if I was there that night, but it seems crazy to do so.

"Thank you, Cora," he says, his tone gentle as his eyes study my face, but in that instant, the shrill ring of my phone disrupts the moment.

I glance at the caller ID—it's my dad. Answering the call nervously, I mutter, "Hey Dad."

"I just got a call from Sheriff Holm about a murder investigation. Can I ask why you aren't at home right now?" he asks, irritation evident in his voice. I don't blame him; he explicitly told me not to leave the house after sunset. I sigh, rubbing my temples. But when I look up, I realise Theo is gone.

"I was at Damon's memorial, Dad. It was at school. There were teachers everywhere," I groan. A pause lingers on the other side of the line, and I hear him exhale.

"I won't ground you, but you're seeing your psychiatrist tomorrow," he says.

"But, Dad..."

"No buts. And you're coming home right now. It's 8 A.M."

He ends the call, and I release a deep sigh. Feeling a mix of frustration and resignation, I start heading back home. As I walk, I can't shake off the lingering thoughts about the suited men and the mysterious events surrounding Damon's death. It's clear there's more to this story than meets the eye.

Not only that, but I still don't remember where I was that night.

13

Eight days.

Word spread like wildfire about Theo's innocence, which made his presence at Damon's funeral less awkward. It's the second funeral I have attended, and it doesn't get any easier. It's a different sorrow from losing my mom, yet the weight of grief feels strangely familiar.

Only the seniors and a few of Damon's teachers were invited, making this funeral more personal than the school memorial. For instance, Mayor Glenn and Dr Fleming were absent. People were sobbing or in utter silence during the eulogy, delivered by Damon's closest people, including Chris's mom. She caught my eye a few times, and she looked utterly devastated. Even those not close to Damon, like our group, shed a few tears.

But Chris was notably absent, and he hasn't been responding to my calls, adding to my anxiety. It's not every day that a seventeen-year-old gets murdered, and it's the second killing in Barren within two weeks.

I feel the unease in the air as people exit the church, the overall mood reaching a new low. Our group congregates outside, a heavy silence settling among us. I've always struggled with finding the right words in the face of death. Fortunately, Helena breaks the oppressive silence.

"I can't believe the Sheriff arrested Theo in front of the whole town, and he was totally innocent," she says, shaking her head. I swallow hard, realising I can't reveal that I was the one who got him out. They might think I'm insane.

"These local cops hardly do anything. And when something does happen, they don't know how to react," Mason adds, disappointment etched on his face. In that instant, a voice cuts through the sombre air.

"Cora!"

From the corner of my eye, I see Theo approaching me, the tightness of his suit barely allowing him to run. All heads turn toward me, and I blink rapidly in disbelief.

"Hey," I manage, feeling my cheeks turn a subtle shade of pink.

"Can I talk to you?" Theo asks, a hint of worry in his voice. I hesitate, not prepared for more bad news.

"Sure," I reply, my heart hammering in my chest. I cast a glance at Helena, who appears shocked by our interaction. He gently takes my arm, steering me away from the group. A moment of hesitation crosses his face as he nibbles on his lip.

"I just wanted to thank you for what you did," he says, his eyes briefly meeting mine. "You really saved my ass."

I respond with a shy smile, casting my gaze downward as we begin to stroll through the cemetery.

"You already told me yesterday," I tease, locking eyes with him. His cheeks flush with embarrassment.

"I know. But I really want to make it up to you. I know it's not much, but I was thinking of grabbing some pizza. I can drop you off at home after."

My cheeks flush beet red, taken aback by his unexpected gesture.

"N-Now?" I stutter. He nervously bites his lip again, an anxious expression crossing his face.

"If you're up for it. Just as friends, of course," he says quietly, avoiding my gaze.

"I'd love to," I reply, my cheeks still pink. A charming smile appears on his lips.

"Awesome. Let me get my car," he says, leading the way to the parking lot.

"Where do you live?" I ask. When I picture Theo's house, the beach comes to mind, not the humid hills of Barren.

"About ten minutes away," he replies.

We reach Theo's car, a navy-blue Nissan that seems to be holding on by a thread. He unlocks the doors and gestures for me to hop in. The familiar scent of his cologne envelopes me as I settle into the worn seat of his car. Theo slides into the driver's seat, bringing the car to life with a turn of the key. We smoothly exit the parking lot, and my gaze can't help but wander to the congregation of people outside the church.

Helena and the others seem engaged in their conversations, blissfully unaware that I left. Rolling down the windows, the evening breeze plays with our hair as we navigate the familiar streets. A sense of freedom brings a soft smile to my lips.

"I couldn't wait to leave that place, honestly," Theo shares, meeting my eyes in the rear-view mirror. "I hate funerals."

"Yeah, me too. What are people saying about the case? I hope they're not bothering you," I say.

Theo shakes his head.

"The football team knows it wasn't me. I had no motive," he responds, looking directly at me. "But there are some who think I did it just because I'm new. Either way, I couldn't care less."

As we drive past the town hall and head towards Evergreen, a subtle unease settles in the pit of my stomach. The surroundings grow more familiar, and I recognise the path we're taking—it's one I've walked many times before. The air feels heavy, and my breath quickens as a sense of recognition sets in. A wave of panic crashes over me as the ivory-coloured house comes into view. It's not just any house—it's my childhood home.

Theo notices my distress, concern furrowing his brows.

"Cora, are you okay?" he asks, worry evident in his voice.

He brings the car to a gentle stop, his eyes filled with panic as I struggle to catch my breath. The weight of memories floods over me, threatening to pull me under. Unable to contain the rising panic, I open the car door and stumble out, gasping for air. The world spins around me as I clutch the car's frame for support.

"Theo, I'm sorry," I manage to choke out between shaky breaths. "I... I need a moment."

Theo joins me, his hand resting gently on my back.

"What's wrong, Cora? I'm here," he comforts, his voice a soothing presence. I avert my gaze in embarrassment, focusing on the muddy earth below. My thoughts spin like a carousel, making it hard to think clearly. I can't believe Theo lives in my childhood home. It feels like someone barged into my private world and messed up the memories I cherished.

I calm myself with a series of slow breaths. When our eyes meet, I see concern reflected in Theo's green gaze.

"That used to be my house," I mutter quietly. His eyes widen in shock.

"What?" he exclaims. "Cora, I had no idea."

I sit on the porch with an exhale, burying my face in my hands out of embarrassment. It's the second time someone has witnessed me having a panic attack, and it feels terrible. Theo sits next to me in silence, his eyes studying me with a mix of concern and understanding. Neither of us utters a word as we gaze at the sunset before us. Evergreen appears serene at this hour, the sunset's vibrant colours casting a warm glow on the treetops. But things feel different—perhaps because this place is no longer ours.

After a few minutes of silence, I turn to look at him. His cheeks are tinged with a hint of pink, and a pang of guilt washes over me for spiralling into panic. The amber and indigo clouds blend into the dark pine trees, casting a tranquil ambiance over the scene.

"I'm really sorry, Cora. I had no idea this was your house. I just... I wanted to make it up to you for what you did yesterday," he says sincerely. "You were the only person that believed me."

I respond with a wry smile. His blue eyes remain focused on me, expressing a sincere honesty.

"I'm genuinely grateful," he adds. I raise a brow at that, playfully elbowing him.

"Theo Rhodes being grateful?" I tease, causing an inevitable grin to spread across his face.

"Oh, come on. It's not that hard to believe," he replies, laughing under his breath. The chirping of crickets fills the air as the sun sets on the horizon, and I anxiously tap my nails against the rubber of my soles.

"I'm sorry for freaking out. It's just that… I grew up in this house, and it's been a very long time since I saw it," I mutter, biting my lip.

"I genuinely had no clue. I feel bad for bringing you here," he admits, looking down at his shoes.

"It's okay. You couldn't have known."

A momentary silence hangs in the air before Theo lets out a sigh.

"My mom bought the house for me and my sister," he explains, squinting at the sky.

"You don't live with your parents?" I ask, glancing at him, but he keeps his gaze fixed on the horizon.

"No, they're still in LA. They recently divorced, and since my sister is in college in Jersey, I thought it would be best if I moved here," he explains. While I may not fully understand his parents' situation, in a way, both of us have experienced a sense of loss within our families.

"I'm sorry to hear about your parents splitting up," I say. Theo responds with a shrug.

"I'm over it," he adds.

Our eyes meet, and I realise he's already looking at me. The sunset's beams accentuate Theo's jawline and cheekbones. Realising our gaze has lingered for too long, both of us swiftly avert our eyes. The silence is shattered by a chime from my phone, almost as if it were a timely sign.

> **Dad**
> *Remember you have your*
> *appointment at 8 P.M. I suggest*
> *you grab some dinner beforehand.*

Shit, I completely forgot. I check the time and realise the appointment is in 45 minutes. I made a promise to my dad that I would go, more for his sake than mine. I haven't dreamt of the forest fire in a couple of days, but that doesn't mean anything. The hallucination I had in the shower proves that what's happening to me isn't just a simple case of night terrors.

"Is everything okay?" Theo asks, casting me a worried glance.

"I'm sorry, I completely forgot I have an appointment," I say, feeling a tinge of guilt. "Can we reschedule?"

"Of course," he says, offering a soft smile. Extending his hand, he offers to help me to my feet. "Do you need a ride?"

"Yes, please," I reply, accepting his hand.

"After freaking you out, it's the least I can do," he jokes, giving me a charming grin.

Theo and I engage in small talk during the drive, his easy-going attitude making me momentarily forget that I'm on the brink of discovering whether I'm clinically insane or not. He casually mentions he's applying to go to Princeton next year, where his sister is. When it comes to college, I have no idea what I'm going to major in—probably English literature.

A soft rain blankets the town as we arrive at the healthcare centre, and a wave of uncertainty washes over me. Should I be honest with my therapist about what I'm seeing? Should I tell her about the recurring dream of the forest fire? If I'm going insane, I have the right to know before it's too late.

Theo pulls up, the soft hum of the car engine fading as he brings it to a stop. I sit there for a moment, gathering my thoughts, the gentle raindrops creating a soothing backdrop.

"That'll be ten bucks," Theo says with a smirk. I roll my eyes at him, but I can't help but smile.

"Thanks, Theo," I say, getting out of his car.

Stepping out into the rain, the healthcare centre stands before me. The soft rain intensifies as I climb the steps, almost as if the weather mirrors the turbulence within me. I take a deep breath, feeling the cool droplets land on my skin before heading inside.

•••••

The rain soaked my clothes during the last ten minutes of my walk back home, almost as if it mirrored my mood. Yanking off my muddy sneakers, I dump my soaked backpack on the floor and swiftly tie my wet hair into a ponytail. I head to the kitchen, where I find my dad vigorously scrubbing the dishes. Our eyes meet instantly, and he stops what he's doing.

"How did it go?" he asks, his tone carrying a hint of anxiety.

"Good," I lie, inspecting the half-empty fridge. "I didn't have the chance to grab dinner."

"There's some leftover pasta from today," he mutters just as I locate the container. Carefully spooning the contents onto a plate, I purposefully avoid my dad's nervous gaze. "What did the therapist say?" he asks.

Even though I expected him to ask, the question still twists my stomach. Fidgeting with the cutlery as my food heats up, I realise it's unavoidable. I must either lie or tell the truth, but I must answer. He takes a seat across from me, his eyes focused on me.

"I didn't tell her much. I kind of froze," I reply.

"Some people take time to open up. Don't worry," he reassures. There's a brief pause before he shifts the conversation. "I know you're grounded, but... I heard you got that boy out of prison."

"He was innocent, and I couldn't just sit and do nothing. Thanks for talking to your manager about it," I say. My dad nonchalantly shrugs.

"Legally, they're allowed to ask for footage, so it wasn't a big deal." He sighs. "I can't imagine what the Martins are going through right now."

"I guess they're not handling it well," I say.

Chris still hasn't replied to my message, and it worries me. Perhaps I should go to his house tomorrow after school. Even if he doesn't feel like talking, at least I'd be there. And, in theory, we are still together, right? The uncertainty nags at me.

"I used to be friends with his father. Back in the day," he exhales, reminiscing. The thought of my father having a beer with Damon's dad seems unimaginable.

A brief pause fills the air as I eat. A part of me wishes I were having pizza with Theo, not microwavable mac and cheese. The way he responded to my panic attack brings a sense of relief. I'm not used to experiencing them in public, but I didn't expect him to be so supportive. Chris, on the other hand, would have somehow taken it personally.

My dad's voice breaks my train of thought.

"I wanted to discuss something with you," he says with a serious tone. The way he speaks makes me feel like it might not be good news.

"What?" I ask, my throat going dry.

"I've been thinking for some time about marrying Isabelle, but after your reaction the other night… I'm not too sure," he explains.

His words leave me momentarily speechless.

"Wait, what?" I manage to choke out, my mind racing to comprehend his words. I feel nauseous. I never expected my dad to consider remarrying, especially since he hardly knows this woman.

My dad's upset gaze is fixed on me, waiting for a response. I take a moment to process his words, the weight of the situation sinking in. The air in the room feels heavy, and I finally manage to find my voice.

"I didn't mean to react that way," I stammer, my mind racing. "I just… It was unexpected. I'm sorry if I made you doubt your decision."

He sighs, a mix of disappointment and understanding in his eyes.

"Cora, it's about ensuring you're comfortable with a change like this. When your mom and I decided to have you, I made a promise to prioritise you. I'm concerned about your well-being."

The realisation hits me that my father's happiness is tangled with mine, and my reaction may have affected more than just that one moment.

"Why are you worried? I'm fine," I say, swallowing hard. An uncomfortable silence stretches between us, his grey eyes clouded with tears. He looks shattered.

"A few months before your mom died, her behaviour was exactly like yours. She was having trouble sleeping, concentrating..."

My breath catches in my throat, and I manage to choke out a stunned, "What?"

My dad's shoulders droop, and he deliberately avoids making eye contact with me. He lets out a deep sigh.

"Your mom was diagnosed with schizophrenia a year before she died," he reveals in a strained voice. "That's why she lost control of the car."

For a moment, my heart stops. I recall the sound of pill bottles rattling, a memory I had suppressed until now. I vividly picture my mom's consistently swollen eyes, along with the haunting memories of her nightmares and frantic screams. The memories come flooding back, and a heavy, sorrowful silence hangs between my dad and me.

"I-I didn't know…" I stammer, my heart pounding against my ribcage.

"You were a child," he says, his voice gentle.

If it weren't for the ten years of therapy after my mom's accident, I might have burst into tears. However, thanks to years of PTSD hypnosis and anxiety medication, I've become numb to it all.

My dad notices my expression, letting out a distressed exhale.

"I'm sorry for bringing it up, kiddo," he mutters.

He rises from the chair, making his way to the couch. As he delicately turns on the TV, I sense he's lost in the painful memories of my mom. There are no words that can fully express what my father and I experienced after her accident.

In that instant, a breaking news alert disrupts my dishwashing, and my eyes dart to the TV screen. Our local reporter, Yolanda Olufsen, stands outside the Barren Police Department, holding a microphone in her hand.

"Curfew has been imposed in Barren County to prevent night crime after seventeen-year-old Damon Martin was shot after a school football game," she announces in a steady tone. "Sheriff Brandon Holm said that this is a matter of civilian safety."

Taking the microphone, Sheriff Holm's brows furrow with concern as he delivers the crucial message.

"All citizens must be in their homes by 23 hours. This is for your safety; it is our job to protect."

A shared look of fear passes between my dad and me as the chilling reality sets in.

The men in black are in Barren.

·····

The grandfather clock strikes midnight as I finish cleaning the kitchen. Surprisingly, the sound doesn't disturb my dad, who remains deeply asleep on the couch. He must be used to it. Glancing over my shoulder, I pull out the psychological report from my backpack, my stomach churning with fear as I begin to read.

PSYCHOLOGICAL REPORT

DEPARTMENT OF MENTAL HEALTH
WOLSNER RD
BARREN COUNTY, NJ

Personal information: **Final diagnosis: SCHIZOFRENIA**

Name: Cora Danvers
Age: 18
Date of birth: 5/3/1999

Denial washes over me, and I crumple the document in my bare hands before heading upstairs. The flashback I had in the shower that prevented Theo from being convicted of murder was real. There may not be a scientific explanation for it, but I refuse to accept the diagnosis I've been given.

I sink onto my bed, frustration overwhelming me as a whirlwind of thoughts swirl in my mind. This turbulent situation is straining my relationship with my dad and influencing his decisions. My mind replays my dad's words: My mom had schizophrenia, lost control, and that's why she died. And now, I've been given the same diagnosis.

There is only one way to bring an end to the chaos.

Searching through my drawers, a little voice warns that I might be going crazy with this, but my intuition drowns it out. I find the map of Barren I printed a few days ago, along with my dream journal and sketch. A profound sense of clarity washes over me as the puzzle pieces start falling into place while I examine the drawing. The pine trees from the dream flash in my mind, and their location becomes immediately clear—it's Evergreen. Clenching my teeth, I realise it covers around 200 acres. In essence, the fire could happen anywhere.

A gust of wind stirs my curtains, and their eerily human-like movements send shivers down my spine. Leaning against the window, I hear the soft sound of footsteps. My blood turns to ice as a figure emerges from the shadows, a hood concealing its identity as it moves toward the gate of Mulkiwa Park.

A knot tightens in my throat as the hooded figure glances over their shoulder, and a gasp escapes me when I realise it's Chris. He swiftly adjusts his hoodie to conceal his face, and I'm left speechless I watch him leap over the fence.

I know Chris well enough to understand that he wants to be left alone, but it's 3:20 A.M., and the town curfew was four hours ago.

14

Seven days.

After talking to my dad last night, I realised that if my mom had schizophrenia, there's a good chance I'm heading down the same road. The internal struggle within me grows by the minute. There's a small voice in my head reassuring me that I'm not losing my mind, but the stakes of not giving the medication a shot are too high. The only way to find out is to take it for a few days. If I don't dream of the forest fire during that time, it'll be official—I have schizophrenia.

I make myself swallow the pill during breakfast and head to school. On my way to my first class, all I hear is Theo and Madison hooking up last night. It seems everyone's already moved on from Damon's death, especially Madison, only a couple of days after his funeral.

By the time second period rolls around, I'm already feeling the side effects of the antipsychotics. My mouth is dry, my ability to concentrate has plummeted and I feel like I could fall asleep at any minute. The weight of my body feels almost insignificant, as if I were a mere corpse. Mr. Woods' voice becomes a distant murmur, merging seamlessly with my thoughts like tides in the ocean.

Even with my mental fog, the unsettling image of Chris sneaking into Mulkiwa Park last night lingers in my memory. He hasn't responded to any of my messages, and it seems that no one else has heard from him since Damon's death. The unease gnaws at me, creating a sense of foreboding that I can't shake.

The sudden, ear-popping noise of the bell startles me, and I jolt upright in my seat, realising I had been dozing off in class. As my classmates rush for the door, I sluggishly make my way, colliding with someone outside—which turns out to be Theo. His ocean blue eyes soften with concern as he notices my fatigued state.

"Hey, are you okay?" he asks, steadying me. I mumble a half-hearted apology, my mind tangled in the medication's lingering effects.

"Just a rough morning," I manage with a faint smile. Theo raises an eyebrow.

"You sure you're all right? You look like you've barely slept," he mutters.

I nod, avoiding eye contact.

"Yeah. I fell asleep at four," I explain, hoping to downplay the situation with a small laugh. Gazing at him with an empty expression, the events of last night come rushing back. A sudden realisation hits, an inexplicable pain pricking at my heart.

Theo and Madison hooked up shortly after he dropped me off at the psychiatrist.

He instantly notices the change in my expression, nervously biting his lip.

"Well, if you ever need someone to talk to, I'm here," he says, giving my arm a reassuring squeeze.

"Don't worry about it," I say, offering a tight-lipped smile. "I hope things are going well between you and Madison."

As I walk away, an unwelcome thought emerges, one that fills me with a sense of fear.

Is it possible I have feelings for Theo?

•••••

Hel and Beth tried having a conversation with me in the cafeteria on several occasions, but their words turned into static noise. The sounds that surround me feel distant, like echoes underwater, and I can't shake the feeling that my emotions are trapped within my body. The world around me appears to be on mute, every sound dulled, and in slow motion.

As the group talked about the new curfew, my thoughts were too slow to come up with a response. They've invited me for dinner this weekend, but it's the last thing I want to do, especially since the forest fire will happen a week from now. In the very early hours of that Monday morning, the moon will reach Waning Gibbous.

I trudge towards the library, my heart still heavy in my chest after the conversation with Theo. It shouldn't bother me that he's with Madison, considering we've always been just friends, but I can't help feeling somewhat upset. Maybe it's the medication making me act a bit off.

As I step into the library, the familiar hush envelops me like a comforting embrace. The scent of books and the soft shuffle of pages offer a momentary escape from the weight of my thoughts. I navigate through the library, scanning for the silent study area where the computers are nestled. The PCs are usually taken by freshmen playing videogames, but my eyes catch a glimpse of a familiar face towards the back. Chris is sitting at one of the desks, his face buried in his hands. There's an air of unease around him, evident in the rhythmic bounce of his leg and the anxious sighs escaping him. In a sudden motion, he gets up, quickly shoving something into his backpack.

"Chris?" I call out, unable to ignore the sudden change in his behaviour. He turns around, his face going pale before a flash of anger replaces it. With a brisk movement, he zips up his backpack, his body language radiating a noticeable aggression.

"Not now, Cora," he growls under his breath, leaving me momentarily taken aback. Before I can even muster a response, Chris rushes out of the library. I'm left perplexed, staring at the seat he occupied just seconds ago.

As my vision fades to black, a confusing feeling of floating overwhelms me. The next thing I know, I'm jolted awake by the metallic taste of blood lingering on my tongue. The fluorescent lights above reveal I'm in Mrs. Sanchez's class. The usual student buzz and lesson hum feel unsettling, adding to my confused and surprised state. Glancing around, I try to piece together the fragments of lost time, my mind struggling to comprehend how I ended up here after the encounter with Chris in the library. I can only recall a few images from my dream. A neon sign shaped like a hand and another resembling a crescent moon stand out vividly in my memory. Even if the antipsychotics are clouding my waking thoughts, my dreams are evolving—each time more colourful and vivid.

"Cora, stay with us," Mrs. Sanchez calls out, realising I've dozed off on my desk. A few classmates snicker, stealing glances in my direction.

"Sorry," I mumble, still groggy from the dream.

A set of eyes watches me from across the room—it's Helena. She gazes at me with a blend of suspicion and concern.

•••••

By the time I walk up the porch steps to my house, the night has already fallen. Swinging open the door, my lips part in surprise as I discover Chris seated on the couch next to my dad. The surprising sight leaves me momentarily stunned, trying to make sense of the strange scene in my living room. Their sitting posture is remarkably alike—with hunched shoulders, spread legs, and an uncomfortable tight-lipped smile when they notice me.

"Hey, sweetie. Chris came to see you," my dad says.

I glance at Chris' outfit—black Nike basketball shorts and an oversized grey hoodie with 'Jersey State' written on it. A pair of Bose headphones hang from his neck, reaching the end of his ruffled hair. His sharp jawline and furrowed brows give him an air of seriousness or anger. It's always a mystery to me.

"Why are you here?" I cautiously ask Chris. Awkwardness hangs in the living room like a thick fog. Suddenly, Chris rises from the couch, leaving me perplexed as he pulls me into a hug.

"I came to say goodbye," he says, releasing me. "Before the tour," he adds, clarifying his words.

My dad shoots me a side glance, indicating it's his cue to leave. Chris and I find ourselves alone in the living room, his green eyes studying my face. Our relationship has always been a chess game—until one of us takes the initiative, we linger in a state of inactivity and contemplation. I decide to make the first move.

"I haven't heard from you in a week. Are you ghosting me?" I ask, my tone laced with anger.

To my surprise, tears begin to well up in his eyes. He releases an anguished exhale, lowering his chin to avoid meeting my gaze.

"No, I'm not. I'm just not the best at coping with loss. You should know that by now," he retorts in a condescending tone. My blood boils at his attitude, and I clench my jaw in frustration.

"You could have at least messaged me saying you were okay. I've been feeling like an idiot waiting for-" Chris cuts me off before I can complete my rant.

"Look, my brother was murdered by a bunch of crooks. Not even the Sheriff knows who it was. I hadn't left my room until today," he explains.

There's a sadness in his voice, a kind I hadn't heard since Chris' parents separated. A sharp pain grips my chest, but it quickly subsides when I catch him in a lie. Chris was at Mulkiwa Park last night, several hours past curfew; he has definitely left his room. But I can't let him know that I'm aware of it.

"What about today in the library? I looked like a total idiot," I interject, nervously biting my bottom lip. Chris rolls his eyes.

"I had class. I didn't want to talk to anyone. Don't be selfish, Cora."

"I don't think it's selfish to communicate and try to make this work," I say, my jaw clenched in frustration. The air in the room becomes charged with our conflicting emotions, a palpable tension hanging between us. He sighs, giving me a pitiful glance.

"I just need some space to process things, Cora," he mutters, the heat of his anger fading away. I interpret it as a signal to calm myself too. Maybe I've been so worried about the forest fire and my medication that I failed to notice Chris's need for space. I inhale deeply, locking eyes with his piercing blue gaze.

"I'm sorry. I guess I'm not used to spending this much time away from you. And you're leaving for two weeks," I murmur. Chris looks at me with a mix of understanding and lingering frustration.

"It's just a short tour. Plus, I need to get out of Barren for a while," he says. Our eyes meet, and for a fleeting moment, a spark reminiscent of our early dating days flickers. But Chris interrupts the moment by rising from the couch.

"Gotta go. My flight's in a few hours," he adds. I nod in understanding, leading him to the door, his suitcase dragging behind him. At the porch, he turns to me, planting a soft kiss on my cheek.

"I'll text you; I promise. I'll get better at replying," Chris assures, flashing a small smile.

"Okay," I reply, my eyes fixed on him descending the porch steps. As I'm about to shut the door, Chris turns his head to steal a last glance at me.

"I love you," he says.

"I love you, too," I mutter hardly above a whisper. But this time, the words leave a metallic taste on my tongue.

He flashes me a smile before his silhouette disappears into the night, a lingering unease settling within me. The memory of him skipping curfew last night gnaws at me, creating an unsettling feeling in the pit of my stomach.

I'm jolted from my thoughts by the sound of my dad clearing his throat behind me. I turn around to find him standing in the hallway with crossed arms, wearing a disapproving look.

"When were you going to tell me you had a boyfriend?" he asks. I hesitate for a moment, caught off guard by my dad's unexpected question.

"It's not like that, Dad. Chris and I... it's complicated," I explain, which is partly the truth. I don't know where Chris and I stand, so it's better not to admit that I kept a one-year relationship from him.

I never mentioned Chris to my dad because he's incredibly overprotective. I can't blame him, considering the challenging childhood I've had; the last thing he wants is someone hurting his daughter. If my mom were still around, I'd share everything with her. But with my dad, it's a whole different story.

"Complicated, huh? You've been seeing him for a year, Cora. You think that would've come up in conversation," my dad remarks, his disapproval evident in his furrowed brows. I sigh, realising Chris must have told him about our relationship. I can't help but wonder what else he could have told him.

"Well, Dad, it's not like I've been keeping it a secret on purpose. Things with Chris are just... uncertain," I explain, trying to ease the tension in the air. My dad arches a brow.

"He told me he's in a band. From what I've heard, he's quite talented," he says. I nod, relieved that my dad doesn't seem overly upset.

"Yeah, Dad. I'm tired, and I have an early class tomorrow. I'll talk to you in the morning," I say. My dad gives me an understanding nod.

"Good night, kiddo."

He leans over to give my cheek a gentle squeeze, just like he always does.

"Goodnight, Dad," I reply, making a dash for the stairs.

As I close the door behind me, the events of the evening swirl in my mind, leaving me with a mix of emotions. I flop onto my bed, staring at the ceiling as I grapple with the uncertainty surrounding Chris and the uneasy feeling in the pit of my stomach. His behaviour confuses me, and I can't quite grasp the full picture. Ignoring me for almost a week and then suddenly meeting my dad raises more questions than answers. Plus, his midnight excursion to Mulkiwa adds another layer of mystery.

What was Chris up to at 3 A.M.?

・・・・・

Six days.

The assembly hall buzzes with muted conversations as students gather, finding their designated spots on the cold metal bleachers of the Great Hall. As Dr. Fleming makes announcements, I sense a few heads turning in my direction. Perplexed, I wonder why all the sudden attention is focused on me. They're probably noticing my weakened physical state from the medication. One noticeable change is that Damon's name seems to have vanished from everyone's lips, including Dr. Fleming's, who previously painted him as a martyr. It's as if society's attention span is shorter than a Snapchat streak.

As the assembly concludes, a rush of people stands up from their seats, but amidst the commotion, someone grabs my arm. My eyes instantly meet Hel's. Her dark chocolate hair looks freshly straightened, and her makeup is flawless. Yet, a hint of anxiety lingers in her expression, as if something is gnawing at her inside.

"I know you might not feel like talking, but... Are you okay?" Helena asks, her eyes filled with concern. Her cautious tone gives off the impression that she's walking on eggshells around me. Maybe she's noticed my soulless expression and my frequent napping in class. Maybe she thinks I'm on drugs.

"You look like you've seen a ghost," I joke, trying to downplay the situation. Helena blinks, processing my attempt at humour. "I'm okay. Just feeling a bit down since Chris left last night," I answer. Her brows arch in surprise.

"So, you're not sad because of..." she starts, then stops herself from finishing the sentence. I shoot her a confused look.

"Because of what?" I choke out, urging her to continue. A heavy tension hangs in the air, causing my head to spin. By now, everyone has left the Great Hall, and Helena and I find ourselves alone. She takes a moment, as if choosing her words carefully.

"Because of what happened with Damon?" Helena finally asks, sounding uneasy. Her cheeks are crimson, but I'm not sure why.

"No. I mean, no offense, but no," I reply, maintaining steady eye contact. Helena nods, lowering her gaze. She seems uncomfortable, but why? Is it the medication playing tricks on my perception of reality?

"Is something wrong?" I ask, swallowing hard. She shakes her head, flashing me a nervous smile.

"Let's go outside. A bit of fresh air might do you good," she utters. She grabs my hand and starts pulling me outside of the hall, but I stop her. My intuition is screaming that something is terribly off. I gently take hold of her shoulders, compelling her to look at me.

"Helena, what's wrong?" I ask, my tone growing stern.

Suddenly, my phone vibrates, and Hel's face turns as pale as a ghost.

chrismatthews9
sent you a video

"Don't open that," Helena says in a breathless voice, her expression tinged with terror.

"Why?" I ask, feeling my heart race in my chest. She places a firm hand on mine to stop me from opening the video.

"Please, just trust me on this," she implores, her eyes filled with a mix of fear and concern. My heart skips a beat as I absorb her words, and a wave of disbelief washes over me.

"What's in the video?" I manage to ask, my voice trembling. She takes a deep breath, hesitating before responding.

"It's something you shouldn't have to see, especially not like this."

The weight of Helena's words lingers, creating a heavy silence between us. I'm at a crossroads, torn between the curiosity of uncovering the truth and listening to Helena's advice. The anticipation intensifies, and my heart pounds relentlessly in my chest.

I open the video.

As the video begins to play, my worst fears unfold before my eyes. It's a scene of Chris in bed with a girl, but not just any girl—Emily, one of the band members he's on tour with. The room spins, and my heart sinks, overwhelmed by the profound sense of betrayal.

I can't breathe.

Overwhelmed by a violent wave of nausea, I hastily scramble to the nearest bathroom. Helena rushes in behind me, guiding me to an open stall as I empty my stomach. A constant stinging pain grips my chest, and Helena rubs my back in soothing circles, attempting to calm me down.

"Cora, I am so sorry. I can't believe..." Helena begins, her voice filled with genuine sympathy. Or is it pity? Embarrassment washes over me, making the situation even more unbearable.

I'm devastated. Chris cheated on me after everything I did for him. I sacrificed so many parts of myself for him, only to have him stab me in the back like this. The pain is profound, and the weight of betrayal feels almost suffocating.

I explode into uncontrolled sobs, my body sliding down to the cold floor. Helena tries to comfort me with soothing words, but the pain is too immense to be soothed. The bathroom door creaks open, and I hear a few people enter, asking what's wrong. But their voices are drowned out by the relentless thoughts racing in my head.

"Does everyone know?" I manage to choke out in between sobs. Pain finds its way onto Helena's face, as if my question had stung her.

"He sent it to the entire school," she confesses, her words hanging heavily in the air. For a moment, my heart stops. Embarrassment seeps into my bones, but it is soon replaced by an increasing anger. Not only did he cheat on me, but he sent it to everyone to humiliate me.

The bathroom spins uncontrollably, a side effect of the antipsychotics and the anguish within me. An icy chill envelopes my soul, and my intuition whispers a truth I'm hesitant to accept—maybe Chris isn't the person I thought he was.

15

By lunchtime, even though my crying has stopped, the news has spread like wildfire. A few people shoot me sympathetic looks as I walk into the cafeteria, my shoulders hunched with embarrassment. The image of Chris and Emily lingers in my mind, their moans haunting my thoughts with distorted echoes.

I slip back into consciousness, realising I'm seated at the lunch table with the group. Their eyes are fixed on me, and I push myself to swallow the last bit of pumpkin pie.

"You know we're here for you, Cora," Matt murmurs, rubbing my back in consolation. Feeling the weight of others' glances, my face reddens, but the swollen puffiness of my eyes keeps me from meeting their gaze.

"Thank you," I reply, my words barely audible.

"I just don't get it. Why would he send that to the entire school?" Beth asks, scrunching her nose in disgust. It's the question lingering in everyone's mind for the past three hours, yet none of us have an answer. All I can feel is a profound sense of humiliation, pushing me to the verge of running away.

"Maybe he was hacked. Either way, it doesn't do him any favours," Matt suggests, earning a nod from Mason.

Now that I reflect on it, Chris had been acting strange ever since that altercation with Damon. He ignored me for a week after Damon's death, and I caught him sneaking around at Mulkiwa. In that instant, a disgusting theory creeps into my mind. Perhaps Chris went to Mulkiwa in the middle of the night to see Emily.

I suddenly recall all the times Chris had band practice and didn't want me to come. The realisation hits me, and I gulp at the thought that he might have been cheating for all these months. The knot of betrayal tightens, and the nagging thought pops into my mind: Did Chris ever truly love me?

Helena's voice breaks through my spiralling thoughts.

"I'm pretty sure that video is illegal. He's underage."

"No," I interject, my words deliberate. "Chris is nineteen."

"Still. Why would he even do that?" Matt asks, raising a brow.

As the question lingers, a heavy silence settles over the group. The frustration builds within me, anger simmering beneath the surface. Each passing moment adds fuel to the fire, and I feel my head reaching its boiling point when my phone suddenly vibrates, jolting me out of the suffocating stillness.

All of their eyes land on me again as I take out my phone, and the anticipation increases as I read the sender's name.

"It's Chris," I mutter breathlessly.

The group collectively exclaims, "What?", their faces displaying a clear expression of surprise. The room seems to hold its breath as I open the message, the screen illuminating with Chris's words.

> **chrismatthews9**
> *cora, i really hope you haven't seen that shit.*

coradanvers
you're a cheating asshole.

"If that didn't put him in his place, I don't know what will," Helena mutters, narrowing her eyes in disgust. Panic continues to surge within my chest, and a sense of suffocation grips me. The cafeteria table begins to blur, and erratic star-like patterns dance before my eyes, causing my breath to catch in my throat. The overwhelming disorientation tightens its grip, amplifying the urgency to escape the dizzying scene.

"Cora, are you okay?" a distorted voice asks, but I can't tell who it belongs to.

The panic finally consumes me, and without a second thought, I bolt out of the cafeteria and the main building. The need to escape pushes me forward, my surroundings blurring as I rush through the crowded hallways.

I sprint towards the football field, my breaths gradually evening out as my vision regains focus. The rhythmic sounds of jocks training fill the air, but I'm too caught up in my own turmoil to take notice. Reaching the bleachers, I seek refuge beneath the metallic structure, attempting to regain my breath in the cool shadows.

A few approaching footsteps pierce through my panic attack, jolting me back to the present. Theo's concerned face comes into view as he approaches me under the bleachers. His eyes reflect worry, and he crouches down to my level.

"Cora, are you okay?" he asks, his voice gentle. I manage a shaky nod, but the distress in my eyes remains evident. Theo, sensing my unease, chooses not to push for more information. Instead, he settles down beside me, offering silent support. My tears have dried up, and my panic attack has subsided, leaving me staring blankly at the ground.

"I had no idea he was cheating on me," I croak, breaking the silence that enveloped us for the past few minutes. Theo's eyes meet mine, sympathy evident in his gaze.

"He's an asshole for doing that. You deserve so much better, Cora."

A heavy sigh escapes me as I lower my chin.

"I can't believe he sent it to the entire school. I feel so humiliated," I confess. Theo shakes his head, his azure eyes studying my face.

"He should feel that way, not you. You're an amazing girl," he reassures. A small, shy smile tugs at the corners of my lips.

"Thanks, Theo."

"That's what friends are for, right?" he says, flashing me a smile.

The peaceful moment is disrupted by the distant rumble of thunder, breaking the silence between us. A light drizzle begins, but the metallic shelter of the bleachers shields us from the cold autumn rain. The rhythmic pattering of raindrops on the metal creates a gentle harmony, blending with the distant thunder. As the rain intensifies, the coach blows the whistle, signalling the football team to head inside. I glance at him for a moment, noticing he's in his football uniform.

"Shit, you missed practice," I mutter. He gives me a sheepish shrug.

"I had to make sure you were okay. Plus, I had a feeling you'd want to talk to me," he says, giving me a playful nudge.

I can't help but chuckle, feeling grateful for the lightness he always brings to the conversation.

"You're so arrogant," I tease. He playfully bites his lip, his eyes gleaming with a mischievous spark.

"I know, but I make you laugh," he grins.

Theo and I share a smile, and for a moment, I forget Chris cheated on me. It's just the two of us sitting under the rain, finding solace in the quiet moment. The memories of Matt and Helena's expressions in the cafeteria, along with the pitiful eyes of others, flood my mind. The most embarrassing part was receiving pity from people who had never noticed me until now.

"I just feel so embarrassed. Everyone was looking at me with pity," I mumble, burying my face in my hands. Theo's comforting hand lands on my shoulder, prompting me to look up.

"You want my honest opinion? Screw them. They're going to forget about all this in two days, just like they forgot about Damon."

A soft smile graces my lips, grateful for his presence. Unlike Helena and Matt's group, he doesn't insist on talking about Chris or has asked me for details.

"Is Madison going to kill me for talking to you?" I ask, chuckling ironically. Being friends with Theo could easily land me on her death list.

Theo gives me a puzzled look.

"Why?" he asks. I fiddle with the rubber soles of my shoes, picking a few pebbles from the cracks to avoid his gaze.

"I heard that you guys hooked up," I mutter. Theo grimaces, scratching his stubble.

"Oh, no. That was just a rumour," he clarifies awkwardly. My mouth drops open in surprise.

"Seriously?" I blurt out. I had expected Theo to be just like any other guy, secretly pining after Madison. But he shakes his head.

"We only kissed a few times. Nothing serious," he chuckles. He shoots me an arrogant smirk. "I gotta say, you sound relieved."

Embarrassment paints my cheeks crimson as I shake my head in denial.

"Why should I? We're just friends," I retort with a scoff.

"True," he murmurs, his gaze shifting back to the now rain-soaked, empty football field. We silently watch the rain, the sound of the bell signalling the end of lunchtime breaking the quiet moment. With a shared glance, he stands up from the damp grass.

"Let's go to class," he suggests, offering his hand. I manage a soft smile before he helps me to my feet.

•••••

They often say that comfort is more convincing when it comes from those we don't expect. Maybe my prejudice against the jocks was inaccurate, at least when it comes to Theo, who appears to be a friend despite his association with The Damnation. Despite everything that happened, I felt like he listened to me more than Helena and her group. Helena messaged me a few times, apologising for gossiping about Chris, but I don't have the energy to reply.

By the time I arrive home from school, the rain has subsided. Throughout the afternoon, a few girls approached me to express their condolences for Chris cheating on me. Despite my efforts to not feel uncomfortable, I couldn't shake off Theo's words: "They will forget about this in two days."

Chris has been persistent, trying to reach me through messages, calls, and even emails all afternoon. His apologies and promises of change continue, but the antipsychotics have left me numb. The Cora from last year might have blamed herself for his cheating, but I'm not her anymore.

Locking the front door, a surge of anger tightens my chest. The overwhelming urge to show up at his house and scream consumes me, but he's thousands of miles away. I feel helpless, unsure of how to channel this intense anger. I find my dad on the couch watching TV, and luckily, he doesn't hear me over the sport commentator's booming voice. Making my way upstairs, I lock my bedroom with a heavy sigh. The pain in my chest resurfaces, but I can't bring myself to cry.

Instead, I gaze out the window at the moon's gentle glow. With the Waning Gibbous phase just days away, I realise I'm on the brink of uncovering the truth about the forest fire.

16

Four days.

In the early hours of the morning, the cold winter air turns my breath into mist, making me wish our gym class was scheduled for a later time. We assemble in a circle before getting split into four softball teams, our teacher addressing a few students about their recent absences. The whispers about Chris and me persist, but this time, I find myself indifferent to them. The anger has faded because, in four days, I'll find out whether I am clinically insane or not.

Ms Whittaker places me on the same team as Beth and Matt, which I am not too excited about, before she blows the first whistle. The teams scatter instantly, and I return to my designated catcher position, the sweaty scent of my leather gloves causing me to wrinkle my nose. My phone buzzes in the pocket of my shorts for the twentieth time in three minutes, and I release a frustrated exhale.

Despite Chris sending me fifty messages in the past two days, pleading for me to call him, I've chosen to ignore every single one. I don't have the energy or headspace to entertain his excuses.

The batter, Jak Oban, takes a powerful swing at the ball, launching it into the air as though it were destined for the stars. With prideful roars, Jak's team celebrates as he dashes from one base to another.

Meanwhile, my team faces challenges trying to grab the ball, with Beth in hot pursuit.

Suddenly, a surprising turn of events captures everyone's attention. Three fully armed police officers storm onto the field, their intimidating expressions instantly hushing the class. Panic spreads through the class as Ms. Whittaker quickly approaches the Sheriff, exchanging hurried words with a worried expression. The atmosphere becomes charged with tension, and curious glances dart between the students. Ms Whittaker's eyes land on Hel, gesturing for her to come over. Hel's eyes widen, and her face turns ghostly pale, a palpable tension filling the air as she nervously makes her way to the teacher.

A bone-chilling realisation creeps into all of us.

The police have started to investigate the students of Barren High.

Helena and the police officers disappear into the thick fog, and an eerie silence falls over the remaining students. They exchange uneasy glances, unsure of what the investigation might reveal about Barren High. An unsettling sensation takes root in the pit of my stomach.

Do the police suspect that the mysterious men in black are among us?

Despite the growing tension in the air, Ms. Whittaker blows her whistle, and the softball game continues. Everyone swiftly returns to their positions, but an air of discomfort lingers amongst them. Jak hits the ball, sending it soaring through the air. But this time, the crowd's enthusiasm is noticeably lower.

As the ball sails through the air, my eyesight blurs, and the noises around me fade into silence. The only sound is the rhythm of my own breaths as I gaze into the abyss of darkness. A shiver runs down my spine as a man's voice pierces through the stillness.

"Helena Corey. What was your relationship with Damon Martin?"

The unfamiliar voice resonates in my head, but it only lasts for moments before vanishing into thin air. It's as if the words were whispered directly into my ear, transporting me to that very moment.

"Cora! Run!" Beth's urgent shout jolts me back to reality, and the air returns to my lungs.

I sprint after the ball, adrenaline coursing through my veins, but the haunting words linger in my mind like an echo I can't shake. The thud of my heart matches the pounding of my footsteps on the ground. Closing the gap, my fingers graze the softball just in time, snatching it from the air before Jak reaches home base. The crowd holds its breath for a split second before bursting into an explosive cheer. My cheeks burn with redness, and each breath feels excruciating as I toss the ball back. The excited cheers of my classmates surround me, but a horrifying fear begins to seep into my veins, casting a dark shadow over the victorious moment.

Despite the antipsychotics, my delusions have returned.

•••••

The police investigation has stirred chaos among the students of Barren High, reaching its peak tension by lunchtime. Half of the seniors have been called in for questioning, but for some reason, they haven't called me in. Maybe it's because I had already shared everything I knew when I helped Theo get out of prison. Either way, the less the police know about me, the better—I still don't have a clear idea of where I was that night. The silver lining is that no one is talking about Chris anymore, which comes as a relief.

As we settle around the cafeteria table as a group, a strange feeling takes root in my chest when we collectively notice Helena's absence. Matt appears the most nervous among them all.

"Has anyone seen Hel today?" he asks. They shake their heads in unison, a sense of discomfort lingering between them.

"Not since softball," Beth replies. Matt bites his lip, fiddling with his phone case as his eyes dart around the cafeteria

"She should be out of class by now," he mutters.

"Let's wait a few minutes. If she's not here, I'll call her," Beth suggests. Mason takes a bite of his apple, the crunching sound making me flinch.

"I'm sure she's fine, Matt," Mason reassures. "She was with us when Damon was shot."

The fragment of the conversation I overheard on the field is etched in my mind, persistently bothering me. It must be a side effect of the medication because I had never experienced hearing voices before.

Helena arrives a few minutes later, her hair tightly pulled back into a ponytail, and her eyeliner smeared. With an anguished sigh, she places her tray on the table.

"Hel, are you okay?" Beth asks, her eyes wide. Matt plants a quick peck on her cheek, but Helena responds by staring blankly at the table.

"Dude, you're scaring us," Daniel exclaims.

Helena snaps out of her trance, her gaze filled with terror as she surveys each of us.

"You guys have no clue what's going on," she says, her voice trembling. An eerie silence falls upon us, and my heartbeat quickens. "Three people were involved in Damon's murder. And they have no idea who they are."

A heavy tension hangs in the air as Helena's revelation lingers. The cafeteria seems to hush into an uneasy stillness, and the weight of her words settles on each of us.

The men in black. They're here, and they could be amongst us.

•••••

As the final bell rings, I quickly rush out of school. The darkness outside intensifies my unease, especially after Helena's trembling revelation about the men in black. I'm more nervous than ever about walking alone at night. It seems like everyone else feels the same way, as both students and staff are also hurrying home. Sheriff Holm has not yet made a public announcement about the three killers, but word spreads rapidly in this town.

As I walk through the main square, I'm surprised to see most of the shops have already shut their doors. Christmas decorations deck the storefronts, yet the interiors lie in darkness. I shudder before crossing the road, finally reaching my street. The pine trees surrounding Mulkiwa Park are frosty, and the bare oak trees make everything seem lifeless. But there's something that breathes life into the scene—the Christmas lights adorning every house. They glow softly, brightening up the sidewalk.

A bittersweet and nostalgic memory from last Christmas creeps into my thoughts, making me bite my inner cheek. It was almost midnight on Christmas Eve when a knock on my window startled me. There was Chris, bundled up in his oversized puffer jacket, a woollen scarf wrapped up to his nose. I teased him about the redness of his nose, playfully calling him Rudolf, while he held a thermos of eggnog with more alcohol than milk.

The memory stings my chest. Was none of that real?

"Cora, wait up!" Hel's loud voice startles me, causing me to jump. She's rushing towards me, her face etched with worry.

"Damn, you scared me," I exhale, our footsteps falling into sync as she catches up. She shoots me an embarrassed smile, tucking her hair behind her ear.

"Sorry. Can I walk with you?" she asks.

"Sure."

We walk in silence for a few minutes, the rhythmic sound of our footsteps echoing on the concrete. I steal a glance at Hel, noticing her furrowed brows and a thoughtful expression in her eyes. She inhales deeply, as though collecting her thoughts.

"You left so suddenly yesterday," she starts, her voice breaking the silence. "I wanted to talk to you about what happened."

"Yeah, sorry for running away. I had a panic attack," I admit, my cheeks flushed with embarrassment. Hel's expression shifts to one of concern, and she slows her pace, giving me her full attention.

"God, I feel so bad right now... We shouldn't have brought up Chris or gotten involved. It was insensitive of us," her eyes reflecting genuine worry.

"Don't worry about it. I'm fine," I reply, lowering my chin. The tension in the air eases slightly as we continue our walk, a cool breeze running through the trees. Hel walks beside me, a moment of silence lingering between us. After a moment, she speaks again.

"I'm here for you, Cora. If you ever want to talk or if there's anything I can do, just let me know," she offers, her voice filled with sincerity.

"Yeah. Thanks," I mumble, avoiding her gaze. Hel gives me an understanding yet somewhat upset look.

"I can't imagine what you're going through. I've been with Matt for as long as I can remember, so I have no idea what breakups are like," she admits, her tone sympathetic. I shrug, feeling the weight of the situation settle on me once again.

"It sucks," I admit. "But it's for the best."

In that moment, my phone buzzes, cutting the heavy atmosphere. I fish it out from my pocket and glance at the screen. I bite my lip, holding back a smile.

> **theorhodes**
> *are you free tonight?*

"Is it Chris?" Hel asks, attempting to glance at my screen.

"No, it's Theo," I mutter. Hel raises an eyebrow, her expression a mix of surprise and intrigue.

"I didn't know you guys talked," she says, curiosity evident in her voice.

"Yeah, we're friends," I reply, a hint of a smile playing on my lips as I type a reply.

coradanvers
what do you have in mind?

theorhodes
*i promised I'd make
it up to you, remember?*

I can't help but smile at Theo's message, and Hel gives me a quizzical look.

"Just friends? It doesn't seem like it," she comments, her words hanging in the air with a sense of observation.

I shrug, looking up from my phone to meet her gaze. Although she's not convinced, I feel it's better to keep my relationship with Theo strictly platonic. I've had enough gossip about me this year.

"It's not what you think," I clarify, hoping to clear any misunderstandings. "It's just refreshing to not talk about Chris for once," I add. Hel flinches, realising it's a subtle dig at her.

"You're right. I'm sorry, Cora," Hel mutters, flashing me an apologetic smile. As we reconcile with a hug, approaching footsteps draw our attention. Mayor Glenn, accompanied by a stunning golden Labrador, strides toward us. The formality in his attitude and clothes contrasts with the casual setting of the street.

"Good evening," the mayor says, nodding politely.

"Good evening, Mayor Glenn," we reply in unison, returning the courtesy. Mayor Glenn walks past us, his dog panting softly by his side. Once he's out of sight, Hel's eyes light up as if she just met Taylor Swift, a wide grin spreading across her face.

"Glenn is such a great man. Did you see him walking his dog like an normal guy?" she squeals. Eager to steer clear of awkwardness, I join in with a laugh at Helena's comment.

•••••

The door creaks open, and my heart skips a beat as I find Theo on the other side, wearing a denim jacket and a snug grey beanie. A grin spreads across his face, reflecting the excitement in my chest.

"Hey. Ready for our adventure?" he asks, his eyes gleaming with warmth. I nod, returning the smile.

"Sure am. We need to be quiet, though. My dad is home," I say in a hushed tone, slightly above a whisper.

We jump into the car, and the moment Theo starts up the engine, the heater kicks in, instantly fogging up the windows. A slow, sensual melody begins to play through the speakers, and a subtle warmth colours my cheeks. I instinctively roll down the windows, allowing the cool air to sweep through the car. Theo, catching my eye, grins playfully as he smoothly pulls out of the driveway.

"Where are we going?" I ask, gazing at the gleaming Christmas lights as we drive. It's only a couple of hours before curfew and the streets are deserted, with most houses illuminated from within.

"Somewhere you've never been before," he says with a smirk. I can't help but laugh at his comment, considering there isn't a corner of Barren I haven't explored.

"Oh, really?" I challenge him, returning his smile.

"Yep. I'm pretty sure I'm the first person to see this place," he says.

"You do know I was born and raised here," I tease, earning a chuckle from him.

"I'll still manage to surprise you. I promise."

Driving through the main street, I can't help but notice how different the environment is compared to the suburbs. Dozens of people are gathered outside the vintage cinema, eagerly waiting for the new Spiderman screening. I recognise a few faces, even some seniors, chatting and laughing as they await their turn. The high-end restaurant next to the cinema is bustling with people enjoying their dinner or sipping on drinks. A sudden, violent gust of wind ruffles my hair into a messy dance, and Theo can't help but burst into laughter.

"You look like a lion," he jokes. I glance at my reflection in the rear-view mirror before I join him in laughter.

We drive past Barren High, the local grocery store, and the new Town Hall that was built in the past year. It's adorned with white stone and glossy windows, giving it an eerie resemblance to The White House. As Theo takes the highway, my brows furrow in confusion.

"Where is this place?" I ask.

"It's right on the border of Barren," he says, locking eyes with me. Theo's hands confidently grip the steering wheel, his movements so smooth that I find myself biting my lip.

In the quiet of the night, the highway is surrounded by the emerald pine trees of Evergreen. Their branches form a calm canopy over the road, and moonlight gently illuminates the path. The air is filled with the soothing scent of pine, creating a peaceful atmosphere as we drive through the serene night.

Theo gestures toward a clearing on the side of the road.

"Look, it's right there," he says.

As we draw closer to the clearing, an aged wooden sign comes into view, welcoming us to a place called *'Whispering Pines Hill'*. Theo's grin widens, excitement shining in his eyes.

"I thought it would be the perfect spot for us tonight," he says, steering the car toward the entrance. As we step out of the car, I find myself gaping at the breath-taking scenery around us. The clearing is bathed in moonlight, and a soft breeze rustles through the whispering pines. The air is fresh and filled with the scent of nature, creating a magical atmosphere. Theo looks at me with a satisfied grin, pleased to share this hidden gem.

"Wow," I breathe, scanning my surroundings.

"Oh, this is nothing. Come," he beams, giving me his hand.

A giddy sensation washes over me as I take his hand. As we approach the hill, the breath-taking views leave me in awe. Jersey City stretches out in the distance, its buildings looking like delicate miniature models from this elevated spot. The scene is mesmerising, bathed in the glow of city lights and the distant murmur of traffic. Perched on the cliff, a simple park bench provides the ideal spot for taking in the picturesque view.

"I-I'm speechless," I stutter, a broad grin lighting up my face. Theo's gaze meets mine, the gentle lights casting shadows on his chiselled features.

"I told you it was worth it," he whispers, a soft smile on his lips.

In that moment, we both realise our hands are intertwined. Theo quickly pulls away, glancing aside with an embarrassed expression. He settles onto the bench, letting his backpack slump to the floor. Unzipping it, he peers inside. I join him, taking a seat and watching as he extracts a couple of blankets.

"No way," I chuckle. "You really came prepared."

Theo hands me a thick blanket, offering a shy smile.

"I promised I'd make it up to you for getting me out of jail. And, well, for accidentally taking you to your childhood home," he says with a hint of humour. I'm left momentarily speechless as I envelop myself in the warmth of the blanket.

"You really didn't have to go through all this trouble," I say, feeling genuinely touched. Theo smirks before rummaging through his backpack again.

"So, I guess I was right—you're not familiar with this part of Barren," he says.

"I wasn't," I reply with a sheepish smile. Theo pulls a thermos from his backpack, taking out several paper cups. His eyes gleam with excitement as he hands one to me.

"Hot chocolate?" he suggests with a playful smirk.

"I can't resist that," I answer. I watch him pour the steaming drink into my cup, warming my hands.

As the rich aroma of hot chocolate envelops us, we both turn our attention to the skyline, the city lights dancing in the distance. A comfortable silence settles between us, accompanied by the occasional sound of traffic far below. The warmth of the blanket and the soothing sip of hot chocolate create a serene moment, making words unnecessary. We simply sit together, wrapped in the tranquillity of the night and the beauty of the cityscape.

"You know, I'm really glad we met," Theo says in a gentle voice, breaking the silence. In that moment, our eyes lock, and the intensity in his gaze makes my heart flutter.

"Really?" I ask, glancing down at my drink, my cheeks flushing.

"Yeah. You're way more than what I expected, Cora," he murmurs, his tone breathy. Our eyes meet once more, and I can't help but feel touched by his words.

"Are you saying you thought I was dull?" I joke, hoping to inject a bit of humour into the conversation. A moment of surprise flickers in his eyes before he realises I was just teasing. A playful grin tugs at the corners of his lips.

"No, not dull at all," he responds. The mood shifts as his expression turns serious, his eyes tracing my face before lingering on my lips. "I guess I never expected us to be friends."

"People can surprise you," I murmur, taking a sip from my cup to distract myself. The thought of Theo glancing at my lips sparks an unfamiliar warmth, one that I hadn't felt with him before.

"You were the only one who believed in me when I was arrested," Theo admits, tapping the metallic thermos with his finger. The sight of Theo being nervous feels unfamiliar, but it adds a touch of character to him. I wish I could tell him what I saw in the shower, but I hold myself back.

"I don't know... I just had this gut feeling you were innocent," I say, playing with the blanket. He shoots me a sidelong glance, letting out a chuckle.

"Gotta always trust your gut," he chimes in with a charming smile.

A tingling sensation envelops me as I find myself unable to look away from him. He catches my gaze, turning to face me as he bites his lip. The intensity of our eye contact makes me hold my breath, my heart racing in my chest.

In that electrifying moment, a memory of Chris flashes through my mind, a pang of guilt and nostalgia intertwining. However, the warmth building inside me serves as a reminder that I haven't felt anything like this in many months. Theo leans towards me slowly, closing the gap until our lips are mere inches away. The air between us becomes charged with anticipation, a moment suspended in time as we hover on the brink of a kiss.

"I can't do this…" Theo whispers, his breath softly grazing my lips.

"What?" I murmur, feeling my pulse quicken. A frustrated sigh escapes his lips, heightening the tension between us.

"Pretend we're just friends," he confesses.

A brief silence hangs in the air, the anticipation building before our lips collide. A gentle moan escapes my lips as Theo deepens the kiss, his tongue delicately brushing against mine. My hands entwine in his hair, and in response, he pulls me onto his lap, intensifying the intimate connection between us.

The world outside fades away, and all that remains is the electric energy of our kiss.

17

Three days.

I stand in the kitchen, morning light filtering through the window. The smell of breakfast lingers as I reach for the pill bottle on the counter. With a sip from my favourite mug, I swallow the medication, but this time with hesitation. The psychiatrist assured me that my delusions would fade, but it's been one week, and nothing has changed. The echoes of what the sheriff told Helena at the field still reverberate in my mind.

We're three days away from Waning Gibbous, and a powerful hunch grips me, reinforcing the idea that I might be onto something. What if Theo is right? What if, despite all logic and reasoning, there are moments when we simply have to trust our gut?

I grab my backpack, strapping it onto my shoulder, but a wave of wooziness washes over me from the medication. As I wait for the bus, memories of last night with Theo echo in my mind. Spending time with him made me realise that I hadn't felt that way in a long time. Maybe I had spent all this time convincing myself that Chris was the love of my life when I shouldn't have. I dropped everything and everyone to be with him, only to be betrayed in the end. The pain stings my chest, but there's a part of me that knows things were over a long time ago, ever since senior year started.

After Theo dropped me off at home, I glanced at my phone to find fifteen new messages from Chris, but I decided to switch my phone off before drifting into sleep. I always thought that the day I'd end things with Chris, I would lose myself. But now that it's over, I'm surprised by the amount of apathy I feel. Maybe it's my medication, but I feel absolutely nothing for Chris anymore—no love, no empathy, nothing. I can't forgive him for what he did.

The bus arrives, and I hop on, finding a seat near the window. The rhythmic hum of the engine blends with the soft chatter of fellow passengers. As the bus pulls away, I stare out the window, lost in my thoughts.

•••••

In the hallway, Helena and the group greet me with smiles as I hurriedly make my way to my first class. The atmosphere feels lighter, and the tension that lingered seems to have eased. It's a relief, and I realise that part of it stems from feeling better about the breakup. In fact, today I am feeling more excitable than before, which is strange. For a moment, I think it's a side effect of the medication, but when I see Theo sitting at his desk as I walk into class, I realise that it's not. His intense gaze lingers on me, igniting memories from last night. A playful smile passes between us as I settle into my desk.

As Mr. Woods begins his lecture, my eyelids start to flutter, but I force myself to jot down thorough notes to stay awake. We move onto our usual exercise, where each student takes turns reading a paragraph from the book we're currently studying. A student called

Lucy starts reading the text, and I find my eyes growing heavier as we progress around the classroom.

When it's finally my turn, I sense my body on the brink of collapse. All eyes are on me, waiting for my turn to begin, and I discreetly pinch my hand under the desk in a desperate attempt to stay awake. I clear my throat, steadying myself, and begin reading the next paragraph. My words emerge slower than expected, and a few chuckles ripple through the classroom.

"Thank you, Cora," Mr. Woods acknowledges once I finish, casting me a slightly concerned look.

"Looks like someone hardly slept," I overhear a feminine voice comment. I clench my jaw, a tinge of embarrassment washing over me.

As the bell rings and students flood out of the classroom, Mr. Woods calls me over to his desk. The last of the students exit, leaving him and me alone. He removes his reading glasses, placing them on the desk before meeting my gaze.

"I'm concerned about your attention in class, Cora," he expresses, his tone filled with genuine worry. I sigh, fiddling with my backpack strap. He's right; I've been falling behind this past week due to my medication.

"Mr. Woods, I can explain," I begin, but in that moment, a yawn escapes my lips.

"You've been falling asleep in class these past two weeks. Is something happening at home?" he asks, arching a concerned brow.

I find myself debating whether I should tell him about my medication, but the truth is, I feel too embarrassed.

"No, everything is fine," I say, pausing to choose my next words carefully. "I've just been taking some allergy medication, and they leave me drowsy."

Mr. Woods shoots me a puzzled look.

"Allergies? Is there still pollen this time of the year?" he asks. Shit, he's right. It's December— not really allergy season.

"Huh," Mr. Woods muses, still not fully convinced. "Well, think about whether taking that medication is really worth it, especially if it's affecting your chances at getting into a good college."

I nod, acknowledging that he's right. If this medication is the solution to my blackouts, it might be causing more harm than good.

"You're not taking any illegal substances, are you?" Mr. Woods asks with a scornful look, leaving me momentarily speechless. Do people think I'm on drugs?

"N-No, sir," I stammer, my words stumbling out. It's a struggle to maintain eye contact as he studies my face, searching for any signs of deception. After a tense few seconds, he nods.

"I'd talk to your doctor, because you shouldn't take those long term," he advises, reaching for something in his drawer. He hands me my most recent pop quiz, and I can't help but wince at the C minus scrawled in red pen.

"See you next week," Mr. Woods says. "Hopefully more alert."

I nod, tucking the sheet into my backpack. I walk out of the classroom with slumped shoulders, the weight of Mr Woods' words weighing heavily on my mind.

·····

By second period, the drowsiness worsens, making it increasingly challenging to stay awake in class. As the sun unexpectedly peeks through the clouds, a ray of light lands just inches from my hand on the desk. It's a pleasant surprise after enduring two weeks of continuous rain. My thoughts are abruptly interrupted by the harsh scraping sound of a chair leg against the linoleum floor. I can't see past the math teacher, absorbed in scribbling equations on the board. Her soft chatter as she teaches feels like distant murmurings, as if I were submerged underwater.

"Cora," somebody whispers, pulling me from my trance. As I turn my gaze toward the neighbouring desk, I see Matt leaning in my direction. His pen taps the calculator rhythmically, and his dark brown curls cascade over a part of his forehead. "How do you do question two?"

"I'm not sure. Sorry," I murmur, keeping my eyes on the examples displayed on the whiteboard. For a moment, the numbers and symbols on the board look like a puzzle, like they're written in a language I can't understand. It's like my mind is too foggy to process it. Suddenly, my phone vibrates inside my coat, and I reach to grab it.

> **chrismatthews9**
> *cora I am so sorry, please let me speak to you.*
>
> **chrismatthews9**
> *she means nothing to me.*
>
> **coradanvers**
> *we're done, chris.*

With watery eyes, I stare at my own text, knowing I did the right thing. As I tuck my phone into my back pocket, the air entering my lungs feels denser, and the pen trembles in my hands.

Throughout all this time, I believed I knew Chris. I defended him when he got drunk at his concerts, skipped class to practice, and even during the fight with Damon. I stood by him, even when he was an asshole to me. Tears begin to blur my vision, distorting the numbers on the page as if they're dancing on the paper. Stars twinkle in front of my eyes, and panic sets in as my vision fades to black.

The fire's roar echoes in my ears, sending shivers down my spine. A taste of bitter ashes lingers on my tongue as the air thickens with each passing moment. Tangerine flames crawl up the pine trees, devouring every inch of bark. Embers rain down on the forest floor, setting it ablaze in a fiery spectacle. The scalding air becomes suffocating, making me violently cough. The crackling fire draws closer, its overwhelming sound urging me to take hesitant steps forward. Sweat glues my clothes to my back, and each breath becomes a painful struggle, making me cough up more ashes.

My eyes snap open with a gasp, the sound piercing the silent classroom. The entire class is staring at me, including Matt, whose eyes are wide in shock.

"Are you okay?" he asks, concern etched across his face. The taste of ashes lingers on my tongue, leaving my throat dry. I stare blankly at him, unsure of how to respond. The medication isn't putting a halt to my hallucinations.

"Cora," Matt repeats, his voice louder this time. The ashy flavour gives way to a metallic taste of copper, and an intense coldness courses through my body.

Matt grabs my arm gently, leading me out of the classroom. The corridor is a blurry haze, and the distant murmur of students fades into a distant echo. It's as if I'm floating alongside my body, observing everything from a distance. He guides me to a quiet corner, concern etched on his face.

"Cora, what happened? You zoned out back there."

I want to respond, to tell him about the forest fire, the taste of ashes and copper, but my words feel trapped in a fog. The world around me remains disconnected, as if I were still lost in a dream. Concern deepens in Matt's eyes as he glances around, searching for help. The corridor begins to spin, but he steadies me.

"I'm going to take you to the nurse, okay? Talk to me if you can," he says.

I manage a nod, or at least I hope I do. Matt becomes my anchor as he guides me through the halls, but the world around me is a swirl of indistinct shapes and muted colours.

We reach the nurse's office, where Mrs. Wheeler greets us with a smile. She examines me while Matt explains the situation, but my mind is too foggy to understand. I focus on the cup of water in my hands, the coolness providing a small anchor in the swirling fog of my mind. Mrs. Wheeler's soothing voice directs me to take slow sips. I follow her instructions, the water providing some relief to my dry throat.

"Your heart rate is above normal," Mrs Wheeler says, putting away her stethoscope. She leads me through a series of deep breaths, and as I sit for a few minutes, my thoughts gradually regain coherence. The fog in my mind begins to dissipate, bringing me back to the present moment.

"I... I don't know what happened," I say, finally becoming aware of my surroundings. Mrs. Wheeler gives me a reassuring smile.

"It's okay, darling. Sometimes our bodies react in unexpected ways. Do you have any history of anxiety or panic attacks?" she asks.

Swallowing the knot in my throat, I nod. This wasn't just a panic attack; I feel completely dissociated.

"Can you tell me what you're feeling right now?"

"I feel... disconnected," I confess. Admitting it makes me feel vulnerable and embarrassed. "It's like I'm watching everything from afar, and none of it feels real."

There's a shared look of concern between Matt and the nurse. Mrs. Wheeler motions for Matt to step out of the room, and he quietly closes the door behind him. She directs her focus back to me, offering a comforting smile.

"I just need to ask you a few questions, Cora," Mrs. Wheeler begins, pulling out a notepad. "How have you been sleeping lately?"

"Too much," I admit, my gaze dropping to my hands. "I can't seem to stay awake."

Mrs. Wheeler nods, jotting down a few notes.

"And how about your overall stress levels? Anything significant happening in your life?"

If I could share even a fraction of the events that unfolded during my senior year, it would leave her utterly stunned. I've found a dead body, my classmate was killed by three hitmen, managed to get Theo out of prison, my dad is getting remarried, and I am haunted by nightmares of a forest fire that might kill me.

"I guess there's just a lot going on," I answer, sighing. "School, personal stuff, it's all overwhelming sometimes."

Mrs. Wheeler scribbles more notes, her expression thoughtful.

"Are you currently taking any medication?"

The dreaded question hangs in the air, and I hesitate before answering.

"Yeah. Uh, Seroquel."

Mrs. Wheeler looks at me with widened eyes, clearly taken aback.

"Antipsychotics?" she asks, surprise evident in her voice. I nod, feeling a wave of embarrassment.

"Yeah, it's for... hallucinations," I say, the words feeling heavy as they leave my lips.

The room falls into a brief silence, my words lingering in the air. Mrs. Wheeler looks at me, her expression a mix of surprise and concern.

"You should discuss these side effects with your doctor. Continuing with the medication could pose risks," she advises. "You should stay here and rest, okay?"

I manage to give her a nod before she opens the door, allowing Matt to come in.

"Hope you're feeling better," Matt says, squeezing my hand in comfort with a smile. I owe him big time—without him, I would have probably died from cardiac arrest.

"Thanks, Matt," I respond with a weak smile. Mrs. Wheeler hands me a plastic cup with an aspirin floating on the surface.

"You can stay here for the afternoon. Get some rest and drink up," she says.

"Thanks," I say, returning a soft smile.

"I'll go grab your bag," Matt says, leaving the room.

I settle onto the patient bed, my eyes fluttering shut as I drift into a deep sleep.

•••••

My eyes snap open, becoming aware of my surroundings. The bedroom is swallowed in darkness, with only the faint glow from the streetlamp outside casting shadows on the walls. Cold sweat beads on my forehead as I sit up, disoriented. I pull the covers tighter around me, trying to dispel the chill that has settled in my bones.

In that silent moment, three words settle on the tip of my tongue.

He's a watcher.

The weight of those words lingers, a puzzle demanding my attention. Questions flood my mind, seeking understanding, but doubt creeps in. It was just a dream, I tell myself. Maybe I heard those words in a song. I can't be losing my mind. I reach for my phone on the bedside table, the screen illuminating my face as I check the time—3:23 AM.

For the first time in a long while, I can't remember my dream. All I remember is those three words.

18

Two days.

As I groggily head downstairs for breakfast, the usual morning calm is disrupted by the distant murmur of voices. I follow the faint sound, and my blood turning to ice when I find five police officers in the living room.

My heart pounds aggressively against my ribcage as I take a few steps back, attempting to stay out of sight. Two officers are interviewing my dad, while the remaining three observe from a distance like guard dogs. They exchange a few hushed words, but I manage to catch a snippet of the conversation.

"Eight years ago," my dad mutters, and I realise he must be talking about my mom.

I take a deep breath before approaching them, and their attention immediately shifts to me. My dad's posture stiffens, and his eyes silently urge me to stay calm.

"What's going on?" I ask, my voice barely above a whisper.

The female officer interviewing my dad scrutinises me with a scornful gaze, narrowing her eyes.

"You must be Cora Danvers," she states. Shifting my weight onto my other foot, I notice I'm still in my pyjamas, amplifying my sense of vulnerability.

"Yeah. Sorry, I just woke up," I mumble, my voice still raspy.

"No problem. We're investigating Damon Martin's case, and we need to review everyone's file in Barren," the officer explains. She gestures for me to take a seat. As I follow, I notice the officers look more daunting from this angle, their uniforms and stern gazes adding an air of authority.

The officer reaches for a cream-colored folder, her fingers deftly flipping through the contents. The weight of the situation settles in the room, and I can't shake off the feeling of being under a microscope. The ticking of the grandfather clock seems to echo louder, creating an unsettling rhythm in the stifling silence. I shift in my seat, waiting for her to break it. She clears her throat, her amber eyes meeting mine.

"Miss Danvers. Your file is quite clean. No felonies, excellent grades…" She continues to scrutinise the folder, her eyes flicking across the pages. The room feels smaller, suffocating, as her gaze remains fixed on the contents. "Although, one thing concerns me."

My heart quickens its pace, uncertainty dancing in my chest. The only thing they could know about me is that I got Theo out of prison.

"Your mother died when you were ten years old. Suicide due to a history of schizophrenia. I have a copy of your psychology report right here," she says, pulling out a sheet.

My eyes dart to my dad, his expression shifting to one of horror as he absorbs the information. Shit. He'll lose his mind if he discovers I was diagnosed with the same condition as my mom.

"Officer, I don't feel comfortable sharing my report with my dad," I blurt. The officer raises an eyebrow, her gaze unwavering.

"Miss Danvers, this is a part of our investigation. We need to gather all relevant information."

My dad's eyes plead with me to comply, but I can't let him know about that diagnosis. It's a secret I've guarded fiercely, even from him.

"I understand, Officer, but it's a sensitive matter. Can we discuss it privately?" I insist.

The air becomes heavy with silence, the tension almost tangible. My dad attempts to catch my gaze, but the officer intervenes before he can. She nods in understanding, breaking the silence with a throat clearing.

"Alright, Miss Danvers. We can discuss this privately. But remember, full cooperation is crucial for our investigation," she asserts, her tone firm. I nod, grateful for the chance to shield my dad from the truth, at least for now. "Mr. Danvers, could you step out for a moment? Cora's psychological report is confidential," she requests.

"Of course," my dad answers. Our eyes lock briefly, and in that fleeting moment, I see the shattered look in my dad's eyes, causing a pang of guilt to surge through my heart.

As my dad reluctantly exits the room, I can't help but feel a mix of anxiety and curiosity about what the officer has uncovered. The door clicks shut behind him, creating a brief cocoon of privacy around us.

The officer leans forward, her expression serious.

"Miss Danvers, I need to ask you some questions. We need your cooperation to understand the full picture."

I gulp nervously, fiddling with my fingers.

"Sure," I reply, my voice showing a hint of anxiety.

"Given your recent diagnosis of schizophrenia, have you had a violent episode in the past?"

I shift uncomfortably in my seat, the weight of her question settling in the room. The clinical tone doesn't soften the impact of the question. Memories of moments when my mind betrayed me flood my thoughts, and I take a moment to collect myself before responding.

"No, I haven't had any violent episodes," I reply, my voice steady despite the unease in my eyes. "The diagnosis is recent, and I've been working closely with my therapist to manage it."

One wrong movement, and they'll be onto me like leeches. I'm aware that they could be searching for a scapegoat just to remove the men in black from the equation.

The officer nods, her gaze focused yet empathetic.

"It's crucial for us to understand your condition comprehensively. Can you share more about the strategies you and your therapist have been using to address your schizophrenia?"

I swallow the lump in my throat.

"I'm currently taking Seroquel," I reply, my tone uneasy. "And I'm under Cognitive Behavioural Therapy, once a week."

She nods, jotting down a few words on her notepad. My anxious eyes dance around the room, wondering what she could be writing.

Will they hold me responsible for Damon's murder? The unstable, daydreaming lunatic of Barren?

The officer looks up, her gaze meeting mine.

"I understand you're in quite a stressful situation right now. Living with one parent, economic problems, mental instability..."

Her words hang in the air, and I can't help but feel a knot tighten in my stomach. Now that she mentions it, it's no surprise they're questioning me. I swallow the lump in my throat, determined to maintain my composure.

"Yes, it's been a tough road," I confess. "But I'm doing my best to navigate through it."

The detective nods, shuffling some papers before redirecting her gaze to me.

"Where were you on the night of Damon Martin's murder?" she asks, her question cutting through the air like a blade.

The gravity of her question presses on me, and my mind turns into a void. The only memory I can recall is finding a stash of money in my locker, Damon's money. I can't let her know I blacked out.

A chilling question creeps in: Is it possible that I was involved?

The fear bubbling inside me is evident, but I know I can't let it show.

"I went home after class. I had to study for a test," I lie, keeping my answer as vague as possible. She remains unconvinced for a second, her gaze fixed on me as she jots something down.

"Did you attend the football game?" the officer asks, probing for more details. I honestly don't know if I attended the football game or not. Regardless, I know I must respond.

With a silent prayer, I reply, "No."

"Have you had recent contact with Damon's half-brother, Chris Matthews?"

My mouth falls open in shock.

"Is Chris considered a suspect?" I blurt, taken aback by her question.

The detective remains silent; she can't provide an answer to that question.

"We're only trying to connect the dots here, Cora. Any details you have about Damon or his relationship with his half-brother would be very useful to us," she answers.

The only piece of information I have about Chris and his relationship with Damon is that he never told me directly. Instead, I had to learn about it from Helena.

"I haven't spoken to Chris since we broke up," I say, which is the truth, but a question lingers: Could Chris have been behind this?

The officer nods, continuing to jot down notes.

"Did he ever have the intention of attacking Damon? Did they argue a lot?" she presses. In that moment, she manages to get on my nerves.

"I'm not the right person to ask about Chris or his family," I reply defensively. Chris cheated on me, but I refuse to throw him under the bus. I take a deep breath, steadying myself as the officer observes my reaction. The atmosphere in the room is tense, and I can feel the weight of her scrutiny.

"I've shared what I can about Chris and my knowledge of Damon's situation," I assert, my voice steady despite the underlying tension.

A few minutes of tense silence hang heavily in the air. The officer, sensing the end of the interrogation, closes her notepad and leans back slightly.

"Thank you for your cooperation, Miss Danvers. We may need to reach out to you again if necessary," she says, rising from the couch. I lead the five officers to the front door, a sense of relief washing over me as the hellish moment comes to an end.

As the door closes behind the officer, I find myself alone in the living room, a blend of relief and anxiety washing over me. The unanswered questions linger, and the uncertainty of the investigation hangs in the air like a heavy fog. A nagging thought lingers in the back of my mind: Why did they ask me about Chris?

Do they suspect I was involved too?

•••••

I've scanned the same page of my AP Econ textbook for what feels like the dozenth time, the concepts slipping through my fingers. The words seem to float on the page, creating a sense of detachment between my mind and the information. The unsettling thought lingers—maybe Mr. Woods and Mrs. Wheeler were right; perhaps this medication is causing more harm than good

I try to read the paragraph again when a gentle knock on my door interrupts me. My dad pokes his head through the door, a hint of concern in his eyes.

"Hey, sweetheart. Can I talk to you?" he asks, his tone gentle.

"Sure, Dad," I reply, closing my textbook to give him my full attention. He takes a seat on the edge of my bed, his worried eyes scanning me.

"I was wondering how you were feeling after the interrogation. Do you want to talk about it?"

I take a deep breath, contemplating how much I want to share.

"Yeah... It was intense. They've been interrogating seniors all week. They were asking about Damon, and it felt like they were trying to connect dots that I couldn't even see," I answer.

"Huh," he mutters, furrowing his brows. "You don't happen to know anything about that, right?"

I shoot him a puzzled glance.

"No, why would I?" I reply, my tone showing a hint of defensiveness.

My dad shrugs, noticing my reaction.

"No reason, I know you kids speak amongst yourselves a lot. Maybe you heard something," he says, his eyes searching mine.

I shake my head, feeling my hands turn cold. For some reason, whenever someone brings up this question, I find myself feeling uncomfortable.

"The only thing that I know is what I saw on that tape. Theo is innocent," I insist, my voice steady despite the unease settling in.

After a brief pause, my dad lets out a deep sigh, shaking his head.

"God... Barren has changed so much in these past couple of years. Three murderers on the loose—it's unbelievable. You know, when I was your age, the scariest thing we had to deal with was the occasional daredevil jumping off the quarry cliffs. Now, it feels like there's danger around every corner."

I nod in understanding, reflecting on the stark difference between his memories and my reality. The truth is, Barren has witnessed too many sinister events in the past three months.

"It's unsettling, Dad. I wish I could make sense of it all."

He nods, and a heavy silence lingers for a few moments. His gaze is hesitant, as if there's something more he wants to say. He finally breaks the silence with a question that catches me off guard.

"What about the medication you're taking? What's that for?"

My mind is blank for a few moments, deciding on an answer. I can't tell him the truth; it would break his heart.

"It's just anxiety medication for school. You know, stress and all," I mutter, unable to meet his gaze.

"Maybe I'm putting too much pressure on you about getting into college," he mutters, a tinge of guilt in his tone.

"No," I say, shaking my head. "It's not that, at all."

"Then what is it?"

I meet his gaze, and the pain in his hazel eyes is evident.

"I just… sometimes things overwhelm me, and I don't know how to react," I answer, trying to find the right words. I wish I could tell him what I am going through, but until I have an answer, I can't.

He studies me for a moment, genuine empathy reflected in his eyes.

"I'm sorry, sweetheart. You know you can talk to me about anything, right? I just want to make sure you're handling all of this okay," he says.

"I appreciate that, Dad," I reply, mustering a smile. "It's a lot to handle, but I'm figuring things out."

He gives me a soft smile, getting up from my bed.

"Alright, sweetheart. Don't hesitate to talk to me if anything's bothering you," he says, giving me his signature cheek pinch.

"Thanks, Dad," I say, a soft smile forming on my lips. He gives me a reassuring smile before leaving my room.

•••••

It's Saturday afternoon, and Hel, Beth and I have gathered at the school library to study for our SATs. However, every couple of math examples, the conversation inevitably shifts toward Damon's case. But their curiosity only fuels the inevitable terror creeping up my spine, which hints that my blackout episode may not be a mere coincidence.

Am I one of the suited figures? Is that why I knew Theo was innocent? Because I was the one responsible? The mere thought of it makes me nauseous.

"Cora, have you done question three?" Hel asks, interrupting the swirling thoughts in my head. Beth doodles a whirlwind on the margin of her notebook, boredom evident in her expression.

"Not yet, sorry," I reply, chewing on my pencil. The thoughts continue to swirl in my head—the money in my locker, the blackout.

D.M. A deal is a deal.

The words seem etched onto my brain as hundreds of possibilities race through my head. Who would want Damon Martin dead?

Perhaps Damon owed somebody money, or he was involved in selling drugs. Maybe that's why they killed him. Either way, the way the men in black entered the picture indicates it was premeditated.

"Hel, can I ask you something?" I ask. Hel looks up from her textbook, her curiosity piqued.

"Sure, but if it's math related, I can't promise I'll have the answers," she says, chuckling. Her smile fades when she notices my serious expression.

"What did the cops ask you about Damon?" I ask, recalling the distant voice I overheard on the softball pitch. It was almost as if I were in the room with her, catching snippets of their conversation.

"Nothing special. They asked if I had seen him after the midterm finals game," Hel replies nonchalantly.

Beth raises a brow, studying me intently.

"Haven't they questioned you yet?" she asks.

"Yeah, earlier this morning," I reply, feeling a bit uneasy. Hel glances between Beth and me, sensing the tension in the air.

"They came to your house? What did they ask you?" Helena asks.

I hesitate, the weight of the morning's interrogation still fresh in my mind.

"Yeah, they did. A lot of questions about Damon and his relationships," I admit, the unease lingering in my voice.

The fear tightens its grip on me as the realisation sinks in—I still don't know what happened that night or where I was. Judging by the current situation, it seems no one else has the answers either.

Beth leans back, an anxious expression on her face.

"This whole situation is getting more and more bizarre. I can't believe they still haven't caught them. Barren's a small town; surely their suspect list can't be that long," Beth says, a mix of frustration and disbelief in her expression.

Hel releases a tense breath, rubbing her temples anxiously. It's unusual to see her in such a state, but the reality of a student being murdered just a few feet away is enough to unsettle anyone. She glances at her exam paper, letting out a frustrated sigh.

"Remind me again why we're in the library at half past seven? Curfew is soon," she moans. In that moment, I notice it's already dark outside, casting an eerie ambience in the library.

"Yeah, we should get going," Beth mumbles, hastily collecting her books. Following suit, I quickly stuff my books into my backpack with a sense of urgency. As we leave the library, an unsettling feeling lingers amongst us. The school, now empty, takes on an eerie and somewhat frightening atmosphere.

In ten minutes, the lights in school will be switched off and, in an hour, the quiet town of Barren will be engulfed by the terror of the night.

If one killer wasn't alarming enough, the thought of three is a recipe for disaster.

19

Tomorrow.

At 4 A.M. on Sunday, I jolt awake with my heart pounding in my chest. In an instant, a wave of energy envelops me, and I realise my thoughts are noticeably clearer. The realisation hits me—my medication must be wearing off.

The events from yesterday flood back into my consciousness: the encounter with the police, the conversation with my dad, studying with Hel and Beth, Damon's case, and the mysterious suited men.

But the most disturbing question lingers: Where was I that night?

Frustration and fear kick in, but a sudden spark of inspiration pulls me out of my thoughts. How do people remember where they left their keys?

"Retrace your steps," I murmur to myself. "I have to go back through what I did that day. I need to remember."

Determination fuels my actions as I throw on a jacket and hastily leave my house.

The school parking lot appears before me, bathed in the soft glow of the moon. The surrounding silence is almost deafening, with not a single soul in sight. The fear of being caught breaking curfew sends a shiver down my spine, but the urgency to remember overrides it.

I take a deep breath, my steps purposeful as I approach the scene of Damon's tragic end. My heart quickens, a blend of anticipation and dread coursing through me. I stand in the quiet emptiness of the parking lot, hoping for the memories to resurface, but as I gaze at the spot where Damon was shot, a frustrating realisation sinks in—my mind is a blank canvas.

"Focus, Cora," I mutter to myself. I inhale deeply, shutting my eyes as I desperately try to centre my thoughts.

The last thing I remember is finding Damon's money in my locker.

D.M. A deal is a deal.

I take a deep breath, following the thread of my logic to understand what I could have done next.

"After giving Damon the money, I could have gone back to class," I whisper to myself, keeping my eyes closed. I visualise myself walking down the corridor, leading me back to Mrs. Kingston's biology class. The lecture continues on microcellular biology, and towards the end she mentions there's a pop quiz scheduled for tomorrow.

What could I have done next?

"I could have had lunch with the group," I continue, concentrated on my visualisation. I start to walk down the corridor with my books, running into Helena and Beth by my locker. They ask if I want to watch the midterm practice during lunch break, and I agree to join them. We head to the football field, where the jocks are practicing for tonight's finals. I deliberately avoid Theo's gaze when his eyes wander in my direction after I witnessed him kissing Madison.

"I go back to class and finish the school day," I say, my voice steady. "Afterward, I head back home."

I visualise saying goodbye to my friends before boarding the bus back home. It's already getting dark, but I manage to reach home before sundown. When I get home, I realise my dad isn't there since he's at work. I head to my room, searching for my dream journal. After a brief search, I find the page with the Waning Gibbous moon.

In that moment, the images start to reconstruct.

After stepping out of the shower, I slipped on one of Chris's hoodies, the comforting scent of his cologne bringing a smile to my face. While running a brush through my damp hair, my phone started buzzing. I answered it instantly after seeing the caller ID.

"Hey babe," Chris said in an affectionate tone. "What are you doing tonight?"

"Not much," I replied, settling onto my bed. "Need to study for tomorrow's biology quiz."

"I can't believe you're taking two AP classes this year," he said. "I'm proud of you, Cora."

"I just want my dad to be happy, you know?" I sighed, placing the dream journal in my lap. My eyes scanned every detail, from the shape of the pine trees to the distant smoke in the picture.

Chris chuckled on the other end of the line.

"Babe, you gotta do it for yourself, not just for your dad," he advised.

"I know," I admitted, biting my lip. "I just wish I was a better daughter."

"Babe, you're a great daughter. You want to talk about shit kids? I take the prize for that one."

I couldn't help but laugh under my breath. It had been forever since Chris and I joked around like that.

"I'm really glad we patched things up," he said warmly after a short silence. "I really missed talking to you like this."

I traced my fingers over the shapes of my drawing, and a strange feeling surged through me. It felt like the drawing was trying to tell me something, but I couldn't figure it out.

"I'm glad too," I said with a smile. "I'm really going to miss you when you're gone."

Chris sighed.

"You have no idea how much I'll miss you. But I promise, I'll be back soon."

Those two weeks without Chris felt like an eternity back then, and a part of me feared what would happen when he left. Perhaps, deep down, I had already sensed that our relationship was coming to an end.

I let out a yawn, making Chris laugh.

"I think it's time for your bedtime, grandma," he teased, I chuckled, leaving my journal on my nightstand before lying down.

"I *am* a grandma, it's not even eleven," I admitted, my eyes drifting to the window. "Do you think the game is still on?"

In that moment, I found myself wondering how Theo was performing in the game. A tinge of annoyance hit me—I didn't want to be thinking about him, not after I saw him hooking up with Madison.

"I'm not sure. Maybe," Chris replied nonchalantly. "What matters is you go to sleep."

"Yeah, I think I'll do that," I said with a sleepy smile. "Night, Chris."

"Goodnight, Cora. I love you," he said, his voice gentle.

"I love you too."

With a final exchange of goodnight wishes, we hung up. As I laid back on my bed, a swirl of emotions enveloped me. The scent of Chris's hoodie lingered, and the images of the drawing danced in my mind before falling asleep.

My eyes snap open, finding myself back in the parking lot. My breaths are uneven, but a relieving realisation sinks in.

I didn't kill Damon.

•••••

The rising sun casts its glow, and a newfound strength courses through me as I rush to my backyard. I find the metallic trashcans nestled against the wall, my heart racing in my chest from the adrenaline. I clutch a small box of matches tightly in one hand and the pill bottle in the other, my determination pushing me forward.

With a determined exhale, I toss the pill bottle into the trashcan, the plastic clattering against the metal. A sense of conclusiveness washes over me as I strike a match, its flame dancing between my fingers. With steady hands, I drop it into the trashcan, watching as the pills catch fire. The glowing embers turn into a powerful flame, melting the plastic pill bottle with its scorching heat.

There's only one way to make sense of this chaos, to prove I'm not losing my mind: waiting for tomorrow, when the moon coincides with the one in my dream.

I observe as the flames devour the plastic pill container, a new wave of acceptance washing over me.

20

Today.

For the first time in a very long time, I step out of my house with a newfound energy pulsing through me. The heavy fog of the antipsychotics is lifting, and with each step towards school, I can feel my mental clarity returning. It's as if a monochrome world is gradually being painted with vibrant hues.

Even if my mood is noticeably better, a nagging thought lingers at the back of my mind—one that reminds me I am hours away from uncovering the truth. Hours away from unravelling the mystery behind the forest fire. But with the anticipation comes anxiety, and a part of me questions my own sanity. The conflicting emotions swirl within, a turbulent mix of excitement and doubt as I approach the school building.

Students pour into the hallway, navigating through the crowd as they rush to their first class. I join the flow, weaving through the sea of cheerful conversations and hurried footsteps. Reaching my locker, I fumble with the combination, the metallic clinks echoing in the bustling corridor. As the door swings open, my books, folders, and a trace of lavender-scented perfume from a neglected notebook greet me.

And there, among the chaos, I spot Theo. He casually leans against the locker next to mine, effortlessly drawing my attention. Our eyes meet, and in that brief connection, the world seems to pause. The lively chatter and hurried footsteps fade into the background, leaving only the two of us in a suspended moment.

A shy smile plays on Theo's lips, mirroring the unspoken tension between us. A grin spreads across my face, and my chest flutters from the intensity of his blue eyes. We haven't been able to speak to each other since we kissed at Whispering Pines Hill, but seeing him now brings a wave of relief.

"Hey. How was your weekend?' he asks, his voice smooth as he gazes at me.

"Besides the police showing up at my house? Pretty good," I reply in a playful tone, closing my locker.

Theo's eyes widen in response.

"Wait, they showed up at your house?" he asks, disbelief evident in his voice. I nod, meeting his azure eyes. His hair is slightly ruffled, and the shirt he's wearing hugs his biceps.

"Yeah. They asked me all sorts of questions about Damon. How about you?" I ask, offering him a smile.

"Well… Compared to *that*, kind of boring," he chuckles, rubbing the back of his neck. His gaze lingers on me for a moment, and a warmth creeps into my cheeks. He nibbles on his lip. "Any plans after school?" he asks.

"I have to help Matt with the school play," I reply. *And I have a forest fire to attend*, I want to add.

The bell rings, snapping me out of the moment. Students scatter to their respective classes, but Theo's intense gaze lingers on mine. He nods, a sly grin playing on his lips.

"Have fun with that," he says, giving me a wink before disappearing into the crowd. I head to my first class with a blushing grin on my face, but the moment is short lived. The forest fire looms on the horizon like an approaching storm.

•••••

The classroom is a sea of focused faces, hunched over their desks, scribbling answers on the econ exam. My eyes keep turning back to the clock, and every passing minute feels unbelievably slow. With each glance, the image of the looming forest fire intensifies in my mind.

Fidgeting with my pen, I can feel the urgency building within me. The words spill onto the paper, driven by a mix of concentration and the gnawing worry about the upcoming disaster. I glance at the clock again, realising that every second spent on the exam is a second closer to the forest fire.

As the exam's end approaches, my writing speed picks up. For the first time in weeks, a surge of mental clarity washes over me, and the words effortlessly flow onto the paper. I can almost taste the ashes on my tongue, and it's as if I can feel the heat on my back from the approaching forest fire.

•••••

The day drags on at an incredibly slow pace, the anticipation reaching its peak by the time the final school bell rings. At lunch, Helena and Beth mentioned they can't help Matt with the play tonight because of cheer practice and art club, leaving me to make my way to the drama hall on my own.

Entering the drama building, the door softly creaking behind me, a strong smell of fabric glue and paint immediately greets me. The hall is in a chaotic state, with dozens of unpainted props scattered on tables, and students busily adjusting their costumes. The dim lights cast a warm glow on the space, revealing Mason and a few guys meticulously fixing the sleeves of Matt's costume. Chuckling at the sight, my laughter catches the attention of the guys. Mason flashes me a perfect grin before strolling up to me in an outfit straight out of the 1800s.

"Welcome! Could you lend a hand suiting up Jean Valjean?" he asks, gesturing with his thumb towards the chaos behind him. I can't help but giggle at the epaulettes on his shoulders, paired with his obviously fake wooden sword.

"What on Earth are you dressed up as?" I ask.

"Javert, ma'am. He's the antagonist," Mason answers with a bow, prompting an even heartier laugh from me.

Mason leads the way as I walk up to the group, where Matt stands, holding his breath. His friends loosen the sleeves of his blouse, his muscles on the verge of bursting the costume altogether.

"Hey, Matt," I greet, my grin widening at the sight of the dedicated team at work.

Matt takes a deep breath and smiles back, the anticipation evident in his eyes.

"Thanks for coming to help. We're almost there," he says. He holds in his breath again, beads of sweat trickling down his forehead.

Raising a brow, I shoot Mason a sidelong glance.

"Too much muscle on him?" I ask, earning a chuckle from Mason.

"Hardly. They're last year's costumes. We did Pirates of Penzance, and that was one of the freshmen's outfits," he replies, causing me to snort.

"Better keep an eye on those buttons. They might pop off mid-show," I tease, causing a loud laugh from Mason. Matt, who's overheard us, rolls his eyes in annoyance.

"Hey, lovebirds! Cut the flirting and lend a hand," Matt exclaims, visibly uncomfortable in the snug costume. Amused by Matt's interruption, Mason and I share a quick glance.

"You look fantastic," Mason encourages, his gaze fixed on Matt's slightly comical appearance. Matt sighs, attempting to run a hand through his messy dark curls, but the sleeves are too tight.

"For fuck's sake. I can't do this. We need new costumes, man," he groans.

Hugo, one of the guys assisting with the sleeves, bursts into laughter.

"Got sixty bucks on you?" he asks.

Matt attempts to shrug, but the blouse prevents him from doing so.

"Man, at this point, I'd pay a hundred for a shirt that fits!" he exclaims in annoyance, eliciting laughter from all of us.

I sweep my gaze across the hall, taking in the sight of people absorbed in their tasks. Some are focused on lights, others engrossed in reading scripts, and a few diligently paint backdrops. The atmosphere is electric as everyone pours their energy into adding the final touches to the Les Misérables production.

"So, Matt. What would you like me to work on?" I ask, redirecting my attention back to him. He paces around the room with his script, making a conscious effort not to move his arms.

"Ah, yeah. Do you wanna work on painting the main street backdrop?" he suggests.

"Sure, I don't mind," I respond with a casual shrug.

"Come, I'll show you," Mason says, tugging at my arm.

Mason leads me backstage, weaving through paint cans, brushes, and a wooden backdrop in progress. The air is filled with the distinct scent of paint, and the backstage area resonates with creative energy. Mason points to the large wooden canvas propped against a wall.

"Here we are. This is the main street backdrop. We need to add some finishing touches and bring it to life," he explains, handing me a paintbrush.

I roll up the sleeves of my jumper, tie my hair into a messy bun, and dip the coarse brush into the brown paint. With gentle brush strokes, I feel a sense of freedom as the paint flows from the brush, adding life and character to the main street backdrop.

"He's really crazy, isn't he?" Mason interrupts with a joke, referring to Matt. I smile at him, continuing my strokes on the canvas.

"You can tell this play is really important to him," I remark.

"I mean, he has to sell all the tickets. Everyone's counting on him to raise money for the Martin family," Mason adds, emphasising the gravity of the situation.

"It was genuinely kind of him," I comment. Not everybody would have donated funds to Damon's family. He may have been popular, but not many people these days are that generous.

Mason sighs, adding a touch of yellow to a flourishing tree.

"I still can't wrap my head around that night, you know? One minute he won the home game, the next he was at the hospital," he reflects, sadness evident in his eyes.

"What exactly happened that night?" I ask, curious to hear his perspective. Now that I know I fell asleep talking to Chris, I'm not as scared about discovering the truth.

Mason shrugs, a thoughtful look in his eyes.

"I mean, it was just a regular night. Beth was cheerleading so that's why we all went. We celebrated the victory; everyone was in high spirits. Damon was thrilled, especially since it was his winning shot that secured the game. We all headed to a little post-game party, and everything seemed normal," Mason recounts, his brush moving methodically across the canvas.

"So, he didn't have any weird interactions or fights with anyone?" I ask, and he shakes his head.

"Not at all. As a matter of fact, everyone was pretty happy," he replies.

"That's strange..." I murmur, chewing on my bottom lip. The idea of assassins targeting a teenage boy still sends a shiver down my spine.

"You heard about the guys in suits, right?" he asks, causing me to pause in my movements.

There's still something so horrifying about the image that I can't get over. Maybe it's the way they shot Damon, three of them at once. Or perhaps it's the way their faces were obscured by shadows, making them impossible to distinguish.

I gulp, returning to my strokes on the canvas.

"Yeah," is all I manage to say, the tension of the conversation lingering in the air.

"Do you think they could have been hired assassins? I mean, Damon's parents are pretty wealthy. They must have had enemies," Mason speculates, his eyes filled with intrigue. It's like Damon Martin's murder added a dose of excitement to people's otherwise mundane lives. All I know is, I shouldn't be talking about it.

I let out a deep exhale.

"I don't know, honestly," I murmur.

"I think Barren isn't what it used to be. There's some dark stuff going on, I swear," Mason states with a solemn tone.

"You're giving me some Twin Peaks vibes," I mutter with a chuckle. Mason shakes his head, refining what he just painted with a thinner brush.

"Well, you never know. Every town has its secrets," he says, arching an eyebrow suggestively.

"Okay, that's seriously cheesy," I chuckle, dipping my brush back into the paint.

"All right, maybe a little," Mason chuckles.

•••••

By the time I get home, the sun has already dipped behind the trees, which intensifies my anxiety. As the moon's ascent continues, I realise I am hours away from uncovering the truth.

I find my dad slouched on the couch, a pilsner in his hand as he watches the news. Hurriedly, I walk up the stairs, my thoughts racing with anxiety. After locking my door, I retrieve my dream journal, my eyes scanning the drawing within. I try to memorise every detail on the page, understanding that each nuance might hold the key to unravelling this mystery.

There's a part of me that believes I'm not insane, that this forest fire has a meaning, but I am yet to find out if it's positive or negative. Could it be that the forest fire will lead to my own demise? Or maybe I am meant to save someone from it.

My eyes wander to the window, left ajar to invite the cool air into my bedroom. The moon hangs in the sky in the Waning Gibbous phase, casting a gentle glow over the surroundings. The soft light spills into my room, creating a serene ambiance.

Doubts begin to creep in. What if there's no fire at all?

I rake my fingers through my blonde bangs, releasing an anxious sigh. When should I head there? How will I even know when it's about to happen?

As I lie down on my bed, uncertainty gnaws at me. The anticipation and doubt swirl within me, creating a turbulent mix of emotions. I can't help but wonder if I'm on the brink of uncovering the truth or descending into madness.

As the moon inches higher in the night sky, I close my eyes, hoping that whatever awaits me on the other side of this mysterious forest fire is something I can face.

•••••

I toss and turn in bed, kicking the bedsheets for what feels like the dozenth time. Rolling over, I check my phone again; it's only a few minutes past midnight. In that moment, my intuition seizes control, an invisible force guiding my actions. The word *'Evergreen'* floods my mind, a silent command urging me into action.

Adrenaline surges through my veins as I hastily throw on clothes and slip into my shoes. Without a second thought, I approach the window, my intuition pushing me forward. Using the nearby tree as support, I climb out and land on the ground below with a gentle thud.

As I cut through the street, my heart races in my chest, the flashlight from the information cabin dangling from my wrist. The night air is crisp, and the only sounds are my hurried footsteps and the occasional rustle of leaves in the breeze. The deserted town square stretches before me, the silence echoing through the empty streets. The flickering lampposts cast long shadows, creating an eerie ambiance.

I stand on the threshold of the Evergreen Forest, my senses heightened by the eerie atmosphere. The realisation hits me—being in a forest at night is scarier than I thought. The darkness amplifies every sound, intensifying the feeling of isolation. With my heart in my throat, darkness engulfs me as I enter the woods, relying on my only source of light to guide myself through the rich wildlife. I tread carefully, the crunch of fallen leaves beneath my feet echoing louder than I'd like. The beam of my flashlight reveals twisted branches and tangled vines, creating eerie shadows that play tricks on my imagination.

As I reach the forest clearing, my old house comes into view. All the lights are switched off, and I assume Theo must be asleep.

In that moment, my blood turns to ice at the sound of leaves crunching behind me. I spin around quickly, my senses on high alert, only to find nothing. Driven by my primal instincts, I cautiously move toward the source of the sound. As I advance, a chill runs down my spine when I realise I'm tracing someone else's footsteps.

The rhythmic sound of the footsteps is bone-chilling, purely because I have no idea *who* I am following. I reach another clearing, my heart stopping when I see nothing ahead of me—no animal, no shadow. Nothing. Just the sombre forest, gazing back at me.

I'm on the verge of heading back to the house when I hear it—the sound that has haunted my dreams for six months.

The crackling of fire.

Panicking, I shine the flashlight around, my heart pounding with sheer dread.

Once again, nothing. No fire.

In that fleeting moment, my surroundings start to blur and distort, the crescendo sound of flames ringing cacophonously in my ears. But in the blink of an eye, the sound fades, leaving me standing in the silent, undisturbed forest.

I run. I don't know why, but I do. The flashlight swings back and forth freely as I delve deeper into Evergreen, the forest floor crunching beneath my feet with each hurried step. The crackling of fire echoes again, louder this time. My pace slows, and my breath sticks to my throat. With fear gripping me, I take a few steps towards it until I reach a small clearing. I hang the flashlight on the nearest tree branch, sweat forming on my forehead as the temperature rises sharply. My lungs feel heavy, and an orange hue appears as smoke billows from the upper canopy.

It's coming towards me.

I see the flames within seconds, ashes tarnishing the air and making me wheeze. The smell of burning wood fills my nostrils, and my eyes cloud from the dense smoke.

I need to leave. Now.

I involuntarily inhale some ashes from the air, triggering a fit of violent coughing. In that moment, a twig suddenly crunches behind me, making my skin crawl as I spin around on my heels.

My breath catches in my throat as I notice a shadow among the pine trees. Instinctively, I reach for my flashlight, casting its beam to reveal the mysterious figure lurking behind me.

My heart stops when I see Theo covering his face from the blinding light, a lighter in one hand and a can of gasoline in the other. His face is etched with sheer terror, an exact reflection of mine.

21

The fire crackling behind me grows louder by the second as I stare wide-eyed at Theo, his face ghostly pale in the flickering glow of the flames. This can't be real; it has to be a nightmare.

"What on Earth are you doing here?!" I shout over the cacophonous roaring of fire, dread coursing through me.

Theo remains frozen in his movements, staring at me in disbelief with his lips parted in shock. Suddenly, a deafening crack pierces the air, and a massive tree crashes down just a few feet away from us.

"Run!" Theo yells, breaking into a sprint.

I don't need a second invitation. Without hesitation, I turn on my heels and sprint alongside him, the fiery chaos behind us casting an ominous glow on the trees. The distant sound of crackling flames and the crashing of burning branches follow us as we plunge deeper into Evergreen, our breaths ragged and hearts pounding. The air thickens with each step, the acrid scent of burning wood and the heat of the spreading fire making me cough.

Our footsteps come to a halt once we reach Theo's house, both of us feeling completely out of breath. Anger, confusion, and fear swirl within me, and I shoot him a furious look, waiting for an explanation.

"What the hell were you doing back there, Theo? Do you even realise what you've done?" I shriek. Terror remains etched on his face as he looks at me, the can of gasoline still in his hands.

"Cora, let me explain," he begins, motioning for me to calm down. "Just come with me. It's not safe out here."

"You just set Evergreen on fire!" I exclaim, my voice trembling with a mix of disbelief and fury.

His jaw tightens, and his eyes dart around nervously. In a flash, he grabs my hand and pulls me towards his garage, catching my breath in my throat. With a swift push, he opens the door, revealing my old garage, now packed with tools and Theo's Nissan.

"You need to call the authorities," I say breathlessly, horror etched in my voice. He sets the empty gasoline can on the sink, wiping sweat off his forehead. Hastily turning on the tap, he fills it with water.

"I've already called them. They're on their way," he replies in a low voice, his back to me. Confusion sets in, and I question why he would take such a step after setting the forest ablaze.

Theo sighs, turning to meet my gaze.

"I had no choice, Cora. I had to burn down Glenn's house," he confesses, a hint of regret in his voice.

For a second, I think I may have misheard him. But, as I stare at him with wide eyes, I realise I wasn't mistaken.

"You... burned down *Mayor Glenn's* house?" I exclaim, fear crawling up my spine.

Theo leans back against the sink, rubbing his temples with a frustrated sigh.

"Please, let me explain," he pleads.

"I'm calling the police," I croak, terror in my voice as I reach for my phone. Theo shakes his head, putting his hand over mine.

"No, you can't do that," he interjects, panic reflected in his eyes. "They'll come after your family."

His words send a shockwave rippling through me, turning my blood to ice.

"My family? What does my family have to do with this?" I stammer, swallowing the knot in my throat. He shoots me a puzzled glance. Suddenly, his eyes widen, as though he has just realised something.

"Wait... You really don't know anything, do you?" he asks, curiously studying my face.

An overwhelming sense of dread engulfs me.

"A-About what?" I stammer, cold sweat dampening my neck. Theo hesitates, as if he's revealed more than intended.

"Why did you come here tonight?" he asks, his words piercing the air. My heart pounds against my ribcage, gulping anxiously. He observes my reaction, his expression instantly turning cautious.

"Did you have a dream about tonight?" he tries again, and my heart skips a beat. Shit. Fear grips me as the colour drains from my face.

"H-How did you know? Did you go through my diary?" I stammer breathlessly. Theo shakes his head with furrowed brows.

"No, of course not." He bites his lip, his eyes momentarily dancing around the room as if hesitating. His eyes soon meet mine again, a gentler look replacing the initial intensity

"Cora... The dream you had... It wasn't just a dream. It was a premonition," he says, biting his lip. "I get them, too.

"What?" I exclaim in disbelief. For a moment, I wonder if he's just messing with me. I study his face, desperately looking for any sign of a joke, but his expression is dead serious. My eyes widen in sheer terror as Theo's words sink in.

There's no way this is possible. This must be a dream.

"I thought you knew after you helped me with my arrest," Theo says, furrowing his brows in confusion.

I shake my head in disbelief, suddenly feeling out of breath. It's as if my lungs had lost air capacity. I numbly sit on the hood of the Nissan, tears clouding my sight. My chest tightens, and I struggle to draw in a breath, the air feeling thin.

Theo rushes to my side, his worried eyes examining me.

"Cora, breathe, it's okay," he mutters, his voice laced in concern.

"Now you're gonna tell me I'm not human, right? That I've been a supernatural being my whole life?" I cry. My words feel surreal, as if my entire perception of the world had changed within seconds. Theo shakes his head, resting a consoling hand on my knee.

"No, Cora. You're very much human. We're not supernatural," he says.

Despite his reassurance, the world around me continues to blur, and panic threatens to consume me. The ground beneath my feet feels shaky, as if I'm standing on the edge of a reality I never knew existed.

In that moment, the distant roar of planes cuts through the chaos, capturing both of our attention. We instinctively turn towards the window, drawn to the source of the sound

"What is that?" I ask, fear evident in my tone. Theo anxiously bites his lip, hurrying back to the sink.

"They're putting out the fire." He screws the canister lid shut, hastily slipping his lighter into one of the drawers. He leans against the sink, his back turned to me as he lets out a frustrated exhale.

Theo's words from a few minutes ago continue to echo in my mind, and a persistent fear nags at me. I find myself caught in a tug-of-war between trusting Theo and the inevitable fear creeping in. If I have premonitions, what am I? And why does Theo also get them?

"None of this makes sense," I mumble to myself, staring blankly at the ground.

Theo turns around, his worried eyes fixed on me.

"Cora, I know it's a lot. I'll explain everything, but you must promise not to tell anyone. They'll come after you," he urges, his eyes pleading.

"Why would anyone come after me? The police? I haven't done anything wrong, Theo. You're the one who killed someone," I fire back, anger simmering in my chest. He clenches his jaw, his intense blue eyes fixed on me.

"I swear on my life I'll explain everything. I just need to get rid of this," he says firmly. Snatching the water-filled canister, he storms out of the garage. I stand momentarily dumbfounded before fear grips my chest, propelling me to chase after him.

The whizzing helicopters in the distance diligently work to put out the fire, and the air is thick with dense smoke. Theo rushes to his shed, grabbing a shovel before delving deeper into the forest. I follow him a few steps behind, my eyes widening as he starts to dig out a hole in the ground. My heart races in my chest as I quickly glance over my shoulder, checking if anyone is observing us—but I'm only met with the eerie darkness of the forest.

"What are you doing?" I ask, uneasiness in my voice.

The rhythmic noise of the shovel cutting through the soil reverberates in the silent forest, the growing tension palpable in the air. His movements are too fast for me to process, and I pray to God the helicopters soaring above won't spot us.

"Burying it so they won't find it," he grunts. Tossing the canister into the hole, he wipes his brow before covering it with dirt. "I filled it with water to get rid of the smell," he adds.

My breaths come out heavy, a mixture of smoke and adrenaline filling my lungs. The weight of the situation presses on me; the knowledge that if we get caught, the consequences would be unbearable.

"Theo," I whisper, anxiety causing my teeth to chatter. "Hurry up, please."

Theo's movements quicken, the last bits of dirt covering the canister. With a final pat, he conceals the makeshift grave, and we both stand there for a moment, the weight of our shared secret hanging in the air. The distant hum of the helicopters begins to grow as they draw nearer.

Theo turns to me, fear reflected in his eyes.

"We need to go," he says, urgency in his voice. "I'll answer every question you have. Just come inside. Please.

I nod, grabbing his arm before we rush back into the garage. Theo leads me inside, the dim light revealing a mix of emotions on his face—regret, fear, and a hint of determination. The scent of gasoline lingers in the air, a stark reminder of the chaos that unfolded moments ago.

We settle on the garage floor with a collective sigh of relief. I bury my hands in my head, the weight of the recent events sinking in. The air in the garage is thick with anticipation as we sit, my breaths slowly returning to normal. My eyes flicker to Theo's, silently demanding the answers he promised.

"You're a clairvoyant," he says, his words piercing the silence.

I burst into laughter at his answer, but it takes me a few seconds to realise he's being serious. I gulp, feeling the colour drain from my face.

"What, like a psychic?" I ask, a hint of panic in my voice.

Theo shakes his head, furrowing his brows as if I had said something offensive.

"No. Psychics are bullshit."

"So... I can't see people's future through a crystal ball," I joke, but he remains expressionless.

"I'm not playing with you, Cora. Your senses are heightened compared to the average person. You have premonitions in the form of dreams, hallucinations..."

"Is this some kind of prank? Did the Damnation set you up to this?" I chuckle, still in denial.

Theo sighs, shaking his head.

"No, Cora. This is not a joke. I promise," he replies.

I search his face for a hint of a smile or any sign of jest, but his expression remains serious. Then, my stomach drops.

The pieces fall into place as I remember what I saw in the shower—the vision of Theo being innocent. The snippets of conversations between Helena and the sheriff during school interrogations and the premonition of Theo and Madison kissing seconds before it happened all rush back, leaving me in a whirlwind of confusion and realisation.

It's biologically impossible. The most logical explanation I have is that my hallucinations could be linked to my medication, but... I'm off them now. Shit. He's not joking.

Theo's stormy-blue eyes glisten as if he could read my thoughts.

"How long have you been dreaming about this?" he asks, studying me.

My breath gets caught in my throat, forcing me to swallow hard.

"Six months."

Theo raises an eyebrow before nodding in understanding.

"What? What does that mean?" I ask, anxiety creeping in. He shrugs, his expression unreadable.

"I mean, it's not uncommon... It means tonight is really important for you." Theo's words hang in the air, leaving me with a sense of unease.

"But why is it important?" I ask, arching a brow. Tonight's events have played out in my dreams for a long time, but what could they symbolise?

Theo's gaze softens, momentarily soothing the anxiety within me. For a second, we're back to the way things were, and I sense the spark between us reigniting.

"Well… You discovered who you are," he says, a flicker of pride in his eyes. We sit in silence for a few minutes, and during that time, I feel normal again. I feel like me, a senior in high school experiencing hallucinations and recurring nightmares. Shit, maybe I was never that normal.

In that moment, distrust creeps back in.

"Hold on. Why did you kill Mayor Glenn?" I demand, shooting him an angry and suspicious look.

Theo releases a heavy sigh, biting his lip.

"I didn't kill the mayor, I left him a warning. I did this to protect my family. And not just mine—yours, too," he says, his tone carrying a hint of irritation.

"A warning for what? And what does my family have to do with all of this?" I say, frustration also getting the better of me. I should be on the phone with the police right now, but for some reason, I can't. It's as if it went against my nature.

"He wanted to hurt people like us," he says sternly, his eyes searching for mine.

"Mayor Glenn wouldn't hurt a fly," I retort, feeling a mix of confusion and disbelief.

Theo arches his brows, as though my statement is utterly absurd.

"That's where you're wrong. He was after us—*all* of us.

"What?" I gasp. I stare at Theo in shock, struggling to piece together the fragments of the puzzle. Arthur Glenn, the man who has devoted his life to improving Barren, is a murderer?

Theo takes a deep breath, as if preparing himself for a difficult explanation.

"Mayor Glenn works for an organisation called the Rogues, a group of hired assassins that are designed to kill us."

"What?" I shriek. No, this can't be. Being a clairvoyant is one thing, but having hired assassins after us? That's beyond surreal. What's next, vampires?

Theo's ocean-blue eyes meet mine, worry evident in his gaze.

"That's why you can't tell anyone about this, Cora. We must be careful and stay hidden," he insists.

A few minutes of silence linger between us, Theo's words weighing heavily on me. This is so messed up that it just can't be real. I can't help but express the unsettling thoughts running through my mind.

"Let me get this straight. The Mayor of Barren, whom I have known my entire life, is a murderer?"

"Yes," Theo answers firmly, his eyes steady on me.

The words hang in the air, sounding surreal even as I say them. The reality I once knew now appears more distorted and twisted than ever before, sending shivers down my spine. Mayor Glenn, a familiar figure in my life, now seems tainted by the revelation of his sinister actions.

Theo checks the time, rising from the ground. He extends his hand toward me.

"It's getting late, and we've got school tomorrow. You should head home," he says.

I take his hand, letting him help me up.

"I don't think I'll be able to sleep after all this," I mutter, a sense of brokenness in my voice.

Pain reflects in Theo's eyes.

"You don't have to understand it now; I know it's a lot to take in," he says. He pauses for a second, biting his lip. "But I only wanted to protect you, Cora. I couldn't let you die."

My eyes widen in shock.

"Wait. What?" I exclaim.

He nods, shooting me a solemn look.

"The mayor was going to kill you in two days. I had a vision about it. He was going to shoot you right here." He gestures to his forehead, sending a shiver down my spine. "That's why I did this. I couldn't let that murderer kill you."

"He... He knew about me?" I stutter.

"Yes," Theo affirms, crossing his arms. "That's why he was after you. It was his job to end your life, Cora. That's what the rogues do."

The garage is engulfed in a profound silence, with Theo's words lingering in the air. As the realisation sinks in, I suddenly feel like I can't breathe, and my surroundings start to sway from side to side.

I was going to die. Mayor Glenn was going to kill me. If Theo hadn't intervened, I would be dead.

Feeling overwhelmed by the situation, my eyes begin to water.

Theo's gaze softens, and he gently pulls me into a comforting embrace.

"I'm sorry you had to find out like this, Cora. I never wanted you to be in danger."

Clinging onto Theo for support, I sob into his chest as tonight's events swirl in my head.

I'm a clairvoyant.

22

I haven't slept a wink. How could I, after finding out what I am?

I missed the school bus and had to sprint to campus to make it in time for the first period. Every little noise, from the toaster's pop to passing cars, makes me jump. Maybe I'm struggling to accept what Theo told me last night. The worst part is I can't tell anyone. And even if I could, it's too surreal for anyone to understand.

I'm a clairvoyant. The word still seems surreal. Oh, God. Everything about last night seems surreal.

As I walk down the halls, it feels like everyone's eyes are on me, but it's impossible because none of them know I'm a clairvoyant.

Holy shit. *I'm a clairvoyant.*

It takes me a few seconds to realise the atmosphere in the hallway is different—heavy with panic, just like the day after Damon was shot. As I pass a group of scrawny freshmen, their hushed conversation reaches my ears.

"Evergreen burned down last night, dude. The fire brigade had to put it out."

I try to keep my composure, pretending to be just as curious as everyone else, but the weight of last night's revelations keeps tugging me back into a state of unease. How much do they know?

Entering history class, I'm enveloped by students' fragmented conversations. I notice that everyone is worried about the forest's condition after the fire, but no one seems to be discussing Mayor Glenn. I wonder if the police have shared any information about the incident's cause.

As the rest of the students pour into the classroom, their conversations create a hum in the air. The topic on everyone's lips is the fire, and a pang of guilt creeps into my bones. I need to clear my mind. Opening my notebook, I force myself to focus on last week's notes, trying to drown out the anxious chatter around me.

The image of Theo burying the petrol container to eliminate the evidence resurfaces, causing me to nervously chew on my lip. I force myself to push the thought away, flipping a few pages back in my notebook to choose another chapter—The Cold War. This one should be easy.

I begin reading the page slowly, concentrating on each word to drown out my thoughts. I become so absorbed in my reading that I don't notice Helena next to me until she speaks.

"Are you freaking out, too?" she asks, fear in her brown eyes.

"About?" I ask, swallowing the knot in my throat. I have to trust Theo and act like I don't know anything.

"You didn't hear? Apparently, a third of Evergreen caught fire last night."

"No way," I say, pretending to be surprised.

The bell's ring echoes, and my stomach drops when I see Theo surrounded by a flock of cheerleaders, as if nothing happened. How can he act so normal after what happened last night? It feels surreal that only 16 hours ago, he shared the biggest secret we would ever keep.

I'm a clairvoyant, and he is too.

Helena must have noticed the expression on my face because she mutters, "Are you sure you guys are just friends?"

"It's complicated," I reply with a forced smile, trying to push the anxious thoughts away. *Theo and I are clairvoyants.*

Helena raises an eyebrow, clearly not buying my attempt to downplay the situation. I deliberately avoid meeting Theo's intense gaze as he takes a seat a few desks away, the cheerful chatter of the cheerleaders trailing after him.

"I don't see the harm. You both like each other," Hel nudges me playfully.

I shrug, unsure if she's right about us liking each other. As of last night, Theo is a clairvoyant who committed arson to stop Mayor Glenn from killing me. It sounds like a plot from a Twilight spinoff, but the unfortunate part is that it's not a movie—it's my reality.

I force myself to go along with my usual excuse, glancing at the girls surrounding his desk.

"You see why," I mutter. I roll my eyes, pretending I'm just a normal teenager with a crush, and not a *clairvoyant* who has just found out the gut-wrenching truth about herself.

"He may be popular, but he likes you," she says, making me sigh.

Mrs. Sanchez hurries into the room, silencing the classroom chatter. As usual, her textbooks are clutched to her chest like a student, and tiny glasses are perched on the tip of her nose.

"Good morning," she greets us almost breathlessly, as if she had to run to class.

As Mrs Sanchez begins the lesson on the fall of the Berlin Wall, my mind is elsewhere. I can't shake the feeling that everything has changed, and I'm caught in a web of secrets and danger. I keep glancing at Theo, who seems unfazed by the events of last night. How can he be so composed? On the other hand, my thoughts are a tangled mess, constantly pressing down on me. I know I should stop thinking about it, but it's impossible. Last night's events haunt me.

Suddenly, the loudspeakers crackle to life, interrupting the class.

"Attention students," Dr Fleming's voice echoes through the room, "I hope you all are safe and sound. We're aware of the forest fire incident last night. The cause is under investigation, and due to the tragic death of Mayor Glenn, the town is in a state of mourning."

A collective gasp sweeps through the class, even catching Mrs. Sanchez off guard, causing her to almost drop her whiteboard marker. Wait, what? I thought Theo said he didn't kill him.

I shoot Theo a glance, whose face has turned ghostly pale.

The principal concludes, "Our condolences to Arthur Glenn's family and friends. If anyone has information, please come forward. Thank you."

The announcement sends the class into a state of panic. My gaze remains fixed on Theo, shaking my head in disgust. The room feels suffocating as my classmates exchange nervous glances, and Mrs Sanchez struggles to regain control of the chaotic atmosphere. I can't believe Theo lied about Mayor Glenn still being alive.

The students' panic only becomes louder when the bell rings, and they all hurriedly get up from their seats, dashing for the door. Helena tries to grab my arm amongst the chaos, but I've already started to run after Theo.

I follow him into the next classroom, fear pulsating in my chest as I close the door behind me. I turn to find Theo leaning against a desk. His blue eyes meet mine, carrying the heavy burden of guilt.

"Did you lie to me?" I demand, anger in my voice.

Theo shifts uncomfortably, avoiding direct eye contact.

"Cora, I swear I didn't kill Mayor Glenn. It's impossible. He wasn't even at his house," he insists, his voice shaky.

I narrow my eyes at him, frustration boiling within.

"How could you possibly know that? The announcement just said he's *dead*," I press.

He takes a deep breath, struggling to find the right words.

"Because he was at his holiday house. My sister saw him there," he confesses.

"Your sister?" I ask, surprise evident in my tone. I had no idea Theo had a sister. "But if he wasn't at home, then why are people saying he's dead?"

Theo shakes his head, a troubled expression clouding his face.

"I don't know, Cora. Maybe he ran away. Maybe something else happened. But I didn't kill him."

As the weight of the revelation settles in the room, an overwhelming feeling washes over me. I release a frustrated sigh, my fingers instinctively rubbing my temples.

"This is too much. The mayor is dead, and I don't know what to believe anymore," I mutter.

Theo sighs, his pain-filled blue eyes meeting mine.

"I understand, Cora. I just need you to trust me. I didn't kill Mayor Glenn, and I don't know why people are saying he's dead. But I'm going to find out the truth," he insists.

As the weight of Theo's words lingers in the air, a knock disrupts the silence, making us jump. We exchange a frightened glance before our eyes fixate on the small window on the door, revealing students waiting outside. I open the door, only to find a group of freshmen on the other side.

"Sorry, we have class in here," a girl with thick glasses and braces apologises.

Theo and I share a quick glance that silently communicates the close call before we exit the room. Making my way to my locker, I unexpectedly collide with Helena, her eyes widened with concern.

"Cora, what's going on? Why is everyone saying Mayor Glenn is dead?" she whispers urgently.

I shoot a quick look at Theo, who remains tight-lipped, before turning back to Helena.

"I don't know. There's too much going on, and I'm just as confused as you are," I reply, biting my lip.

Theo takes this as his cue to leave, walking away without saying a word. Once he's out of earshot, Helena's brows furrow with worry.

"Did Theo tell you anything?" she whispers.

I hesitate for a moment, torn between the weight of the truth and the desire to protect Theo.

"No, uh, we weren't talking about that," I lie, but my voice trembles.

Helena's face brightens.

"Oh, my God. Were you guys having 'the talk?'" she shrieks.

My eyes widen, and I find myself momentarily at a loss for words. In that moment, it feels as if I've been backed against the wall. If Helena knew what we were talking about, it would take the school ten minutes to find out. We'd probably end up in a psychiatric ward first, and then in prison.

"No. I mean, yes. More or less," I stammer, realising it's too late to back out now. Shit. I may have just shot myself in the foot.

"So you guys are dating now?" Helena exclaims, clapping her hands in excitement.

I swallow the knot in my throat, doing a mental recap of what happened last night. Theo saved my life. Mayor Glenn would have shot me in a day and a half if it hadn't been for him. Mayor Glenn is dead, but did Theo kill him? Mayor Glenn is a rogue.

I'm a clairvoyant. I'm a fucking clairvoyant.

I look at Helena, who is excitedly waiting for an answer. I can't let anyone suspect anything. Maybe it's better to distract her with something like this than raise doubts as to why Theo and I spend so much time together.

"Yeah, I guess we are," I lie, nervously biting my lip.

Helena beams at me, giving me a tight hug.

"I am so happy for you, sis. So glad you're over Chris," she chirps. I'm taken aback by her sudden excitement, but there's a part of me that feels relieved she bought it.

"Promise me you won't tell anyone, though," I say with a serious look. The last thing I want is for the entire school to find out, including Theo. Shit. How am I going to explain this to him?

Helena's eyes momentarily widen in surprise, but she nods.

"I promise," she says.

I'm about to ask her how Les Misérables is going when everyone's attention shifts to the main entrance. My jaw drops to the floor when The Rebellions stride down the hallway. Their intimidating expressions, leather jackets, band merchandise, and ripped jeans all exude confidence. They seem transformed, almost like celebrities. I'm left in stunned silence as they walk past Helena and me, Chris completely ignoring my existence.

Helena elbows me to grab my attention.

"Weren't they on tour?" Helena whispers, shock evident in her tone.

The band's presence leaves me stunned, much like the rest of the students in the hallway.

"He completely ignored me," I whisper to Helena, a sharp pain radiating from my chest. I had somehow expected Chris to at least acknowledge me, but I guess after our breakup, I might be dead to him.

Helena shoots me a worried look.

"You shouldn't talk to him. Remember what he did?" she asks, arching her brow.

The pain in my chest intensifies as I watch Chris talking to a few girls. He seems entirely different, not in terms of physical appearance, but there's a shift in the air around him. The familiar good-boy vibe has been stripped away, replaced by a raw, confident aura. Helena's words echo in my mind, reminding me of the pain Chris caused. Still, curiosity gets the better of me, and I find myself following him with my eyes.

As the students disperse, I notice Chris glancing in my direction. Our eyes briefly lock, and a silent tension lingers between us.

Helena pulls at my arm, breaking the moment.

"Come on, Cora. Let's get to class," she urges, but my curiosity pushes against her advice.

Ignoring her plea, I break away and head toward Chris at his locker. As I approach, he glances up, a guarded expression on his face.

"Chris," I start, uncertainty in my voice. "Can we talk?"

He looks at me for a moment, then closes his locker without saying a word. We move to a quieter corner of the hallway, away from the bustling students.

"What do you want, Cora?" Chris asks, his tone distant.

"I just... I didn't expect you to ignore me like that," I admit, searching his eyes for any sign of the boy I used to know.

He scoffs, a bitter smile playing on his lips.

"You didn't expect me to ignore you? What did you expect after breaking up with me over text?" he grumbles.

"You cheated on me," I remind him, my voice firm. "Don't make me the villain here."

He looks down, guilt etched on his face.

"I know and I am so sorry I did that to you. But we could have made it work, and you didn't want to."

"I thought you were on tour," I say, shifting the conversation away from the painful memories. Chris may have broken my heart, but there's still a part of me that wants to stay in contact.

"I was, yeah. We had to postpone it," he admits, his gaze meeting mine. There's a vulnerability in his eyes that I haven't seen in a while.

"Why?" I ask, genuinely curious.

"My mom died," he states, the words hitting me like a heavy blow.

The air is sucked out of my lungs, and for a moment, I can't believe what I just heard. But the agony in his expression makes the reality of the situation painfully clear

"W-what?" I stammer in disbelief.

The revelation leaves me speechless, the pain in Chris's eyes mirroring the ache in my own chest. How could his mom have died? She was relatively young and healthy. I bite my lip, forcing myself to not ask questions.

Chris shrugs, as if trying to downplay the magnitude of the loss.

"Dr Fleming revoked my expulsion because she died. Said my education is important, especially now," he explains, the weight of grief evident in his voice.

"Oh, my God. I'm so sorry, Chris..." I murmur, the urge to console him overwhelming me.

For a fleeting moment, I forget about the past—that he didn't cheat on me with Emily or that we've broken up. I'm on the verge of reaching out for a comforting hug when I catch sight of Theo observing from afar, arms crossed.

"It's okay," Chris replies, forcing a smile.

An awkward silence lingers, and though instinct tells me to offer comfort, I resist. We're still tiptoeing on the fragile shards of our broken relationship.

"I should have been there for you," I express, regret tainting my tone. Chris shakes his head, his emerald eyes meeting mine.

"I'm okay. Look, I know it's not the best time to ask you about this, but... Can we still be friends at least?"

If circumstances were different, I might have hesitated, but given the recent losses he endured, Damon and now his mom, I cave in.

"Of course," I assure him, earning a soft smile in return.

"Okay, great. Anyway, I'll see you around?" he asks, gently touching my arm.

"Yeah," I reply, smiling back.

As Chris shuts his locker, my eyes drift to Theo, whose scornful gaze is still on me. If I didn't know any better, he looks jealous. It seems like he's about to approach me when Chris turns to catch my eye.

"By the way, are you free tonight? I feel like we have a lot to talk about," he asks.

I glance back at Theo, noticing the anger in his expression. It's amusing; earlier this morning, he was flirting with dozens of girls, and now he's jealous because I'm talking to Chris.

"Yeah, I'm free," I reply, flashing Chris a quick smile.

"Good. Should we head to class?" he asks, shyly rubbing the back of his neck. I catch a glimpse of the Chris I once knew—the guy who used to bring me cinnamon rolls whenever I felt down.

"Yeah. Math, right?"

"Yeah," he replies, offering a warm smile.

But despite the nostalgia, after everything that happened, I won't give Chris a second chance. Only as friends.

As Chris and I walk towards our math class, Theo's gaze remains fixed on me. It's a strange feeling, being caught between two worlds—Chris, my past, and Theo, my present.

23

As Helena, the group, and I make our way to the lunch hall, the buzz of whispers and hushed conversations about Chris fills the air. It's evident that his return is the hot topic of the day, and the student body is a relentless force when it comes to gossip.

My eyes scan the crowded tables as we walk in, finding Chris sitting just a few tables away with the other band members. I notice the discomfort on his face as he munches on an apple, hardly paying attention to what his friends are saying.

Hel nudges me, breaking my thoughts.

"There he is. Back in the spotlight," she says, a hint of sarcasm in her voice.

As we sit down at our usual table, I can feel the collective gaze of the cafeteria drifting toward Chris. The atmosphere is charged, and it's as if the cafeteria has become a stage for a drama we never auditioned for.

I glance at Chris, wondering how he's handling the attention and the judgment of the entire school. Returning to a place that once felt like home must be overwhelming, especially with the added burden of recent losses. I can't help but feel a pang of sympathy for him.

As we settle into our seats, the shock on the faces of Helena, Matt, Beth, and Mason is palpable. It's as if they've seen a ghost—a ghost with a complicated history that we never quite managed to bury. Helena wears a frown that could rival a storm cloud.

"Why is he even back?" Matt mutters, his eyes fixed on Chris.

"Dr Fleming revoked his expulsion because of his mom's death," I explain, trying to keep my tone neutral. The group exchanges glances, and it's clear that none of us expected this twist in the narrative.

Helena, however, doesn't hide her discontent.

"Cora, seriously? You're just chatting with him like nothing happened?

I let out a sigh, feeling the weight of their judgment.

"We were friends before everything went south, Helena. I can't just ignore him," I explain.

"But he cheated on you, Cora!" Helena's frustration is evident, her eyes flashing with anger.

"I know," I admit, my gaze dropping to the table. "And I haven't forgotten that. But he's going through a lot right now."

Helena's disappointment is palpable, and I can sense the rift widening between us.

"I just don't want you getting hurt again, Cora. And Chris is the type of guy that will," she insists.

I sigh, frustration finding its way onto my face.

"I won't, Hel. I've moved on."

I nudge Helena with my foot under the table, a silent reminder of what I shared with her earlier about Theo. She shoots me an apologetic look, a sudden realisation crossing her face. Maybe it wasn't a bad idea lying about Theo being my boyfriend.

I decide to shift the conversation to a lighter topic to lighten the mood.

"By the way, when is Les Misérables?" I ask.

Matt, who was lost in devouring his sandwich, looks up in excitement.

"It's tomorrow night. I'm counting on you to be there," he says with a playful nudge.

"Tomorrow night? That's awesome! Count me in," I reply with a smile, grateful for the change in conversation. But in that moment, Mason brings up the topic I had been dreading.

"Is no one going to address the elephant in the room here?" he asks, his eyes wide. "Mayor Glenn is dead, y'all."

The mood instantly shifts, and a heavy silence falls over the table. Mason's words hang in the air, a stark reminder of the recent events that have rocked our small town. Beth's eyes widen, and she glances around the table, waiting for someone to break the silence. Helena shifts uncomfortably in her seat, clearly caught off guard by the abrupt change in topic.

Finally, Matt breaks the silence with a nervous laugh.

"Well, that's one way to kill the vibe."

But Mason doesn't back down.

"Seriously, guys. What do we know about it? It's not like one of our mayors die every day."

I absentmindedly play with my water bottle to avoid their gazes, which luckily nobody notices. A sense of guilt washes over me, even though I'm innocent. My mind is a battleground, torn between the desire to trust that Theo didn't kill Glenn and the nagging suspicion that he might have.

Can Theo really be capable of such an act?

I run a quick mental recap: He kept my secret about Robert Harris' flashlight, he helped Damon when he was shot... Yet, he also set Mayor Glenn's house on fire. But then again, he claims he did it to save my life.

I'm also concerned that my feelings for him might cloud my judgement, making me blindingly believe him. The questions persist in my mind, leaving me lightheaded. Maybe having proof of my clairvoyant abilities will be the key to settling my doubts and trusting him completely.

The conversation takes an unexpected turn as theories about Mayor Glenn's death begin to circulate.

"A lot of people have gas leaks at home, right?" Matt says, contemplating the idea. "Maybe he left a cigarette or something. Boom! Accidental explosion."

"I heard he had some enemies. Maybe it was foul play," Beth chimes in.

Mason raises an eyebrow.

"Enemies? Come on, Beth. Everyone loves Mayor Glenn."

Helena leans forward, her curiosity piqued.

"But what if it was something more mysterious? Like something supernatural?" she asks, a spark of excitement in her eyes.

My stomach drops, instantly feeling the weight of Theo's secret. Panic flushes my cheeks, and I force myself to down the rest of my water bottle.

Matt lets out a cackle, shooting Helena a glance.

"Babe, you've been watching too much The Vampire Diaries," he teases.

Embarrassment colours her cheeks, and she playfully swats Matt's arm.

"Oh, come on! Isn't it weird that we've had three murders in two months? Maybe vampires are real," she suggests.

A moment of silence hangs in the air before the group erupts into laughter.

"Good one, Hel," Mason chuckles, shaking his head.

As we collect our scraps, the group's banter returns to its usual tone, easing the tension that momentarily hung in the air.

I don't know if vampires are real yet, but clairvoyants seem to be.

•••••

theorhodes
can we talk?

I read the message, releasing a sigh as I zip up my skirt. These past 24 hours have been a rollercoaster, and I need a break from it all. Tonight, I just want to be around normal people, without any conspiracy theories or supernatural drama. I've agreed to meet Chris at The Grub, one of the very few diners at Barren. I spent four weeks last summer working as a waitress for Old Mary, and ever since, the old 50s diner has become Chris and my go-to date destination.

With Theo's message lingering in my head, I make my way downstairs. I find my dad peacefully asleep on the couch, the soft melody of his snores filling the living room. With a quiet sigh, I make my way to the door.

The evening air is crisp as I step out into the quiet streets of Barren. A few dimly lit streetlamps cast long shadows on the pavement, and the distant hum of a passing car and the occasional rustle of leaves are the only sounds breaking the stillness. I pull my jacket a little tighter around me, the chill nipping at my cheeks. As I walk through the town, I pass by familiar storefronts, their soft lights illuminating the street

The retro neon sign of The Grub comes into view, beckoning me to enter. As I step inside, the aroma of fried bacon, cheap coffee, and grilled steak greets me, triggering memories of the countless times I've been here with Chris. We spent most of our free time in this diner, savouring strawberry milkshakes and strong coffees to kill our boredom.

I find a free booth at the back, next to the antique jukebox, which, in the age of Spotify and iTunes, now appears obsolete. A smile lights up my face as Old Mary approaches my booth, notepad in hand.

"Goodness! Look who's back!" she exclaims, her smile carving wrinkles around the corners of her mouth.

"Hi, Mary. How are you?" I respond with a polite smile.

"Ah, you know how it is. Same old, same old. I was just thinking about you the other day. Fancy a cup of coffee?" she offers, her Jersey accent adding a touch of warmth to the invitation.

"Actually, I'm waiting for a friend," I reply.

In that very moment, Chris strolls into the diner, his dark brown hair tousled as if he just rolled out of bed. He's wearing a basic white shirt with a flannel layered on top—remarkably, it's the first time I've seen him not wearing a hoodie. He locates my booth, making his way toward me.

Old Mary's smile brightens as Chris joins me.

"It's been a while since I saw both of you! Still planning on heading to Pennsylvania for Christmas?" she asks, clearly unaware of the events that have unfolded in the past months.

"Hi Mary," Chris greets her with a genuine smile. "And I'm afraid not, we're just friends now."

Old Mary gives us a startled look, as if we had just shattered her dreams. I clear my throat awkwardly, sensing the tension lingering between us.

"Could we have some burgers and smoothies?" I ask, forcing a smile.

Mary takes a few seconds to recover from the revelation before nodding in acknowledgment.

"O-Of course," she stammers before walking away.

Chris remains expressionless, his gaze fixed on me as if trying to read my thoughts.

"It's been so long since we came here, huh?" he asks, breaking the silence. A sudden realisation hits me—I was wrong; I can't just pretend last night didn't happen. I'm a clairvoyant, and nothing will ever be the same.

"Yeah," I respond. "How have you been coping since..." I hesitate, unsure if it's too early to broach the subject.

Chris releases a sigh, his gaze briefly wandering.

"Surviving, honestly," he mutters, a hint of weariness in his voice. It's painful to see Chris in this state, especially knowing that his mom was the only family he had left.

"How did it happen?" I ask, feeling my eyes welling up.

He exhales, leaning back into the booth.

"She had an accident," he answers, the weight of the words hanging in the air. "I don't really want to talk about it, if I'm honest," he adds, his serious gaze locking with mine.

I nod in understanding, sensing the sombre atmosphere settling between us.

"How are you? How's everything going?" he asks, shifting the focus to me.

My mind goes blank for a few seconds as I struggle with how to answer. Sharing even a fragment of the events that unfolded in the past 24 hours feels like it would land me a one-way ticket to the nearest mental institution.

"I'm hanging in there," I manage, mustering a forced smile. "Most of my afternoons are consumed by SAT prep with Helena and the group."

Chris raises a brow.

"Helena Corey?" he asks, seeming surprised.

"Yeah. Why?"

"No, nothing. I didn't know you liked girls like her," he says, disapproval tainting his voice.

"What do you mean 'girls like her'?" I ask defensively.

"She's kind of a gossip," he says with a shrug, making me frown.

"You're acting like you don't talk about other people with your friends," I fire back. It's surprising to see him acting this way, especially since he used to complain about me not having friends when we were together.

Chris shakes his head, taking out a napkin from the dispenser.

"That's different," he mutters.

I can't help but scoff at the hypocrisy of his comment.

"It's exactly the same. That's having double standards," I retort.

In that moment, Old Mary arrives with our food, her usual smile back on her face. We mutter a thank you before Chris dives into his burger, maintaining a stoic silence. As we both dig into our meals, the tension remains palpable in the air. I glance at him, uncertain of what words would mend the growing distance between us. Old Mary, sensing the awkwardness, discreetly leaves our milkshakes on the table a few minutes later with a comforting smile.

Chris breaks the silence, wiping some ketchup from his mouth as he looks at me.

"Look, Cora... I'm genuinely sorry for what I did and how I treated you. I was completely selfish, and I didn't appreciate what I had. I've even quit drinking for good. My mom was always against it, and now that she's gone... I feel like I owe her that."

His declaration momentarily leaves me speechless, and I take a sip of my milkshake, using the moment to compose myself. I certainly wasn't expecting that.

"I'm glad to hear you're doing that for her," I manage to reply, offering a small but genuine smile. In all honesty, I can't help but feel immense sympathy for him. Losing his mom, his sole remaining family, and dealing with the impact of Damon's death—it's a heavy burden. I realise I'm all he has now.

Chris nods, polishing off the last of his fries. His green eyes study my face, as though he's thinking about something.

"What?" I ask, feeling a hint of nervousness.

"What's happening between you and Theo Rhodes?" he asks, his question causing my heart to quicken its pace.

Honestly, I'm utterly clueless about Theo and me, except for the fact that we're both clairvoyants. The topic of our relationship never came up before the forest fire, and even though there might be something there, the current circumstances make everything feel too complicated.

I pause, taking a moment to gather my thoughts before responding. The last thing I want is for Chris to suspect anything and confront Theo.

"Chris, Theo and I are just friends," I answer, watching his expression closely.

His tense expression softens, and he looks at me with a mix of relief and understanding.

"Just friends?" he asks, the worry dissipating from his voice.

"Yeah, just friends," I confirm.

Chris buries his hands in his face, letting out a sigh of relief.

"I swear to God, I thought you were having a thing," he laughs. His emerald eyes fix on mine, and the laughter fades, replaced by a serious gaze. "I'd be careful with him, if I were you."

A surge of anger courses through me, causing my muscles to tense.

"Why?" I ask, shooting him a glance.

His eyes narrow, bitterness seeping into his gaze. Maybe he is the jealous type after all.

"He hooked up with Madison Cortese right after my brother was murdered," he booms, making me flinch.

I take a deep breath, my voice steady as I respond.

"Madison and Damon broke up months before it happened. If anything, you should be mad at her," I answer. "He's been a really good friend to me, Chris."

He runs a hand through his hair, clenching his jaw.

"I just don't want you to get hurt," he says, a touch of irritation in his voice. I look at the boy who made me cry countless times and ended up cheating on me.

"Don't worry. I'll be fine," I reply, forcing a tight smile. "Anyway, tell me about the tour. I'm dying to hear about it."

In an instant, his face lights up, the annoyance from moments ago melting away.

"God, this tour has been incredible; I have so much to tell you," he beams.

He starts sharing stories from the tour—the challenges of sleeping on tour buses, the interactions with fans, and the occasional arguments with his bandmates. Though it doesn't particularly interest me, I listen politely. By the time we ask for the bill, I'm certain that I don't miss being with him anymore.

The realisation that my life has dramatically changed overnight sinks in. There's no escaping the truth—I'm a clairvoyant now, and the concept of normalcy feels like a distant memory, no matter how hard I try to deny it.

After splitting the bill, we find ourselves standing outside the diner. The crisp evening air envelops us, and the distant hum of cars forms a backdrop to our awkward farewell. After tonight's conversation, it's clearer than ever that my feelings for him have faded.

Chris gazes at me, his eyes reflecting a blend of nostalgia and uncertainty.

"It was good seeing you again, Cora," he says, his words lingering in the cold night sky.

"Yeah, you too, Chris," I reply, a bittersweet smile playing on my lips. It feels strange not kissing each other goodbye, and an awkward moment of silence hangs between us.

"Do you want me to walk you home? It's late," he offers, his eyes fixed on me.

I shake my head with a polite smile, remembering that Theo needs to talk to me.

"No, it's alright. I've got it covered. Take care, Chris."

Chris gives me a surprised look, but he nods, respecting my decision.

"Text me when you're home," he says, offering a small smile.

I watch him stroll away with his hands in his pockets, his breath creating mist in the crisp night air. After his shadow vanishes into the night, I retrieve my phone to text Theo. The glow of the screen illuminates my face as I type.

coradanvers
sorry, just seen this.
you wanted to talk about
something?

theorhodes
can i meet you at my house
in an hour?

24

As I head towards Theo's house, the remnants of the forest fire become unmistakably apparent. Dry leaves crunch beneath my feet, now accompanied by soot and ashes. The acrid scent of ashes lingers in the air, a vivid reminder of the recent blaze. But the most noticeable change is the thick yellow tape wrapped around parts of the forest, bearing the cautionary message, 'POLICE LINE DO NOT CROSS.'

Despite the tape, I approach the front door with a mix of nostalgia and anxiety, eager to know why Theo wants to talk an hour after curfew. A soft knock on the door resonates through the house, and as Theo opens it, his azure eyes reflect a blend of relief and gratitude.

"Hey," he greets, a hint of warmth in his voice.

"Hi," I reply with a soft smile. "Sorry for the delay; I was having dinner."

He briefly studies my face, as if trying to decipher something.

"No problem, come in."

Theo invites me in, and I take a moment to absorb my surroundings. The living room, once filled with the comforting memories of my childhood, now has a different ambiance and décor. Theo's furniture now brings a more modern touch, in white and light blue hues, but the homely atmosphere still lingers. We settle onto the couch, unsure how to feel about the changes, but somewhat relieved to be able to see it again.

After a few minutes of silence, Theo brings his lip between his teeth.

"I firstly wanted to apologise for dropping such a huge bomb on you last night. I had no idea you were a clairvoyant, too," he explains, looking down at his hands.

I bite my inner cheek, unsure of what to say. He's turned my life upside down within minutes, and the likelihood of returning to normality seems distant and elusive. Even during dinner with Chris, a persistent lump in my throat reminded me that I will never be able to share my new reality with anyone.

Theo notices my silence, his concerned eyes flickering to mine.

"Secondly, I also want to be transparent with you. I have no clue what happened to Glenn, but you need to trust me. I only gave him a warning so he wouldn't kill you, and my sister helped me ensure he wasn't at home. I would never kill anyone, that's not who we are."

The weight of his words hangs in the air, tension palpable between us. Part of me is inclined to believe him, considering all we've been through together in the past few months. However, another part of me resists, terrified of embracing the idea that I'm different.

I take a deep breath, a sudden determination flowing through me.

"There's only one way I'll believe you," I challenge him with a spark in my eyes.

"What is it?" he asks, giving me a nervous glance.

"Prove to me that I'm a clairvoyant," I assert.

Theo's eyes widen in surprise, and for a moment, he seems taken aback by my request. But after a brief pause, he nods. He retrieves a gold ring from his pocket, gently placing it in the palm of my hand. As I look at the antique piece, a wave of apprehension passes through me.

"What's this?" I ask.

"I need you to hold this ring. Like this, okay?" Theo instructs, demonstrating by curling his own fist.

I tighten my grip around the ring, a sense of anxiety tingling within me.

"Uh... Okay," I chuckle, feeling somewhat sceptical.

"Now, close your eyes and focus. Try to sense anything about the ring. Any images, feelings, or thoughts," he guides me.

I take a deep breath, shutting my eyes and concentrating on the gold band in my hand. It feels cool against my skin, and for a moment, I'm just aware of its physical presence. But as I focus on its energy, my heart quickens, and images start to flicker through my mind like scenes from a surreal movie.

At first, I see a couple— a guy and a blonde girl, holding hands and walking down the familiar halls of Barren High. They smile at each other, their eyes filled with love, an intimate moment captured in time.

Then, the setting changes abruptly, and a disturbing, gut-wrenching scene unfolds. I see a woman hanging from the ceiling, her lifeless form swaying eerily.

My eyes snap open in shock, a bone-chilling cold rushing through my veins. Theo gently grabs my wrist, his concerned gaze meeting mine. I become aware of blood trickling down my wrist from holding the ring too tightly.

"Shit. Are you okay?" he asks, biting his lip as he tries to wipe away the blood.

A series of uncontrollable shivers travel down my spine, making my teeth chatter. My breaths are ragged from the disturbing images, leaving me momentarily speechless. What I witnessed wasn't a daydream or a hallucination. It felt like I had glimpsed into someone's life, their memories vividly playing before my eyes.

"What... What was that?" I stammer, my voice trembling.

Theo wraps his arms around me, pulling me into a comforting embrace.

"Shh, it's okay," he murmurs, his voice soothing. "The first time is always rough."

I hold onto him, the warmth of his embrace slowly easing the unbearable cold that had gripped me moments ago. Despite the lingering images in my mind, Theo's presence provides a sense of security. Gradually, my breathing steadies, and the shivers that once racked my body begin to subside.

"Take your time," Theo whispers, his fingers gently rubbing circles on my back. "Seeing those visions can be overwhelming, especially in the beginning."

I nod against his shoulder, gradually regaining my composure. The image of the woman begins to fade from my mind, but the unsettling feeling lingers, a haunting reminder of what I have just experienced. I pull away slightly, looking into Theo's eyes. The concern in his azure gaze is evident, and for a moment, neither of us says anything. I feel a magnetic pull between us, making my heart race.

"What was that?" I ask breathlessly.

He pulls away from me, but his gaze remains focused on me.

"That was Mayor Glenn's ring. It's called psychometry. You can sense information about an object by touching it. The visions you experienced are impressions left on the ring, the emotions and events connected to it," he explains.

As Theo's words hang in the air, the pieces of the puzzle all seem to click. I'm not dealing with schizophrenia or any mental illness.

I'm a clairvoyant. The images, the visions—it's all real.

"Oh, my God, Theo. You were right," I exclaim with wide eyes.

The words echo in my head like a broken record. *Theo wasn't lying. I'm a clairvoyant. Theo wasn't lying. I'm a clairvoyant. Theo wasn't lying. I'm a clairvoyant.*

Theo nods, his expression a mix of understanding and reassurance.

"It's a lot to take in, I know. Mayor Glenn is a major player among the rogues," he explains.

"The people that want us dead," I clarify, swallowing the knot in my throat. At first, there was a part of me that doubted him, but now it's crystal clear—I can't believe I didn't see it earlier.

Theo nods in agreement.

"Exactly. I need to show you this," he says, taking out a folded sheet from his pocket and handing it to me. Unfolding it, my eyes widen at the mayor's mugshot, surrounded by handwritten notes. A sinking feeling sets in as I scan the list of names beneath his image.

"Who are these people?" I ask, an inevitable wave of dread washing over me.

"People he's killed."

His words make my heart skip a beat.

"What?" I exclaim, feeling the colour drain from my face.

I scan through the names in panic once more, but none of them ring a bell. There are about twenty, a mix of male and female names. In that moment, the chilling truth settles in.

Mayor Glenn is a murderer. A serial killer.

"Were they clairvoyants?" I ask, the word still feeling unfamiliar on my tongue.

Theo nods solemnly.

"Most of them, yes. Some were just in the wrong place at the wrong time," he explains. He pauses, his serious gaze focused on me. "This is why we need to be careful about who we trust. We can't let anyone know about us."

I gulp, a wave of fear washing over me. It's as if the world I knew has transformed overnight.

"Why do the rogues want to kill us?" I ask.

"Because we're very powerful. Using psychometry, we can discover anyone's past based on the connection between them and an object. We can foresee events, know when people are going to die… It's like being the grim reaper. They want that power in their hands. And if we don't want to work for them, they will kill us," he explains.

I blink repeatedly, trying to take in all this new information. Maybe living in denial was easier, but as Theo's words sink in, the pieces of the puzzle start to connect. It's utterly disturbing to discover that Mayor Glenn, the man who vowed to protect Barren, harbours so many dark secrets.

"I had no idea how dangerous Mayor Glenn was… Everyone in Barren loves him," I mutter, a mix of disbelief and unease tainting my voice.

Theo nods, a hint of disappointment on his face.

"A vast majority of politicians are. You know the woman you saw in the vision?" he asks. The term 'vision' still seems surreal. I nod, recalling the blonde woman who was seeing Glenn. "She found out what Glenn was up to. That's why he killed her."

The revelation sends a chill down my spine.

"He killed her just for finding out?" I ask, my disbelief escalating.

"Yes, he drove her to suicide so she wouldn't talk. Mayor Glenn eliminated anyone who posed a threat to his secrets. That's why we need to be cautious," he says.

I'm left momentarily speechless, struggling to absorb the shocking news. Theo's eyes meet mine, worry clouding his gaze.

"You were going to be next, Cora. That's why I burned down his house, to give him a warning," he explains. He bites his lip, lowering his gaze in guilt. "I couldn't just watch you die."

In that vulnerable moment, our eyes lock, and I sense a deeper connection beyond the shared danger. Theo's concern for me is palpable, and a mixture of gratitude and something more lingers in the air.

"You risked everything for me," I say softly, my voice filled with a newfound understanding. Theo was only protecting me from Glenn. If I knew someone was in danger of dying, I, too, would do whatever it takes to save them.

Theo's gaze softens, his face mere inches from mine.

"I couldn't stand the thought of losing you, Cora," he whispers, making my heart leap.

In the intensity of the moment, the gravity of our situation fades, replaced by a different kind of tension—the magnetic attraction that has lingered between us since the night we met.

"Thank you, Theo. For everything."

As the atmosphere between us thickens with unspoken emotions, I feel the anticipation building between us. Just as our lips are about to meet, a distant rumble of thunder echoes through the air, shattering the moment. Theo pulls away, his face reflecting a mix of longing and regret. I can't help but feel my heart clench, disappointed that our moment was cut short.

We sit in silence for a few minutes, the rhythmic tap of raindrops on the windows creating a sullen backdrop. Suddenly, I realise we haven't talked about our relationship since we kissed at *Whispering Pines*. I'm unsure if being together is the right choice since it might complicate things. Yet, there's an undeniable pull towards him that I just can't ignore.

Theo breaks the silence with a sigh.

"I get it. You don't want to see me anymore," he says, the pain in his voice stinging my heart.

I gently place my hand on his cheek, guiding his gaze towards me.

"No, Theo, it's not that. I just need time to process everything. It's not about us; it's about me figuring things out," I say, my voice gentle.

He nods, a spark of hope igniting in his azure eyes.

"I totally understand. Take as long as you need." His features soften, a sense of understanding in his gaze. "I guess I have no idea what it's like to find out you're a clairvoyant. I've always known."

I shoot him a surprised glance.

"Really? Are your parents clairvoyant, too?"

Theo nods.

"Both of them are, and my sister as well."

"Wow... Your family dinners must be quite interesting," I say with a laugh.

Theo chuckles, his eyes lighting up with amusement.

"You have no idea. It's a regular clairvoyant convention at the dinner table."

We share a brief laugh, the tension easing a bit. It's strange to think that Theo has been part of this world his whole life, yet our paths only converged recently.

"But seriously," he continues, his expression turning more serious. "I'm here for you, Cora. Whatever you need, whether it's about being a clairvoyant or just dealing with everything, I'm here.

His sincerity makes my heart flutter, and I flash him a grateful smile.

"Thanks, Theo. It means a lot."

In that instant, a memory from this morning floods back. Shit. Theo instantly notices the sudden change in my expression, shooting me a concerned look.

"Hey, what's up?"

I take a deep breath, debating whether to share my earlier conversation with Helena. Eventually, I choose honesty, despite the possibility that he might hate me.

"I told Helena earlier that we're dating," I reply, biting my lip.

Theo's eyes widen in surprise.

"What?"

I sigh, nervously fiddling with my fingers.

"I know, I'm sorry. I just didn't want her to suspect anything, and I'm sorry if—"

He gently rests his hand on my thigh, making my eyes meet his.

"Cora…"

"Yeah?" I ask, my breath caught in my throat from his touch. He bites his lip, the intensity of his gaze sending my heart racing.

"I'm fine with it. In fact, it might save us a lot of trouble," he answers in a low voice.

"So you're not mad at me?" I ask, taken aback.

He shakes his head, a sly smirk forming on his lips.

"I don't mind fake dating you for the time being," he teases, his eyes sparkling with amusement.

My face warms up as we share a playful grin. The rain drums on outside, and a sudden thunderclap draws our attention to the window. Theo stands up from the couch, reaching out his hand to me.

"It's pouring out there. Let me give you a ride home," he suggests. I gladly accept his hand, a smile playing on my lips.

"Thanks, I really appreciate it."

We head towards the garage, the sound of raindrops on the roof creating a soothing rhythm. He opens the door to his Nissan for me, revealing the warm and inviting interior that smells like his cologne. As he starts the engine, the gentle hum of the car surrounds us, but just before he opens the garage door, he turns to glance at me.

"One last thing," he mutters softly, sending my heart racing.

"Yeah?" I whisper, my gaze fixed on him.

"Learning to control is crucial. If we don't, the visions can drive us to madness—even suicide," he says.

The weight of his words lingers, leaving me stunned for a few seconds. A chill passes through me, the fear of that possibility gripping me. The garage door opens, echoing the familiar rusty sound it made whenever my dad used to open it. We pull out of the garage, instantly enveloped by the heavy rain and the darkness of the forest.

The soft glow of the dashboard illuminates his focused expression as he navigates the rain-soaked streets. I can't help but steal glances at him as he drives, captivated by the way his blue eyes glisten through the raindrops on the windshield. As Theo brings the car to a stop in front of my home, the rain continues its rhythmic dance on the roof. We sit in a comfortable silence for a few moments, the air filled with a subtle anticipation.

"Thanks for the ride. And for everything else," I say, a smile gracing my lips.

He turns to face me, his ocean eyes locking onto mine.

"It's nothing. I had a great time tonight," he mutters, his gaze briefly lingering on my lips.

"I did too," I reply, feeling a gentle flutter in my chest.

A smile plays on the corners of his lips, his eyes lighting up in the dimness of the car. In that moment, I choose to take a chance. Closing the gap between us, our lips meet in a passionate and lingering kiss. As our bodies respond to each other, everything starts to fade away. I forget about being clairvoyant, the dangers of pushing the limits, and the threats from the rogues and Mayor Glenn. Theo's hands travel up my torso, pulling me closer to him. I let out a soft moan, my hands running through his hair as we deepen the kiss. The tension between us intensifies, causing the car windows to fog.

Just a few hours ago, I was terrified of being a clairvoyant, feeling uneasy around everyone, including Chris. But realising I'm not alone in this, having Theo by my side, brings forth a sense of empowerment I had never recognised within me before.

Breaking away from the kiss, a breathless smile lingers on both our faces. The windows, still fogged from the intensity of the moment, cast a dreamlike spell on the car's interior. Our eyes meet, the lingering desire between us palpable.

"Wow," Theo whispers, his voice carrying a mix of surprise and longing.

"Yeah," I reply, my breath still catching up.

The heavy rain outside serves as a backdrop as we lock eyes, my heart racing at a thousand beats per minute.

"I'll see you at school tomorrow," he says, still breathless.

I nod, a soft smile forming on my face. As I lean in for a hug, he catches me off guard with another passionate kiss. Moaning, I reluctantly pull away, meeting his gaze.

"Goodnight," I murmur, biting my lip.

"Goodnight, Cora," he replies, his eyes still ablaze with the intensity of the moment.

I step out of the car, hurrying up the porch steps as heavy rain soaks me within seconds. As I reach the door, I hear Theo's car driving away, the hum of its engine fading into the night. Still buzzing with adrenaline from moments ago, I unlock the front door, an inevitable smile lighting up my face.

25

After spending time with Theo last night, I'm gradually processing the events of the past two days. In fact, today is surprisingly one of the few days since the semester began where I don't feel overwhelming anxiety. Perhaps acceptance is the most powerful stage in the five stages of grief after all. But, in the back of my mind, knowing that there's a group of sinister people that aim to eradicate us fills me with horror. Now, I understand the importance of not telling anyone what we are.

As I navigate through the busy hallway, students chatter lively amongst themselves, making quick stops at their lockers before heading to the lunch hall. However, in an instant, chaos breaks loose.

A nervous murmur ripples through the students, escalating into angry protests as they gather near the bulletin board. Navigating through the crowd, I try to see what's happening, my heart racing as I fear for the worst. My eyes widen as I spot a student hanging a poster on the wall—one that announces, *'Election day, January 9th.'*

It's only been 48 hours since they announced Mayor Glenn's supposed death, and the town is already on the hunt for a new candidate. Just like Damon's death, people have quickly moved on. The realisation makes my gut wrench.

As students voice their protests, viewing the poster as insensitive, the haunting image of the woman hanging from the ceiling resurfaces in my mind. None of the people defending him are aware of who Mayor Glenn is and the atrocities he has committed. Most importantly, none of them know he was planning to kill me today.

Pushing past the irritated crowd, I make my way towards the lunch hall. As I enter, the familiar aroma of burgers, bolognese and fish fills the air. My eyes scan the room, searching for my friends amongst the sea of students. Spotting Helena and the group at a corner table, relief washes over me. I settle into the seat beside Mason, who greets me with a broad grin.

"Hey, Cora," he says.

"Hey, guys," I reply, scanning the table. I notice Matt is missing, causing me to furrow my brows. "Where's Matt?"

Helena rolls her eyes, popping a fry into her mouth.

"He's with the nurse because of a cold. You know... actors. A cold was never a big deal in my household," she answers, earning a chuckle from Beth.

"She's not wrong," Beth adds with a smile.

Helena's chestnut eyes flicker to me, causing her to pause mid-bite. She studies my face as if piecing together a puzzle, her eyes widening in realisation.

"You look different," she breathes.

Her comment catches me off guard, and I feel my cheeks flush in response. What could she possibly mean by that?

"Yeah?" I reply, an anxious smile playing on my lips. "Different how?"

Helena leans back, squinting slightly.

"Can't put my finger on it, but something's changed. Did you do something last night?" she asks.

I feel my cheeks redden even more, memories of Theo and me passionately kissing in his car resurfacing.

Beth nods in agreement, pulling me out of my thoughts

"Yeah, I noticed it too. There's a certain... glow about you, Cora."

It must be the new clairvoyant glow; I ironically think to myself.

I glance at Mason, who shrugs, equally puzzled.

"Maybe she's just radiant from dodging election drama," he suggests with a playful grin.

"Oh my God, yeah. Did you see the poster?" Hel asks, her eyes wide in shock.

"Yeah," I reply, clenching my jaw.

I wonder how they'd all react if they knew what I know about Glenn. The cold chill that crawled up my spine after looking into his ring lingers in my memory, even though Theo assured me it's normal during the first visions.

My thoughts are interrupted by Beth's eyes on me.

"Are you going to Les Misérables tonight?" she asks, finishing her OJ.

"Of course," I reply, flashing a smile. Maybe engaging in normal activities is the right move despite my situation.

"Oh my God, thank you, Cora," Hel gushes, grabbing my hands. "Matt has put so much effort into it, and he'd be thrilled to have you there."

The group falls into a sudden silence as Theo makes his way to our table, his piercing blue eyes locked onto me. Clad in a black tee that highlights his muscles, he takes a seat beside me, and I can almost taste the tension intensifying between us. The group's atmosphere immediately shifts, clearly taken aback by his unexpected appearance.

"Hey," Theo says, his eyes lingering on me.

The air between us becomes charged, and I'm left breathless for a few seconds, wondering why he's making it so obvious. Then, the realisation hits me—I told him that Helena thinks we're dating.

Managing to recompose myself, I clear my throat.

"Hi. You wanna come to Les Misérables?" I ask with a playful glint in my eyes. I shoot Helena a quick glance, and her jaw is practically on the floor.

A smile tugs at the corners of Theo's lips.

"Sounds like a plan. Count me in."

"Perfect, see you tonight, then," I say, flashing him my best smile.

My heart almost leaps out of my chest when he gives me an irresistible smirk before walking away. The group stares at me in disbelief, their eyes wide with shock. Even Helena, who already knew about our 'relationship' is utterly astounded.

"Wait, what just happened?" Beth whispers.

Helena bites her lip to prevent a smile, trying to contain her joy.

"How did you manage to convince a *jock* to attend the school production?" Mason asks in disbelief.

Their reactions make me laugh, hoping it will distract them from Mayor Glenn, even if it's just for a few seconds. I can't risk anyone finding out what happened that night, not only because of Theo, but because I was also somewhat involved.

"Guys, it's nothing. Please be chill," I say, feeling a little uneasy.

"That was *not* nothing," Beth insists, raising a suspicious brow. "Something's definitely going on between you two."

"Guys, just because I invited him to Les Mis doesn't mean we're dating," I say, shooting Helena a knowing look.

It's one thing to almost get caught and make up stories about my connection with Theo, but becoming the central gossip at school is a different story altogether.

Helena and Beth exchange a glance, both pursing their lips. The awkwardness is suddenly interrupted by the bell's ring, and I let out a sigh of relief. The chaotic lunchtime rush begins as students scatter from the tables, and I seize the opportunity to slip away from the group's curious gazes. Gathering my things, I make my way to the next class, but Helena's voice stops me.

"Cora!" she calls out, causing me to turn on my heels. "See you at seven," she declares, a broad grin stretching across her face. I smile back, offering her a wave before exiting the hall.

•••••

As I leave the school building, the chaotic energy from this morning about the upcoming elections has escalated even further. The air is thick with tension, and the hallway is full of angry whispers and frustrated faces. I had expected people to move on by now, but Mayor Glenn's death seems to have had a stronger impact on the students than I imagined. The idea of people defending him stirs anger within me, and I wish I could shout about all his sinister acts. However, I know I can't, and even if I did, they wouldn't believe me.

The weight of the secret about Mayor Glenn and the forest fire rests heavily on my shoulders, and I'm unsure how difficult it will be to keep. Unlike Damon's death, there hasn't been a public announcement from the sheriff about Glenn, which I find suspicious. Maybe Theo was right, and there's more to the story that we don't know.

A growing unease settles in my chest as I walk home. The darkness outside intensifies, casting eerie shadows on the streets. The farther I get from the school building, the quieter my surroundings become, sending a shiver down my spine.

A sudden, bone-chilling thought strikes me. What if the suited men who killed Damon were rogues? Was Damon a clairvoyant? No, it's impossible. Damon Martin is incapable of keeping a secret, especially one as life changing as that.

The questions swirl in my head, but they are suddenly interrupted by the buzzing of my phone.

> **chris** *now*
> *heyy wassup? I was wondering
> if you wanted to hang out
> tonight.*

Shit. Perhaps having dinner with him last night was a mistake; he might have gotten the wrong idea about us. Now that things are sort of happening with Theo, it wouldn't be wise to spend time with Chris again. Yet, I can't shake the sympathy I feel for him. Maybe all he needs is a friend right now.

I chew on my lip, thinking of a reply that won't be like shooting myself in the foot.

me
sorry, I can't. I have les mis tonight.

chris
since when do you like drama?

me
I'm going for matt. he's worked really hard on this play..

chris
k. at what time is it? I can drive you there

me
don't worry, it's fine see you at school :)

I approach my house, a tinge of guilt settling within me for turning Chris down. I debate whether I made the right choice, wondering if being there for him is more important than avoiding potential complications. I unlock the door with a sigh, realising I only have a couple of hours until the play.

I head to my room, the anticipation building as I choose an outfit for the night. Tonight marks Theo and I's first appearance together, and I want it to be somewhat memorable—despite the chaos surrounding us. I settle on a stylish yet casual ensemble, a tennis skirt and a sweater, hoping to strike the right balance between laid-back and put-together.

As I get dressed, I can't help but feel a mixture of excitement and nervousness. I find comfort in the fact that I'm in a better place than I was two weeks ago, grappling with my diagnosis and adjusting to the medication. After struggling to accept being a clairvoyant, I've finally come to terms with it. I know there's a lot to learn, but there's a sense of empowerment in understanding my potential.

All I need to do is keep it a secret and prevent anyone from finding out about the forest fire.

•••••

I head downstairs and find my dad on the couch, watching TV. The soft glow of the screen illuminates his face, and I hesitate at the bottom of the stairs. I've been avoiding him since the forest fire, too scared to face him. Keeping my clairvoyance a secret becomes even more challenging when it comes to my dad. We've never been particularly close but hiding something as significant as this is difficult to manage.

"Hey, Cora. How was school?" he asks, glancing at me over his shoulder.

"It was... eventful," I reply with a subtle smile, not wanting to delve into the details. I'm too scared to ask him if he heard about Glenn and the elections. "I've got the school play tonight. Is it okay if I head out?"

Dad looks at me with understanding. He must be relieved that I've made friends this year.

"Of course, sweetheart. Just be safe, okay?" he says, concern etched in his eyes.

"Will do, Dad," I assure him, grabbing my coat and heading towards the door.

The cold winter evening welcomes me as I step outside. The air is crisp, and a gentle breeze prompts me to pull my coat tighter around myself. The streets are quiet, and the only sound resonating is the rhythmic clicking of my boots against the asphalt. I take out my phone to text Theo, letting him know I'm on my way.

> **theo**
> *are you sure you don't want me to pick you up?*
>
> **me**
> *no it's fine! Be there in 10*
>
> **theo**
> *okay, see you soon*

I continue my walk, the faint glow of streetlights casting elongated shadows on the pavement. Suddenly, I hear rapid footsteps behind me, making my blood run cold. Before I can react, a strong hand clamps over my mouth, stifling any potential cry for help. Panic grips me as a black bag is forcefully pulled over my head, plunging me into an abyss of total darkness. Desperation fills me as I attempt to scream, but my efforts are futile. A cold, metallic sensation presses against my throat, sending shivers down my spine.

In the suffocating blackness, a chilling voice warns, "Stay silent, or the plot takes an unexpected turn."

My feeble attempts of fighting back come to a halt as a sharp needle pierces my skin.

26

My eyes snap open, clarity returning to my vision. A surge of intense panic grips me when I realise I'm locked in an unfamiliar dark basement. An involuntary scream escapes me, only to be cruelly stifled by the duct tape tightly covering my mouth. The musty stench of mould fills my nostrils, and the dryness of my throat forces a cough. My wrists ache, bound behind my back with a coarse rope that ties me to a chair. Muffled sobs escape me as a sense of vertigo overwhelms me while I take in the grim surroundings.

Dozens of large cardboard boxes surround me, creating a claustrophobic atmosphere, while a horrifying knife display looms behind me, sending a sense of dread that tightens my throat. Feeble rays of light seep through a minuscule window on the distant wall, its distance unreachable. I muster all my strength to loosen the rope around my wrists, but it's futile. The coarse fibres bite into my skin, leaving me helpless.

Where the hell am I?

Most importantly, how long have I been here?

I frantically scan the room, my eyes darting around in search of any potential means of escape. The dim light filtering through the small window creates eerie shadows, adding to the overall sense of dread. The tight bindings on my wrists and the oppressive atmosphere amplify the fear that courses through my veins. Desperation grips me as I realise the dire situation I'm in.

The sudden creak of a door opening startles me, and two figures wearing sheep masks and a grey suits step into the dimly lit room. My heart races, and I can feel beads of sweat forming on my forehead. Trapped, I can only watch in terror as they approach, the grotesque masks concealing any hint of emotion. My attempts to speak are futile, the tape over my mouth muffling my cries.

I instinctively start to wriggle in the chair, desperate to escape the impending danger. However, my attempts are abruptly halted as the first man clamps a taser against my neck. The surge of electricity courses through me, every muscle contracting in agonising pain. I gasp for a breath as the attacker retreats, the numbing current of electricity lingering on my skin.

"You've been running for way too long, Cora," one of them snarls in a robotic tone, his voice altered by a machine. With a threatening gesture, he waves the sharp blade in front of my eyes, prompting an asphyxiated yelp to escape my lips.

The chilling stare of the second hitman sends waves of terror down my spine, his cobalt eyes radiating malevolence behind the mask.

"You have to cooperate with us now," the other hisses.

"We can do this the easy way, or the hard way," Knife man threatens.

Fear coils in my stomach, icy tendrils crawling up my spine as he menacingly hovers the blade between my eyes. The air is thick with my muffled screams, beads of anxious sweat dampening my face.

Just when I think he's about to cut me, Knife man briskly pulls away, leaving me in a state of breathless anticipation and heightened fear. Suddenly, a worn-out ragdoll is thrusted into my face, its eerie, beady black eyes sending a shiver down my spine.

"Tell us what you see, Cora. Tell us!" the second man commands, his voice demanding obedience.

My heart beats uncontrollably as I stare at the doll in horror, feeling intimidated by their twisted game. My terror intensifies as Knife man reaches for my wrists, but shock sets in when I suddenly feel them go free. Confusion kicks in as the doll is forced into my trembling hands, the tension thickening in the air.

"What do you see, Cora?" the second man demands.

With a brisk movement, the tape is ripped from my mouth, causing me to gasp for air. Fear courses through my veins as I lock eyes with the doll, its lifeless gaze piercing into my soul.

"I-I see... a doll," I stammer, my voice shaky.

The second man growls, his anger palpable even through the mask.

"Look inside the doll!" he shouts, making me flinch.

I gulp nervously, my hands trembling as I examine the worn-out doll. Then, the realisation dawns on me. He wants me to use my abilities.

Desperately focusing on the doll, I recall what Theo had taught me only a few days ago. With a trembling breath, I try to focus on the image of the doll before closing my eyes, but the image refuses to take shape. The sudden jolt of the taser sends shockwaves through my body, a primal scream tearing from my throat. As the electric current courses through me, I convulse in the chair, every muscle tensing and releasing uncontrollably.

"What do you see?!" Knife man's shout pierces the air, reverberating through the room.

"If you do not cooperate, you will be dead. We cannot let impure beings roam the Earth," the second man growls menacingly, the anger palpable even through the twisted sheep mask.

The air is charged with tension as they wait for a response, the relentless hum of the taser still lingering in the room. My breaths are ragged as the doll is shoved into my face once again, an overwhelming horror kicking in.

If I can't give them what they want, I will die. It has to work.

Clutching the worn-out doll, a cold and eerie sensation seeps through my body, fear intensifying with each passing second. I close my eyes, attempting to control my panicked breaths while squeezing the doll with all my strength.

Come on, Cora, you can do this.

I desperately try to visualise the doll in my mind—the unorganised, straw-like hair, the beady eyes, and rosy lips. Within seconds, the familiar ice-cold sensation rushes through me, sending shivers down my spine and creating goosebumps on my skin. An adrenaline rush takes over as a vivid scene begins to materialise before my eyes, the overwhelming intensity propelling me backward into my seat.

The vivid scene unfolds in my mind—a well-lit living room adorned with luxurious furniture. An unfamiliar woman sobs on the man's shoulder while he reads a letter, his eyes mirroring the despair etched on his wife's face. A few words are scrawled on the letter, pricking the hair on my skin.

Follow the instructions if you want your daughter back.

Dread tightens in my stomach when the scene takes a turn for the worst. The man and woman dangle from a noose, their hands entwined, suspended in a macabre dance as their lifeless bodies sway back and forth.

My eyes snap open, and a gasp escapes my lips. The familiar ice-cold sensation grips me, making my teeth chatter as I desperately gasp for air. Warmth slowly seeps back into my body with each measured breath, yet a chilling reality persists—the cold, ruthless edge of a knife pressed menacingly against my throat.

The hitman's hiss pierces the air, his grip on the knife tightening.

"What did you see?" he demands. The hitman fixes his gaze on me, an unwavering intensity that sends my heart into a frenzied race.

"A-A man and a woman," I stammer. "Th-they hung themselves. They read a letter." Each word escapes my lips with a tremor, the gravity of the vision still haunting me.

The masked men share a fleeting glance, and then one of them ruthlessly stomps on my foot. A scream erupts from my lungs as excruciating pain crawls its way up my leg.

"Were they dead?" Knife man growls, his voice demanding answers.

Physically unable to speak, the mixture of pain and oxygen deprivation create a nauseating concoction within me. With every ounce of remaining energy, I muster a weak nod, aware that another jolt from the taser could kill me. In one swift motion, they secure my wrists once more with the unforgiving grip of coarse rope, its fibres gnawing at my flesh.

A desperate cry escapes my lips.

"Please, you don't have to do this," I beg, the vulnerability in my tone palpable. "What do you want from me?"

Cruelly silenced by the reapplication of duct tape, my chair is violently kicked against the wall, the impact sending shockwaves through my battered body. As the men vanish into the shadows, I gasp for air, my ribs aching from the relentless abuse. In this dark and hostile reality, the truth becomes painfully clear.

I've been captured by the rogues.

27

The torture is relentless.

In just two days, the rogues have given me a dozen objects to peer into—watches, earrings, shoestrings, even a piece of fingernail. Insomnia and malnourishment erode my capacity to obey their orders, yet neither of them has a glint of mercy towards me. Just as Theo warned, the rogues' condition is straightforward: I must either cave in and work for them, or they will end my life. Constant beatings and verbal assaults have tainted my skin with bruises and scars, and any lingering hope of escape has been obliterated. If someone were to see my face now, it would probably cause screams of terror.

The door creaks open, but my swollen eyelids distort my vision, rendering it impossible to tell who enters the room. Approaching footsteps echo through the space, yet the unbearable pain in my neck hinders me from lifting my gaze. A plastic cup is pressed against my lips, forcing me to drink a small amount of water—barely enough to sustain life. The rogue leaves the room with a resounding slam, the darkness engulfing me once again.

I've been trying to figure out where I am for days, but it's futile. The unsettling truth lingers—I could be held hostage anywhere, and the likelihood of anyone finding me grows dimmer with each passing moment.

The basement is cloaked in suffocating darkness, the air dense with a damp chill. The musty scent of rusty metal and sewage fills the space, triggering waves of nausea with each breath. Dim moonlight filters through the narrow window, casting feeble shadows on the cold concrete floor.

My mental stability crumbles with each passing hour, haunted by the sheep-masked men and the regret of not having told my dad the truth. The last thing he heard from me was that I was on my way to Les Misérables. He must be worried sick. I never said goodbye to him, nor expressed how much I love him. I never said how grateful I am for befriending Hel, Beth, and the others this year. But most of all, I regret not getting into Theo's car that night. The thought of him makes my heart ache, a mix of emotions swirling in my chest.

When I first met him that night at Mulkiwa Park, I never expected us to become so close, let alone share such a secret. It felt fated, the way our friendship evolved into something more, and the coincidence that my vision of the forest fire led to me discovering who I truly am.

I doubted him on the night of the forest fire, thinking he was playing a prank on me. Now, I realise how right he was. The rogues are far worse than I imagined, and I should have believed him. I never expressed my gratitude for having him by my side when I found out I was clairvoyant, nor how I feel about him.

The heart-wrenching realisation sets in, one that dictates my grim fate. I refuse to take innocent lives, especially those who are like me.

Tears well up in my eyes, knowing that it's only a matter of time before the rogues end my life.

My eyelids feel heavy from constant sleep deprivation, and my body is drained of energy. After the long battle to stay awake, the burden of physical and mental exhaustion becomes too much for me to bear. Within minutes, I surrender to exhaustion.

•••••

A sudden loud bang jolts me awake, causing goose bumps to ripple across my skin. My eyes dart towards the direction of the sound, my heart racing in my chest as I brace for the worst. In the suffocating darkness, the bone-chilling chilling realisation sinks in—they're going to kill me.

Suddenly, the door swings open with a forceful kick, its echo reverberating through the basement. A crack of light spills into the darkness, and my swollen eyes strain to adjust. As the silhouette becomes clearer, utter disbelief washes over me. For a second, I think I might be hallucinating, but when his ocean blue eyes meet mine, the reality sinks in—it's really him.

It's Theo.

"Come on, we don't have much time," he urgently says, rushing towards me.

Panic tightens its grip on my chest, fuelled by a mix of fear and anticipation. His eyes are filled with panic as he frantically unties the rope around my wrists and rips the duct tape from my lips. The sudden freedom makes me gasp, but my head still swirls with dizziness. The air fills with furious shouts and heavy stomping, instantly turning my blood to ice. They're coming.

With a quick and purposeful kick, Theo sends several boxes toward the door, securely creating a barricade. In a fleeting second, his panic-filled eyes lock with mine before he darts towards the narrow basement window. A moment of silence hangs in the air before he smashes it with his bare fist, and I shriek in horror when I notice the blood dripping from it. Pain is etched on his face as he rushes over, encircling me with his arm before helping me get up.

The door suddenly echoes with a series of violent bangs, making us gasp in terror. The imminent threat becomes palpable—it's only a matter of seconds before they break in

"Let's go!" Theo urges, ushering me toward the window.

He moves with urgency, gripping my waist and lifting me towards the windowpane. Adrenaline courses through me as I pull myself out, but the razor-edged shards of broken glass ruthlessly carve into my thigh. An agonised sob escapes my lips, tears distorting my vision. As I crash onto the damp grass outside, a sudden realisation jolts through me—I'm stranded in the heart of a forest, but it's not Evergreen.

Despite the burning pain in my thigh, I muster the strength to help Theo through the window. The tension thickens as he lands on the grass, and just then, a gunshot shatters the air.

Fear instantly grips my chest, propelling us into a sprint. We navigate through the dense forest, driven by adrenaline and the grim realisation that danger trails close behind. The only audible sounds are our heavy breaths and heartbeats, and every rustle of leaves heightens the sense of imminent threat.

Breathing heavily, we come to a halt as the echoes of the rogues' footsteps and yelling fade into the night. The stillness of the forest surrounds us, a soft glow of the moon seeping through the trees. Theo's eyes lock onto mine as we both struggle to catch our breath, panic still evident in our gazes.

"Cora, are you okay?" Theo asks, his voice filled with concern.

In an instant, my energy plummets, and the excruciating pain on my thigh returns. I lift my skirt with trembling hands, stifling a shriek at the sight of the cut.

"Shit," I exclaim, a wave of dizziness washing over me. Panic flashes across Theo's face before he quickly wraps an arm around me, supporting my weakened stance.

"Babe, it's okay. You'll be okay. I promise," he soothingly whispers into my hair.

In that moment, a surge of dizziness overwhelms me, and my body abruptly crumples to the floor.

28

My eyes flutter open, and I gradually become aware of my surroundings as consciousness returns. I take in the sterile scent of the hospital room, realising I'm surrounded by white walls and the rhythmic beep of a heart monitor. I glance at the table next to my bed, adorned with get-well-soon cards and balloons, which makes me wonder how long I have been here.

The room seems to spin as I sit up, and an immediate sharp pain creeps up my spine. I wince, gently touching the wounds on my back. A wave of unsettling memories flashes before my eyes, but in that moment, I notice my dad asleep in one of the chairs.

"Dad?" I croak, making his eyes to snap open. Relief instantly brightens his face, and tears of gratitude well up in my eyes as he envelops me in a warm, tight embrace. His soft cries against my hair shatter my heart into a billion pieces, and guilt settles in the pit of my stomach.

"I'm so glad you're okay," he sniffles, his teary gaze meeting mine. "Where on earth have you been?"

"I'm sorry," I stammer, my voice raspy from crying. My heart clenches with the realisation that I can never tell him the truth—about my clairvoyance, about Theo, about the rogues. I'm forced to keep him in the dark for the rest of my life to protect him.

My dad buries his head in his hands, releasing an anxious sigh.

"I was worried sick. The police have been searching everywhere for you," he says. He looks into my eyes once more, but this time, his expression is stern. "Did Chris do this to you?"

I am momentarily taken aback by his question. I never thought something like that would cross my dad's mind. I stammer, struggling to find the right words.

"No, Dad. Chris didn't do this to me. I went hiking," I lie, but the trembling in my voice makes it difficult to believe. Lying my way out of this is going to be a challenge.

A flash of frustration appears on my dad's face as he crosses his arms over his chest.

"Hiking? You were on your way to the school play."

Damn it, I really didn't think this through.

I shake my head, anxiety intensifying the pounding in my chest.

"Dad—"

"Someone did this to you. I don't know if you got mugged or something else, but you need to tell me," he insists, narrowing his eyes.

In that moment, the image of the basement resurfaces. The putrid scent of sewage is almost palpable, and the ghostly sensation of the tight rope around my wrists lingers. Tears start to cloud my sight, and a knot forms in my throat.

My dad's expression suddenly softens, as if he's realised he's pushed too hard. He sighs, reaching for my hand.

"I'm sorry, sweetheart. You don't have to tell me if you're not ready," he murmurs, pain evident in his voice. He sighs once more, gazing down at our intertwined hands. "I'm terrible at this, I know. If your mom were here, she'd know what to say.

My heart stings at the mention of her, feeling an overwhelming sense of guilt for making him feel this way.

"I'll let the doctor know you're awake," he mumbles before rising from his seat.

He leaves the room, and I'm left alone with the weight of unspoken words hanging in the air. I glance around, trying to gather my thoughts and make sense of the fragments of memories that haunt me. As minutes pass, anxiety builds within me, wondering what questions the doctor might have and how much I'm willing to reveal.

Releasing a slow, measured exhale, I carefully sit up to avoid a head rush. My hand glides down my exposed back, and I flinch when my fingers encounter the stitches on my skin.

"Fuck," I whisper, but my curse is cut off by the creak of the opening door.

The doctor enters, an Asian man in his mid 30s, wearing a pristine white coat that drapes over his frame. His jet-black hair is neatly combed, and a pair of glasses rest on the bridge of his nose. He greets me with a warm smile.

"Good to see you awake, Miss Danvers. My name is Dr Li. How are you feeling?"

"I'm holding up. When can I go home?" I ask, my voice somewhat hoarse.

"You'll be staying here overnight. We don't have any updates as of now," he explains.

I nod, feeling a bit uneasy. Staying overnight at the hospital is unfamiliar territory for me but considering the stitches on my back, it might be a wise decision.

Dr Li raises a brow, flipping through my patient report.

"Can you provide more details about what happened, Miss Danvers?"

Dr Li's gaze remains focused on me, awaiting an explanation. I take a deep breath, aware that I need to craft a more credible story than the one I told my dad.

"It's a bit complicated," I begin cautiously. "I was out for a walk, and I must have taken a wrong turn. I ended up in a secluded area where I tripped and fell, injuring my back."

Dr Li raises an eyebrow, his expression indicating a mix of scepticism and understanding.

"A secluded area? That sounds unusual. Were there any witnesses or specific details you remember?"

I hesitate, choosing my words carefully.

"It was a less-travelled path, and unfortunately, no one was around. It happened so quickly, and I found myself here."

He nods, jotting down notes on his clipboard.

"Accidents can happen unexpectedly. We'll continue to monitor your condition, and if you recall any additional details, please don't hesitate to share."

I nod, anxiously chewing my lip.

"I've just informed your father about the procedure for looking after the wounds. We'll remove the stitches on your back in two weeks. For the bruising, I've prescribed you a cream," he adds.

"Thank you," I respond politely.

Dr Li heads for the door, and as he reaches it, he turns to meet my gaze.

"You have a visitor," he informs me before walking away.

As Theo and I lock eyes, an overwhelming sense of relief floods the room. The tension that had gripped the atmosphere loosens its hold, replaced by almost tangible wave of comfort. If I weren't connected to the medical machines, I would leap into his arms right now.

"Cora," he says breathlessly, cutting the distance between us. "Thank God you're okay."

He wraps me in a tight hug, prompting tears of joy to well up in my eyes. I exhale in relief, immersing myself in the familiar scent of his cologne. Our eyes connect as I gently cradle his face, tracing my finger against his bottom lip. The intensity of his azure gaze deepens, and I find myself unable to resist kissing him. His touch is tender on my skin as he reciprocates, careful and considerate of the wounds on my body.

For a fleeting moment, the memory of the rogues kidnapping me and the brutal assault fades away. It's just Theo and me our bodies longing for each other as we kiss on my hospital bed.

As we draw back, we gaze breathlessly at each other, the profound connection between us still palpable.

"What happened? How did I get here?" I stammer, nervously biting my lip. All I can remember is that he found me and saved my life from the evil clutches of the rogues.

He gently tucks a couple of strands of my hair behind my ear, his worried eyes studying me intently.

"After you passed out, I drove you to the hospital. Luckily, we were only a few miles away from Barren. I told them I found you in Evergreen, but I didn't know what had happened," he explains.

I breathe a sigh of relief, relieved that Theo's story somewhat matches what I told Dr Li.

"I just can't believe you're here," I whisper, our lips still just inches away from each other.

In that moment, the memory of the rogues' abuse resurfaces in my mind, sending a cold shudder down my spine. I genuinely believed I was as good as dead—that nobody would find me. I suddenly realise that being clairvoyant has its power, but it also comes with a price.

Theo brings me back from my thoughts with a tender touch on my face, his eyes reflecting concern.

"I did everything I could to find you. I waited outside school for almost an hour, but you never showed up. I went to your house to check on you and found your dad, and he had no idea where you were either. We tried calling you, but your phone was off. We went to the police station together, and I just had this horrible gut feeling…"

I bite my lip, feeling guilty for putting both my dad and Theo through this. They must have been so worried about me.

Theo lets out a sigh before adding, "Then I noticed Chris' car parked outside the station, and he seemed to be talking to someone on the phone-"

"Wait. What does Chris have to do with this?"

He rubs his chin in hesitation, lowering his gaze.

"I wanted to tell you, but I wasn't sure," he mutters in a low voice. His words send an unsettling sensation down my spine.

"Tell me what?" I croak, feeling my throat tighten. Our eyes lock, the seriousness of his expression causing my heart to race.

"Chris is your watcher."

"What? What does that even mean?" I exclaim, a sudden wave of uneasiness washing over me.

"Every clairvoyant in the rogues' system has one. They assign someone to observe the clairvoyant so that when they become aware of their abilities, which is what we call *perceptive,* they can manipulate them into joining the rogues."

Theo's words hang heavily in the air, an unnerving feeling settling in the pit of my stomach. The idea that Chris, my ex-boyfriend, could be involved with the rogues throws me into a whirlwind of disbelief and fear. I shake my head repeatedly, struggling to accept what Theo has just revealed.

"There's no way," I stammer, my voice catching in my throat. Chris can't be a part of the rogues. It's impossible.

Theo's expression remains serious, his gaze unwavering.

"It's true, Cora. The second he got back from tour, I knew he was your watcher. Mayor Glenn's death brought him back," he explains.

His words send shockwaves through me, and I continue to shake my head, my heart racing at a thousand beats per minute.

"Stop," I sob, tears welling up in my eyes. "Chris came back because his mom died."

Theo gives me a sullen glance, sighing.

"That has to be a lie," he states.

"Why would he lie about his mom dying?" I exclaim defensively, the weight of the situation pressing on my shoulders. Chris and I shared almost a year together, and I feel like I know him better than anyone else. The thought that he could lie about his mom's death, especially when she was the only family he had left, is inconceivable.

He runs a hand through his hair, frustration evident in his eyes.

"I don't know, Cora. Maybe it was a cover. The rogues are cunning, and they know how to manipulate situations."

The weight in his voice makes me ponder the extent of their manipulation. I bite my lip, the terrorising flashbacks from the basement flooding my mind once again. If Theo hadn't found me, they would have beaten me to death. The realisation sends a shiver down my spine.

"Trust me on this. Now that you're *perceptive*, his job is to watch you at all times," he insists, his tone carrying seriousness and concern.

In that instant, a specific memory resurfaces—the one where I woke up with three words on my mind.

He's a watcher.

At that time, I didn't understand what it meant, but the word now feels hauntingly familiar. The pieces start to connect, and a chilling realisation creeps into my bones.

I shoot Theo a panicked glance, my chest tightening.

"That's why Chris wanted to see me that night."

Theo's eyes widen, a mix of surprise and anger crossing his face.

"What?"

"He said he'd drive me to Les Mis. I-I said no. Even if we're not together, I didn't want to ruin things between us, Theo." My words tumble out, hurried, and filled with desperation, hoping he'll believe me. The last thing I want is for him to lose trust in me, especially if it's because of Chris.

Theo sighs, rubbing his temples as he processes the information. The room becomes heavy with the weight of the revelation, and for a moment, silence engulfs us. He finally breaks the silence, his voice carrying a mix of concern and frustration.

"I need you to understand that Chris is not who you think he is. If he's a part of the rogues, he's dangerous, and we need to figure out how to deal with this. Your safety is the priority."

His words hang in the air, and I'm left grappling with the unsettling truth that someone I once trusted may have been part of a sinister plan. The room suddenly feels suffocating, causing dizziness to wash over me.

In an instant, everything clicks into place. Chris had witnessed my blackouts numerous times, yet he never labelled me as crazy. He never freaked out whenever I lost track of time. But most of all, when I blacked out and woke up in Jersey City, he knew exactly where I was.

"He's known about me his entire life," I choke out, the weight of the revelation settling heavily on my shoulders.

Theo bites his lip, a glimmer of empathy in his eyes.

"That's what watchers do. They make sure that when you're *perceptive*, that you have no one else to turn to but the rogues."

My eyes well up with tears, and a lump forms in my throat. I had placed complete trust in Chris from the start. I had trusted him about so many personal aspects of my life, even sharing the painful details of my mom's death. The sting of the betrayal tightens my chest, leaving me feeling vulnerable and exposed.

"I… I thought I knew him. I really thought he was a good person, Theo," I mutter.

He sighs, offering comfort by placing his hand over mine.

"I'm really sorry, Cora. I really wanted to tell you."

We exchange a solemn glance, but our moment is cut short by a light knock on the door. Dr Li appears, poking his head into the room.

"I'm sorry Mr Rhodes, but Miss Danvers needs some rest," he says.

"I'm gonna be right outside, okay?" Theo assures, gently pecking my forehead. His delicate gesture flushes my cheeks, and I respond with a soft smile.

As Dr Li ushers Theo out, I am left alone with the haunting memories of the basement, the vivid scenes of the torture replaying in my mind. I take a deep breath, trying to shake off the lingering dread that clings to my senses.

The stitches on my back throb with a dull ache, a constant reminder of the rogues' relentless abuse. I shift uncomfortably, trying to find a more pain-free position on the hospital bed. As I lie there, the truth about Chris and the rogues settles in. The person who I once thought was the love of my life turned out to be a pawn in a sinister game. I feel betrayed, vulnerable, and a sense of isolation creeps over me.

I close my eyes, hoping it will drown out the angry yells of the rogues echoing in my mind.

29

"I'm afraid the situation is more serious than our initial assessments," Dr Li's words echo in a hollow, detached tone.

"That can't be. My daughter isn't in those circumstances," my dad chokes, his voice trembling.

"The medical results indicate otherwise. It is in her best interest, as well as yours, that we find a solution."

•••••

I wake up what feels like hours later, my eyes gradually opening to the hospital room's bright lights. The steady rhythm of the heart monitor fills my ears, and a sigh of relief escapes me as I spot Theo in the chair, scrolling through his phone. Our eyes meet, and I see a blend of relief and concern in his gaze.

"How long was I asleep?" I mumble, still a bit groggy.

"A couple of hours," he responds. "How are you feeling?"

I make an effort to sit up on the bed, but a sudden sharp pain shoots up my back, and I can't help but wince.

"I'm feeling a little bit better," I murmur, not wanting to cause any worry.

A soft smile graces his lips.

"I'm glad. Your dad went off to work, and I promised him I'd keep an eye on you."

I feel my cheeks instantly flush, a tinge of embarrassment colouring my face. For some reason, I can't picture Theo talking to my dad, and I find myself wondering if he thinks we're together.

"Thank you," I say with a shy smile.

He gazes at me, a hint of pain evident in his azure eyes.

"No need to thank me. He was so worried about you, and so was I," he admits, fiddling with his fingers.

Suddenly, a wave of anguish engulfs me, accompanied by a pang of guilt. I despise the fact that I've put Theo and my dad through all of this, especially considering it was partly my fault. I should have been aware that walking alone at night wasn't a safe choice.

"I'm sorry. I should have gotten in the car with you," I mutter, my lip quivering.

Shaking his head, Theo settles onto the bed. He gently holds my bruised hand, pressing a comforting kiss onto it. My tear-filled eyes meet his, the hollow pain stinging in my chest.

"Hey," he murmurs, sadness in his tone. "None of this is your fault."

I nod, wiping away a few tears. In that moment, Theo's phone buzzes in his pocket, catching me off guard. He sighs, casting me a worried glance before reaching for it. A wave of unease washes over me as I see his expression becoming increasingly concerned. Acting quickly, he grabs the TV remote and switches on the small TV in my room. As the screen flickers to life, my eyes widen in shock and disbelief. A photograph of a middle-aged couple appears, and I instantly recognise them.

"Reputable banker Hughes Allen and his wife Lindsey were found dead last night in their home in Newton, New Jersey. Their final thoughts were with their daughter, as indicated in their suicide letter: 'We only want to be with our daughter, whose mind is already with God'. Authorities confirm there was no evidence of foul play."

The reporter's words send a shiver down my spine, bringing back the haunting image of the couple hanging from the ceiling. My stomach churns with terror as a sudden realisation dawns upon me.

The Allen family. That's what the rogues forced me to see.

The rogues' motives become strikingly clear—they needed to make sure that the Allens were dead, and that's precisely why they needed me.

The question is, how were the Allens involved with the rogues?

The reporter adds, "The couple's only daughter has been at Alheim Hill Mental Hospital for the past ten years, and it is believed to have triggered their tragic demise."

A sequence of photographs depicting a raven-haired girl follows, and the anguish in her brown eyes creates a profound sense of unease within me. A suffocating sensation envelops me as if the air is being sucked out of the room. The vivid and disturbing flashbacks of the Allens swinging from a noose surge into my mind, forming goose bumps on my skin. My breaths become shallow, making it difficult to draw in air.

"Babe, are you okay?" Theo's voice interrupts my anxious thoughts. He gently gives my hand a squeeze, his eyes filled with worry.

I try to shake away the flashbacks, but it feels impossible. They've consumed me entirely. I release a deep sigh, my lip quivering as I muster the courage to tell him the truth.

"N-no," I stammer, my eyes filling with tears. "The rogues forced me to look into the Allens' belongings and... I saw that they hung themselves because of their daughter..."

A moment of silence hangs in the air as Theo's face turns incredibly pale. He swallows hard, but in an instant, a flicker of anger replaces his initial shock.

"Those bastards," he mutters through gritted teeth. He rises abruptly from the bed, clenching his jaw. "I can't let him get away with this."

A wave of dread crashes over me as he storms toward the door.

"Where are you going?" I ask, my heart racing in my chest.

He stops in his tracks, the intensity of his anger softening as his gaze meets mine.

"I'm going to find Chris, and I swear he will pay for doing this to you," he says, an unwavering determination in his tone.

"No, please don't! Let me talk to him. This has to be some kind of mistake. I'm certain he has no idea what he's gotten himself into," I plead, panic evident in my voice.

Theo's eyebrows furrow in disbelief.

"Talk to him? After what he's done?"

I take a deep breath, trying to steady myself. There must be some sort of explanation for all of this. Chris might work for the rogues, but there's a part of me that believes he would never intentionally harm me.

"I know it sounds crazy, but if there's a chance I can get through to him, make him stop... Maybe it doesn't have to be this way," I try to explain.

Theo rubs his temples in frustration, scepticism etched across his face.

"How can you trust him, after everything he's done, Cora?" There's a certain pain in his voice that tells me he doesn't appreciate me siding with Chris.

"I don't trust him, but I know him. There's a part of him that might still listen. I need to try."

A brief, tense silence lingers in the air before Theo sighs, a certain pain reflected in his eyes.

"You need to stay here and rest. You've been through too much already," he insists.

"I can't just sit here and do nothing," I argue, my eyes welling up with tears. Our gazes lock, and I can sense the pity and sympathy in his eyes. But then, he shakes his head.

"I'll sort this out, I promise."

"Theo!" I call out, but he's already stormed out of the room.

In that moment, the door swings open, and Dr Li walks in. His expression shifts from routine professionalism to concern as he notices the distress on my face.

"What's going on, Miss Danvers?" Dr Li asks, his eyes scanning the room for any signs of trouble.

"I need to get out," I insist urgently, the desperation evident in my voice.

"You need to stay here, Miss Danvers," he asserts, a glint of something more than concern in his eyes.

Ignoring his advice, I try to leave the room, but before I can take more than a step, Dr Li swiftly injects a sedative into my arm. As the drug takes effect, the world blurs, and my legs give way beneath me. The last thing I see before succumbing to unconsciousness is Dr Li's stern expression.

•••••

"I'm in complete shock, doctor."

"We can help her, but she requires clinical help. She is in a state of mania and she's not responding well to the medication."

"I just can't believe this… She was doing better…"

"We will take care of her, Mr Danvers. I will make sure of it."

•••••

I gradually wake up to the bitter taste of copper on my tongue, feeling unusually groggy. As I become aware of my surroundings, a wave of terror engulfs my fragile body. My bed is encircled by a team of nurses, their faces concealed by the shadows of the room. At the foot of my bed, Dr Li stands with a clipboard in his hands, a sinister look in his eyes.

"What's going on?" I stutter, instinctively sitting upright.

"Good morning, Miss Danvers. We're here to take care of you until you recover," a nurse says in a soothing tone.

"Recover from what?" I ask, furrowing my brows in confusion.

She removes the heart monitor and intravenous drip, her movements urgent and rushed. A horrifying realisation sinks deep into my bones. They're going to take me somewhere, and my instincts warn me that I won't like it. My throat tightens, and I nervously shift my gaze from one nurse to the next.

"N-No, you must be mistaken. I-I haven't done anything," I stammer, panic seeping into my voice.

"Don't worry Miss Danvers. Your father agreed that this is the best decision," another nurse reassures with a smile.

"What decision?" I exclaim, a cold chill running down my spine.

In that moment, the nurse seizes my arms, her artificial nails cutting into my flesh. A scream escapes me as panic takes hold, and I desperately try to break free from her grip. My blood turns to ice when the other nurse hands her a syringe.

"Someone help me! Please don't hurt me!"

I make a frantic attempt to squirm out of their grasp as the needle inches towards my arm, but my body is too weak to put up a fight.

"Take her belongings," Dr Li orders.

"Please! I am not-"

Without warning, the needle pierces the flesh of my arm, its pinching sensation draining the colour from my cheeks. The room slowly becomes hazy, my cries growing softer before everything fades to black.

30

As I open my eyes, the first thing I notice is the white-tiled ceiling above me. Confusion grips me as I try to make sense of the unfamiliar surroundings, my head spinning with dizziness. My heart pounds in my chest, and panic courses through me as I realise I'm unable to move. Leather straps tightly bind me to the bed, their coarseness digging into my wrists. I frantically glance around the room, a sense of dread washing over me as I take in my surroundings.

I find myself trapped within a cell, its walls composed of dark green brick, covered in thick layers of grime. The air is heavy with the sickening stench of sewage, making my stomach churn uncomfortably. Behind my rusting headboard lies a grimy toilet—and nothing else.

"Theo?" I call out, my voice shaky with fear.

There's no response, just the eerie silence of the sterile room. Dread settles in the pit of my stomach as I realise I'm alone, trapped in this nightmare with no idea how I got here or where Theo might be.

With trembling hands and uneven breaths, I try wriggling out of the harness, the bed screeching in protest. I slump back onto the bed with a frustrated exhale, realising that my efforts are futile.

"Help!" I scream at the top of my lungs. "Somebody help!

My desperate cries bounce off the hollow walls, but deep down, I know they won't be heard. An inevitable wave of dread washes over me as the realisation sinks in. Once again, the rogues have captured me.

I fight against the restraints, but they remain firm, slicing into my skin and sending waves of pain rippling through my body. Cold sweat forms on my neck as I come to the realisation that there's no way to break free.

Tears well up in my eyes, my chest tightening with anguish. The last thing I recall is the nurses injecting me with a tranquiliser in my hospital room. But a haunting question lingers in my mind: Where is Theo? If the rogues did something to him, I swear to God...

Suddenly, the door to my cell creaks open, immediately putting me on high alert. A woman in a medical uniform enters, her age marked by deep wrinkles as she stares at me with lifeless eyes.

"Where am I? What do you want from me?" I wail, my voice trembling as I struggle against the restraints. The nurse's eyes remain fixed on me, devoid of any emotion. With methodical calmness, she leans over and begins unfastening my handcuffs, ignoring my protests.

The next thing I know, I'm being dragged down a series of halls that seem to grow darker with each step. Fear tightens its grip on me as we navigate past the rows of patient rooms, their doors closed but the faint sounds of psychotic wails filtering through. The sight of unfamiliar medical equipment only adds to my growing unease.

Finally, we arrive at a large room with rows of chairs and a cafeteria stall. The fluorescent lights overhead cast harsh shadows, giving the space an eerie atmosphere. My attention is immediately drawn to the patients scattered throughout the room, each engaged in their own repetitive and unsettling gestures. A shiver runs down my spine as the realisation sinks in—I'm in a psychiatric hospital.

The nurse leads me to one of the coffee tables, urging me to take a seat. I seize the opportunity to glance out of a nearby window, but fear grips me when all I see are towering trees, stretching endlessly into the distance.

My eyes anxiously scan the room, a knot tightening in my throat as I absorb the unsettling scene. A man moves his head in a spasmodic manner, while another woman is maniacally chewing on her arm. Across the room, another patient rocks back and forth in her seat, lost in her own world of distress.

This is what hell looks like—and I'm not even dead.

The nurse briskly elbows my chest, and I let out a cry of pain. I glance at her petrifying face, but her brittle voice diminishes any remaining courage I have left.

"Breakfast," she commands, pointing at a queue of people ahead of me that seem to resemble zombies.

Reluctantly, I join the queue, feeling a sense of dread creeping over me as I observe the vacant expressions and sluggish movements of those ahead. The atmosphere is heavy with despair, and I can't shake the feeling that I've been plunged into a nightmare from which there's no waking up. As I inch closer to the food counter, a wave of nausea washes over me, and I can't bring myself to take another step forward.

I watch my nurse as she joins her colleagues on the other side of the room. The nurses form a single file, their backs pressed against the wall—their eyes dark and menacing, resembling gargoyles perched in the shadows. I wonder if any of them know I'm a clairvoyant, and I wonder if they're rogues.

I'm suddenly jolted as something slams against my back, and a cold liquid trickles down my robe. I turn around to find a woman with a deep scowl on her face, holding a tray with a half-empty glass of orange juice. Despite my muttered apology, her deathly glare freezes me in place.

Maybe this is going to be much worse than I thought. Either I'll end up just like them, lost in madness, or one of them is going to kill me.

I grab one of the food trays just seconds before the lunch lady dumps stale oats on it. Grimacing, I quickly move out of the queue.

Is there any way of getting out of here? This must be illegal. They can't keep us here against our will.

I need to get out of here or I'll lose my mind. These people will drain my sanity. I sink back into the chair I was almost forced to sit on, on the verge of tears. Is this what all of this is about? Do the rogues want me to go insane here?

My thoughts are abruptly interrupted by a loud rattle. An elderly nurse stands before me, holding a plastic cup in her trembling hands.

"Cora Danvers. Your medication," she orders, extending the cup to me. Inside are two large pills—one red and one orange. I stare at her in utter confusion.

"What's the medication for?" I ask, my voice barely audible. The nurse presses her lips into a thin line, pushing the cup closer to me.

"You've got the wrong person. I'm not ill," I plead, shaking my head. The nurse remains stoic, forcing the cup into my hands with a lifeless expression.

"Take your medication, Miss Danvers, or you'll be taken into a closed unit," the nurse warns sternly.

"Who gave you the right-" I begin to yell, but the nurse grabs my chin. I choke as she forces the pills down my throat, my coughs violent and uncontrollable. With an icy glare, I watch as the nurse walks away.

Feeling a mix of anger and frustration boiling within me, I slump back into the chair, my mind racing with questions and uncertainties.

What kind of place is this? Why am I being treated like a patient? And where on earth is Theo? As I sit there, surrounded by the eerie atmosphere of the psychiatric hospital, a sense of dread settles over me. It's clear that escaping this place won't be easy, but I refuse to give up hope. Somehow, someway, I'll find a way out of here and uncover the truth behind this nightmare.

A sudden idea pops into my mind: maybe my dad can get me out of here.

"Hey!" I yell at the nurses, who stare blankly into space as if under hypnosis. "I have the right to a phone call."

A nearby female patient lets out a witch-like cackle, startling me. I shoot her a glance, but immediately regret it. Her glass eye, too large for her eyelid, stares back at me with an eerie intensity.

"They don't care about none of that, princess," the woman says, her tone filled with mockery.

I gulp, shrinking back into my seat. As the pills take effect, a drowsy haze envelops me. My eyelids grow heavy, and my thoughts become fuzzy. It feels like a thick fog is clouding my mind. I fight to stay awake, but the urge to sleep becomes almost overwhelming. I almost think I'm dreaming when a male nurse escorts a group of male patients into the hall.

With Theo among them.

I stare at him in disbelief, a whirlwind of thoughts flooding my mind. He's okay. How did he get here? How did the rogues find him?

My heart tightens as I notice the bruises on his collarbone, creeping up from beneath his patient robe. His eyes seem vacant and lifeless, with dark bags shadowing them. He doesn't notice me until I call out his name, his reaction slowed by the drugs.

"Thank God you're here," he says, his voice slightly slurred.

We embrace instinctively, finding solace in each other's arms as a sense of relief washes over us.

"No contact!" a nurse snarls at us, abruptly interrupting our moment. As we reluctantly pull away from each other, Theo's worried gaze meets mine

"We need to find a way out of here," he whispers urgently. "But first, we need to figure out what they've done to us."

I nod, my mind racing with a mix of fear and determination.

"Agreed," I mutter.

"You have no idea how worried I was. I thought you were dead," he mumbles, his eyes filled with concern.

"I was terrified, too. How did you end up here? What happened?" I whisper, my eyes brimming with tears.

"I was heading to find Chris, but then the wheel jammed on the highway. Everything went black. They said I was suicidal and crashed the car. You know I'm not. I swear I lost control of the car—I don't know how," he explains, his words rushed and tense.

I'm left momentarily speechless, struggling to process his words. The rogues must have been behind that. They must have discovered he's a clairvoyant when he came to visit me at the hospital. Shit. This is all my fault.

My lip quivers, tears clouding my vision.

"I'm so sorry, Theo. This is all my fault," I croak, my voice filled with guilt.

Theo's expression softens, and he reaches out to gently wipe away my tears.

"Hey, don't blame yourself," he says, his voice soothing. "We'll figure this out together, okay?"

I nod, feeling a glimmer of hope amidst the chaos. We may be trapped in this nightmare, but as long as we have each other, we can find a way out.

Theo glances at the nurse monitoring us before leaning in close to my ear.

"We need to plan an escape," he whispers urgently. "All I know is they can't legally detain us for more than 72 hours without a certified therapist's approval."

"If only the law mattered in this place," I mutter. "They forced me to take some medication."

Theo bites his lip anxiously.

"You're right. Me too," he admits, his voice laced with unease.

A shiver runs down my spine as I remember the grim conditions of my room, the scent of rust and sewage lingering in my memory.

"Something tells me the rogues run this place. No one in their right mind would keep a place like this open," I say.

Theo nods in agreement, his eyes filled with worry.

"It wouldn't surprise me. I don't want to stick around and find out what they want from us," he says, biting his lip. He scans the room, his gaze darting from one corner to another. "We need to plan an escape."

Suddenly, a piercing alarm fills the hall, startling us. The nurses swiftly move towards the patients, ushering them to form a line as breakfast comes to an end. Theo and I exchange a worried glance before our nurses forcefully separate us, pushing us in opposite directions.

Something tells me that the nightmare has only just begun.

•••••

As the nurse leads me down the hallways with a tight and uneasy grip on my arm, Theo's words continue to swirl in my head.

"We need to plan an escape."

But how? The nurses have us under constant surveillance, never letting us out of their sight. And with each dose of medication, my mind grows more sluggish. It's only a matter of time before I'm too numb to think, trapped in this hellhole indefinitely. I have to find a solution before it's too late.

My pulse quickens as I realise we're taking a different route, and my intuition warns me she's not leading me back to my room.

"Where are we going?" I ask, my voice trembling with fear.

Ignoring my question, the nurse leads me past patient cells and a communal bathroom until we reach a door labelled *'Staff.'* Anxiety grips me as she gently knocks, fearing what awaits inside.

Upon entering, I find myself in an office furnished with a metallic desk, cabinets, and chairs. One-sided windows overlook the common room, allowing for observation without being seen. Behind the desk sits a woman with sleek black hair and piercing green eyes, giving off an aura that suggests she's not particularly friendly.

The woman regards me with a cold stare, her lips pressed into a thin line. I swallow nervously, suddenly feeling like a trapped animal under her gaze.

"Sit," she commands, gesturing to a chair in front of her desk.

I obey, sinking into the seat with a sense of dread settling in the pit of my stomach. The nurse stands silently beside me, her presence only adding to my unease.

"What's your name?" the woman asks, her voice sharp and authoritative.

"Cora... Cora Danvers," I reply, my voice barely above a whisper.

She nods, jotting something down on a piece of paper in front of her.

"And do you know why you're here, Cora Danvers?"

I shake my head, unable to find my voice. The woman's cynical smirk leads me to a chilling realisation. I know what she is. She's one of them. Fear tightens my throat, making it difficult to breathe.

"I'm Aurelia Dibra, your appointed therapist during your stay at Alheim Hill."

My eyes widen as I hear the name of the institution. It only takes a couple of seconds for me to realise where I've heard it before.

The Allen family, I think to myself, suddenly making the connection. *Their daughter is a patient here.*

Aurelia continues, her smile strained as she taps the cap of her pen against her desk.

"You were brought here for observation," she states, her tone firm. "We need to ensure that you're not a danger to yourself or others."

"I'm not... I'm not a danger," I stammer, my hands trembling in my lap. If she's a rogue, I need to be extremely careful.

Aurelia raises an eyebrow, her expression sceptical.

"We'll see about that," she says, shooting me a look. "For now, you'll remain under close watch. Any attempts to escape or cause trouble will be met with consequences."

A sense of dread washes over me as Aurelia's menacing words sink in. Knowing the rogues and their ballpark, I am terrified of finding out what those consequences could be.

"Tell me about yourself," Aurelia prompts, a smirk playing at the corners of her lips.

I blink rapidly, unsure of how to respond without revealing the truth. I know that whatever I say will be used against me; that's what the rogues do. They want intel on me, anything that might give them the upper hand.

As Aurelia stares at me expectantly, a sense of unease settles in the pit of my stomach. I can't afford to slip up, not when the stakes are this high.

"I just want to go home," I finally murmur, crossing my arms over my chest defensively. It's a safe enough response, one that reveals nothing. But even as the words leave my lips, I can't shake the feeling that Aurelia sees right through me.

Her dry chuckle sends a chill down my spine, and I instinctively shrink back in my chair.

"You can't go home. It's not safe for someone like you," she mutters, her eyes glimmering with a hint of menace.

I gulp, weighing my options. This woman could be my only chance of escaping this hellhole, or she could be the reason for my demise.

"What do you want from me?" I ask, mustering a hint of courage.

Aurelia leans back in her chair, her smirk widening.

"Simple. Cooperation," she replies smoothly, her eyes locking onto mine with an unsettling intensity. "You follow the rules, answer my questions truthfully, and perhaps your stay here won't be as unpleasant as it could be."

Her words hang heavy in the air, and I swallow hard, weighing my options. Cooperation might buy me some time but trusting her feels like stepping into a lion's den blindfolded. Yet, going against her could be even worse. I need to tread carefully, play the game smartly if I want any chance of surviving.

"Tell me about your past," she says, flipping open a light-brown folder that I know contains information about me. Panic surges through my body at the realisation that she wants to know everything about me. I can't let her. I keep my gaze low while speaking.

"I don't remember much of it."

"Try to think, Miss Danvers," Aurelia presses, tapping her pen impatiently.

"I really don't remember," I insist, clenching my jaw.

"Don't play games with me, Cora. Tell me about your family," Aurelia demands, her tone growing sharper. The thought of Aurelia hurting my dad ignites a surge of anger within me.

"No," I reply firmly, meeting her gaze defiantly. Screw being polite; I won't let this woman control me.

As our eyes lock in an intense stare, the tension between Aurelia and me becomes palpable. Suddenly, she seizes a fistful of my hair, violently yanking me towards her. Pain shoots through my scalp as Aurelia's grip tightens, her nails digging into my skin. I struggle against her hold, but her strength overwhelms me.

"You will cooperate, Miss Danvers," she hisses, her face inches from mine. "Or you'll regret it."

Fear courses through me, but I refuse to let her see my vulnerability. With a defiant glare, I muster all the strength I have left and manage to push her away.

"I won't be intimidated by you," I retort, my voice trembling but resolute.

Aurelia's eyes narrow, a dangerous glint flickering within them.

"We'll see about that," she says bitterly as she releases her grip on my hair. With one final glare, Aurelia straightens herself, smoothing out her clothes before dismissing me with a sudden gesture.

"You may leave," she says, gesturing towards the door. "Your therapy sessions will be daily, so come prepared."

As the nurse guides me out of Aurelia's office, her final words linger in my mind like a haunting echo. Was it a warning, a threat, or just a statement of fact?

Either way, I'm terrified.

31

Aurelia Dibra may not have abilities like mine, but she is far more menacing and manipulative. The moment I saw her, my intuition screamed that she was a rogue, and the way she spoke and ran the therapy session confirmed it.

As soon as my nurse locked me back in my cell, a sense of dread washed over me. Aurelia is no ordinary rogue; she's far more dangerous. She has the unnerving ability to manipulate and control others effortlessly, bending them to her will with a mere snap of her fingers.

I need to find a way to warn Theo before she gets to him, to ensure he doesn't crack under her pressure.

As I lie down on the rusty bed, my mind remains foggy from this morning's medication. The lack of windows leaves me clueless about the time, and the constant stench of sewage only adds to my dizziness.

I need to get out of this hellhole as soon as possible. But how? The medication's drowsiness robs me of any rational ideas.

Just as I start to doze off, the creak of my cell door jolts me awake, and my nurse strides in with her usual expressionless look. I sit up defensively, my mind racing with unease.

"Dinner is in the mess hall," she utters, her voice devoid of any emotion. I suddenly realise that the last thing I ate was a feeble sandwich in my cell, and my stomach grumbles in protest.

With a firm grip on my arm, she leads me through the dimly lit corridors of Alheim Hill. As night falls, the atmosphere becomes a thousand times more terrifying. Shadows seem to come alive, and I can't shake the feeling of ghosts roaming the halls.

We finally reach the mess hall, a spacious and well-lit room with rows of benches and dining tables neatly set up. Despite its resemblance to a majestic dining hall, the unsettling sounds of patients' cries and the lingering odour of stale food fill the air, creating a chilling atmosphere.

I scan the room, searching desperately for Theo. Relief floods through me when I spot him at the back, by the buffet station. As I approach, I notice him staring at the green soup on his plate, absentmindedly scraping its surface with a spoon.

"Theo," I whisper, catching his attention.

His blue eyes light up as he sees me, and he almost reaches out for a hug before restraining himself. After what happened last time, it's best to keep a distance, no matter how hard that might be.

"Thank God you're here. I swear I'm going mad," he says as he nervously chews on his lip.

"Let's find some seats," I suggest, scanning the room for empty tables.

Theo nods in agreement, and we make our way to a partially vacant table. We choose seats away from the other patients, feeling their curious gazes on us. Sitting beside him, I grimace at the sight of our plates. While the soup looks like pea soup, its scent is anything but appetising. Theo leans in closer, ensuring no one overhears us.

"I've figured it out," he whispers, catching my attention.

I raise an eyebrow in response.

"Figured out what?" I whisper back, tearing off a piece of bread. It takes effort to swallow it, but I know it's better than the pea soup.

"The escape. It's just a matter of getting down to the morgue," he explains quietly.

"The morgue?" I ask, perplexed.

Theo nods, lifting a cup of water to his lips.

"They transport the deceased patients in a van to a nearby cemetery. Down the hill, there's a main road. We make a run for it, and we're gone," he explains

It's a solid plan, undoubtedly better than anything I could have come up with, but it almost feels too good to be true.

"Won't they inspect the body bags before loading them into the van? Plus, how are we going to get down to the morgue? That place is restricted," I murmur. I recall the dark stairwell leading to the morgue while I was taken back to my room after therapy, and it didn't seem easy to access.

"That's where you come in. We only need a card to get in," he explains, lowering his voice even further. "Also, this place was built in the 30s. It's not a supermax prison."

With a newfound sense of hope, I nod slowly, understanding his plan. Despite the risks and uncertainties, it's the closest thing to freedom we've had since we got here. Maybe we can actually leave this place.

Aurelia's terrifying gaze flashes in my mind, reminding me of what I needed to tell Theo.

"Hey, I need to tell you something. Have you been to the therapy sessions yet?" I ask, but before Theo can answer, a deranged man suddenly takes the seat next to me. Feeling uneasy, I shrink into my seat, avoiding eye contact with him.

"I've got it first thing tomorrow," Theo responds, giving the man a wary glance.

"Please promise me you'll be careful," I plead urgently.

"Why?" Theo asks, his brow furrowing in confusion.

I sigh, leaning closer to him to ensure the man next to me won't overhear.

"She's a rogue," I whisper, my breath barely grazing his ear. Being this close to him makes my legs tremble, but in this moment, survival is our sole focus.

"Shit... I'll be careful," Theo responds, his brows shooting up in alarm.

We share a nervous glance before the blaring alarm signals the end of dinner.

•••••

As I'm escorted back to my cell, my gaze lingers on the stairwell leading to the morgue. The sight is petrifying, almost resembling a stairway to hell—but what truly grabs my attention is the lack of guards.

Maybe Theo's plan could work. All we need is the key card, but how can I get it?

I observe my nurse closely as she unlocks my cell with a blue key card, wondering if it's the same one used for the morgue. The nurse dismisses me with a quick nod before ushering me into my cell, closing the door behind me with a resounding thud. I drowsily lie down on the bed, the rusty springs creaking beneath me. My gaze drifts to the cracked ceiling above, and I realise it hasn't even been twenty-four hours since I woke up in this hellhole.

What worries me the most is that the more time passes, the more they'll sedate me, until I'm reduced to little more than an amoeba.

One thing is certain—I can't stay here.

I sigh, combing my fingers through my tangled hair.

I've spent the entire day locked in this cell, with only meals in the cafeteria and mess hall as a break. Today, they didn't even take us to the communal showers, making me wonder if they'll allow it tomorrow.

I miss Barren—the pine trees scattered throughout town, their fresh scent lingering in the air. I miss the inviting aroma of fries and grilled burgers at The Grub, with Old Mary tirelessly serving coffees day and night.

I miss school. I wonder how Helena, Beth, and the others are doing.

But most of all, I miss my dad. I can't help but worry about him. Disappearing twice in a week must have him in a panic. I wonder if police are looking for me. Maybe he knows where I am, but he's unable to do anything about it.

Having Theo here provides some comfort; at least I'm not alone in this mess. But running away forever isn't a feasible option. There must be another way to make life feel normal again. Perhaps I can talk to Chris. Maybe I can even negotiate with him.

Feeling the effects of both sleep deprivation and medication, I notice my thoughts slowing down. Wiping away some tears with my sleeve, I force myself to close my eyes, praying for some much-needed sleep.

·····

My eyes flutter open, feeling a chill run down my spine as I recognise Aurelia's cold, metallic office. The air feels heavy, filled with an icy tension that makes my skin crawl. I suddenly notice Aurelia seated at her desk, and a wave of dread washes over me as I realise who she's with.

"Mr. Rhodes," she begins, a sly smile curling her lips, "I have something you might find interesting."

She pulls out a document from her desk drawer and dangles it in front of him. Theo shifts uncomfortably, his eyes narrowing as he reaches for the document.

"What is this?" he asks, worry in his voice.

Aurelia's blood-red lips curl into a sinister smile.

"Oh, just a little insurance policy," she replies coyly. "A document detailing certain... indiscretions of yours, shall we say?"

Theo's face drains of colour as he scans the document, each word deepening the furrow of his brow. His gaze flickers to her, anger evident in his eyes.

"You wouldn't dare," he says through gritted teeth.

Aurelia leans back in her chair, a smug expression spreading across her face.

"Oh, wouldn't I?" she purrs. "You're in quite a predicament, Theo. And unless you do what I ask, this document might end up in the wrong hands."

Theo's jaw clenches as he stares down at the piece of paper in his hands.

"You're crazy. Do you realise how much is at stake here? This could all blow up in your face," he mutters under his breath.

Aurelia seems unfazed by Theo's anger, crossing her arms calmly.

"Let's be rational. You and Little Miss Cora need to get your priorities straight," Aurelia says with a sly smile, her green eyes glinting with mischief.

"After all, there's much to gain from cooperation, and much to lose from resistance."

Theo's eyes simmer with anger as he glares at her, the tension palpable between them. He's on the verge of doing something he will regret—I can sense it.

"I'm not doing this," he finally says, pushing the document away.

"I'm afraid you have no choice," Aurelia retorts, her tone dripping with menace as she leans forward, her eyes boring into his. "Or the whole world will find out that you're a killer."

Theo's jaw clenches at her words, his fists balling at his sides.

"I didn't kill Arthur Glenn," he insists. "And I know that for a fact."

Aurelia chuckles under her breath before her expression changes abruptly. She slams her fist against the desk, causing Theo to flinch.

"Look, Theo. You should have been dead a long, long time ago," she says sharply, her teeth gritted in rage. But this time, Theo doesn't flinch. Instead, he furrows his brows in confusion, which turns Aurelia's anger into a smile.

The air is heavy with tense silence until she lets out a devilish cackle.

"You have no idea, don't you? Who do you think we were after that night? Damon Martin, a feeble jock, or you?"

In that moment, my sight blurs, suddenly yanking me out of the vision. I fight to catch my breath, grasping the bed frame for stability as the truth crashes over me like a wave of nausea.

The rogues weren't after Damon that night. They were after Theo.

That's why Theo was safe until they saw him at the hospital with me. They thought he was dead—until now.

"This is all my fault," I whisper to myself, guilt flooding my eyes with tears.

I need to get Theo out of here before they kill him. There's no time to waste.

•••••

It's been twenty-four hours since I woke up at Alheim.

Breakfast is a nightmare, not only because it's a reminder that I've been trapped in this hellish place for twenty-four hours, but also because I haven't seen Theo yet.

As I wait in line for some stale oats and coffee, the overwhelming fear of something terrible happening tightens my chest. The coldness of Alheim Hill seeps through its old walls, pushing patients and nurses to rely on hot drinks for warmth. I scan the breakfast queue, my gaze settling on a nurse pouring scorching coffee into her mug. I need to swipe the key card from one of them before it's too late.

My eyes quickly scan the nurse, wondering where the key card might be. It's probably in her pocket, but I don't have much time to hypothesise. I move forward a few spots in the queue, keeping my head low to blend in.

The smell of acidic coffee and burnt toast makes my stomach churn as I grab some toast before continuing down the line. I remain focused on the nurse in front of me as she reaches for a muffin, providing the perfect opportunity to check her pockets. I suppress my excitement as I discreetly reach into her pocket, slipping the key card into my bra.

I casually grab a muffin, trying not to draw any attention to myself. The nurse ahead of me continues along the line, unaware of what just happened. Now, I just need to wait for the right moment to use it.

I grab a seat at an empty table, my eyes darting around the room in search of Theo once more. Taking a sip of tea, I instantly scald my tongue, causing me to wince and blow on it. However, impatience gnaws at me, and nausea churns in my gut as the minutes tick by without any sign of Theo. If Aurelia did something to him, I swear to God...

Theo's pale face during my vision filled me with dread. The rogues must have found a way to incriminate Theo, even though there was no evidence that Mayor Glenn died that night. I remember Theo telling me that his sister had ensured Glenn was away that weekend. But could he have been mistaken? The mere thought makes me gulp.

A few tense minutes pass before Theo walks in with the other patients, his expression weary and his steps slower than usual. I let out a deep sigh of relief, grateful that he's okay.

I need to give him the key card without anyone noticing. Watching him grab a cup of coffee, I nervously lick my lips, pondering how to give it to him discreetly. Glancing around, I check for any watching nurses. Then, I notice a pile of books on a nearby coffee table. Snatching the nearest one, I quickly tuck the stolen card between its pages. I sink into one of the couches, feigning interest in the book.

Theo approaches with a sombre expression, settling beside me.

"You were right, Cora..." he murmurs.

My heart shatters as he withdraws his hands from his pockets, revealing the bruises on his hands and wrists. The deep bags under his eyes, evidence of narcotics and insomnia, become more pronounced with each passing hour.

"Oh my God... Are you okay?" I ask, gently reaching for his battered hands.

He shrugs, but his eyes betray his true feelings.

"Yeah, I'll be okay," he mutters, shoving his hands back into his pockets.

I bite my lip worriedly at his state, realising the gravity of our situation. The rogues are slowly killing us, and it's crucial that we find a way to escape. With a sense of urgency, I hand him the hardcover version of Wuthering Heights.

"What's this?" he asks, glancing at the book with curiosity.

"Take it to your room. Read it from start to end," I whisper urgently.

He locks eyes with me for a few moments before nodding in understanding.

"When's your therapy session?" he asks, his eyes clouded with worry. He's terrified of Aurelia and what she might do—and I am, too.

"Now, after breakfast," I mutter, sighing heavily.

Theo nods, briefly looking down at the empty cup in his hands.

"Please be careful," he says, biting his lip.

We exchange a longing glance, wishing there was a way to support each other. Right now, all we have is a blue key card, which I can only hope will help us get to the morgue.

In that moment, the ear-piercing alarm blares through the speakers.

32

After what I saw in my vision last night, Aurelia is the last person I want to see right now. I knew she was dangerous from the first time I laid eyes on her, but after seeing the bruises on Theo's arms, my fear of being near her has only grown.

Cold sweat forms on the back of my neck as the nurse opens the office door, terrified of what is to come. Aurelia sits calmly at her desk, her gaze steady as she watches me enter. Despite my fear, I muster the courage to meet her serpent-like eyes, determined not to let her see the turmoil within me. I try to steady my nerves as I take a seat, but the anxiety still churns in my stomach.

Aurelia's lips curve into an inauthentic smile.

"Good morning, Cora Danvers," she says, her voice smooth. The way she addresses me with my full name makes me uneasy, as if she's looking into the depths of my soul.

"Good morning," I murmur. After seeing how Aurelia brutally treated Theo, I realise the importance of staying on her good side.

"I wanted to show you something," she says, pulling out a sheet of paper from her drawer.

My mind races with apprehension as she unfolds the paper, revealing what appears to be a detailed psychological report. My heart drops when I recognise the signature at the bottom of the page—it's the psychiatrist who prescribed me the pills a few months ago.

"It says here that you were diagnosed in the fall with psychosis, blackouts, delusions of grandeur..." Aurelia begins, her words echoing in the tense silence of the room. Her green eyes lock with mine, the seriousness in them tightening my throat.

"I'm afraid that with this diagnosis, I cannot release you from Alheim Hill," she concludes, her voice firm. The thought of spending the rest of my life within these walls, surrounded by uncertainty and darkness, fills me with deep dread.

I gulp, mustering some courage.

"That report is false. I am not mentally ill," I assert, maintaining a steady voice.

A moment of tense silence fills the room, Aurelia's face devoid of expression before she bursts into laughter. She leans back in her chair, a Cheshire cat smile spreading across her face.

"Then what are you?" she purrs, her tone dripping with amusement, like a predator toying with its prey.

This is exactly what the rogues want from us: to convince us that we are not clairvoyant, that we are mentally ill, and beyond saving. But their greatest mistake was bringing Theo and me together because now I see through their facade. They want to frame Theo for Mayor Glenn's death and confine me to this wretched place for life, all to feed on me like vultures.

I tighten my jaw, fixing my gaze on Aurelia's amused expression.

"I'm not signing this," I say firmly, sliding the document back across the desk. "I'm not mentally ill."

A tense pause hangs between us before Aurelia nods, her expression unreadable.

"I can give you until tomorrow. You know, to think it over," she says casually, but her tone lacks sincerity. Then, her gaze locks with mine. "I'd think about your dad, though. It's not easy for him to cope with this."

Anger gushes through my veins as her words sink under my skin. Is she threatening me?

"What do you mean?" I murmur through gritted teeth.

In that moment, the tension is shattered by the blaring alarm echoing throughout the facility. Worry instantly spreads across Aurelia's face as my nurse abruptly enters the room and seizes me. I scream as I'm dragged out of Aurelia's office and taken to the canteen, where the rest of the patients are gathered. The scene is chaotic, filled with frightened faces and the clamour of voices. I struggle against the nurse's grip, but it's futile. Panic surges through me as I realise something must be terribly wrong for such a commotion.

The nurses line us up, aggressively ordering us to put our hands behind our heads and fall to our knees. Fear tightens my chest as I scan the crowded canteen, hoping to find Theo amongst the sea of faces. My heart leaps as I finally locate him among the crowd, a few rows ahead. Our eyes lock, and we exchange a worried glance, both unsure of what this is all about.

The room goes quiet as a man in his late fifties steps toward, his posture stern and authoritative. Deep wrinkles line his face, and he sports a thick moustache that gives him a retro look, almost like a character from a 1970s adult movie. However, the taser in his hands erases any possibility of amusement.

"Attention," he announces sternly. "One of the nurses is missing a key card, so we are going to check every one of you. The person found with the key will be punished in isolation for three weeks."

His gaze fixates on me, causing a lump to form in my throat. Did he see me take the key card from the nurse? But the moment is short-lived because his eyes continue to scan the faces of the crowd, shifting away from me.

With a snap of his fingers, the nurses start searching the patients, patting them from top to bottom. My eyes dart to Theo, who's in the second row and next in line to be searched.

A horrifying realisation dawns on me: He has the card on him. If we get caught, Aurelia will surely kill us.

Nausea grips me as the nurse approaches him, a whirlwind of panicked thoughts swirling in my mind.

We've lost. We're dead. The rogues have won.

Time seems to freeze as the nurse begins to search him, my breath caught in my throat. Theo remains tense as she starts patting his arms, but my heart sinks to my stomach when she finds something wedged under his tricep.

"I've got something!" she exclaims, drawing everyone's attention.

The tension is palpable as she digs her hand into Theo's sleeve, only to retrieve a tissue. I release the breath I was holding, feeling relief wash over me. The nurse clicks her tongue bitterly, shooting him a cold glare before moving on to the next person.

Theo subtly turns to me, signalling towards the bin where I know the card is hidden.

•••••

Aurelia has granted me twenty-four hours to sign the document declaring me mentally ill. This means we must speed up our escape plan before those twenty-four hours are up—or we will be trapped in this hellhole forever.

We were incredibly lucky Theo managed to hide the key card inside one of the bins, but I know we don't have much time before they empty the trash. Since the card wasn't found on any of the patients, we've all been punished with an hour of cleaning each. I've been tasked with cleaning the massive windows in the hall, but anything beats being stuck in my solitary cell.

I pick up the window cleaning spray, tossing a filthy rag into one of the buckets before wiping sweat from my brow. Letting out a deep sigh, I glance over my shoulder at the grandfather clock for the thousandth time. There are ten minutes left before my shift is over, and fifteen until they open the lunch hall.

A hollow cough interrupts my thoughts, and I turn to meet a girl's gaze. Her tight, curly hair covers half of her face, while bruises stain her caramel skin. Her facial features appear bony from malnutrition, much like the other patients. She lowers her chin in shame, forming a thin line with her lips before looking away.

I resume wiping the window in a circular motion, my mind falling into a trance as I try to pinpoint where I've seen that gaze before. I feel like I've seen it somewhere, but I can't quite put my finger on it.

My eyes drift to the trash can where Theo stashed the card, anxiety twisting my stomach. There isn't much time left before we execute our escape plan—and if we screw up the slightest detail, we will die in the hands of the rogues

The siren finally blares through the cafeteria, marking the end of my cleaning shift. I toss the Windex-soaked rag into the bucket and wipe my hands on my uniform as the line of patients floods into the hall.

A wave of relief floods over me as I lock eyes with Theo, who bites his lip to fight back a smile. I grab a couple of cold sandwiches from the lunch bar before joining him at the table.

"Hey," he says, taking a bite of his stale sandwich. "How was it with..." he trails off. He's talking about Aurelia, who was luckily interrupted by the siren.

I let out a frustrated sigh.

"Could have been better, but could have been worse," I reply quietly. In that instant, the final piece of the puzzle clicks in my head, causing me to nervously chew my lip.

I know who that girl is.

Glancing over my shoulder to ensure we're not being watched, I lean in close to Theo.

"Do you remember the Allen family?" I whisper. He nods, his piercing blue eyes studying mine. I gesture towards the girl sitting a few tables away, her back facing us. "I think that's their daughter."

Theo briefly looks at her, furrowing his brows, before turning his attention back to me.

"Are you sure?" he asks.

I nod, the vision the rogues forced me to see that day still fresh in my mind.

"She looks just like her mother," I whisper, my gaze fixed on the girl. I bite my lip, knowing what I'm about to say is risky. "We need to get her out of here."

Theo scratches his stubble, letting out a heavy sigh.

"This might fuck up the whole plan, Cora," he mutters.

"We can't risk leaving her here. If she's one of us, she needs to come with us," I insist.

He bites his lip nervously, aware that we could be putting our own lives at risk.

He's right; it could greatly complicate things. But there's a part of me that simply can't abandon this orphan girl in this dreadful place, especially if she's a clairvoyant.

In that moment, I feel the intensity of someone's gaze on the back of my neck, as if they were scrutinising us. Turning around, I realise one of the nurses is staring at me from across the room. If we're not careful, Aurelia will kill us before we even have a chance to escape.

I quickly pick up a magazine from 1996 lying on the coffee table, feigning interest in its contents.

"Are we being watched?" Theo whispers, though he already knows the answer.

My eyes remain fixed on the coffee-stained page, waiting for the nurse to look away. Instead, she strides over to us, a deep scowl etched on her face. I gulp nervously, dropping the magazine to meet her gaze.

"Is there a problem?" I ask casually, despite the tension prickling the back of my neck.

The nurse stares blankly at me, holding a plastic cup in her hands.

"Your medication," she orders, her voice firm as she extends the cup toward me. I raise the pills to my lips, pretending to swallow as I tilt my head back. I discreetly let the pills fall into my sleeve, hiding from the nurse's watchful gaze. She shoots me a bitter glance before walking away, her movements seeming robotic.

Theo looks at me, his eyes narrowed in confusion.

"You took it? But I—" he starts, but I interrupt him by pressing a finger against my lips, revealing the pills hidden in my sleeve. His expression shifts from surprise to a sly smile, but it quickly fades. He clenches his jaw, his gaze fixed on the trashcan.

"We don't have much time before they take out the trash. We need that key card," he whispers urgently.

We watch as a man lifts the lid before tossing his food scraps, making me scrunch my nose in disgust.

"We have to leave tonight," I murmur.

•••••

The sound of running water from the communal showers fills me with dread as I enter. Dense steam rises in the cold air, creating an atmosphere akin to a sauna. The floor tiles, tinged with a rosy hue, bear traces of mildew from lack of hygiene, making me grateful for the slippers I've been given.

My muscles tense as I glance at the naked women around me. Many of them have bruises and cuts from the tortures they've endured, which makes me realise that perhaps Aurelia was soft on me.

Lowering my gaze to avoid awkwardness, I find a free shower stall next to the toilet cubicles, hoping not to draw too much attention.

The water droplets hit my face as I close my eyes, their warmth offering an unfamiliar sensation. For a moment, I imagine myself in the comfort of my own shower at home, a fleeting sense of relaxation washing over me. However, as soon as I open my eyes, the sounds of the other patients fill my ears, and the chaos of the institution returns in full force.

I catch sight of a familiar face in my peripheral vision, and my attention turns to the girl from this morning. She's shivering as she holds onto her body tightly under the shower. I soon realise that her hot water tap isn't fully turned on.

"Here," I offer, adjusting the knob. As the steamy water begins to flow, the girl lets out a sigh of relief.

"Thank you," she whispers, her voice barely audible over the sound of the running water. She closes her eyes, allowing the warm water to cascade over her, washing away the tension in her muscles.

Maybe this is the right moment to find out if she is indeed related to the Allen family.

"What's your name?" I ask softly.

The girl hesitates for a moment, her eyes darting around nervously. Finally, she replies in a hushed tone, "Alexis."

It's impossible to tell if she's an Allen just from her first name, but I don't want to press too much. Another idea comes to mind.

I reach for her wrist, hoping to glean some insight into her past. Her eyes widen in shock at my touch, and she quickly jerks her arm away, letting out an audible gasp. She stares at me with a look of disgust, as if I were some kind of monster.

"Who... Who are you?" she splutters, her voice trembling with confusion and fear. Snatching her towel from the hook, she rushes across the room, her movements frantic with alarm.

"Shit," I mutter under my breath. She must have seen my past instead. Either way, it means my intuition was right. She's Alexis Allen, the daughter of the Allen family.

I'm on the verge of explaining that we're the same when a nurse storms toward me with a deep scowl etched on her face.

"What the hell did you do, Danvers?" she growls, her gaze darting between Alexis and me.

My attention remains fixed on Alexis, who clutches her towel tightly against her chest, her expression resembling that of a deer caught in headlights.

If she speaks, our escape plan is ruined.

33

We have six hours until our escape, and the fear coursing through my veins has never been more palpable. Alexis could potentially derail everything by speaking about me, making every move I make from here on out crucial.

The dinner hall is a chaotic scene, filled with the clamour of patients banging their spoons against their plates, loudly chewing their food, and muttering gibberish. As always, the hot drinks stand is bustling with people, each one eager to warm themselves with a drink in hand. Spotting Theo amidst the crowd as he pours himself a cup of coffee, nerves flood through me.

My eyes rake the crowd as I search for my nurse, knowing that time is of the essence. Spotting her approaching the drink stand just a few feet from Theo, I make my way over, my legs trembling with anxiety. I reach for a paper cup and pour myself some coffee, then discreetly drop the pills I saved from this morning into the drink. With a spoon, I mix the contents, ensuring they dissolve completely

Next step.

As I advance in the line, a sudden thud followed by the sound of liquid hitting the floor echoes through the lunch hall. The nurse nearby gasps loudly, prompting me to glance at the dark brown stain spreading across the tiled floor.

"Shit. Sorry," someone mumbles. I quickly turn my gaze to Theo, noticing that his cup is now dripping with spilled coffee.

"You spilled all of my coffee!" the nurse shrills, shooting him an icy glare.

He offers another apology, quickly grabbing some napkins from the nearby bench and helping the nurse in wiping her apron.

"Here, ma'am. This one is still hot," I interject, swiftly handing her my cup. My nurse gives me a side glance before snatching the cup from my hand.

"Make sure you watch your step next time," she growls at Theo, who's on his knees wiping the floor with a rag. Then, she turns to me, a surprising smile appearing on her lips. It almost makes her seem human.

"It's good to see you're starting to change your attitude towards this place," she says.

I flash a grin, observing her as she sips her coffee. In thirty minutes, she'll be in for a surprise. As the nurse finishes her coffee and walks away, relief washes over us. I exchange a glance with Theo, silently acknowledging that our plan is still on track.

We make sure to sit at separate tables, close enough to communicate without drawing suspicion. As we choke down our awful dinner, a sense of determination fills the air.

This time, we know we're going to escape.

•••••

The blaring alarm echoes through the halls as my nurse escorts me back to my cell, marking the end of another day. But if everything goes according to plan, this could be our last moments at Alheim Hill.

The nurse yawns for the third time in a minute, her eyes puffy from exhaustion, sending a wave of adrenaline through me. The pills I slipped into her coffee have worked, signalling the start of our countdown.

Our footsteps come to a halt as we reach my cell, the nurse yawning once more. I seize the opportunity, quickly grabbing her arm to prevent her from ushering me inside.

"Hey, um… I just remembered something. I left my watch in the cafeteria," I murmur, deliberately drawing out each word to give the impression that she's on the verge of falling asleep.

The nurse blinks, her eyes struggling to stay open. She's clearly drugged out of her mind, just like she's been drugging us for days.

"I'll come with you," she starts, but my grip tightens on her arm.

"No need! I know where to find it," I insist with an inauthentic smile.

She hesitates, but the sedatives are far too powerful for her to resist. She nods slowly, her movements sluggish.

"Fine," she mumbles, her voice heavy with drowsiness. "But be quick about it."

I nod eagerly, trying to contain my excitement. This is it—the moment we've been waiting for. I have half a minute before she passes out on the floor.

With adrenaline coursing through my veins, I sprint towards the cafeteria, desperately scanning the area for the bin amidst the stacked chairs. The darkness makes it hard to distinguish objects, but I can't afford to waste a second.

As I approach the bin, a putrid smell hits my nostrils, making me gag. Ignoring the stench, I rummage through the trash, my fingers brushing against slimy leftovers and discarded wrappers. Then, just as I'm about to lose hope, my hand closes around a familiar plastic card.

The key card! I snatch it out of the bin, relief flooding through me despite the foul door.

Now, it's time to get out of here before anyone notices I'm missing.

With my heart pounding in my chest, I rush down the corridor towards the morgue stairwell, clutching the key card tightly in my hand. As I turn the final corner before reaching the stairs, I let out an involuntary gasp as I collide with someone. My pupils dilate with shock as I meet Theo's petrified gaze, his expression mirroring my own astonishment.

"You scared the shit out of me," I pant, casting a nervous glance over my shoulder.

Theo's breaths come out in quick, shallow pants as he grips my arm, his fingers digging into my skin.

"We need to hurry," he whispers urgently, his eyes darting around the dimly lit corridor.

I hand him the blue key card, relief washing over his face. Our eyes lock, a shared understanding passing between us—we're one step closer to freedom.

As we rush down the stairwell leading down to the morgue, it feels like descending into the depths of hell itself, each step filled with a mounting sense of dread. We reach a metal door labelled 'Morgue', its intimidating appearance sending a shiver down my spine. Cold air escapes from underneath, causing my breath to fog and goose bumps to form on my skin.

The tension is thick as Theo swipes the key card, and I pray to God that it will grant us access to the morgue. We hold our breath, every passing second feeling like an eternity. Then, at last, there's a beep, followed by a blinking green light. We push the door open with a creak, but a shiver runs down my spine as I realise we're not alone. The sound of approaching footsteps from behind makes my blood turn to ice. We spin around, our eyes widening in fear at the sight of a shadowy figure at the top of the stairs.

"It's you, isn't it?" a female voice says. Theo's grip tightens my arm, ready to make a run for it, but I soon recognise who it is.

"Alexis? What the hell are you doing here?" I hiss through gritted teeth, hoping she hasn't sabotaged our plan.

Theo's eyes dart between Alexis to me, irritation evident in his expression. This is exactly what he warned me about.

"We have to go, Cora," he whispers urgently, nervously tugging my arm.

Alexis' silhouette looms over the stairs, casting an eerie shadow.

"I had a dream about you. You broke me out of here," she mutters, fear evident in her voice.

I share a glance with Theo, who pleads with me not to help her, but eventually gives in with a sigh.

"Quick, let's go!" Theo urges, ushering us into the morgue and swiftly closing the door behind us.

As we step inside, the blast of cold air from the air-conditioning hits us instantly, but it's accompanied by the unmistakable stench of decaying bodies. The combination is nauseating, causing bile to rise in my throat and my teeth to chatter uncontrollably in response to the freezing temperature of the room.

Alexis' eyes dart around nervously as Theo and I rummage through the drawers for the body bags.

"Guys, what's the plan?" she asks, her voice tinged with fear.

My hands shake as I pull out the body bags from one of the drawers, the crinkle of the plastic echoing in the silent room. I lay them out on the cold metal table, my heart pounding with anticipation. Quickly, I hand Alexis a bag, her eyes wide with panic.

"Take this. Get inside the drawer and slip it over you," I urge, knowing time is running out.

She gulps nervously before giving me a nod. Meanwhile, Theo rushes to the refrigerator, swiftly opening and closing drawers until he finds three that are empty.

"We need to hide in the refrigerator until 5 A.M. That's when they take the dead patients to the cemetery," Theo explains breathlessly, glancing back at us.

We gaze at the three drawers, a chilling silence settling between us. It's a terrifying sight, and I doubt there will be enough oxygen for the four hours we need to spend inside. Despite the daunting prospect, we know we have no other choice. With a heavy heart, I step forward and open one of the drawers, revealing its narrow interior. I exchange a glance with Theo, who is already sliding the body bag on. Alexis stares at me with parted lips, as if she's in a trance.

I take a deep breath and climb inside, the cramped space pressing against me uncomfortably. Darkness envelops me as I slide the body bag over myself, the plastic rustling with each movement. The sensation of claustrophobia grips me instantly, worsened by the refrigerator's icy chill that makes my teeth chatter uncontrollably. A wave of nausea overwhelms me, and panic flushes my face.

As I struggle to steady my breathing in the confined space, I hear the muffled sound of Alexis crying nearby. Her sobs echo off the walls of the refrigerator, adding to the suffocating atmosphere. My heart sinks with guilt, knowing that we've dragged her into this dangerous situation.

"Alexis, it's going to be okay," I hear Theo's muffled voice say. "Just please don't cry. They will hear us."

The sound of Alexis' muffled sobs gradually fades, dissipating into the stillness of the cramped space. I close my eyes, trying to block out the overwhelming sensation of claustrophobia, but it only seems to intensify with each passing second. Sweat beads form on my forehead as I struggle to control my breathing, the cold air of the refrigerator doing little to alleviate the oppressive atmosphere.

The thoughts race through my mind like a speeding train: We will die here. We won't make it. There isn't enough oxygen. There must be another way.

"Theo?" I cry out, my hands trembling as they press against the cold walls. "I can't do this."

"Baby, everything will be fine, trust me," he reassures me, though my instincts tell me otherwise. The walls feel like they're closing in on me, each breath becoming suffocatingly shallow.

"No, I can't. I feel like there's no air," I gasp, the panic rising in my voice.

"Please, just hold on," he mutters, his voice strained. I sense that he's also struggling for air.

Alexis starts to sob again, her cries echoing in the cramped space. Each breath feels like a struggle, fear coursing through my quivering body. If these are truly our final moments, then honesty is all that remains.

"Theo?" I call out, my voice trembling.

"Yeah?"

"I love you," I whisper, my voice barely audible. "If we don't make it out alive, I need you to know that."

There's a moment of silence before I hear a sniffle.

"I love you too, Cora," Theo whispers back, his voice raspy. "We'll make it through this. Just hang in there."

In that instant, the eerie silence of the morgue is shattered by the piercing sound of an alarm. It blares through the institution ruthlessly, penetrating every crack in the wall and travelling through the ventilation systems, obliterating any other sound that exists.

"What's going on?" Alexis's voice rings out, followed by the sound of her ripping off her body bag. She's panicking, but any slip-up could mean death at Aurelia's hands.

"I don't know, but we need to stay put or they'll hear us," Theo shouts, his voice tense with urgency.

My heart races at an alarming speed, the piercing wail of the alarm engulfing all other sounds. I screw my eyes shut, trying to centre myself amidst the chaos. Suddenly, everything goes silent, leaving only the echo of my own breaths.

Think, Cora. Think. There must be a way out of this. We can't stay here any longer. In less than ten minutes, they'll find us, I'm certain of it.

We have to act fast.

With a sense of urgency, I unzip the body bag and cautiously slide out, feeling the icy air rush against my skin. My eyes dart around the dimly lit room as the alarm continues to blare, desperately searching for any means of escape.

"Cora?" Theo's voice echoes from inside the refrigerator, filled with concern. "What are you doing?"

"What's happening?" Alexis shrieks, her voice filled with fear.

My mind races with a whirlwind of thoughts, panic gripping me as the alarm blares on.

The rogues. Death. The Allen family. My dad. Damon Martin.

Panic courses through my veins, bile threatening to rise up my throat at the terrifying thought of being killed by Aurelia.

The rogues. Death. The Allen family. Death. Aurelia Dibra. Death.

My thoughts race as I continue to scan my surroundings, my body entering fight or flight mode. There's an operating table, utensils, a sink, and a small window.

Theo grunts, pushing the drawer open with his feet.

"Cora?" he calls out, his face etched with fear. Alexis soon follows, her breaths heavy as she crawls out of her drawer.

But there's no time to waste.

I sprint towards the window, the relentless alarm muffling all other sounds. I notice it leads to the recreation field, surrounded by a wire fence. We can make a run for it, and in less than a minute…

A spark of hope ignites within me. It's risky, but far better than facing Aurelia's wrath in the morgue within the next ten minutes.

"Guys," I say breathlessly. "I think I've got it."

Theo and Alexis exchange a glance, but I've already rushed towards the operating table. With swift movements, I rummage through the drawers, examining the hundreds of autopsy utensils. I grab what I believe to be a rib cutter, feeling a cold chill run down my spine.

I turn towards Theo and Alexis, my heart pounding in my chest.

"Follow me," I say, my voice steady despite the adrenaline coursing through me.

But in that moment, a deafening yell from upstairs knocks the air out of my lungs. Our focus shifts towards the door, dread creeping over us as light seeps through the cracks. The cacophony of loud thumps and shouts from the guards only indicates one thing.

It won't take long before they find us.

34

Alexis sobs in panic, tears staining her crimson cheeks as the alarm continues to wail. Holding my breath, I watch the morgue door, the distant sounds of yelling and thumping chilling me to the bone.

We need to act quickly; time is running out.

"They're probably doing a headcount," Theo whispers, his voice strained with concern.

"We need to leave. Now," I declare urgently.

With determination fuelling my every step, I stride towards the window, my heart pounding in my chest. The alarm's blare seems to grow louder with each passing second, driving my sense of urgency even higher. As I reach the window, I glance back at Theo and Alexis, gesturing for them to follow.

I immediately swing the metallic rib cutter against the glass with all my strength. The sound of shattering echoes through the room as the glass fractures into hundreds of pieces, clearing the way for our escape.

"Come on! Let's go!" I shout as I pull myself up, grabbing onto the window frame. Shards of glass pierce my palms, causing me to grunt in pain. Blood trickles down my wrist as I push through the cracked window, landing with a thud on the damp grass. The crisp winter air chills my heavy breaths as I take in my surroundings.

Theo makes it out next, then Alexis.

Without hesitation, we sprint across the open field, the wail of the alarm fading into the distance. However, the sound of our footsteps pounding against the earth is drowned out by the sudden, jarring crack of a gunshot.

My blood turns to ice, but the rush of adrenaline drives me forward. Gripping the rib cutter tightly, I muster all my strength to pry open the wired fence. With determination, I slash through the wires, ignoring the stinging pain in my hands. Theo and Alexis join in, ripping apart the corroded wire to create an opening for our escape.

As the sound of approaching footsteps intensifies, our frantic efforts to breach the fence become more urgent, while the shouts and bangs from the building grow louder.

We need to run. Now.

"Shoot them!" one of the guards yells from the morgue, his tone dripping with rage. "Shoot them *now*!"

With a shiver coursing down my spine, I instinctively seize Alexis and Theo. Time seems to slow as we dash through the breach in the fence, driven by our instinct to sprint straight ahead. Racing across the empty road, we swiftly head towards the looming dark forest on the horizon.

As we plunge deeper into the forest, the echoes of gunshots and screams fade into the distance behind us, none of us daring to look back.

•••••

After what feels like hours, we gradually slow our footsteps, the gentle breeze sweeping through the lush forest. We check once again for any signs of pursuit, but all we see are the trees and the serene silence around us.

"I can't believe we made it," Theo breathes out between heavy pants. "That was incredibly close."

"We did it," I say breathlessly, a sense of disbelief tinged with relief in my voice.

Catching my breath, I lift my gaze to the sunrise above our heads. Its warm glow paints the sky with hues of pink and orange, momentarily easing the fear and tension of our escape. I inhale the refreshing scent of pine trees, realisation dawns: we're in The Pinelands, but the question remains—where exactly?

"Where are we?" Alexis asks, her words echoing my thoughts.

Theo shakes his head, a puzzled expression creasing his brow.

"I'm not sure..."

I survey our surroundings, searching for any familiar landmarks, but the forest stretches endlessly in every direction, offering no clues to our location.

"And where are we going now?" Alexis asks, her eyes filled with worry. Our plan was to escape the tortures of Alheim, but we didn't give much thought to what happens afterwards.

Theo sighs, wiping sweat from his forehead with his patient uniform.

"I think our best shot is heading to my house. We can hide in my basement until we figure out our next steps," he explains, his soft ocean eyes fixed on me.

I nod, understanding that despite the risks, returning to Barren is our only option for now.

"We need to find a highway," I say. "It's our best chance to figure out how to get back home."

Theo lets out a deep breath, his shoulders visibly relaxing.

"Yeah, let's keep moving," he says, his eyes scanning the forest ahead.

With a nod of agreement, we set off once again, our footsteps echoing through the forest as we navigate through the trees, guided by the soft light of dawn.

The morning sun casts long shadows through the trees, creating an eerie yet beautiful atmosphere around us. But as we walk, I can't shake the feeling of being watched. Every rustle of leaves and distant caw of a crow sends a shiver down my spine, fuelling my paranoia. Nevertheless, I push those unsettling thoughts aside, focusing on our goal: finding a highway and reaching safety.

After what seems like an eternity of walking, we finally emerge from the dense foliage onto a narrow dirt path. In the distance, the faint sound of traffic and the outline of buildings mark the presence of civilisation.

"Guys, we're getting close," I announce, gesturing towards the distant skyline. "Let's keep moving."

As we continue along the dirt path, the sound of traffic grows louder until we finally reach the edge of the forest. Before us stretches a highway, its lanes bustling with cars zooming past. Relief floods through me at the sight of civilisation.

Then, my eyes catch something—a road sign just ahead. Squinting, I read the words: *"Cassville."*

A surge of hope fills my chest. Cassville is a nearby town, a familiar name.

"We're close to Cassville," I say, excitement tingling in my voice. "It's just a town away from Barren."

The three of us exchange a relieved glance, even if the danger is nowhere near over.

•••••

Once we spot the sign *"Welcome to Barren,"* we make sure to enter through Evergreen Forest to avoid being seen. If anyone catches sight of three teenagers in mental patient uniforms, it won't take them more than ten seconds to call the police.

We had to explain to Alexis how we ended up at Alheim and about the group of people hunting us for our abilities. At first, she was in disbelief, but then she told us that when she grabbed my arm in the communal showers, she saw everything. I tried to avoid overwhelming her with too much information but provided enough for her to grasp the situation.

I didn't expect her reaction to be so calm, especially considering how difficult it was for me to assimilate when Theo told me. However, I realise that she might still be too drugged to fully grasp the consequences of our situation. I didn't have the courage to tell her about her parents, but I know it's only a matter of time before she asks.

Our weary footsteps come to a stop as we reach the forest clearing, the ivory-toned house becoming visible on the horizon.

Every time I lay eyes on my childhood home, memories flood back like a gust of wind hitting my face. My dad had built it years before I was born; he told me he had spent a year working with the construction team to ensure it was perfect for us.

And indeed, it was.

As we approach the porch steps, Theo disappears briefly into the foliage and returns with a spare key hidden among the shrubs. With a sigh of relief, we unlock the door and follow him inside. The musty scent of the old house welcomes us, a stark contrast to the crisp outdoor air.

The dim light filtering through the curtains casts long shadows across the furniture, reminding me of countless memories spent within these walls—including the newer ones with Theo. It's surreal to be back here, considering I hadn't set foot in this house since the night of the forest fire. Despite the uncertainty of our situation, being back in my childhood home brings a sense of peace I hadn't felt in a long time.

"Let's head to the basement. We should be safe there for now," Theo says, his voice echoing in the living room. "Let's rest and figure out our next move."

With a nod, we follow him down to the basement, our footsteps echoing softly on the creaky wooden stairs.

The door opens with a screech, and my breath catches in my throat as a woman with a baseball bat nearly swings it at Theo's head with an ear-piercing scream. Alexis and I shriek from the shock as Theo quickly ducks, narrowly avoiding the swing of the bat.

"What the fuck, Phoebe?" Theo shouts, his voice filled with shock and confusion.

The girl, who appears to be in her mid-twenties, studies us with wide eyes. Lowering the bat, her expression shifts from anger to relief. Then, she throws herself into Theo's arms, catching me completely off guard.

"Theo! Where the hell were you? And who are they?" she blurts out.

She pulls away from the hug, gently cupping Theo's cheeks. A wave of discomfort washes over me as I speechlessly wonder who this girl might be, an uncomfortable silence settling between us as she eyes the mental patient uniforms we're wearing.

"They're clairvoyants. I can explain everything," Theo says, turning to face us. "This is my sister, Phoebe."

It takes me a few seconds to register it. At first glance, it seems impossible that they are related: Phoebe with her gorgeous blonde wavy hair, and Theo with his dark brown hair. But as I look closer, I notice they share a similar facial structure—a sharp jawline with a cleft chin and ocean-blue eyes.

"Hey, I'm Cora," I greet her, offering my best smile. However, much to my surprise, she shoots me a cold look before letting us inside. Exchanging a glance with Theo and Alexis, I'm relieved I wasn't the only one who found her rude.

The basement has definitely improved since I was last here. There's an old leather couch with piles of pillows and blankets, a long coffee table, a narrow filing cabinet, and numerous cardboard boxes stocked with food and supplies. I remember when I was growing up, this place was off-limits because my dad stored all his guitars here.

Phoebe sinks into the leather couch, cocooned in blankets and pillows, her brows furrowed as she opens her laptop. It's clear from her expression that our presence isn't exactly welcome.

"What are you doing here, Phoebes? I thought you had exams," Theo asks, settling beside her.

She meets her brother's gaze, the seriousness in her expression making me gulp nervously.

"We're in deep trouble, Theo. This time, it's serious," Phoebe says.

"What? What do you mean?" Theo asks, his brows knitting together in concern. He knows it can't get much worse than this.

Phoebe sighs, rubbing her arms anxiously. She reaches for a letter from the coffee table, handing it to him.

"They've found out where I live. I received this letter from Alheim Hill Psychiatric Hospital a few days ago."

"Fuck... They found out you're at Princeton?" he asks, his brows furrowing as he reads the letter.

"Wait, how do you know about Alheim?" I ask, shooting Phoebe a look. If she knew about this from the beginning, why wouldn't she tell Theo?

"Everyone knows about Alheim," Phoebe snaps, rolling her eyes at me. "They use the facility for recruitment. They numb you with pills, basically restarting your brain."

My eyes widen as the pieces of the puzzle start falling into place. It explains why we were among so many patients, yet the focus seemed to be on us. The patients were all listening to us at all times, gathering information.

"Why are you pissed off? We didn't willingly put ourselves in that situation," Theo retorts, his arms crossed in irritation.

"Because, Theo! I explicitly warned you to stay away from this girl," she snaps, pointing a finger in my direction. My eyes narrow in confusion. Did she know about my abilities from the start?

"What?" I gasp, surprised. Theo shakes his head, coming to my defence.

"It's not her fault. We were both targeted."

"What about her?" Phoebe asks, now pointing her finger at Alexis, whose cheeks instantly redden in embarrassment. I lock eyes with her, silently offering support.

"She's Alexis Allen. She was sent to Alheim when she was ten, falsely accused of being schizophrenic," I explain, sensing Alexis's discomfort.

"She's like us," Theo adds.

"Is she really?" Phoebe challenges with a laugh. "Prove it."

Theo exhales in exasperation, but before he can respond, I step in.

"Are you serious? We should be gathering everything we can and getting out of here," I snap, my frustration evident.

Theo nods in agreement.

"She's right. Barren isn't safe anymore, especially with her watcher around," he says.

Phoebe scoffs in disbelief.

"Her watcher is still alive? For God's sake, Theo, get yourself together," she groans, making my blood boil.

Theo shoots her an angry glance, causing her to recoil with a sigh.

"Look, I'm sorry... I completely panicked when I got the letter from Alheim. I genuinely thought you were dead," she murmurs softly.

Her rapid mood shifts are bizarre, I think to myself.

Theo crosses his arms over his chest, his stern gaze fixed on his sister.

"Well, they almost killed us," he states bluntly. "If we had left Alheim a day later, we would be six foot under, being mercilessly eaten by worms. Aurelia would have made sure of that."

Theo's words hang heavy in the air, the gravity of the situation sinking in.

"Aurelia?" Phoebe repeats, her voice barely above a whisper. "You mean, Aurelia Dibra?"

Theo nods grimly, lowering his chin.

My eyes widen in disbelief. I would have never imagined they had heard of Aurelia. She must be a powerful rogue, just as I suspected.

Phoebe rises from the couch, her troubled expression evident as she paces back and forth.

"This complicates things," she mutters under her breath. "We need to act fast."

I exchange a worried glance with Alexis, realising the gravity of our situation has just intensified.

"So, what do we do now?" I ask, my voice tinged with concern. "It won't take Chris long before he finds out we escaped."

"I want to go back home," Alexis cries in a childlike voice. My heart clenches in despair, knowing we have to tell her the truth.

"Alexis... Your parents..." I struggle to speak, the words sticking in my throat like glue.

Her eyes fill with tears, overwhelmed by dread.

"What?" she croaks, her voice barely audible.

I hesitate, knowing there's no easy way to say this.

"They were killed by the rogues. I'm sorry," I say softly

Her lip begins to quiver, and soon, she's frantically sobbing into her hands.

"So, I can't go home?" she cries out, her voice choked with grief.

I shake my head, my heart heavy with sorrow.

"No. The rogues know where you live," I respond, watching her fragile emotional state.

I can feel the weight of the world crashing down on her. I witnessed the death of her parents first-hand, but I don't think I'll ever be able to tell her. There was nothing I could have done to stop it, yet somehow, I feel responsible for their deaths.

As Alexis continues to cry, I move closer and wrap my arms around her, offering what little comfort I can. My heart aches for her. Alexis is utterly alone in the world. Since she was ten years old, she's been trapped at Alheim Hill, subjected to the ruthless control of the rogues.

"She's clearly not aware of what she can do," I overhear Phoebe say.

My blood boils at her comment, and I shoot her a filthy look.

"What's your problem?" I snap.

Phoebe clenches her jaw, crossing her arms over her chest. She seems taken aback by my comment.

"You brought an *unperceptive*. That's my problem," she retorts sharply.

"She's not unperceptive; we've only just told her she's a clairvoyant. She just found out her parents are dead, for God's sake," I fire back.

Theo rolls his eyes, clearly annoyed by our bickering.

"Just mentor her, Phoebe. It's not the end of the world," he says, his patience wearing thin.

Phoebe shoots him a sharp glance.

"It may as well be the end of the world. Where on Earth can we go? The rogues know I go to Princeton, and returning to LA is out of the question," she retorts, her frustration palpable.

"When you say 'we', I hope you're including Cora and Alexis," Theo argues, his tone edged with frustration. Phoebe's face remains stoic, unaffected by his glare. "You weren't, were you?"

Phoebe sighs, rubbing her chin thoughtfully before reluctantly meeting his gaze.

"This is risky, Theo. We can't just take in lost people. This could blow up in our faces," she counters, her tone firm.

"None of us are lost," I interject, feeling the tension thickening between us.

"Okay, then. Where can we go?" she snaps back.

"We've got a few hours to figure it out. We should stay in the basement and gather what we need before we leave. Do we all agree?" Theo suggests, trying to diffuse the tension.

A moment of silence hangs in the air as Alexis and I nod in agreement, while Phoebe remains with her arms crossed over her chest.

"What if we asked mom?" Theo suggests, sharing a glance with his sister.

She immediately shakes her head.

"It's far too dangerous."

"Where is she?" I ask, curiosity evident on my face. Theo had never mentioned anything about her, except that she lived in Los Angeles.

"She's in hiding," Phoebe replies.

Suddenly, everything falls into place. The rogues found her, and Theo was forced to leave his family behind. That's why he came to Barren.

Theo rises from the couch, his steps measured as he paces around the room lost in thought. The silence stretches on for a few minutes before he finally breaks it.

"We need to find a place far from civilisation. Somewhere the rogues can't easily reach us while we figure out our next steps," he declares.

In that moment, the gravity of his words sinks in. We're leaving Barren for good. The mere thought leaves me with a lump in my throat. I don't know if I can leave my dad behind, especially after everything he's gone through.

I glance at Theo, hoping to find some reassurance in his eyes, but all I see is determination. Phoebe seems lost in her own thoughts, her brow furrowed with worry. Alexis sits quietly, her eyes downcast, perhaps grappling with her own fears and uncertainties.

"We can't stay here any longer," Theo says, breaking the heavy silence. "It's too risky. We need to find somewhere safe, somewhere off the grid. And we need to leave now, before Chris finds us."

His words hang in the air, each one carrying the weight of our uncertain future. Leaving Barren means leaving behind everything we've ever known, everything familiar and comforting. But staying here means risking our lives every day, constantly looking over our shoulders, never knowing when the rogues might find us.

I take a deep breath, trying to push back the wave of anxiety threatening to overwhelm me.

"Okay," I say, my voice barely above a whisper. "Let's do it. But if we're leaving, we can't go around looking like this," I utter, grabbing the skirt of my patient uniform.

"I'll go get some clothes. We should be the same size," Phoebe volunteers, rising from the couch.

Phoebe leaves the room, her footsteps echoing faintly as she ascends the stairs. Theo and I exchange a glance, both of us feeling the weight of the upcoming departure. Alexis remains silent, lost in her own thoughts. It's a solemn moment, filled with uncertainty and fear.

Every time I think of my dad, sheer dread courses through my veins. He must be collapsing without me. After all, I'm his only daughter and his only family. This is what the rogues do. They tear us from our families, making them think we're insane so they won't come looking for us. We're left with no option but to disappear to stay alive.

"I need to tell my dad," I mutter, breaking the silence. "He still thinks I'm at Alheim. I need to let him know I'm okay."

Theo's expression softens, his blue eyes locking onto mine.

"Don't worry, we'll find a way to reach him safely," he assures me. "We can call him from a public phone booth."

Just then, the door swings open, and Phoebe enters with a tall stack of clothes in her arms.

"It's all I've got," she says, dropping them onto the table.

I quickly examine the pile, grateful for anything other than the patient uniform.

35

I wake up to the feeling of Theo's arms wrapped around me, his warm breath brushing against the nape of my neck as he sleeps. A soft smile graces my lips. For a fleeting moment, the weight of the past few weeks is lifted from my shoulders. I forget about the capture by the rogues, the torment at Alheim, and the fact that we have no choice but to leave Barren for good.

My eyes scan the dimly lit basement, catching sight of Alexis snoring on the other couch, while Phoebe has settled on the floor. A cynical thought crosses my mind: what if she's not a clairvoyant, but actually a vampire?

Theo stirs beside me, his movements slow as he wakes up. A soft moan escapes his lips before he pecks my neck. I glance over at him and meet his sleepy gaze, unable to resist smiling back at his smirk.

"You have no idea how much I missed you," he whispers, his hands gently patterns on my back.

"I missed you too," I smile, but in that moment, the worrying thoughts come rushing back. I lower my gaze, biting my lip anxiously. "I was so scared, Theo. I thought Aurelia did something to you."

His touch is tender as he raises my chin, our eyes locking.

"What matters is we're out of that shithole," he whispers, pulling me closer to him. "We're together now, and we'll figure everything out, okay?"

I nod, my heart fluttering with emotions. Since we exchanged those three words at the morgue, I've felt an even stronger connection with him. But now, there's a fear of losing him that I've never experienced before.

"Theo..." I whisper, my voice barely audible as I lower my gaze. "I don't know if I can leave Barren."

"I know, baby," he murmurs, his voice soft and comforting. "It's not easy for me either, but the rogues know where we are. It's far more dangerous if we stay, even for your dad."

I bite my lip, knowing he's right. The rogues are hunting us down, and it wouldn't take them long before they find us again. Barren is too small for any of us to stay unnoticed, but that doesn't make leaving any easier.

Theo notices the worry in my eyes and gently cups my cheeks.

"Hey, I'm right here with you, okay?" he reassures me softly.

In that moment, our lips hungrily crash together. A soft moan escapes his lips as his hands trail down my back, pulling me closer to his chest. I can't help but feel a burning desire for him, longing to have him this close to me always. My legs instinctively wrap around his torso, feeling his warmth against me. However, a pained grunt escapes his lips as he gently pulls away, his blue eyes meeting mine.

"Are you okay?" I ask, my voice raspy with concern.

He exhales heavily, lifting his hoodie. My eyes widen as I take in the bruises and cuts on his skin. Anger rushes through my veins, wanting to kill Aurelia for doing this to him.

"It's not as bad as it looks," Theo murmurs, noticing my reaction.

"We need to treat this," I insist, shaking my head in concern. I sit up, my eyes urgently scanning the room. "Do you have a first aid kit?"

"Babe, it's fine," he whispers, gently tugging my arm. I know he's trying not to worry me, but I can't bear to see him in pain.

I shoot him a pleading look before he sighs.

"It's in the downstairs bathroom."

In a flash, I hurry up the basement stairs, my footsteps echoing in the silence. Reaching the bathroom, I swiftly open the drawers, searching for the first aid kit. As I rummage through toiletries and supplies, I hear someone approaching from behind, their steps soft against the floorboards.

"Here, let me help," Theo offers, reaching past me to grab the first aid kit.

"What are you doing here? You should be lying down," I say, turning to face him with concern in my eyes.

He tucks a strand of hair behind my ear, his face now inches from mine.

"I didn't want to wake Alexis and Phoebe up," he whispers.

My pulse quickens from his proximity, feeling the air thicken around us.

"Take off your hoodie," I say, trying to maintain composure. A devilish smile forms on his lips, and I feel my cheeks instantly go red.

"Okay," he says, complying with my request. He takes off his hoodie, revealing his defined body. Despite being covered in bruises, I find myself staring at him speechlessly, mesmerised by him. A playful smirk graces Theo's lips, but I quickly clear my throat to refocus.

"Let's get these wounds cleaned up," I say, opening the first aid kit.

With gentle hands, I apply antiseptic to his cuts and bruises, careful not to cause him any further discomfort. Theo's eyes never leave mine, the intensity behind them stirring a rush of emotions within me.

"I'm really sorry Aurelia did this to you…" I say softly, my voice tinged with guilt.

Theo's gaze softens, his hand reaching out to gently cup my chin, urging me to meet his eyes.

"It's not your fault. You were right, she's far more dangerous than we imagined," he reassures. Despite his words, I can't shake the guilt gnawing at me.

"I still feel like it is my fault," I murmur, my fingers tracing the edges of his bandages nervously.

"Why?" Theo's voice is gentle, coaxing me to open up.

"They saw you with me at the hospital, and they must have figured out we were together…" I confess, my gaze dropping to the floor.

His eyes lock with mine before he sighs, his expression filled with understanding.

"It doesn't matter. I'm just glad you're here with me. Plus, we saved Alexis together," he says, his touch comforting as he squeezes my waist.

I let out a sigh, closing the first aid kit.

"Can I ask you something?" I meet his gaze, feeling a hint of uncertainty.

"Sure," he replies, slipping on his hoodie.

"Why does your sister hate me?" I ask, feeling somewhat embarrassed.

"She doesn't... She's just overprotective," he explains, his eyes searching mine. "I know she can be a pain, but she has more experience with the rogues than any of us."

I nod, a moment of silence lingering between us. Even though I'm not entirely convinced, I choose to change the subject. I don't want to speak negatively of his sister.

"I had a vision about you talking to Aurelia, the night she beat you up," I confess. "She said they were after you the night Damon died."

Pain flickers in Theo's blue eyes.

"Damon shouldn't have died..." he murmurs, his voice heavy with regret.

I'm not used to seeing Theo upset, and it tugs at my heartstrings. I inch closer to him until our bodies are almost touching.

"Theo... That wasn't your fault. You know how ruthless the rogues can be," I mutter, attempting to comfort him. But he's unable to meet my gaze, his jaw clenched tightly.

"That should have been me, Cora," he says in a low voice. "But they took the life of an innocent teenager instead."

"You're also an innocent teenager," I remind him, gently cupping his cheeks. His teary eyes meet mine, and the pain reflected in them breaks my heart. Without a word, I pull him into a tight embrace, holding him close as he buries his face in my shoulder. There has to be a way to break free from this dreadful situation.

"What if we figure out something with Chris?" I suggest, my voice barely above a whisper.

Theo pulls back slightly, his expression turning curious.

"What do you mean?" he asks, furrowing his brows.

"Chris has resources," I continue, feeling a glimmer of hope. "Maybe he can help us come up with a plan to stay in Barren or deal with the rogues. We can't keep running forever."

Theo clenches his jaw, his body tensing with scepticism.

"What makes you think he would do something like that?" he questions, his tone guarded.

"He was my boyfriend. He must at least have some sympathy," I argue.

He sighs, rubbing his temples.

"He was your watcher. You can't trust them, no matter who it is. The whole thing was staged," he explains.

Even though I know Chris works for the rogues, a part of me refuses to accept that it was all fake. How could someone pretend to be in love?

"It might not have been," I say with a gulp, the words sticking in my throat.

Theo's expression softens, sympathy evident in his eyes.

"I understand it's hard to accept, but trust me, it's better to face the truth," he says gently, reaching out to squeeze my hand.

I exhale, knowing he's right.

I recall the times when Chris caused problems in school, doing his best to isolate me from everyone else. I remember the negative things he said about Helena when I began spending time with her, and how unsettled he seemed when I started forming new friendships. The hardest part to accept is that I never saw through his facade. I genuinely believed he was a good person and even thought I was in love with him.

Every time I think about being with Chris, I'm reminded of the weakness I felt. I remember feeling lost without him, like I couldn't accomplish anything on my own. Our relationship was toxic—there's no denying it. The worst part is that people constantly warned me about it, but I chose not to see it until it was too late.

"I just wish I had realised sooner," I mutter, biting my lip.

"You have no idea how many times I wanted to tell you," he confesses.

"I don't understand why I defended him for so long," I murmur, my voice tinged with self-doubt. "I feel incredibly naive."

"You're not. Manipulative people have a way of making you see only their good side, no matter what they do. And the rogues are experts at that," he reassures me. He takes my hands, pulling me closer to him. Our eyes meet, the intensity in his gaze sending my heart racing.

The way I feel about Theo is completely different from how I felt about Chris. With Theo, even if the world were falling apart around us, I know he'd never leave my side.

In that moment, I'm irresistibly drawn to him, as if pulled by a magnetic force. Our lips collide eagerly, and his tongue gently intertwines with mine. His arms tighten around my waist, and a soft moan escapes his lips, igniting a fire within me. I've wanted to hold him like this for weeks, to feel his hands exploring every inch of my body, to revel in the warmth of his skin against mine. As he intensifies the kiss, he pushes me against the bathroom door, eliciting a moan from my lips. I instinctively wrap my legs around him, feeling his warmth between my thighs.

"Are you sure about this?" he whispers in a raspy voice, sending shivers down my spine. My hands travel down his torso, fiddling with the hem of his boxers.

"I've never been surer about anything," I say, unable to tear my gaze away from him.

We lock eyes for a few intense seconds, the tension thickening the air around us. Then, our lips find each other again, our bodies responding with even more hunger. His hands explore my body, planting kisses on my neck that make me arch my back. With a groan, he tightens his grip on my waist as he reaches for a condom with his other hand. He steadies himself, pressing his hips against mine.

"I love you, you know that?" he whispers, his voice dripping with desire.

"I love you, too," I whisper back, our words tainted by the passion between us. A moan escapes his lips as he thrusts against me, prompting me to bite my lip to prevent anyone from hearing us.

36

I never imagined my first time with Theo would be so incredible. I thought it might be awkward, like in the past, but it felt completely natural. During those four days at Alheim, the fear of losing him consumed me, but being so close to him now gives me hope that we can overcome the evil clutches of the rogues.

As we head down to the basement, both Phoebe and Alexis are already up, sorting through boxes of food and supplies for our departure.

"Where were you guys?" Phoebe asks, glancing back at us.

My cheeks instantly flush, hoping that neither of them heard us. Luckily, Theo is quick to reply.

"They beat me up pretty bad at Alheim, Cora was helping me patch up."

Worry flashes across Phoebe's face, pausing her actions as she looks at her younger brother.

"They beat you? Holy shit..." Phoebe exclaims.

Theo shrugs, attempting to downplay the seriousness of the conversation.

"I'm fine, she's a great nurse," he says, squeezing my hand.

I bite my lip to contain a smile, feeling a giddy sensation in my stomach. Phoebe's eyes flicker between Theo and me, as if she's trying to piece something together.

"We need to start packing. I'm gonna find a place to stay," she declares, reaching for her laptop.

Theo nods, taking a seat next to her on the couch.

"I can help you with that. We need to find a safe place to stay, as far away from Barren as possible," he says, studying Phoebe's screen.

I approach Alexis, whose expression still holds the same fear as the moment I met her. In a way, she reminds me of how I felt when I discovered I was a clairvoyant—the feeling of being in danger and seeing the world through a different lens. The difference is that I wasn't sedated, tortured, and damaged for years.

"Did you get some sleep?" I ask, giving her a small smile. She shrugs, loading some canned food into the cardboard box.

"I guess it's not easy to sleep when you find out you're an orphan," she murmurs.

My heart drops, feeling nothing but sympathy towards her. I gently squeeze her shoulder, hoping to offer some comfort.

"Hey. You're one of us. We're in this together," I say reassuringly.

She responds with a sad smile before continuing to stack cans into the box.

"Alright..." Phoebe murmurs, her gaze fixed on her screen. "Looks like there's an Airbnb a few miles away from Newton."

I've never been to Newton before, all I know is that it's four hours away from Barren.

"Is it safe?" I ask, my voice tinged with concern as I glance at Phoebe.

"Should be. I'm using my fake ID to book it," she replies, her fingers flying over the keyboard.

"You have a fake ID?" Alexis' eyebrows shoot up in surprise.

"It's one of the measures we have to take to stop the rogues from tailing us," Phoebe explains, her tone blunt. She glances at Theo before adding, "You and I have them, so we're covered. But Alexis and... Carla, right?" Her eyes dart to me, clearly aiming to provoke a reaction.

Instantly, a surge of anger courses through me. Before all this, I might have ignored comments like that, but since the rogues, there's a part of me that refuses to accept any disrespect.

"Can you just tell me what your problem is with me?" I snap, my jaw clenched tightly.

"My brother is in danger because of you," Phoebe declares, her gaze drifting to Theo, anger burning in her eyes. "I told you, Theo, but you wouldn't listen."

"Phoebe.." Theo warns but she continues.

"We're in this mess because of her, and you know it."

Her words sting like venom, as if she were a wild serpent that has just attacked me, intensifying the tension between us. As my heart rate accelerates and adrenaline surges through my body, I enter fight mode.

Suddenly, a wave of dizziness washes over me. My ears ring, drowning out the argument between Phoebe and Theo, as I find myself consumed by a vision, a new setting materialising around me.

I find myself standing in the centre of the highway, enveloped in darkness and silence. The desolate road stretches endlessly ahead, and my gaze fixes on a faint light in the distance. As it draws nearer, growing brighter yet blinding, the ear-splitting screech of tires overwhelms me. Before I can react, I'm knocked unconscious, instantly engulfed by a bone-chilling darkness.

My eyes snap open, my heart lurching at the sight before me. There, sprawled on the unforgiving pavement, lies a body stained with blood. As my sight focuses, a chill runs down my spine as I realise who it is.

It's my dad.

His once-familiar features are twisted in pain, his lifeless eyes staring blankly ahead. The world seems to blur around me, the sounds of traffic fading into the background as I kneel beside him, my mind reeling with disbelief. The wailing of ambulance sirens floods my ears as the scene begins to dim, until finally, it fades to black.

My eyes snap open with a gasp, struggling to catch my breath as I realise I'm back in the basement. Alexis, Theo, and Phoebe gaze at me in horror, their eyes widened, and lips parted in shock.

"What happened?" Theo asks urgently, hurrying over to me. His worried gaze scans me as if trying to read my mind, but my throat has gone dry from terror. Panic continues to swell in my chest, suffocating me as if I were drowning.

It takes me a few moments to find my voice.

"My dad is in the hospital," I manage to choke out, tears streaming down my cheeks.

A heavy silence settles over us as Theo, Phoebe, and Alexis exchange shocked glances.

·····

Phoebe and I have been bickering for the past half hour about me visiting my dad at the hospital, as if it's her decision to make. I'm at my breaking point with her constant arguments, and one thing is for certain—I'll never leave my only family, no matter the risk.

"I don't think you understand the gravity of our situation, Cora," Phoebe insists, irritation evident in her tone. "The rogues are everywhere. Anyone can snitch on you. This is an awful idea. It's a trap."

I clench my jaw at her words, my eyes darting around the room as I struggle to maintain composure. Anger bubbles in my chest, my fists tightening. I can't take this anymore.

"Look, Phoebe!" I shout, cutting through the clamour around me. "It's my dad we're talking about. You can't expect me to sit here and do nothing."

Alexis shrinks into her seat like a scared deer, while Theo remains stern with his arms crossed. Phoebe raises an eyebrow, probably insulting me in her thoughts.

Phoebe has no idea about the guilt I'm experiencing. My dad is in the hospital because of me; our escape from Alheim led the rogues right to him. She doesn't know that if I had discovered my abilities earlier, I might have prevented my mom's death in that car crash. I could have possibly saved Alexis' parents too. All those lives were at risk, and I couldn't do anything to help them. And I won't let my dad suffer the same fate.

My eyes lock with Theo's, silently pleading for his support. He must understand; he knows the weight of being responsible for someone's death. But to my surprise, he sighs, lowering his gaze.

"Babe, Phoebe is right," he murmurs softly. "They're trying to lure us."

My heart sinks, feeling an unfamiliar tension settle between us. I genuinely believed he would support me.

Phoebe shoots me a sly glance, but I stand my ground, refusing to give in.

"I don't care, I'm going. I'm not letting them kill him," I declare, rising from the couch. If it means facing danger alone, then so be it.

"Fine. But I'm coming with you," Theo says, his eyes filled with determination. Phoebe gives him a deathly glare, but he brushes it off.

"No. It's too dangerous," I argue, but he shakes his head.

"You're not going there alone," he insists, his voice firm. With purposeful strides, he grabs his leather jacket from the couch, his muscles tensing as if preparing for a battle.

Phoebe's face flushes with a mix of anger and disappointment as she approaches her brother.

"This is a suicide mission. Don't you realise they're waiting for you in there?" Phoebe argues. but I've already made up my mind.

I need to see if my dad is okay.

37

The hospital's slate-grey floors and the cold glow of linoleum lights send an unsettling shiver down my spine. Usually, at this time, dozens of patients would be walking around or seated in wheelchairs, with nurses calling up their assigned patients, and the air would be filled with the pungent aroma of coffee wafting from the machine.

But not this time. The atmosphere is markedly different, almost as if the hospital has been abandoned. Only one woman occupied the front desk, who directed me to my dad's room without hesitation.

I can't shake the feeling of an eerie presence watching me as I navigate the empty corridors, adding an extra layer of unease to the already sombre atmosphere. I take the lift to the second floor, the metallic clanking of the structure creating an unsettling melody.

The elevator chimes, and as the doors open, I find myself facing another deserted hallway. The scent of freshly cleaned floors, which is just the sharp smell of bleach, twists my stomach. My heart sinks into my chest as I locate Room 203, realising I have no clue about my next move. Opening the door, an immediate stabbing sensation pierces my heart. The room is dimly lit, with only a small lamp on the table near the door. My dad lies motionless on the bed, the soft hum of the heart monitor filling the room. An IV drip is connected to his arm, and I notice his swollen eyelids and a purple bruise on his jaw. Witnessing him in such a state brings a suffocating pain to my chest.

"Dad?" I choke out, rushing towards him. My hands are cold as I reach for his, but he doesn't react to my touch.

My tears fall onto the clean, white bedsheets, gently touching his wounded face. I wish I could tell him about the situation, that I'm a clairvoyant and that the rogues are after me. I wish I could reassure him that everything will be okay, but the truth is, I'm unsure of that myself.

As I sit by my dad's bedside, I grapple with the painful reality before me; the only way to keep him safe is to leave Barren for good and never look back. I wipe away my tears, knowing that I have no choice. My heart aches, torn between the love for my dad and the harsh truth that his safety may only be found in my absence.

I rise from the bed with a heavy sigh, planting a gentle kiss on his forehead before mustering the strength to leave. As the door closes behind me, a sudden realisation sends a chill down my spine.

The rogues won't back down unless we give in to them. Until we do, they'll harm or torture the people we care about. They will never let any of us be happy, or even at peace.

I walk down the corridor, a surge of anger coursing through me as I search for the exit. In that moment, something in the corner of my eye grabs my attention—a familiar face that leaves me speechless.

Helena.

She looks at me with wide eyes, and I notice she's dressed in a nurse uniform. Though she appears a bit older than the last time we met, her eyes convey a mix of innocence and fear.

"Cora? Where the hell have you been? I-" she exclaims, her voice trembling. She abruptly stops, staring at me as if she's just seen a ghost. To be fair, I've been missing for four weeks without a plausible explanation.

"I ran away," I answer, my tone flat. Ever since the rogues kidnapped me on my way to Les Misérables, it feels like a part of me has lost touch with the normal world, including my old friendships.

Helena remains wide-eyed, almost as if she's analysing my answer.

I try walking away, but Helena's grip on my arm stops me in my tracks. She looks at me with a firm expression, silently asking for an explanation.

"Cora, please," she pleads, her eyes searching mine for answers. "You can't just drop off the grid like that and expect us not to worry. What happened? Where have you been?"

I meet her gaze, torn between the desire to trust her and the fear of her possibly betraying me. The words stick in my throat, a complex mixture of emotions swirling within me.

Helena has been there for me since day one, welcoming me into her circle of friends and offering her support. She stood by me through tough times, like when Chris cheated on me, when I was on antipsychotics, and even during the aftermath of the forest fire.

However, Theo's words linger in my mind, warning me that we can't trust anyone with our secret, or our loved ones will get hurt— just like my dad. The image of his weakened state brings me back to the present moment. In defence, I jerk my arm away, shooting Helena a warning look.

"Leave me alone, Helena," I reply flatly.

I walk away with clenched fists, a mixture of emotions churning within me. I have no choice but to distance myself from the world, even if it hurts. My steps quicken as I scan for the exit, knowing that I don't have much time before the rogues find me.

As I turn the corner in search of the lift, a wave of terror grips my stomach when I find myself face to face with Chris. His jaw is clenched, and a fierce, fiery gaze burns in his eyes as he blocks the path to the fire exit. I've never seen him exude such an intimidating presence, and it terrifies me.

In that instant, the sound of approaching footsteps intensifies, and Theo emerges from the other side of the corridor. Relief washes over him as he sees me, but the moment is short-lived. His expression swiftly transforms into anger as he glances at Chris.

Theo advances towards me, his eyes meeting mine with a sense of urgency.

"The lifts don't work. That's our only exit," he informs, concern in his tone.

The realisation sinks in as Theo's words hang in the air. We have no choice but to confront Chris, who will undoubtedly put up a fight. I feel a mix of apprehension and determination, knowing that facing him won't be easy, especially considering the anger simmering in his gaze.

Theo takes a steadying breath, his expression serious.

"We need to be careful. Stay together, and let's figure out how to calm things down without making it worse," he suggests, but I shake my head. I've had enough of playing fair, especially since he's responsible for my dad's car accident.

My fists clench as an inevitable anger bubbles within me.

"What do you want, Chris?" I demand, my voice resonating through the empty hallway.

In that instant, the lights above us dim, casting an eerie silence over the corridor.

Chris responds with a cynical chuckle.

"Yelling won't change anything, Cora. This place is deserted," he remarks.

"You almost killed my dad!" I angrily shout, tears brimming in my eyes. He made the rogues do this. He told them where my dad was. All of this is his fault.

Chris' expression remains stoic, his eyes bearing a hint of defiance.

"We had to get you here one way or another. It was actually your best friend Helena who ratted you out," he says, a sly smirk playing on his lips.

The revelation sends a jolt through me, a mix of betrayal and disbelief coursing through my veins. I turn to Theo, searching for confirmation or denial in his eyes, but his angry gaze remains fixed on Chris. The tension in the air becomes electrifying as we stand in the corridor, aware that it's only a matter of seconds before chaos unfolds.

"Step away from the exit, Chris. It doesn't have to be this way," Theo warns in a low voice.

Chris chuckles, unfazed by Theo's menacing gaze and words.

"Over my dead body," he retorts.

"Don't cry when I kick your ass, then," Theo fires back, a smirk playing on his lips.

Without warning, Chris seizes Theo's shirt, his fingers tightening around the fabric. With a swift, forceful motion, he shoves Theo against the wall, the impact echoing with a resounding crunch. Reacting quickly, Theo retaliates. His fist connects with Chris's temple, causing him to stagger back. I remain frozen as they fight, the atmosphere thick with a palpable tension.

Enraged, Chris regains his composure and charges forward. With a furious determination, he presses Theo against the wall, the collision creating a jarring thud. Theo grimaces, but his resilience remains evident as he spits blood onto the linoleum floor.

"Don't you wanna be in a band? Be someone? You know they won't let you," he growls. "You're a slave to their game, Chris."

A moment of tension hangs between them before a sudden anger flashes across Chris' face. He grunts, wiping blood from his lip.

"I know who I am," he hisses, raising his fist as he prepares to strike Theo.

I need to think quickly. Beating each other up won't lead to any answers. If I don't intervene, they might end up killing each other.

In a desperate attempt to break up the fight, my eyes dart around the corridor. Spotting a fire extinguisher in the corner of my eye, I grab it and rush toward Chris. With a swift motion, I bring the extinguisher down, aiming for a non-lethal strike to stop the escalating violence. The metallic thud echoes through the corridor as the extinguisher connects with Chris, breaking the momentum of the fight.

Yells of pain escape Chris as he reels from the blow, causing him to release his grip on Theo. Seizing the opportunity, Theo kicks open the fire emergency door with determination, signalling for me to follow him. We rush down the stairs with a surge of adrenaline, conscious that time is ticking before Chris calls for backup. In that moment, everything accelerates—our ragged breaths, heavy footsteps, and the metallic clanking as Chris chases us down the stairs.

Theo forcefully pushes open the door at the bottom of the stairs, and we spill out into the daylight. In the brief pause before our next move, I exchange a determined glance with Theo before breaking into a sprint. Chris' footsteps echo behind us as we run, weaving through the quiet streets and alleys toward Evergreen. Theo and I share a knowing glance before dashing into the forest, instantly enveloped by the canopy of trees. As we sprint through the greenery, the only sounds echoing are our breaths, and Chris' footsteps gradually vanish into the forest's stillness.

My lungs feel heavy as we burst into a clearing, forcing us to stop and take a moment to regain our breath. With heavy panting, I glance over my shoulder, searching for any signs of danger. It appears that, for the moment, the rogues have lost track of us.

As we catch our breath, Theo takes out his phone, a determined look on his face. He dials a number, bringing the phone to his ear. I watch as he waits for someone to answer, but there's only silence on the other end. Theo furrows his brows, cursing under his breath.

"My phone's dead. We need to tell Phoebe and Alexis to get out of here as soon as possible," Theo says urgently, his footsteps quickening.

With my heart in my throat, I break into a sprint, following him deeper into the forest. In that moment, a heart-clenching realisation dawns on me. Our time in Barren is running out. The rogues know where my dad is, and in due time, they will find us again. Worst of all, Chris was the one that helped them out. The extent of betrayal and harm he's caused goes beyond words now.

The leaves crunch under our feet as we run, and our heavy breaths cut through the silent tension of the forest. Yet, the unshakable feeling that we're being followed keeps us on edge, causing us to check over our shoulders every few seconds.

Theo's house finally comes into view, still evoking a sense of nostalgia each time I lay eyes on it. He swiftly unlocks the basement door, which opens with a loud screech. Phoebe and Alexis rise from the couch, assuming a defensive stance as if they were anticipating an attack. Relief washes over their faces when they realise it's just us. Theo swiftly retrieves his backpack from a stack of boxes without pausing to glance at Phoebe or Alexis.

"What happened?" Alexis asks, her voice quivering.

"We were cornered by a rogue. We need to leave immediately," Theo mutters, rearranging some boxes filled with canned food.

"I warned you it was a bad idea!" Phoebe exclaims, hastily gathering her belongings.

Alexis stands frozen amid the chaos, panic evident in her eyes.

"Alexis, we need to leave. Now," I command, hurriedly packing a duffel bag with clean clothes and canned goods.

"Where?" she croaks, but we continue to pack swiftly for our escape. Time is running out fast, but the question lingers: Where do we go from here? My house isn't safe, and neither is Theo's. We're trapped in this hellhole with no place to hide.

Panic tightens its grip on me, my breaths becoming shallower by the second. These panic attacks seem to be happening more frequently as time passes and our situation worsens. I need to think. Where could we go?

Theo quickly senses my panic attack, placing a comforting hand on my shoulder.

"Don't worry, babe. We'll figure it out. Let's focus on getting out of here first," he says calmly. However, my eyes sting with tears, and the room feels like it's spinning around me.

"I can't, Theo. My dad was run over by a rogue," I croak, wiping away tears.

Theo clenches his jaw, pain evident in his blue eyes.

"I know, baby. That's why we need to leave," he says, pulling me into a comforting hug.

A few tears dampen Theo's shoulder as I find comfort in his embrace. He plants a gentle kiss on my head before we reluctantly pull away from each other. Dark bruises stain his jaw, and a cut marks his lip. Chris should never have hurt him like that. Guilt stings my chest, swallowing the knot in my throat. I should have faced Chris on my own.

In that instant, a loud bang echoes from outside, startling all of us. Phoebe's voice, shaky and tinged with worry, shatters the heavy silence.

"Guys… Are you sure you weren't being followed?"

A palpable tension hangs in the air as we exchange nervous glances, uncertainty written on our faces.

"I… I think so," Theo stammers.

"Are you a hundred percent sure?" Phoebe presses, her concern intensifying.

The tension in the room thickens, an incoming sense of unease settling among us. Theo's nervous eyes meet mine, his bottom lip nervously caught between his teeth. He knows we've made a grave mistake.

There's a time bomb about to explode, and we all know it.

Just as the tension reaches its peak, the doorbell rings.

38

The unexpected ringing lingers in the air, casting a chilling tension among the four of us. Our eyes fixate on the flimsy basement door, each of us gripped by an increasing sense of dread. If the rogues have found us, it's a dead end. The seconds drag on like hours as we remain frozen, silently praying that anyone but the rogues is on the other side of the door.

But in that instant, the doorbell rings again. After two seconds, it chimes a few more times.

Panic sets in. Fear grips us. Adrenaline surges through our veins.

Theo moves fast, snatching a baseball bat before rushing toward the basement door. Phoebe, her jaw still dropped in shock, immediately springs into action. She swiftly shoves some cardboard boxes into place, barricading the door.

Adrenaline seeps into my bones as I scan my surroundings, searching for anything that could serve as a weapon. With urgency, I direct Alexis to take cover behind the couch before grabbing a robust metal pipe from a pile of discarded materials. I hurry over to Theo, prepared to use the pipe for defence.

A heavy silence envelops us, and we exchange nervous glances. Minutes stretch into what feels like hours as our eyes remain fixed on the door, anticipating the next ring of the bell. But nothing comes.

The tension continues to escalate as another ten minutes drag by in unsettling silence.

"Are you sure they're not inside?" Alexis whispers, her words piercing through the quiet. I gulp, contemplating the unsettling possibility.

"I'll go check," Theo whispers, but I quickly shake my head.

"No way. That's too dangerous. They will shoot you," I interject, a surge of fear tightening my chest. I can't bear the thought of losing Theo.

"Nobody is going anywhere. We need to stick together," Phoebe orders.

The tension in the basement thickens as Phoebe's commanding words hang in the air. Just as Theo tightens his grip on the baseball bat, a sudden shift in his expression catches our attention. His eyes glaze over, and the bat slips from his grasp, clattering to the floor.

"Theo?" I call out, his empty expression intensifying my anxiety. I instinctively grab his arm, feeling his body tense like steel. He breathes rapidly, each inhale resembling a panicked gasp.

"Give him space. He's having a vision," Phoebe instructs sternly, her gaze fixed on Theo. I shoot her a scowl before turning my attention back to him.

Theo's vacant gaze gives the impression that he's mentally absent, and his body remains rigid and unresponsive. It's as if he's caught up in a different world, absorbed in whatever vision is unfolding in his mind.

I've never witnessed anyone experiencing a premonition, and I realise how frightening I must look when I have one.

Within seconds, his breathing starts to steady, and the tension that gripped his body starts to ease. As I squeeze his ice-cold hand, his eyes snap open at my touch. He meets my concerned gaze, panic evident in his eyes.

"What happened?" I nervously ask, intertwining my fingers with his.

Alexis' jaw drops in complete disbelief at what she just witnessed, while Phoebe's expression reflects concern rather than fear.

Theo's gaze moves hesitantly from one face to another, as if summoning the courage to reveal what he's seen.

"It's Chris. He's about to break in."

•••••

"What do we do now?"

"He's gonna kill us!"

Alexis and Phoebe's panicked voices blend into a cacophony, causing the room to spin around me as fear tightens its grip.

No matter what we do, our outcome remains the same.

Our lives will always be at risk.

As their voices reach an ear-piercing crescendo, I can feel the pressure building in my chest. Unable to contain it any longer, a scream involuntarily escapes from me, shattering the tension in the air.

"Guys! Can you shut up?" I shout, bringing a sudden silence to the room.

Phoebe shoots me an offended look before letting out a scoff.

"Are you serious? Your watcher is literally outside trying to kill us," Phoebe snaps, scowling at me. I know she silently blames me for dragging them into this mess. After all, she was the first person against the idea of visiting my dad at the hospital.

"I know, but can we focus, please?" I urge, trying to steer the conversation back to a practical solution. "We need a plan. We can't just stay here and wait for him to break in."

Phoebe sighs, realising the weight of the situation.

"You're right. We need to do something," she says, her hazel eyes burning with determination.

"What's the plan then?" Alexis asks, her eyes darting from one face to another.

A tense silence hangs in the air for a few moments as Theo clenches his jaw, seemingly hesitant to speak.

"We need to kill Chris," he finally states his words cutting through the tense atmosphere.

My eyes widen in disbelief, a cold sense of dread washing over me.

"What? There's no way we're killing Chris!" I exclaim, my voice rising in protest.

Phoebe and Theo exchange glances, as if they silently hoped I would agree. They can't be serious.

"Cora, he won't stop until one of us is dead. It's kill or be killed," Theo says, and Phoebe nods in agreement.

"He's right, we have no choice," she adds.

I angrily shake my head, shooting her a disapproving look.

"Excuse me? We are NOT killing Chris."

Phoebe releases a frustrated exhale, a fiery intensity flickering in her hazel eyes.

"Listen, Cora, he won't quit until he tracks you down. And once he finds you, he will find the rest of us."

An intense desire to curse at her wells up within me, but I muster the strength to hold back. I made a promise to Theo that I'd try to get along with his sister.

Alexis, who had been observing the conflict from a distance, gives us a stern look.

"I say we kill him. Those people killed my parents," she declares, crossing her arms over her chest. Just five minutes ago, she was a terrified girl hiding behind the couch, and now she's advocating for Chris's death?

I can't believe this.

"Alexis, he did not kill them. He's innocent," I interject, anger swelling in my chest.

Theo chuckles under his breath, a hint of irritation in his eyes.

"He's not innocent, Cora. He kidnapped you, handed you to the rogues, put both of us in Alheim, almost killed us, and nearly killed your dad," he fires back.

My lip trembles as the weight of his words sinks in. He's right; the person I once trusted the most in this world has betrayed me repeatedly. But no matter who Chris has become and how deeply he is involved with the rogues, I can't bring myself to kill him. Not even after he tried to kill my dad.

"I ... I can't let you guys kill him. I'll figure it out, I-"

The sudden, shrill noise of breaking glass violently interrupts my words, and a collective scream pierces the air as panic takes hold of us. Phoebe and Theo act instinctively, pushing against the door with determined force to create a makeshift barricade.

A few heart-stopping seconds of tense silence fill the room. Suddenly, the calm is shattered by a series of loud, aggressive bangs against the door. Fear tightens its grip within me as the realisation sets in—it's Chris trying to break in.

Phoebe and Theo fight back in terror, forcefully pressing against the door in a gut-wrenching struggle to keep the threat at bay. Fear churns in my stomach as I clutch Theo's bat, preparing to defend myself, while Alexis grabs the scrap pipe.

The chilling realisation sinks in—this could be the end.

The relentless banging outside continues, and Phoebe and Theo's forceful grunts echo in the air. Phoebe's face has paled, the realisation hitting her that it's a dead end. Chris will tear down the door, hinge by hinge.

I must concentrate. I need to maintain control.

Rushing to help Phoebe and Theo, time appears to freeze when the sharp report of a gunshot echoes through the basement. As my eyes reopen, an involuntary gasp escapes my lips. Blood stains Theo's shirt, his pained grunts filling the air as he fights to keep the door shut. Phoebe, her lips slightly parted, stares in shock at her injured brother, her body tense with disbelief. Theo groans loudly, screwing his eyes shut, pouring every ounce of his strength to maintain the barricade.

The violent thumps suddenly stop, but the relief is short lasting. The raw terror inside me intensifies as the basement lights are switched off.

39

My vision regains focus, shock settling into my core as I take in my surroundings. In the darkness, I can vaguely see the outline of the basement, and a gasp escapes my lips as I realise I'm tied to a chair. My distress deepens as I see Theo, Phoebe, and Alexis in the same situation. The rogues have found us again. Perhaps this time, there's no way to escape. My heart skips a beat as Chris emerges from the shadows with a gun, a wicked grin on his face.

"You can't run anymore," he taunts, his serpent eyes fixing on me. "This is the reality you have to face."

The basement's shadows make it hard to see the others' faces, but Theo's anguished grunts and blood-stained shirt only suggest one thing.

We're screwed.

A surge of anger courses through my body as the feeling of betrayal sinks in. When I learned Chris was my watcher, I genuinely believed he was lost, clueless about the situation he had stepped into. I saw him as just a teenager manipulated by the rogues and their twisted ideology. However, the darkness in his eyes now suggests he might not be who I thought he was. He's no longer the bass player for The Rebellions who secretly enjoyed strawberry mojitos; he's the villain.

With a menacing posture, Chris kneels before me, his eyes gleaming with malice. A hostile tension hangs in the air as our eyes meet before he rips off the duct tape from my lips. Tears brim in my eyes from the gesture, but I muster the strength to keep my composure.

There must be a way to break down Chris's ego. Verbal abuse? No, that would be foolish; I'd end up dead. Think, Cora. Think.

He wants me to be angry. Anger is what got us here in the first place. We challenged him, and now our lives are at stake.

Chris' gaze remains locked on me, like a leopard anticipating my next move. Maybe I should try a different strategy, one that will catch him off guard. While he may have us at gunpoint, I have something he doesn't—clairvoyant abilities. I can reverse this situation if I play my cards right.

I bite my lip, forcing tears to well up in my eyes.

"I can't believe you betrayed me like this, Chris. Don't you feel bad about what you're doing?" I ask, my voice quivering.

Chris narrows his eyes, his jaw clenched as he retorts, "Actually, I do. I feel nothing but pity for you miserable bastards."

Theo releases an angry grunt, the sound muffled by the tape on his lips. Chris chuckles under his breath at Theo before leaning towards me. His intimidating green eyes send a shiver down my spine, his face mere inches from mine.

"You're all a damn menace to society. For hundreds of years, you people have been changing outcomes," he hisses. "Your evil nature of changing the future to benefit your own damn selves stops those who deserve power from having it. You are all the reason our world isn't moving forward."

I am momentarily rendered speechless by his words. I'm surprised that this is the narrative the rogues feed people like Chris about us, portraying us as evil, selfish beings.

"What?" I ask, furrowing my brows in disbelief.

Chris laughs, dismissively rolling his eyes at me.

"You have no idea, do you? Who do you think started the Cold War? It was because one of you predicted it. You helped the Russians gain power. And George Bush? You think Americans voted for him?" He coldly cackles. "No. You clairvoyants made him the President of the United States. You sick-"

"That's such bullshit. The government must have manipulated us to make sure he won. They were the ones who desired it to happen; they just used us to achieve their goals," I interject, earning a glare from Chris.

"That's where you're wrong." He releases a manic laugh, shaking his head as if I were ignorant. "Your people have started so many wars because you get involved. You interfere with nature, with destiny. You alter reality to get your way. You're the reason corruption exists today," he babbles.

I shake my head in disapproval and disgust. The rogues are clearly skilled at brainwashing, but I must stand firm.

"Chris, that doesn't make any sense..." I utter, sighing. "Doesn't it anger you that your own government exploits innocent people for their own benefit?"

A brief silence fills the air, as if he's considering my perspective, and for a moment, I think that my plan worked. But that glimmer of hope shatters as Chris erupts into laughter—a wicked sound reverberating through the basement. A visible wave of anger courses through Chris, causing fear to crawl up my spine. His eyes narrow, and I brace myself for whatever might come next.

Before I can react, he lunges at Theo. A sickening thud echoes through the basement as Chris delivers a brutal blow to Theo's already injured body. Fear and helplessness consume me as I witness the violent scene unfolding before my eyes.

I watch in horror as blood drips down Theo's jaw.

"Please, don't hurt him!" I cry out, my heart clenching.

Chris suddenly seizes Theo's neck, flames of rage in his eyes.

"You're a slippery one, aren't you?" he taunts with a chuckle. Despite the abuse, Theo remains motionless, not showing any resistance. It's almost as if he anticipated a situation like this. A cry of fear escapes my chest as Chris delivers another brutal blow on Theo's face.

"Stop!" I yell, but my words are powerless. Chris smirks, his sadistic pleasure evident in the twisted curve of his lips. Ignoring my plea, he continues attacking Theo, relentless and merciless. Each blow sends shockwaves through the room, and I feel a growing sense of helplessness.

Phoebe's eyes widen in horror, and Alexis struggles against her restraints, frustration and fear etched across her face. I can't stand by and watch Chris keep beating Theo.

"Please, Chris! Stop!" I plead, tears streaming down my cheeks.

Chris drops his hands to his side, momentarily regaining his breath. The room is filled with an eerie silence as we all process the brutality that just occurred. Theo remains still, blood trickling down his face, and my heart aches for him.

"You were supposed to die months ago, you know that? Instead, they killed my stepbrother," Chris breathes, his body trembling as he speaks. He then spits on Theo, resembling a cobra attacking its prey, but Theo doesn't even flinch. He maintains his angry glare on Chris.

Driven by a cruel satisfaction, Chris moves in on Theo and forcefully tears the tape from his mouth. Theo winces in pain, but he glares defiantly at Chris. A few seconds of tension linger, thick with simmering resentment between them.

Surprisingly, Theo chuckles, his expression transforming instantly to one of superiority and control.

"Your gang is so incompetent they didn't even realise who they killed," Theo taunts, smirking.

Chris's face turns crimson, intense rage consuming him. He's on the verge of exploding.

"Chris-"

My words are interrupted by the gut-wrenching sound of bones cracking as Chris' fist connects to Theo's jaw.

"Stop!" I scream, tears welling in my eyes as Theo weakly slumps back into the chair. Blood surges from the wound on his cheek, but his furious gaze remains fixed on Chris.

"You better savour that laughter," Chris threatens Theo, their faces just inches apart. "Because after tonight, you'll never laugh again."

Dread courses up my spine as Chris raises his fist for another strike.

"Chris, please don't do this!" I shriek, my voice quivering in fear.

"I have to kill him!" Chris roars, the madness in his eyes intensifying. "He's the reason my stepbrother is dead!"

Theo scowls defiantly through the blood on his face, and Chris, consumed by rage, raises his fist for another brutal blow. Before he can strike, I find myself shouting desperate words, hoping to break through the chaos.

"Chris, listen! Killing Theo won't change what happened to your stepbrother. It won't bring him back. You're letting hatred control you, and it's tearing everything apart. There's still a chance to stop this madness. Please, for all our sakes, just think about what you're doing."

The basement falls silent, the weight of my words hanging in the air. Chris lowers his fist to his sides, turning his attention towards me. His appearance is haunting, as if a dark force has taken hold of him—dark bags frame his puffy eyelids, and his complexion lacks its usual colour. He advances toward me like a predator, radiating a malevolence that sends shivers down my spine.

Just when I think he's about to shout at me, his eyes well up with tears.

"You and I... We were meant to be together, Cora. I could have protected you from all of this. But you chose the wrong side."

Chris' words momentarily leave me speechless, my heart clenching in pain. The man before me is unrecognisable, but a glimpse of the 'old Chris' surfaces in his emerald irises. For a brief moment, I see a hint of remorse in his expression, as if he's remembering the nights we spent at the cinema, enjoying hot dogs at The Grub, and watching sunsets from his bedroom window.

But the moment is short-lived as his eyes shift to his next victim.

"Alexis Allen. Pathetic. The rogues wouldn't even want you, anyway," Chris chuckles, lifting her chin with his finger. Her sealed lips tremble, and her eyes well up in despair.

"Leave her alone, Chris. She has nothing to do with this," I protest, but he ignores me.

"You should have stayed at Alheim. You should have remained an amoeba. Now you're just a parasite," Chris snarls, causing Alexis to flinch. Fear is mirrored in her wide eyes, tears dampening her rosy cheeks. He chuckles at her vulnerable state, stroking her cheek to further intimidate her.

Chris then shifts his attention to his last victim, Phoebe.

"Don't even think about speaking to her," Theo warns, anger flashing in his eyes.

Chris ignores him, taking a few menacing steps towards her.

Phoebe's blonde bangs cling to her face from sweat, but she defiantly growls at Chris through the duct tape. Chris beams at her, amused by her brave response.

"You're just as clueless as the rest of them. Being the eldest doesn't change the fact that you know nothing," he snarls at her. A visible shiver runs down Phoebe's spine as Chris looms closer, and she sinks into the chair in fear.

Cold sweat forms on the nape of my neck as I realise the power Chris has over us. Phoebe's expression is broken, as if she has cracked under Chris' violence. He's exploiting all of us, preying on our weaknesses, and he won't stop until we are left with nothing.

I need to think. Otherwise, we won't survive.

Closing my eyes, I block out Chris' furious shouts, chanting 'concentrate' in my mind. There must be a way out of this. I refuse to accept this as my fate. It can't end like this.

I curl my fists tightly, the coarse rope digging into the flesh of my wrists. I inhale slowly and deeply, trying to clear my mind of any thoughts. A tingling sensation courses through my body, and Chris' words dissolve, leaving my mind in total silence. Darkness surrounds me, and the only sound is the rhythmic beat of my own breathing. Red spots dance across my vision, briefly obscuring my sight before clarity returns.

I can see the basement in my mind's eye.

The dimness makes Chris' expression hard to distinguish, but a wicked smile plays on his lips. Alexis sobs into the duct tape, sheer terror reflected in her doe eyes. Phoebe bitterly scowls at Chris, while Theo's physical state worsens by the minute, his head tilted back from anguish. Amongst them, I see myself with a blank expression.

A terrorising realisation grips me. I'm observing the scene from outside my body, as if a thin glass separates me from reality. I've become a silent observer, witnessing everything from a distance.

Am I dissociating? Have I detached myself from my body?

In that moment, a glistening object on a shelf next to Chris captures my attention. Taking a few cautious steps, I'm taken aback when I realise it's a handgun—loaded and ready for use. Looking at my tied-up self, I suddenly realise what Chris' intentions were from the beginning.

He wanted to kill us—one by one. I can't allow it. No, I won't allow it.

The unsettling yet familiar tingling crawls up my spine, signalling that the vision is coming to an end. The image fades to black, and my eyes snap open with a gasp.

Feverish chills cascade down my spine as I snap back to reality, grappling with the weight of what I've just seen. I need to stop Chris at any cost, even if my body trembles with terror in the process. I glance over at Theo, whose face is now ghostly pale from blood loss.

I don't have much time. I need to get Theo to the hospital, but how do I do it?

Swallowing the knot in my throat, I force myself to meet Chris' menacing gaze.

"You have no idea what you're doing, Chris. All of this is going to catch up with you, sooner or later," I mutter coldly.

Chris smirks, unfazed by my words. He strides towards the shelf, his hand reaching for the gun I saw in my vision. My heart races, realising the danger is escalating by the second. I need to act fast before the situation spirals further out of control. His grip tightens on the gun as he takes a step closer, relishing the fear in my eyes. The room feels suffocating, tension hanging thick in the air.

"Save your threats, Cora. You're in no position to make promises about what's coming," he retorts, his voice dripping with malice.

I glance at Theo, silently pleading for him to stay strong. His pale face shows the pain he's enduring, but his eyes reflect determination. There has to be a way out of this, a plan to turn the tables.

"Chris, think about it. What are you gaining from all of this? Revenge won't fill the void. There's a chance to change, to break free from this cycle," I implore, desperation seeping into my voice.

He laughs.

"Change? The only change is that you all are going to die here tonight, just like Damon did."

He waves the glistening gun in the air as if it were a mere toy. As he advances toward me, the room seems to close in. Panic surges through me, and I scan the room for any potential means of escape. The stakes are high, and I need to find a way to turn the tables on Chris and ensure our survival.

"This could have been different if you stayed quiet. If you had just played along or thought, 'I guess I'm crazy,' this would have never happened," Chris mutters with a dry laugh.

I gulp, realising what he's referring to. He's talking about the blackouts, before I became perceptive. He knew what was happening to me, which is why he never freaked out. He was responsible for controlling me. Manipulating me. And not once did I question his deeds.

"What's wrong, Cora? Cat got your tongue?" Chris taunts, a sly smirk playing on his lips.

I only have a couple of seconds to turn this situation around. I dig my nails into the flesh of my hand, forcing tears to spring to my eyes.

"I'm still in love with you, Chris."

40

Desperation and fear surge through me as my words hang heavily in the air. An intense silence descends in the basement, leaving everyone, including Theo, wide-eyed and stunned.

It's a calculated risk, but I need to create an opening. Maybe this approach will save us all. If it means protecting everyone by pretending I am still in love with Chris and forgiving him, then so be it.

A flicker of surprise dances in Chris' eyes, a vulnerability I haven't seen in a long time. For a moment, the atmosphere shifts. It's as if time itself slows down. I watch as Chris, caught off guard, tries to process my unexpected confession.

"What?" he chokes breathlessly, the handgun still in his grasp and pointed at me. I force myself to maintain a steady gaze, my heart pounding in my chest.

"I love you. I thought you loved me, too," I mutter, biting my lip.

A tense silence settles in the air, and I catch Theo's angry gaze fixed on Chris from the corner of my eye. A lone tear rolls down Chris' cheek, his expression softening in response to my words. The anger and hatred that consumed him moments ago seem to have dissolved, and it's as if the old Chris—the one I once loved—has returned. He lowers the handgun with trembling hands, his face revealing the depth of his pain.

With a swift move, I free my wrists from the ropes as I stomp on Chris' foot. He staggers forward with a shriek, and seizing the opportunity, I grab the gun with one hand and wrap my arm around his neck with the other. I aim the gun at Chris' head, my heart pounding relentlessly in my chest. Chris, with wide eyes and breath caught in his throat, realises the tables have turned.

"It's over, Chris. We won't be your victims anymore," I assert, my voice resonating with determination and fear.

Theo's voice breaks the escalating tension in the room.

"Cora! What the hell are you doing?" he pants, fear etched on his face.

My finger hovers over the trigger, and Chris looks at me with wide, terrified eyes. I feel the weight of the gun in my hand, reminding me of the seriousness of my actions. The room falls silent, the air thick with tension.

I meet Theo's gaze, his eyes pleading me. He wants to stop me—but right now, I can't be stopped. I'm only able to focus on Chris, whose body trembles in fear as I press the gun against his temple.

"Cora, put the gun down. We don't want anyone else to get hurt," he implores, his voice desperate.

My mind races, torn between the fear of what Chris might do and the realisation that I now hold the power to end this nightmare. I take a deep breath, trying to steady my trembling hands.

In that instant, a wave of whispers and echoes fills my head, sending the room into a dizzying spiral. I see red, and a multitude of random images swirl before my eyes. I wince, pressing my free hand against my temple to block out the chaos unfolding inside my head. Chris seizes the opportunity, lunging towards me to wrestle the gun out of my hands. Reacting on pure instinct, I tighten my grip on the trigger, and the basement is filled with the deafening roar of a gunshot.

Chris grunts in pain, his body collapsing to the ground. Blood pours from his leg as the room falls into a shocked and heavy silence. I stare down at the gun in my trembling hand, my heart pounding, the weight of the reality crashing over me.

I shot Chris.

•••••

I'm engulfed in darkness for what feels like hours. As my consciousness and sight slowly return, I'm met with a horrifying realisation—I'm standing in the middle of a chaotic, unfamiliar pedestrian crossing. A sea of people surrounds me, and the blaring sound of a nearby ambulance fills my ears. The honk of a car horn snaps me out of my trance, urging me to cross the road.

Catching my breath, a sense of unease washes over me as I take in my surroundings. Towering skyscrapers dominate the skyline, and the air resonates with the chaotic symphony of cars and taxis. A series of questions buzz through my mind, heightening my anxiety.

Where am I?

My question finds an answer the moment I spot the Goldman Sachs Tower in the distance. I'm in Jersey City.

How did I end up here?

The last thing I recall was shooting Chris' leg. I must have blacked out. Shit. I need to piece together what happened.

The city swirls around me as panic sets in, and I instinctively bring my hands to my temples. In that moment, the realisation hits me: the last time I was here, I had a haunting flashback of my mom's death, exactly one year ago. The memories rush back, sending a shiver down my spine.

It was the end of the school day, and as I walked home, a nagging thought crept into the back of my mind. In a matter of seconds, it transformed into a chorus of voices and the ear-piercing sound of tires screeching. My breaths started to become ragged, and my chest tightened in panic.

The next thing I remembered was regaining consciousness on Hudson Street. Chris called me, his voice filled with worry, asking where I was. I explained that I was lost and didn't know the way home. Within half an hour, he found me and brought me back home in his car.

My dad yelled at me for not telling him where I went, but I sat there numb, unable to speak. The worst part was, I couldn't even tell him because I didn't know the answer myself. I remember the lingering hollowness that stayed with me for hours after.

A sudden realisation dawns on me—that day, I blacked out because I had a vision about my mom's death. Theo explained that blackouts occur because when we experience a vision, it blocks our line of sight. It's like watching two movies at the same time—it's impossible.

As I continue to navigate the bustling streets, a growing sense of unease takes hold of me. I find myself drawn towards a narrow, vandalised alleyway; its entrance shadowed by the towering buildings. As I approach cautiously, anxiety tightens my chest. The narrow, dark alleyway seems to swallow the sounds of the city, leaving me with a sense of isolation. The walls are covered in graffiti, and dozens of adverts are scattered on the ground.

"Help the homeless today" "6m Americans are jobless"

As I walk deeper, a feeling of growing danger crawls up my spine. On instinct, I quicken my pace towards the main road, glancing over my shoulder to check if anyone is following me. I step back into the city's chaos, the cacophony of car sounds and people chattering filling the air. As I swiftly cross the road, Newport Station comes into view, and a realisation slowly sinks in.

There's no way I abandoned the group and made it here on my own—not after everything that happened. This has to be a vision. But an even more horrifying truth settles in my chest: What is this vision going to show me?

My body takes control as I navigate through the crowd of people hurrying to their destinations after a long day. A sudden dryness in my throat urges me towards a small hotdog stand with wisps of smoke rising from it. I grab a few bills from my pocket, and the vendor hands me an almost-frozen bottle in return. As I take a refreshing sip, I spot a blinding purple neon sign behind the hot dog stand. In bold letters, it reads *"Psychic Readings Available"*.

Like a moth to a flame, I find myself approaching the psychic store, its glowing purple lights blinding me. A soft chime resonates as

I step inside, instantly enveloped by the mystical ambiance of the store. The air is infused with the soothing scent of incense, gently wafting through the store. Shelves display an array of candles, their flickering flames casting a warm glow on the artefacts showcased. Pendulums dangle delicately, swaying with a mysterious energy, while crystals of different shapes and hues catch the light, scattering reflections around the space.

I am left momentarily mesmerised by my surroundings until I sense someone's eyes on me. A woman with curly black hair and mocha skin greets me from the front desk with a friendly smile.

"By the Gods! You're here!" she chirps, her face lighting up. I'm left puzzled by her sudden reaction, curious about who she might be. Do I know this woman?

"I'm sorry, what?" I ask, furrowing my brows.

The woman beams at me, wrinkles forming around her eyes and the corners of her lips.

"You're here for your reading!" she replies in a sing-song tone, clapping her hands.

Before I can respond, she bounces towards the back of her shop. I hesitate before following her, a sense of eeriness crawling up my spine. I am led into a private reading room with purple walls, adorned with glass ornaments and coloured crystals. I sit across from her at her desk, my gaze fixed on her as she pulls out a silver pouch. The woman lays out the thick tarot cards on the glass table, flipping the first one over. A sudden anxiety grips me as the image of a jester is revealed.

"Ah, yes... The Fool represents your past," she remarks, her gaze lingering on the card. "It's not a bad thing, my dear. The Fool signifies change. In the past, you were innocent and naive. See the jester at the verge of falling off a cliff? But if you look closely, he's gazing at the sky."

I focus intently on the card. The jester has one foot perched on the edge of a cliff, gazing at the sun above him with a foolish grin. A part of me resonates with the card, yet the other part remains sceptical about this woman's abilities.

"It symbolises your unawareness of your surroundings, a lack of true judgment. It marks the beginning of a new era," the psychic continues.

Anticipation fills the air as she turns over the second card, and my heart sinks when The Devil card is revealed. That can't be good.

With panic in my eyes, I try to read the psychic's reaction, but she appears unphased by it.

"The Devil is your present. It doesn't necessarily mean negativity, but a sense of frustration and oppression. You feel trapped in a hell-like situation, and you've welcomed the darkness within you. It's as if life is pressuring you into making the wrong choices, straining your hope for the future."

I gulp, trying to ease the tightness in my throat. If this is about the rogues, she's right. Ever since I became perceptive, it's felt like my back is constantly against the wall.

The woman flips over the final card, unveiling a tall tower with lightning bolts striking its top. Two people are tumbling from the tower, their faces expressing sheer panic as they descend into a deep chasm. Definitely not what I was hoping for.

"Ah, The Tower. As you can see, it is collapsing around them. The lightning bolt represents a moment of truth that will strike you. It will be unexpected yet illuminating, marking the end of an era," she explains.

I sit in stunned silence for a few minutes, my gaze fixed on the three cards laid out in front of me. The pessimistic tone of the reading sends shivers down my back, and visible goose bumps form on my arms. Could she be right? If the psychic's prediction is true, the tower of safety I had created will collapse in the future. An even darker thought creeps into my mind: what could that possibly mean?

The woman gathers the cards, rising from her seat before leaving the room. I follow her to the front desk, still speechless from the reading.

"40 dollars, please," she says, slipping a piece of gum into her mouth.

I can't help but flinch at the price, quickly searching for my wallet. As I hand her the cash, our hands accidentally touch, and in that unexpected moment, a panicked gasp escapes her lips.

"Is everything alright?" I stutter, feeling confused.

Her eyes widen in fear as she gazes at me, an uncomfortable tension lingering between us.

"I never thought I'd see you again," she mutters almost as if she's out of breath.

"What?" I exclaim, a dryness settling in my throat.

A moment of hesitation passes before her stern gaze reconnects with mine.

"You look just like your mother."

41

I stare in disbelief at the psychic, feeling a dryness creep into my throat from the unexpected revelation.

"You know my mom?" I manage to choke out, my voice trembling with disbelief. How could this woman, living in Jersey City, possibly know her? The thought of it makes me feel nauseous.

In that moment, a distant memory resurfaces—one that has always been painful to recall. I see my mom's tombstone, with delicate rays of sun landing on her coffin like a veil of protection. My dad's teary eyes were vacant, his face scrunched with sorrow.

A surge of anger bubbles in my chest as I gaze at the psychic. She must be lying to get more money out of me. She knows nothing about me and my mom. The woman notices my reaction, her curious brown eyes studying me intently

"Yes. Your mother and I were friends in high school. My name is Kaya," she explains.

I gaze at her in utter disbelief, my chest tightening with pain. Thousands of questions race through my mind, but only one escapes my lips.

"Why did you leave Barren?"

Kaya's eyes dance around the room, as if she were hesitant to share the answer. She retrieves a deck of tarot cards from the counter, her calloused fingers skilfully shuffling them.

"Sometimes, the future traps us. We get stuck in quicksand..." she mutters. Her expression turns grave as her eyes meet mine again. "My life was in danger. You know what they're capable of."

Her words seem ambiguous, leaving me puzzled.

"Who is capable of what?" I ask.

Kaya's card shuffling comes to a halt, leaving the pile face down on the counter.

"The rogues."

As her words linger in the air, Phoebe's words echo in my mind, reminding me to be vigilant. *"The rogues are anywhere and everywhere. Anyone can snitch on you."*

My brows furrow in concern, and suddenly I feel a pang of fear. Is Kaya one of them?

"How do you know about the rogues? Who do you work for?" I ask, my tone defensive.

After being kidnapped by the rogues multiple times, I've come to the realisation that we can't trust anyone. It's us against them. Light versus darkness. Innocence versus evil. Clairvoyants versus the rogues.

Kaya's silent stare quickens my heartbeat. The tension between us is palpable, and fear grips me as I instinctively scan the surroundings for any signs of danger.

Then, suddenly, her serious expression transforms into a dimpled smile.

"My dear, you've misunderstood. I know who you are; I saw you when you were just a baby. The reason I left Barren was because of who I am."

"What?" I gasp, my voice quivering. Is it possible that I've misjudged her entirely?

Kaya responds with a warm smile, gesturing to our surroundings.

"I'm a clairvoyant," she reveals. "My grandmother's shop is what keeps me alive. I have protection here," she gestures toward a glass ornament above the cashier. "The evil eye protects those who believe."

As Kaya's words sink in, the pieces of the puzzle start to fit together, and a sense of relief washes over me. Kaya isn't the enemy, but rather someone who's been through similar struggles as me.

"What do you mean by protection?" I ask, feeling a hint of embarrassment for my misjudgement.

Kaya's expression turns sombre, pain reflected in her brown eyes.

"I cannot return to Barren," she admits gravely. "In every situation, a gun is pointed at my head. The only thing I know is that I'm safe here."

I gaze at her in stunned silence, processing the weight of her words. The mere thought of my fate being like hers tightens my throat. What if one day I find myself caught in the same quicksand?

Suddenly, everything clicks into place. The rogues found her, and she was forced to flee Barren. To escape their clutches, she was reduced to a mere performance monkey, undermining her abilities.

A sudden determination floods through me. I must destroy the rogues, even if it's the last thing I do. I refuse to be trapped like her.

Kaya's voice breaks through my thoughts.

"Wait," she urges. She points toward my chest, and it takes me a moment to realise she's referring to the necklace hanging around my neck. I shoot her a puzzled look, cupping the pendant with my hand. Dainty silver leaves dangle from it, with a small emerald encrusted in its centre.

"What about it?" I ask, confused.

Kaya's intense gaze remains fixed on me as she says, "Look inside when you're ready."

•••••

"Cora?" a distant voice calls out.

"Is she okay?"

The voices are muffled and distorted, but I'm unable to respond to them. Darkness engulfs my sight for what feels like hours until a tingling sensation begins to prickle at the back of my eyes.

As I slowly open my eyes, I realise that I'm sitting in Theo's car, the familiar surroundings gradually coming into focus. I notice that we're driving out of Evergreen along the main highway, the pine trees whizzing past us. I'm suddenly hit with a dull headache at the back of my head, and as I sit up, a wave of dizziness washes over me.

"Theo?" I croak. Theo's eyes instantly lock with mine, and he quickly pulls the car over with a brisk movement, causing me to gasp.

His concerned gaze searches mine, his hands quickly cupping my cheeks. Our lips meet in a rush of relief, breathy and urgent after the tension of the past few hours. Running my fingers through his ruffled hair, our lips synchronise as if they had never spent time apart.

"Babe, are you alright? I was so worried," he murmurs, his worried ocean eyes studying me intently.

"What happened?" I manage to ask.

"You passed out. It seemed like you fainted, but it was more like you were asleep," he explains, his voice tinged with concern.

"Where are the others?" I ask, my concern evident as I glance over my shoulder.

"I told Phoebe we'd meet them at Newton. They're dealing with Alexis' watcher. Having Chris tailing us is bad enough," Theo responds.

A sudden wave of realisation hits me like a ton of bricks.

"I shot Chris..." I utter breathlessly, the weight of my actions sinking in. Pulling back from his embrace, Theo's blue eyes shimmer with a mix of longing and protectiveness.

"Don't worry about that. You did what you had to do," he reassures me.

"Where is he?" My voice carries a note of panic as I search Theo's eyes for an answer.

"Phoebe and Alexis took care of him," he answers, his voice calm despite the gravity of the situation. A shocked look crosses my face, a cold shiver running down my spine.

"Don't worry, he's not dead. After you shot him, they tied him up and left him in Evergreen," he explains.

I release a sigh of relief, sinking back into the seat as I run my hand through my hair.

"I have no idea what happened, Theo," I confess, my voice heavy with regret. "I didn't want to shoot him." The words spill out of me in a rush, as if they were a torrent I couldn't hold back any longer. The vision of being in New Jersey with that psychic feels distant and unreal—or was it just a dream?

"You probably passed out from shock. You're also sleep deprived," he explains.

Suddenly, the memory of Chris shooting Theo floods back, and my heart races as I gently touch his wound.

"Are you alright? Chris shot you."

"I'm fine, luckily it was just a flesh wound. Look," he says, lifting his shirt to reveal a clean gauze on his stomach. "I grabbed the First-Aid kit." With a gentle smile, he pulls his shirt back down and wraps his arms around me. The tightness in my chest eases as I inhale Theo's cologne.

"I'm just glad you're okay," he whispers, his azure eyes fixed on me. Warmth fills my core as I reach out to stroke his cheek.

"I'm glad you are, too," I smile, but guilt begins to gnaw at me. "God, this is all my fault. I should have never put your life in danger like that," I admit, my voice quivering as I lower my gaze.

Theo shakes his head, then gently lifts my chin with his fingers, guiding me to meet his gaze once more.

"Babe, listen to me. None of this is your fault. Chris found us," Theo reassures, his voice firm.

"I shouldn't have let you come with me to the hospital. My dad's accident was my responsibility. Now he knows about all of us and it's because of me," I mutter, feeling my eyes water with regret.

"You had to make sure your dad was okay. You risked your life to protect him," Theo counters, his tone filled with understanding. He traces patterns on my skin, his touch bringing comfort—something I've been lacking lately.

"Babe, if you hadn't shot him, we would all be dead," he says.

He's right. Perhaps Chris would have killed us one by one if I hadn't fought back. But despite the necessity of my actions, there's a part of me that feels regret. I never wanted to harm Chris, no matter the circumstances.

"This gift is a curse," I mumble, defeat tainting my words. Perhaps Kaya is right—there seems to be no way to escape them.

But who is Kaya? Panic courses through my veins once more. If it was a vision, when am I going to experience it?

Theo shakes his head.

"It's not. Sure, we're hunted by those bastards, but we can change this around. We're stronger than them," he insists.

"I don't think we can change outcomes, Theo," I mumble weakly, recalling Kaya's words. *Sometimes, the future traps us. We get stuck in quicksand...*

"Of course we can. That's exactly why the rogues want us," he explains, squeezing my forearm in reassurance. "We just need to stick together."

I swallow the knot in my throat, still not entirely convinced. Maybe I shouldn't tell him about what I saw, not until I figure out what it means. All I know is that if it was a vision, they're becoming stronger each time, just like Theo said they would.

"Why didn't you go help Alexis and Phoebe?" I ask, nervously chewing on my lip. "Phoebe said it—I'm endangering your life," I admit, a pang of guilt in my voice. Theo shakes his head, gently stroking my cheek with his thumb.

"There was no way I was going to leave you." Anxiety tinges his voice, his expression reflecting his fear. "I was terrified. You were out for an hour. I thought you might have hit your head."

I bite my lip, still consumed by guilt.

"I don't remember anything," I mutter, though the memory of the vision lingers vividly in my mind. I've never met Kaya before, nor have I experienced such a lucid and detailed premonition.

Theo's worried eyes study me, but I find myself unable to muster the courage to share what I saw. It's as if the determination and bravery I felt just hours ago have vanished into thin air.

"Are you okay to leave? Chris must be minutes away from calling for backup. If he hasn't already…" he says, a hint of urgency in his voice. He knows we don't have much time before he finds us again.

I nod, feeling a surge of energy coursing through my body as Theo revs up the engine. But in that mere instant, my eyesight begins to blur, and a new setting develops before me.

As Chris awakens in Evergreen, his features twist with pain and fury. An angry growl escapes his lips as he takes in his surroundings, his eyes flashing with rage. Despite his limp, he moves forward with determination in each step.

"Cora," he hisses, his voice dripping with malice.

As my eyes snap open with a gasp, a bone-chilling realisation sinks into my bones.

Chris is coming for me.

42

Theo's blue eyes are clouded with worry, his hands gripping the steering wheel tightly as he waits for me to speak.

"What did you see?" he asks, his voice trembling with apprehension, as if he's too frightened to hear the answer.

Chris' angry, breathy voice echoes in my head like a siren, sending shivers down my spine. My hands tremble with terror as adrenaline surges through me, heightening my alertness. The stark reality hits me: either Chris will call for backup, or he will take matters into his own hands and end my life.

"It's Chris. We need to get out of here," I croak, my voice strained with urgency.

Theo's response is immediate; he steps on the gas, accelerating the car with determination. The engine roars as we speed back onto the highway, leaving the shadows of Evergreen behind us. As dawn breaks, the outlines of the trees gradually sharpen, signalling the approach of daylight. We're running out of time. Within half an hour, the first rays of light will illuminate the town of Barren, leaving us vulnerable and exposed to Chris's pursuit.

After what happened in the basement, I'm well aware that Chris is capable of more than just kidnapping. This time, he's out for revenge, and it's clear that his ultimate goal may be to end our lives.

Theo's stern gaze remains fixed on the road ahead, his jaw clenched tightly with tension.

"We need to leave Barren," he says, his tone sombre. His words strike me like a ton of bricks, rendering me momentarily speechless as the gravity of the situation sinks in.

Leaving Barren means abandoning everything I've known—my past, my family, my friendships. Just as Kaya warned, it feels like I'm sinking into the quicksand of uncertainty. I swallow the lump in my throat, summoning some courage. Perhaps it's time to be rational—if it means ensuring our survival.

"You're right. We can't keep playing this cat and mouse game with Chris. It's only a matter of time before he catches up to us," I mutter, my voice filled with defeat.

Theo's gaze lingers on me for a moment before he nods, his breath escaping in a heavy sigh. He checks the time on the dashboard clock.

"We've got until 6:15 A.M. to get out of town. It'll be easier for Chris to track us once daylight breaks," he notes.

"Alright," I murmur.

As we drive in silence along the highway cutting through Evergreen, a tangible tension fills the air, each of us grappling with the weight of our next steps. I knew this moment was inevitable. Ever since Theo told me about the rogues, it felt like a ticking time bomb waiting to explode. The quicksand keeps pulling me deeper and deeper. Panic tightens my throat as I remember Kaya's words, which now replay constantly in my mind.

Think, Cora, think. We can't panic now. There must be a way out of this.

"We need to make sure Chris doesn't follow us to Newton," I assert, breaking the heavy silence.

"Agree," Theo replies. "There has to be a way to get him off our backs."

As I bite my lip, my gaze sets on the passing pine trees outside the window, lost in thought. The rhythmic motion of the trees blurring by mirrors the whirlwind of ideas swirling in my mind as I search for a solution.

In that moment, a tingling sensation starts behind my eyes, like ants crawling in my brain. Within seconds, an image begins to take shape before me: an old wooden cabin deep in the woods. It only takes a few seconds for me to recognise it—it's our summer holiday cabin.

"Everything okay?" Theo's voice interrupts, snapping me back to reality.

An idea suddenly sparks in my mind.

"Theo, I've got it," I blurt out, feeling a surge of excitement and relief. "There's a small town called Meadville in Pennsylvania, roughly six hours from here. We have a holiday cabin deep in the woods. Chris would never think to look for us there, and I think it's safer than Newton."

Theo's eyes widen with surprise as he glances over at me.

"Really? Could we stay there?" he asks, a glimmer of hope evident in his voice.

I nod eagerly.

"Yes, it's been empty for years. It's secluded, completely off the grid. We used to go there every summer when I was a kid. No one knows about it except my dad and I."

Theo's expression softens with relief.

"That could work. It's far enough from Barren and secluded enough to keep us safe for a while," he agrees.

A sense of determination fills me as I lean back in my seat, the weight of uncertainty lifting from my shoulders.

"Let's head to Meadville then. We'll regroup there and figure out our next move," I suggest, a newfound sense of hope.

"I'll tell Phoebe to meet us there," he says.

•••••

As we head towards the Interstate, we realise we have no choice but to pass through town. It's a risky move, considering Chris might have eyes everywhere, but there's no alternative. I need to make a quick pit stop back home to grab the cabin keys, and Theo needs to refuel before we hit the road. Theo's eyes flicker with concern as we enter Barren. It's the crack of dawn and the streets are eerily quiet, devoid of the usual hustle and bustle. Every shadow seems to hide a potential threat, and I can feel my heart racing with each passing moment. But we have to stay focused, keep our wits about us. There's no turning back now.

My unease intensifies as we near my house, each familiar spot stirring memories I'd rather forget. We purposely avoid driving past the school, needing to steer clear of any unwanted attention. Every passer by heightens the risk of Chris discovering our whereabouts. As my small, two-story house comes into view, a knot begins to form in my stomach. But I don't have time to dwell on it; instead, I rush out of Theo's car and into the house.

My actions are rushed as I search through my dad's drawers, desperately searching for the keys. I force myself to avoid looking at my surroundings, knowing that dwelling on memories will only make it harder to leave. With a sigh of relief, I finally locate the keys and hurry back outside.

Jumping back into Theo's car, he swiftly revs up the engine, the sound of the motor echoing in the quiet street. Tears well up in my eyes as we pull out, my chest tightening with anguish that I can't suppress.

Theo notices my shattered expression in the rear-view mirror and reaches over to squeeze my hand tightly, understanding the turmoil I'm going through about leaving my dad behind.

"Babe, your dad will be okay. I promise," he reassures me, his voice filled with conviction. But deep down, I can't shake off the worry gnawing at my heart.

Theo turns right onto the main street, heading towards the old petrol station. We quickly pull our hoodies over our heads to shield ourselves from being recognised as we drive, the first gentle rays of sunshine breaking through the clouds above us. Time is running out, and we must act quickly. Our only chance of survival is to escape the quicksand Kaya was talking about.

Taking a deep breath, I wipe away some tears from my eyes.

"Okay. How do we do this?" I ask, trying to steady my voice as we pull up to the petrol station.

Theo bites his lip nervously, his gaze darting around for any signs of the rogues lurking nearby.

"We need money and gas," he explains, his voice urgent. "I'll go get some cash for the upcoming days, and then I'll top up the petrol. We need to get out of the state as fast as we can."

His plan seems solid, but the speed at which everything is unfolding leaves me feeling overwhelmed. I sigh, my gaze falling to my lap. Sensing my distress, Theo gives my thigh a reassuring squeeze.

"I'll be back in a second. Stay in the car," Theo instructs before stepping out, leaving me alone in the stillness of the vehicle. I anxiously survey the petrol station for any signs of danger as I wait for Theo, my leg bouncing with nervous energy. I have this uneasy feeling that something is about to happen any minute, but there's no one in sight.

In that moment, something catches my attention from the corner of my eye. My heart skips a beat as I notice a picture of me glued to one of the columns of the petrol station. My breath catches in my throat as I realise it's not just any picture of me—it's a missing person's report. Mine.

Tears cloud my sight as I rush out of the car, my hands trembling as I rip the poster from the wall. I stare at my picture on the report, taken from my dad's birthday celebration six months ago.

"Hey, what's that?"

I look up immediately, meeting Theo's worried gaze.

"Theo," I manage to choke out, my voice trembling as I hold up the missing person's report with my picture on it. He takes it out of my hands, his face going pale.

"Shit. This isn't good, Cora. He's looking for you," he says, his tone heavy with concern.

My world seems to be collapsing, and I can't hold back the tears. I wish I didn't have to put my dad through this. Theo reaches out, wrapping his arms around me in a comforting embrace.

"Hey, it's going to be okay," he murmurs softly, his voice soothing amidst the chaos. "We'll figure this out together.

As he holds me close, his comforting touch slowly calms the storm raging inside me. He clutches me to his chest, his soft breaths against my hair bringing a sense of solace.

"I'm so sorry, Cora… I wish none of this were happening," Theo murmurs, his voice utterly broken.

In that moment, I realise that both of our lives have been ripped to shreds. In this dark timeline, Theo and I only have each other. It's the end of an era, one that, like Kaya, I know I'll have to let go of.

Theo's gaze meets mine with determination as he pulls away slightly. Despite the tears welling in his eyes, his voice remains firm.

"We need to leave now," he says. "We can't stay here any longer. Let's get back on the road and head to Meadville. We'll be safe there."

I nod, wiping away my tears and taking a deep breath to steady myself.

Slumping back into the passenger seat of Theo's Nissan, my spirits plummet to an all-time low. There is no going back—this is the outcome of our actions. Theo and I exchange a glance before he turns on the engine. It's as if he's seeking reassurance from me, but I can offer none in this moment of panic.

As the first rays of sunlight filter into the alleyway, I squint against their intensity, only to have them abruptly blocked by a shadow. We let out a gasp when we see Chris standing in the way, his expression dark and menacing. Panic surges through me, and I grip the edge of my seat, my breath catching in my throat.

"Shit," I curse, my blood turning to ice.

Shadows obscure his face, his irises appearing black in the dim light. His expression remains unreadable, but I can only assume he's consumed with rage. My heart violently thumps in my chest, each beat a drumroll of impending doom. Perhaps this was my fate since the very beginning.

"Cora... If he doesn't move, I'm going to have to hit him," Theo's voice cuts through the silence, filled with urgency and fear. Our hearts race as Chris begins stumbling towards us, his movements resembling those of a zombie.

"He seems unarmed," I whisper, my gaze fixed on Chris. As if an external force controlled my actions, I fumble for the car door.

"Cora, don't!" Theo's urgent voice echoes.

Despite the warning, I step out of the car with my heart pounding in my chest and my legs trembling with fear. Chris's figure looms ominously in front of me, his eyes piercing into mine with an intensity that sends shivers down my spine.

"Stay back, Cora!" Theo's voice rings out, but it feels distant, drowned out by the rush of blood in my ears.

I take a tentative step forward, my breath coming in short, shallow gasps. Chris remains motionless, his cold gaze fixed on me. His presence feels heavy, suffocating me with its malevolence.

But I can't let fear paralyse me. With every fibre of my being screaming at me to run, I stand my ground, steeling myself for whatever comes next.

The adrenaline rush tingles my skin as I continue to approach him, his face partially obscured in the shadows. I hear Theo slam the door shut, his footsteps quickening behind me. Chris' gaze remains on the floor, utterly expressionless, his hands numbly by his sides.

"What do you want from me, Chris? What on Earth do you want from me!" I shout, my patience wearing thin, but Chris remains immobile.

Beside me, Theo's breaths are heavy as he grabs my arm.

"Please, get back inside the car. We don't know if he's armed," he pleads, his tone steady. Despite his words, my focus remains fixed on Chris, who has yet to respond or make a move.

Tension hangs heavy among the three of us for a few moments. Then, unexpectedly, Chris takes a few strides toward me. It's as if a dark aura envelops him like a black cloud, swallowing any hint of light around him. The streetlamp casts a partial illumination on his face—and to my astonishment, tears streak his cheeks.

"Cora... I wanted to say I'm sorry. For everything I've done," Chris croaks out, his voice strained with remorse.

I blink in disbelief, unsure if my ears are playing tricks on me. But Theo's stunned expression confirms that I heard Chris correctly.

"What?" Theo exclaims, surprise evident in his tone.

43

Chris wipes his eyes with the back of his sleeve, his expression a mixture of sorrow and regret. He's crumbling before us, as if he's lost all hope. Tears well in his eyes as his lip quivers, taking a careful step towards us. The streetlight illuminates his face, and I gasp when I see bruises and cuts marring his pale skin, as if he had been beaten.

"They killed my mom, and they were threatening me," he cries, his voice trembling with emotion. "Now that I've lost everyone I cared about, I'm done," he continues, his voice filled with resolve. "I'm done working for them. I'm done with hurting people, especially you."

His words leave me speechless, a hurricane of emotions churning inside me. The rogues have torn his life to shreds without him realising it. First, they killed Damon, and now the only family he had left, his mom. How could such cruel individuals exist? How could they manipulate a nineteen-year-old until he has nothing left?

"T-They killed your mom?" I manage to stutter, my voice filled with disbelief and horror. An unbearable sense of guilt floods over me. If only I could have convinced Chris to leave the rogues, if only I had done something to stop them.

Chris lets out a soft sob, his jaw clenching in anguish.

"I have nothing to fight for anymore, Cora," he croaks, his voice heavy with defeat. My heart clenches in distress, tears blurring my vision. I never imagined those words would escape his lips.

"Of course you do, Chris. Come join us, we can protect you," I blurt out, my words hurried. I glance back at Theo, noticing the anger blazing in his eyes. I know Theo doesn't trust him, but the guilt weighing on me is unbearable.

Chris bites his lip, a glimmer of hope in his watery eyes.

"Do you really mean that?" he asks, his voice strained.

"Of course, come with us," I say, trying to make eye contact with Theo, but his angry gaze remains fixated on Chris.

"You don't know how much that means to me," Chris cries, his voice thick with emotion. The relief shining in his eyes sends a flutter through my heart; in that moment, I no longer feel like I've let him down.

Suddenly, determination flickers in his gaze.

"There's a way. There's a way to end them," Chris stutters hurriedly, but before he can finish, a loud gunshot shatters the air. I instinctively cover my ears as the sound reverberates through the alleyway, feeling a chill run down my spine. As I open eyes, I gasp in horror at the crimson stain spreading across Chris' shirt. He stares at the wound in disbelief, collapsing to his knees as the colour drains from his face.

"Oh, my God! Chris!" I cry out, sprinting towards him.

I lift Chris' shirt, flinching at the severity of the wound as his body trembles with pain. The bullet tore through his stomach, and the pooling of blood on his shirt is unstoppable. Theo rushes to help me apply pressure to Chris' stomach. His panicked expression mirrors my own fear, his face drained of colour.

"Someone must have heard the gunshot. We don't have much time," Theo says, his voice filled with urgency. My sobs are uncontrollable, my own tears mixing with the blood as Chris grunts in pain.

"Chris..." I plead, the sound barely escaping my lips. Blood stains my hands as his breaths grow shallow, his strength fading rapidly. He's not going to make it.

"Chris, stay with me," I urge, my voice trembling as I apply pressure to his wound. "Theo, call an ambulance!"

"He's losing a lot of blood; I don't think we should draw more atten-" Theo begins, his voice filled with concern.

"Just do it!" I bark at him, my patience running thin as desperation claws at my chest.

Theo's eyes widen in surprise at my outburst, but I can't afford to be rational right now. He dashes to his car to fetch his phone, leaving me alone with Chris, whose body is becoming increasingly limp. Chris makes a choking sound, his grip on my hand tightening in desperation.

"Cora... I'm sorry. I lied to you..." he wails, his voice strained with pain. His strength is beginning to wane, mirrored by the draining colour from his face. A heavy weight presses down on my chest, suffocating me with each breath.

"I know, Chris. I'm sorry, too," I whisper, my voice cracking with emotion as tears blur my vision. I wish none of this were real. My agonised sobs pierce the air, a raw expression of the anguish tearing me apart.

Chris's emerald eyes remain fixed on mine, his lips parting as he starts to drift into a distant stare.

"I l-lo... Loved you," he stutters, his voice barely audible.

In that moment, time seems to stand still. The weight of Chris's words hangs heavy in the air, wrapping around us like a cloak of bittersweet memories. My heart aches with the intensity of his confession, mingling with the unbearable pain of knowing that our time together is slipping away.

Tears blur my vision as I reach out to touch his face, tracing the contours of his features as if trying to etch them into my memory forever. His gaze remains fixed on mine, a silent plea for understanding, for acceptance, for forgiveness.

But there are no words left to say, no actions left to take. We are two souls, now tainted by the cruel hand fate has dealt us. And as Chris's strength fades and his breaths grow faint, I realise that this is our final goodbye.

With trembling hands, I lean in to press my lips gently against his forehead.

"I forgive you, Chris. I forgive you," I murmur softly, offering him the release of forgiveness in his final moments.

"Don't worry... I'll be with.. Damon... Mom..." Chris mutters, a bittersweet smile breaking through the tears on his face.

His mention of Damon and his mom pierces my heart even deeper, intensifying my anguished sobs. In desperation, I cling to him even tighter, as if I could defy the inevitable and keep him with me a little longer.

And then, in one heart-wrenching moment, Chris's body goes still.

"No, no, no!!" I scream, my stomach sinking as I shake him, desperate for any sign of life. But there's no response. It's too late.

Tears stream down my face, landing on Chris' lifeless body as I let out a desperate cry. As his body grows cold in my arms, I'm consumed by a profound sense of emptiness. Theo rushes over to me, his breath quickening as he realises what's happened, a curse escaping his lips in a hushed breath.

Chris is dead.

•••••

The truth about Chris was revealed minutes before he died. When I found out he was my watcher, I truly believed Chris was destined to be a villain. But as the ambulance sirens neared the scene of the crime, I realised I had been wrong all along.

Chris was alone, with no one to turn to. The rogues had taken the lives of his stepbrother and his mom solely to keep him under their control. The rogues exploited him until he was no use to them. That's what the rogues do.

The ambulance never made it in time. We hastily placed him in Theo's trunk and drove off before anyone could notice us.

It's 8 A.M. now, and three hours have passed since we laid him to rest in Evergreen. Yet, as we buried him, I wished we could have buried Chris beside Damon.

Theo and I have reached our last resort: hiding in Mayor Glenn's rusty shed until we can figure out a solution. It's the only place where we know we won't be found. This time, we need to carefully plan each step to avoid mistakes. We also need to rest, as it's been two days since either of us slept.

Soon, we will start our new lives as fugitives—but I can't leave without finding Chris' murderer.

I struggle to sit up from the pile of clothes we've used as a makeshift bed, my body too exhausted to move. Swallowing the lump in my throat, I feel utterly hollow and broken. A constant ache stings my chest, and my eyes are swollen from endless tears.

As Theo groans in his sleep, clinging to one of the blankets we rescued from his basement, I reach for Phoebe's laptop. Theo mentioned that Phoebe had installed multiple VPNs to keep us hidden from the rogues. I examine a folder containing articles, documents, and photographs I've compiled over the past hour. It's everything I know about the rogues, including the Allen family case, psychological reports from Alheim, and about Chris' murder.

My gaze flickers across numerous old newspaper clippings, police reports, and online forums, determined to find Chris' killer. Every piece of information I discover feels like a vital puzzle piece, bringing me one step closer to revealing the truth. A surge of determination floods through me, giving me newfound strength. I must do this for Chris, and I won't give up until justice is served.

The research is there. While the rogues may think they've covered their tracks flawlessly, I've noticed a few tiny details. My sole focus is finding a lead—anything that can bring me closer to one of them.

The memories from the burial flood back like a sudden bolt of lightning. The rain soaked my hair, sending moisture trickling down my neck. I stood numbly as Theo dug a hole in the ground with Glenn's shovel, the sound reverberating through the still forest. In that moment, I felt a heavy sense of sorrow and disbelief wash over me. Each shovel of dirt was a stark reminder that soon, Chris' body would return to the earth.

I let out a defeated sigh and leave the laptop on a toolbox near me, feeling the heaviness in my eyelids. I need to find the killer, even if it's the last thing I do. I glance over at Theo, who is still sound asleep, and crawl underneath the blanket with him. As I stare at the shed's ceiling, the repetitive sound of shovelling echoes in my ears like a constant torture.

•••••

I wake up a couple of hours later, my temples damp with sweat from the vivid nightmares of Chris being shot. Even in my dreams, I can't seem to shake the memory from my head. I sit up, my back aching from the hardness of the floor. Looking around for any signs of Theo, I feel my throat tighten when I realise he's not around.

"Theo?" I croak, my heart racing in panic.

I listen intently, but there's no response. Panic begins to rise within me as I call out his name again, louder this time. Still, there's no answer. Dread settles in as I realise Theo is nowhere to be found. Quickly, I scramble to my feet, my heart pounding with worry.

I rush outside the shed, scanning the area frantically. And there, a few feet away, I see Theo standing under a tree, his back turned to me as he talks on the phone. Relief floods through me, but it's quickly replaced by curiosity. Who is he talking to?

"Theo?" I call out, my voice tinged with worry.

He quickly spins around on his heels, his blue eyes locking with mine. Theo's expression is tense as he mutters something into the phone before ending the call. He strides over to me, concern etched on his face.

"Hey, baby. Are you okay?" he asks, enveloping me in a comforting embrace. The scent of his cologne brings a momentary relief, easing the tension in the air.

"Yeah. Who were you talking to?" I ask.

"Phoebe," he replies, averting his gaze. There's a hint of unease in his voice, as if he's just heard unsettling news. "They got rid of Alexis' watcher."

"And?" I prompt, sensing there's more to the story.

Theo hesitates, his ocean eyes meeting mine with seriousness. It's as if he's about to reveal something I don't want to hear.

"We need to go to your holiday cabin and leave Barren for good," he states firmly.

Theo's words leave me momentarily stunned. Despite his suggestion, I know I must stick to my plan. While he may never agree to it, I can't shake the torment of Chris' murder until I find his killer.

"No," I whisper, shaking my head with determination. "I can't leave Barren until I find the son of a bitch that killed Chris."

Theo sighs, his hand running through his stubble.

"Cora, what you're saying is incredibly risky. Hunting down a rogue is like signing your own death warrant. I can't support this," he says firmly, but I shake my head in defiance.

"We've already signed our warrant. The man who shot Chris saw us. He knows we're alive," I argue, desperation creeping into my voice.

Another sigh escapes his lips, his eyes revealing a hint of concern.

"But if we go looking for them, we'll find them. We're basically walking into their trap, Cora. For what, revenge?"

"It's not just about revenge, Theo. It's about doing what's right. Chris deserves justice, and I won't rest until we find his killer."

As he takes a deep breath, I detect a hint of jealousy in his gaze. I understand it's a sensitive topic because Chris was my ex-boyfriend, but I won't rest until I solve this.

After a moment of tense silence, Theo caves in. He sighs, rubbing his temples in frustration.

"Fine, but we're leaving tonight. What do you want to do?

"We need to reverse the roles," I reply firmly.

44

Ever since Chris' death, everything around me seems unfamiliar. Even as I gaze through Mayor Glenn's living room window, Evergreen Forest feels like it's miles away. The house, which was once engulfed by the flames, now wears a coat of soot and shadows, and only a handful of his antique furniture survived. The only things that are still in decent shape is a blackboard, taking up almost half the walls, and a metal filing cabinet. Exhaustion clouds my vision as I lower myself onto the partly burned carpet, crossing my legs.

Theo made me promise I wouldn't do this without him, but I don't have a choice. Chris' death haunts my dreams, and until I do this, it won't stop happening. This is undoubtedly dangerous, but there are no alternatives, no shortcuts, no plan B.

Not only did I promise Theo, but I promised myself not to make things worse, but sometimes breaking promises is necessary to solve something like this.

My eyelids start to flutter, and I blink rapidly to stay awake. Taking in the stale air that was once filled with embers, I dig my nails into the palms of my hands. I must stay awake; it's the only way this will work. Memories of Chris and I together rush through my mind at the speed of lightning.

"Think, Cora. Think," I whisper to myself, praying this will work. Theo mentioned that the best way to engrave yourself into the past is through sleep deprivation. I exhale deeply before gently shutting my eyes.

The killer. Chris' killer. That's where my focus needs to be. I must find out who it was. Allowing my mind a momentary drift, I tighten my fists and take another round of steady breaths.

The shadow of the killer from the alleyway resurfaces in my mind, but the image is fuzzy around the edges. It's too distant in time. That's the tricky part with time—memories get blurrier as more of it slips away.

I open my eyes and reach into my pocket, where I've kept a piece of Chris' shirt. I tore it seconds before Theo lowered his body into the grave. Clutching the fabric tightly in my fist, I make sure my eyes are sealed shut before drawing in another breath. A moment of hushed darkness envelops me, and all I can hear is the rhythmic thumping of my heartbeat

Gradually, the darkness shifts, morphing into a scene—the image of the empty alleyway seeping into my vision. The wind rustles my hair as the scene comes into focus, centring on Chris. He speaks, but I can't hear him—only the sound of my own breaths. Theo stands behind me, terrorised by Chris' presence. Yet, Chris's crying reveals a different truth—he's not a threat but a victim of a tragic situation.

In that moment, I spot a shadow at the alleyway's end—impossible to overlook this time. Time appears to grind to a sudden halt, as if someone hit 'slow-motion' on a video. Chris' lips move slowly, but my attention stays fixed on the shadow. A tingling sensation courses through my body, finally granting me control within the vision.

A gleaming object catches my eye—it's the gun in the attacker's hand, ready to be fired—followed by the ear-piercing gunshot. The noise reverberates through the alleyway, but I make a conscious effort not to flinch this time. The sound is muted once more as Chris drops to his knees, a wave of panic settling within me, just like the first time it occurred. The familiar ache of loss fills me, but the tingling sensation on my skin returns—the vision coming to an end.

Gasping for air, I realise I am back in Mayor Glenn's study room, with my legs crossed and the bloodied cloth clenched in my hand. A persistent chill runs through my body like sharp lightning bolts—the icy aftermath of a vision that always snaps me back to reality. My attention shifts to the floor covered in my newspaper clippings, the adrenaline rush still in my veins.

I run to the blackboard, hastily sketching a rough portrait of Chris' attacker: brows slightly uneven and furrowed, a subtle scar above the lip, deep blue eyes, and a malicious smirk that sends shivers down my spine.

•••••

The line between moral and immoral begins to blur as I stare at the now-blooming Evergreen Forest. The moon hangs in the clear night sky above me, and leaves crunch beneath my feet as I venture further into the woods. My steps pause as I find myself encircled by the dense pines and oaks. I open my hands, palms facing the sky above my head.

Inhale, exhale—that's the only way I'll be able to track him down. I am getting closer; I can sense it. With a few more steps, the cool air raises the hair on the back of my neck, and the eerie atmosphere of the forest sends shivers down my spine. I reach into my pocket, pulling out the bloody piece of torn shirt. Adrenaline leaves my head spinning. Not only that, but this marks my second dive into my memories.

"Unlocking the past is dangerous," Theo had warned me during one of our training sessions. *"The more you do it, the more it hurts."*

He taught me that the safest way to delve into the past is by retracing one's steps—which is exactly what I'm doing. Heading towards the main street, the forest's quietness brings a sense of comfort, even though I'm sleep-deprived and on the hunt for a killer.

Ever since I was a child, my father warned me that Evergreen, though peaceful during the day, was no place for the night. He was right, but I have no other option but to embrace the forest's silence. The crunch of twigs startles me, making my heart skip a beat. Turning around slowly, I release a soft exhale, realising it's just a burrowing animal.

With my heart pounding in my chest, I realise I've gotten distracted, and the memory of the killer has slipped to the back of my mind. I need to delve into my memories again. Glancing at the cloth in my hands, I take a few deep breaths, preparing myself for the plunge once more.

I close my eyes once again, immersing myself in the memory of the night of the murder. The dimly lit alleyway was cluttered with garbage from Demazio's, the pizzeria next to the petrol station. Theo's car was parked just a few feet away from where I stood, the engine softly humming in the background. In that moment, Chris appears in the scene, his face twisted with pain. But this time, my attention isn't on Chris' suffering—it's on the man behind him. The gun. I can see the gun now.

The gunshot echoes, and Chris' body thuds to the floor. The scene unfolds much quicker this time, making it challenging for me to keep up. In the memory, I rush over to Chris, but this time, my present self feels detached. From the outside, I witness my past self pleading for help, with Theo standing behind as he urges me to leave. But this time, my attention fixates on the man, who has started running away from the scene. My breath catches in my throat as I realise I'm following him.

The scene of Theo and me helping Chris in the alleyway fades into the distance as I cross the street, a couple of steps behind the man who took my first boyfriend's life. The memory may not be reality, but I still feel the humidity clinging to my clothes and hair.

The man covers himself with his hood, concealing his identity from onlookers. He slips behind some apartments, his silhouette merging into the darkness of another alleyway. Breathless, I push myself to keep up the pursuit, following him inside the alleyway. The streetlamp flickers above me as my eyes focus on the backdoor of an abandoned building, where the man comes to a halt.

He checks his surroundings to ensure nobody is nearby before rapping on the door a few times. The door swings open, and the rogue steps inside the building. I hurry behind him, slipping into the building just before the door shuts. The humidity inside is stifling, almost suffocating. Chipped paint clings to the walls of the empty warehouse, sending shivers down my spine. I stifle a cough against the accumulated dust and the persistent humidity.

The killer heads towards the storage room of the warehouse, and I dash after him, attempting to match his pace. He unlocks the door, and a solitary yellow light spills onto the basement floor. In that moment, I let out an involuntary gasp. Thank God nobody can hear me. Inside the storage room sits a man in a leather chair. He appears to be in his late forties, with a shaved head and wearing an expensive suit. A cut on his forehead gives him a fierce, aggressive look, as if he'd been clawed by a lion.

The killer lowers his hoodie, unveiling his entire face. My heart pounds in my throat with rage as I stare at the face of the man who took Chris's life. He looks exactly like in a drawing I sketched, with thick furrowed brows and a scar above his lip. He appears somewhat older than me, maybe in his mid-twenties. His platinum hair is styled into a slight quiff, held in place by a bandana that keeps it away from his face. A nose ring adds a touch of decoration, but there's something in his facial expression that makes him appear scared. From a distance, one wouldn't easily label him as a killer.

"Did you do it?" the older man asks, his voice carrying the raspy tone of a seasoned smoker.

"Yes," the rogue replies, both his tone and facial expression devoid of emotion. A hush falls over the room before the suited man reaches for a suitcase, tossing it onto the table. He shoots the rogue a glance before effortlessly popping open the latches with his fingers.

Money. Over a hundred thousand in cash. The rogue's fingers caress the stacks of bills, his eyes gleaming with a mix of excitement and satisfaction. The older man watches him closely, a knowing smirk playing on his lips.

"Consider it a reward for a job well done. Make sure nobody sees you walk home. Understood?" he says, settling back into his chair.

"Yes, sir," the rogue responds, snapping the suitcase closed.

Suddenly, my eyes snap open. I gasp for air, finding myself back in the clearing of Evergreen. Why was I abruptly kicked out from the vision?

Maybe I need to get closer to the scene.

My steps shift into a run as I dash through the forest toward town. With uneven breaths, I eventually reach the parking lot outside The Grub, the site of the shooting. The adrenaline seeps into my bones as I move towards the last location where I physically saw the rogue—the alleyway.

Screwing my eyes shut, I tightly grip Chris' shirt. The next vision unfolds—a neon sign reading Motel 126, but the image is only visible for a fleeting moment.

I recognise that motel—it's an abandoned one only a few miles away from Barren, which means I'm getting close. I know he's still there, but this time I won't let him out of my grasp.

45

The stench of the cheap motel bathroom fills my nostrils as I climb through the window, the floorboards creaking beneath my feet. A wave of dizziness washes over me from the poor air quality the adrenaline accumulated in my veins. I tread softly towards the bedroom, noticing that the door has been left slightly ajar. The room is dimly lit, with a few rays of light filtering through the windows. I notice a creaky bed and a small nightstand, and cheap takeout meals are scattered across the rotting carpet. As my eyes adjust, I notice a figure beneath the covers—it's a man.

I've found him. But how do I seize control of the situation?

My eyes wander to his nightstand, and to my surprise, I find his wallet and a shining revolver. Of course, every serial killer needs a gun next to their bed. I quickly glance at the ID, which reads Elijah Steppord. My breath catches momentarily as I put a name to the man who murdered Chris. Adrenaline courses through my veins, reigniting the anger inside me. Silently, I grab the revolver.

The rogue stirs in his sleep, but his eyes snap open at the ominous click of the safety being disengaged. Yet, this time, it's too late for him. The gun is now cocked and aimed at him, and strangely, he doesn't even flinch. The shadows obscure his facial expression, but the piercings on his face seem to gleam at me.

"Don't fucking move," I hiss, flicking the light on the nightstand table. The platinum-blond rogue raises his hands, his lips pursed as he glares at me. His expression shows no sign of terror, only rage. Lowering my gaze for a moment, my heart sinks when I recognise the gun in my hands.

It's the gun he used to shoot Chris.

My anger pulses through me, overpowering any rational thoughts. I find a duffel bag by the bed, keeping my gun pointed at his head as I unzip it. My eyes widen at the stacks of money, knives, and ropes inside. With adrenaline coursing through my veins, I tie the rogue's wrists to the bed's headboard. He doesn't resist, probably because a gun is pointed at his skull. I take a few steps back, my hands trembling as I point the gun at him.

"Confess, you asshole!" I shout, my voice echoing through the room.

The rogue laughs, his blue eyes glinting with mischief, like a cat toying with his prey.

"Confess?" he challenges. "Confess to what?"

My eyes narrow in anger. He shouldn't be this confident, especially with a gun aimed at his skull. My grip tightens on the gun, and the anger keeps simmering in my chest, pushing me to continue.

"Confess that you've murdered countless innocent people for money. You don't discriminate—old, young, it doesn't matter to you. Money is all you care about."

The rogue smirks, an unsettling calmness in his attitude.

"You've got it all wrong, sweetheart. I'm just a pawn in a much bigger game," he purrs. I tighten my grip on the gun, my patience wearing thin.

"Cut the crap. I saw the money, the weapons. You're no pawn. You're a killer for hire."

He leans back, still bound to the bed. A sinister gleam in his eyes sends a shiver down my spine.

"Maybe I am. But there's always someone pulling the strings, and I just dance to the tune," he says. Frustration bubbles within me.

"Who's behind all this?" I growl. The rogue grins, revealing a set of unnervingly white teeth.

"If I told you, I'd be signing my own death warrant."

A surge of anger courses through me, but I take a deep breath.

"You're going to talk. I'll make sure of it," I insist, clenching my jaw. He laughs, a low, mocking sound.

"You think threats will work? Go ahead, shoot me. It won't change a thing."

The room is filled with tension, the gravity of the situation pressing on me. I must find a way to make him talk. I pull out the shitty burner phone Phoebe gave me, hitting the record button.

"Confess that you murdered Christian Matthews on the 8th of March," I demand.

He shakes his head in amusement, a mocking smile playing on his lips.

"You really don't want the police to find out. You'll all be used as performing monkeys."

The threat hangs in the air, and a chill runs down my spine. I can't let fear consume me. I need to stay focused and make him reveal everything.

"Who are you working for?" I repeat, waving the gun at him. A smirk tugs the corner of his lips.

"You," he answers, his voice lingering in the silent room. "We work for nobody and for everybody. That's how society survives."

Suddenly, my heart skips a beat. The usual ringing in my ears, signalling a premonition, starts. My body freezes, the gun still pointed at the rogue's head seconds before my vision blurs. The ringing persists until a new image takes shape, and everything falls into silence as I realise where I am.

I find myself in a white room, a single source of light hanging from the ceiling. My shock intensifies as I notice a dozen men standing before me. They're lined up in a precise formation, clad in black army gear with visors hiding their faces. In perfect unison, each man draws a shotgun, aiming it directly at me. In that instant, the world around me slows down. The firing squad gets the command to shoot, their guns clicking in eerie unison. Pain courses through my body as a dozen bullets pierce my flesh, and my vision succumbs to darkness once more.

I let out a loud gasp, my eyes snapping open. My hands shake uncontrollably, the gun wavering in my grip. For the first time, I see fear in the rogue's eyes, his jaw dropped.

Kaya. Kaya was right. The firing squad. They're coming for me now.

The sudden crash of the motel room door startles me. In that split second, I fear it might be the police barging in. But as my eyes widen, relief and horror wash over me at the sight of Theo standing in the doorway.

"What are you doing here?" I blurt out. Theo's face pales as his eyes dart between the gun in my hands and the rogue restrained on the bed. In a low voice filled with a mix of concern and confusion, he utters, "Cora... what are you doing?"

The weight of his question hangs in the air, and I can sense the urgency for an explanation in his gaze.

"H-How did you find me?" I stammer, my nervousness showing despite my efforts to stay calm.

"I had a vision," Theo says softly, his eyes fixed on the gun in my trembling hands. The realisation that anger has consumed me dawns on him, and his gaze transforms into a mix of fear and concern. The air in the room becomes thick with unspoken questions and a tension that hangs between us.

I can't allow him to change my mind. I know I must end this once and for all before it's too late. As I turn my attention back to the rogue, my hands keep trembling with the weight of the premonition.

"Kaya is right," I whisper, the gun still aimed at the rogue's forehead. "Sometimes, the future traps us. We get stuck in quicksand," I repeat, echoing her words from my vision.

Confusion clouds Theo's face.

"What? Who's Kaya? Put the gun down, Cora," Theo insists, but his words sound like meaningless noise in my ears.

Kaya's haunting words continue to echo inside my head, dragging me further into a state of paralysing madness. The image of the firing squad replays in my mind, and my surroundings start to blur.

"You can't escape," the rogue taunts, beads of sweat trickling down the side of his neck. I squeeze my eyes shut, anger boiling inside me like a simmering kettle.

"No!" Theo's scream startles me, and I immediately snap my eyes open. I don't understand why he yelled until I see a crimson pool on the rogue's chest.

Fuck. I shot him. I didn't even hear the gunshot. I'm losing it.

"Why did you do that, Cora? We could have forced him to tell the rogues we're dead!" Theo yells, grabbing the revolver from my hands.

The truth is, I've lost my mind. He pulls me out of the motel room, but I can only stare blankly at my hands, now stained with the rogue's blood. Theo's shouts urging us to leave before anyone sees us sound distorted in my mind.

I feel nothing. Not a single drop of remorse.

•••••

"Cora, please say something," Theo pleads for the fiftieth time in the past twenty minutes. "You're scaring me."

"I have nothing left to live for now," I mumble, staring blankly at the dashboard of Theo's car. We left the rogue in the motel room and rushed to his car in the parking lot. Theo's worried expression deepens as he glances at me, his hands gripping the steering wheel.

"Don't say that, please. Tell me what happened."

I remain silent for a few seconds, my gaze fixed on the dashboard. The weight of what transpired at the motel room hangs heavily in the air. The car's engine hums softly, a stark contrast to the chaos within me.

"I don't know what happened," I utter, feeling a disconnect between my mind and body. The rogue looked lifeless, as if all colour had been drained from his skin.

Theo inhales deeply, running an anxious hand through his hair.

"We need a plan. We need to keep moving, stay one step ahead of the rogues."

"I don't care anymore," I mutter, my voice barely audible. I remain numb, unable to shake off the feeling. Once you've witnessed your own death, it's only a matter of time before it happens.

Theo's eyes reflect a mix of concern and determination.

"Cora, we can't let this define us. There's still a chance to make things right," he says.

I meet his gaze briefly, the emptiness in my eyes unsettling even to myself. The car pulls onto the highway, and as the scenery blurs outside, I wonder if escape is ever truly possible.

"You're wrong. No matter what we do," I say with a broken voice.

"What? What do you mean?" Theo asks, trying to lock eyes with me. A quiet pause fills the space as the image of the platinum-blond rogue with face tattoos and earrings floods my thoughts.

What if I killed him? I must have.

"Cora, please talk to me. You're clearly not in control of your own actions right now," Theo insists, pulling me away from my thoughts.

"Do you believe fate can be changed?" I ask, my voice croaky and detached. Theo's brows furrow as he processes my question.

"What? I mean, it depends. Why, what's happened?" he asks, his expression filled with concern. I can't bring myself to tell him that I witnessed my own death before my eyes. I gaze absentmindedly at the pine trees passing by as we drive, the dark grey sky mirroring my inner turmoil.

The realisation suddenly hits me.

"I shot a rogue," I croak, my eyes starting to water. "I wanted to kill someone, Theo. Why did I do that?"

Theo locks eyes with me, his expression mirroring the brokenness I feel inside. He releases a frustrated exhale, nervously biting his lip.

"I don't know, but the rogues are on our tails. We need to leave Barren. We're heading to Pennsylvania," he mutters, his gaze fixed on the empty road ahead.

"What if they find us there?" I ask, fear tainting my voice. "Maybe our fate can't be changed."

If the rogues find us, we'll be cornered with nowhere left to hide. I shift my gaze downward, noting the rogue's blood staining my white Converse—a reminder that won't wash away.

Theo's hand finds mine, offering a gentle reassurance.

"We'll figure this out, Cora. I promise you. But Barren isn't safe anymore."

As Theo's words echo in the confined space of the car, a sense of urgency grips us. Everything is happening too fast, slipping through our fingers like sand. I feel the weight of our options, each one a crucial point in our destiny.

"We need to decide," Theo says, his voice breaking through the chaotic whirlwind of my thoughts. "We can't stay here, but we need a plan."

I look at him, and a silent agreement passes between us. It's time to decide, to grab onto whatever control we can amidst the chaos.

In that instant, Kaya's soft, creamy voice fills my ears.

Look inside once you're ready.

My necklace. Pulling on the chain, I bring the medallion closer, its cool metal against my fingertips. The intricate patterns etched on its surface seem to shimmer as if concealing a secret. I tighten my grip on the necklace, the medallion pressing into the soft palm of my hand. Closing my eyes, I take a deep breath. The familiar tingling sensation in my arms and legs envelops me as the once-clear grey road ahead begins to blur.

A young woman in her late teens stands at the entrance of the Barren High School sign, her dirty blonde hair gently tousled by the warm summer breeze. She's around my height, with slim shoulders and a slender figure. The perspective of the image shifts: I'm now experiencing it from the girl's point of view. She walks down the corridor, holding hands with a boy around her age. He accompanies her to the classroom, and she gives him a quick peck on the lips before entering. In that moment, I notice the mole on the side of his cheek. The guy she's with is Mayor Glenn.

A chilling realisation courses through my veins.

My mom. The blonde woman is my mom. My mother was seeing Mayor Glenn.

The image transitions to the football field, the night sky casting an ethereal glow. We're on the bleachers, but this time, we're not holding hands. In fact, we're sitting quite far apart. A palpable tension fills the air, leaving my throat dry with discomfort.

"I need to talk to you about something, Arthur," my mom says, her tone uneasy. She's overwhelmed by uncertainty and fear.

"What is it? You know you can trust me," Glenn's voice echoes. He squeezes my mother's hand, but she flinches. Her heart races in her chest as she musters the courage to speak.

"I've been having visions..."

"What do you mean?" he asks, raising his brows.

"I can't explain it, but... glimpses of things that haven't happened yet."

Discomfort washes over Glenn's face.

"What? Like what?"

My mom bites her lip, struggling to find the words. Her heart races at an alarming pace.

"Your family... I saw something about them..." A surge of nausea rises in my throat. "They traffic firearms. Is it true?"

Glenn's expression tightens, a mix of surprise and defensiveness.

"Where did you get this idea? You're insane!" he spits.

His shouts become distorted, and the image of the bleachers blurs until I'm surrounded by darkness.

In an instant, a familiar scene overwhelms my vision, and a chill runs through my veins as I realise that it has transported me to the gates of Alheim Hill Mental Hospital. Rain beats down on the umbrella my mother clutches as she gazes in terror at her new home.

Glenn steps out of a polished Porsche, leading my mom toward the gates. She's heartbroken; the only man she trusted has betrayed her. To make matters worse, she is now dismissed as mentally ill for sharing what she saw. My mom's eyes reflect deep sorrow as she gazes at Glenn, her expression a mix of disappointment and heartache.

"You don't have to do this. You know I'm right," she croaks. Tear tracks stain her cheeks, and her voice trembles with both sadness and desperation.

Glenn's face remains emotionless, unmoved by my mom's emotional plea. He responds with a cold and detached tone.

"You need help, Diana. This is for your own good," he states, his words sounding final. through the air with an air of finality. The lack of empathy in his response only makes my mom feel worse, increasing the pain of betrayal. Without a second thought, he abandons her in the rain, swiftly returning to his car.

The following scene sends shivers down my spine. I witness my mother hanging from the ceiling of her room at Alheim, a belt around her neck. It's the same vision I experienced a few months ago while holding Glenn's gold ring, but the pain is even more intense this time. The image starts to fade into black, suggesting the vision is concluding, but I refuse to stop looking into her past.

That can't be right. Her supposed suicide occurred years before she met my dad and had me. My mom died in a car crash, meaning the suicide attempt didn't work.

I take a deep breath, determined to delve further into her past. I tighten my grip on the medallion, beads of sweat trickling down my forehead.

Another vision takes shape, this time crystal clear, as if the memory has been perfectly preserved. It's Evergreen Forest—I can sense it from the fragrance of pine and oak trees. My mom is sprinting deeper into Evergreen, her heartbeat echoing as if she's being pursued. She glances back one last time at the wrecked car before vanishing into the woods.

Suddenly, I'm pulled out of the vision as if a strong gust of wind has swept me away. My eyes open with a gasp, and my heart races in my chest as I stare blankly at Theo's dashboard.

My mom is alive.

46

"Cora? Please tell me what's going on."

Theo's voice echoes within the confines of the car, a nauseating sensation washing over me. We've pulled over on the highway, just a couple of miles away from Barren. Ever since I found out my mom is alive, I can't seem to catch my breath.

"My..." I start, but my throat feels parched, like sandpaper. "My mom... she's alive," I manage to blurt out. Even as the words escape my lips, they feel unreal.

Theo's eyes widen in disbelief, his expression changing from confusion to astonishment.

"What?" he breathes out, his voice barely above a whisper. The colour drains from his face as he struggles to comprehend the magnitude of what I've just revealed.

"I... She was like me, Theo," I stammer, still in complete disbelief.

"And she's alive? That's fantastic," he says, but he doesn't seem to understand. My facial expression must show my uncertainty because he quickly adds, "Right?"

I shake my head, tears beginning to well up in my eyes.

"You don't understand, Theo. My mom has been alive all this time, and she never told us," I say, my words tinged with frustration.

"Maybe she had a good reason. She must have done it to protect you," he says, shooting me a sympathetic glance.

But I'm unable to think rationally at the moment. All I sense is a boiling bubble of anger within me, ready to explode at any moment.

"Protect me?" I scoff. "She made my life unbearable. I suffered from depression, anxiety, and insomnia for years. I had no friends at school. I'm irrevocably messed up because of her."

Theo flinches at my outburst, his expression tense as he bites his lip. After a brief silence, he lets out a sigh.

"Baby, I know you're upset, but we need to leave Barren right now. The rogues are on our heels, and we can't afford them finding us again," he mutters, his voice laced with urgency.

In that moment, the weight of the world seems to collapse onto my shoulders. All this time, Chris was lying to me. He knew what I was, and all he did was manipulate me, planning to hand me over to the rogues when it was convenient for him. And now, on top of that, I've discovered that my mom has been lying to me for the past eight years, pretending she died just so she could walk away from us. I feel nothing but pain, my heart clenching as tears well up in my eyes.

"I can't do this," I mutter, my hand trembling as I reach for the door handle. "I just can't." Just as I'm about to step out of the car, Theo gently grabs my arm.

My gaze meets his azure eyes, and for a moment, time seems to stand still. Despite my anger and disappointment, the longing in his gaze brings me some comfort.

"You're not alone. I'm right here," he whispers.

The gentleness of his voice leaves me feeling vulnerable, and in an instant, my anger is replaced by intense sadness. I find myself overcome with emotion, tears streaming down my cheeks. Does my dad know about her fake death? Does he know she's a clairvoyant? Has everyone been lying to me all along?

Sensing my distress, Theo wraps his arms around me in a comforting embrace.

"I hate her, Theo. I hate her for doing this to me," I sob, my voice thick with emotion.

A sudden rush of guilt overwhelms me as I grasp the reality of my actions.

"I... I killed somebody. I killed that rogue," I stammer, my lip quivering.

Theo pulls away from the embrace, his hands gently cupping my cheeks. His blue eyes meet mine, trying to comfort me.

"Hey," he whispers softly, "We don't know if he's dead. Either way, what happened tonight is the very reason why we need to stay grounded."

"Grounded..." I murmur, letting out a sad laugh. "How can I even think about being grounded when hitmen are chasing me? I've already got one foot in the grave."

Theo shoots me a puzzled look, furrowing his brows.

"Wait... What do you mean?" he asks, his tone tinged with dread.

I tear my gaze away from his, biting my lip in hesitation. I can't keep this from him any longer.

"I had a vision. A-About what Kaya says my fate will be. What her fate is," I explain, my words rushing out.

Theo shakes his head in confusion, struggling to keep up.

"Wait, you're not making any sense. Who's Kaya?"

"She's a clairvoyant. I had a vision about her-"

"When did this happen?" he asks, his eyes filled with concern.

"When I blacked out after shooting Chris," I murmur, unable to meet his gaze. "I saw my own death, Theo. A firing squad, bullets tearing through me."

Theo's eyes widen in shock, his mouth slightly agape as he processes my words. It's a rare sight to see him so visibly scared, and it sends a shiver down my spine.

"Why didn't you tell me when you had the vision?" he asks, his voice trembling with fear and uncertainty.

"What difference would it make?" I argue, frustration lacing my words.

"Because fate can be changed," Theo insists, his voice firm.

"No, it can't. Our fate is engraved in stone. There's nothing we can do about it. That's what Kaya told me," I insist, my tone resolute.

He releases a nervous exhale, his gaze fixated on the empty road ahead as he clutches the steering wheel tightly, his knuckles growing white with tension.

"Visions can be misleading. We can change our path, rewrite our story," he murmurs. But doubt lingers in his eyes, mirroring the uncertainty that now clouds my own thoughts.

Suddenly, the memory of shooting the rogue rushes back. As I arrived at the abandoned motel, I felt myself losing control completely—as if I had transformed into something dark and uncontrollable, something barely human.

I take a shaky breath, my fingers trembling as they graze over the worn fabric of my jeans.

"I don't know what happened at the motel. I have no idea who I am becoming, Theo," I confess, the weight of uncertainty heavy in my words.

Theo's expression darkens, his features clouded with concern as he looks at me.

"You're scared, Cora. I get that. We all are," he says softly.

I shake my head, recognising it's more than mere fear. I sense myself losing touch with reality, being pulled into a dark abyss.

"I killed somebody. And sooner or later, all of this will catch up to me. The rogue was right—there is no escape. There's no way of changing my fate."

The weight of my confession hangs heavy in the air as I utter those words, each syllable a stark reminder of the irreversible actions I've taken. Theo's gaze softens, understanding the gravity of my words.

"You can't keep blaming yourself, Cora," he murmurs, concern in his voice. "We've all made choices we're not proud of, but dwelling on them won't change anything. We have to focus on what's ahead, on finding a way to navigate through this mess together."

I nod slowly, absorbing his words, but the guilt still gnaws at the edges of my consciousness, refusing to be silenced. Deep down, I know he's right, but the fear of what lies ahead is overwhelming.

"And what if I can't change my fate?" I whisper, the words barely audible even to my own ears.

Theo's expression softens further, his eyes reflecting a mix of pain and determination.

"If what you saw is real, we'll face it together. There's no way I'm letting you die," he assures me, his words a beacon of hope cutting through the darkness that surrounds us.

His voice grows urgent as he continues, "But right now, we need to get out of Barren, especially now that you're in danger. We can't afford to stay here any longer."

His words sink in, reminding me of the danger lurking nearby. I nod, realising that our safety depends on leaving Barren and facing whatever lies ahead.

"You're right," I murmur softly, my fingers tracing the intricate patterns on the necklace in my hands.

For eight years, I've worn this necklace without realising the damage it could cause. With the realisation that my days are numbered, a surge of rage courses through me, and I can't help but blame my mom for everything. Now more than ever, I need to find her.

"Before I die, I need to find my mom," I declare, bitterness lacing my voice. "I want her to understand the pain she's caused me."

Theo's voice breaks through my swirling thoughts, pulling me back to the present moment.

"You're not going to die, Cora," he assures, his voice steady and comforting. "And we'll find her together."

"But first, we need to get out of here," he adds, a sense of urgency in his tone.

I glance around the desolate landscape, feeling a shiver run down my spine. Theo is right. Barren holds too many painful memories, too many secrets lurking in the shadows. It's time to leave this place behind and embark on a journey to find the truth, to find my mom.

•••••

Theo pulls over the car in a clearing a few miles from the Barren border, near *Whispering Pines*. A wave of anxiety washes over me as the realisation hits like a sledgehammer: from now on, Barren will be a place I can never return to.

This is the final goodbye.

"Let's stretch our legs and head out in ten minutes," Theo says, eyeing me with concern, "Once we're on the highway, we can take turns driving to catch up on sleep."

"Okay," I reply softly, feeling the exhaustion weighing heavily on me.

As we step out of the car, the cool evening breeze wraps around us, carrying the gentle scent of pine trees. We stretch our legs, the tension from the long drive gradually fading away. Theo keeps a watchful eye while I take in the fresh air. My heart fills with sadness, knowing that it's only a matter of minutes before we leave. It's strange to think these might be my last moments in Barren. These past few months have flashed before my eyes, taking a turn for the worst.

I can only hope that the people I care about will be safe while I'm gone, but the truth is, I can't be sure. With a sigh, I get back into the car, exhaustion washing over me like a tidal wave. As I sink back into the passenger seat, my heart feels heavy with emotion. Theo joins me, concern etched across his face.

"Hey," he says softly. "Are you okay?"

If only I could find the words. I feel caught in quicksand, pulled into a void of emptiness. Chris's death, my encounter with the rogue, and the revelation about my mom being not only alive but a clairvoyant, have torn me apart.

"No," I manage to utter, my lower lip trembling. "I don't want to leave."

Theo's expression fills with pain as he softly cradles my cheeks, his touch sending a comforting warmth through me. He's terrified of losing me, but there's a part of me that doesn't believe I can escape my fate.

"I know, babe. But we can't stay here anymore. We need to make sure you're safe," he murmurs.

I look down at my hands, feeling my heart clench in my chest.

"I'm scared, Theo," I mutter softly, my voice barely above a whisper.

Our eyes meet, the pain evident in both of our gazes.

"I am, too. But I promise you, I will do anything I can to save you," he murmurs. But the truth is, neither of us knows what the future holds.

If someone had told me two months ago that I would shoot a rogue, I would have thought they were insane. That's the thing about life, nothing is certain. One day, you think you've got life all figured out—you're a grade A student with dreams for the future. But the next, you're a clairvoyant, and you see your own death flash before your eyes.

Fiddling with my necklace, I feel its weight in my hand. It's as if my life has come full circle—my mom is now alive, yet I am facing my own death.

I let out a deep sigh, feeling the weight of the world on my shoulders.

"I just feel so hopeless," I admit, unable to meet his gaze.

Theo gives my thigh a gentle squeeze, his warm touch bringing me comfort.

"I know that Chris' death really took a toll on you. It's normal, he was your first love," he says, lowering his gaze. Suddenly, guilt washes over me as I realise that speaking about my ex makes him uncomfortable. "But going after that rogue was dangerous. Now we have an even bigger secret to hide."

"I know…" I murmur, biting my lip.

"The good thing is we have a place to stay. Things will be easier once we get to your holiday house in Pennsylvania. We can figure out our next move from there," he explains.

"Yeah..." I whisper, a sinking feeling settling in. Deep down, I know it's only a matter of time before they find us there too.

The worry in Theo's eyes suggests that perhaps I shouldn't have told him about the firing squad. I understand his panic; I'd feel the same if I learned that someone I cared about was facing imminent death.

"We will find a way," he murmurs, as if he could read my mind. "I'm just glad you are here with me."

He leans in, his proximity sending shivers down my spine as our lips meet in a passionate kiss. Our mouths meld together, and with each lingering kiss, my desire for him deepens. His hands roam, caressing my thighs, hips, and waist with a gentle, electrifying touch.

"Theo…" I moan, feeling the heat between us with each kiss.

"All I want is for you to be safe," he whispers, his hand creeping up my shirt. His sapphire eyes glisten with hunger in the dimness of the car, making my legs tremble. The windows have started to fog, creating an intimate atmosphere between us. I slide over, straddling him in the driver's seat. His breath escapes in a sigh before our lips meet in a passionate kiss.

If these are some of the last moments we have together before I face the firing squad, I want to savour every second with him.

•••••

As night falls, the forest plunges into bitter coldness, but the heat inside the car remains. We decided to wait until night-time to leave, making it more challenging for any rogues to tail us.

As I stare at the quiet forest ahead, a series of anxious thoughts race through my mind, creating a whirlwind of uncertainty and fear. Whatever happens now, we can't return to Barren. Will anyone miss me at school? How are we going to survive as fugitives? Will the rogues go after my dad again? The questions gnaw at me, each one creating more fear than the last.

"Ready to go?" Theo's voice breaks through my thoughts, his blue eyes fixed on mine.

I nod, clearing my mind of any lingering thoughts before he turns on the engine. The familiar hum fills the car's interior as he rolls down the windows slightly to clear the fog. The cool night breeze envelops us, carrying the gentle chirping of crickets—an unexpected sound for this early in spring.

Theo guides us back onto the highway, and silence settles between us as he drives. Once we pass the *'Leaving soon?'* sign, I sink into the passenger seat with a heavy sigh. Our gazes meet in the rear-view mirror, his blue eyes shining in the darkness of the night.

We both understand that whatever happens next, going back to Barren is out of the question. I never got to say goodbye to my dad or any of my friends, but after Chris' death and my encounter with the rogue, I've forged my own destiny.

As we move farther from Barren, a wave of sadness washes over me, causing an ache in my chest. The dark highway stretches ahead, amplifying my sense of isolation. Lost in my thoughts, a cold shiver runs down my spine. Suddenly, the interior of Theo's car fades to black.

A new scene unfolds before my eyes, one that is too haunting to forget. The trees cast eerie shadows over rows of tombstones, while the grey sky sets a tone of loss and sorrow. The melancholic cries of crows in the distance send shivers down my spine, their haunting calls echoing through the solemn air. My attention is drawn to a specific tombstone, and my blood turns to ice as the inscription comes into view.

Cora Danvers (2000 - 2018)

(TO BE CONTINUED...)

Printed in Great Britain
by Amazon